UNITING
THE BALANCE BRINGER

THE BALANCE BRINGER CHRONICLES
BOOK FIVE

USA TODAY BESTSELLING AUTHOR
DEBRA KRISTI

Paperback ISBN: 978-1-942191-54-4 /eBook ISBN: 978-1-942191-51-3
Cover design by Rebecca Frank of Bewitching Book Cover
Professional editing by Eden Plantz

Uniting: The Balance Bringer– 1st ed.
Visit the author: http://www.debrakristi.com/

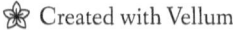 Created with Vellum

Also By Debra Kristi:

THE BALANCE BRINGER CHRONICLES:

Becoming: The Balance Bringer

Awakening: The Balance Bringer

Empowering: The Balance Bringer

Igniting: The Balance Bringer

Uniting: The Balance Bringer

THE BALANCE BRINGER ORIGINS:

The Mystic Maker

The First Balance Bringer

The Would Be Queen

GIFTED GIRLS SERIES:

Magical Miri, Book One

Bewitching Belle, Book Two

Nowhere Nara, Book Three

Clever Chloe, Book Four

Fatal Freya, Book Five

MOORIGAD DRAGON COLLECTION:

The Moorigad Dragon, Part One Moorigad Collection

Reap Not the Dragon, Part Two Moorigad Collection

Plight of the Dragon, Part Three Moorigad Collection

Moorigad, Parts One–Three

CURSED ANGEL COLLECTION:

Blood Promise: Cursed Angel Blood Promise

UNITING
THE BALANCE BRINGER

THE BALANCE BRINGER CHRONICLES
BOOK FIVE

USA TODAY BESTSELLING AUTHOR
DEBRA KRISTI

For Christy
And every reader who loves a great fantasy escape.

"Success is not final; failure is not fatal: It is the courage to continue that counts" — ***Winston S. Churchill***

Ivey City

HUSHMAN'S MEADOW

LISTLESS R

GRA
GO

NARFOLK
BAY

N

HIDDENKEL

PALINOT WOODLANDS

e King's
ral Castle

AUGUR
CLIFFSIDE
DOMICILE

inot ◇

■ Maitias
Garrison

■ Guardoone Point

■ Royal Fae
Castle Estate

QUEEN'S CROSSING

FIRES
OF GUARDOONE

■ Tower South

■ Time Keep
at Season's Cape

ONE

Izza is neither alive nor dead. She exists in a space between. Between worlds. Between beginnings and endings. Separated from tangible experiences and relationships.

A younger version of myself, but with the pointy ears I only recently grew into, her blonde hair and kaleidoscope eyes are the same that I once had, before my hair streaked with gold and my eyes chose their color, one green and one blue.

She has been forgotten by all but me... and Raundel, one of my favorite surly elves, with whom my many past selves have a long history.

Izza is not one of them with such a past, for she suffered her fate before Raundel could find and save her. Before he could protect her from the misfortune that awaited. She became the unrealized Balance Bringer. A thirteen-year-old girl lost to time and trapped in space. Until I discovered her, *Gaea knows* how long after her physical life had ended.

She hugs me fiercely, then drops her arms and steps away.

"We always knew you would return for me. You are not like the others. We are bonded, and you remember."

Bonded the last time we met, during my Balance Bringer ritual in the Lagoon of Lucidity, beneath the Remembrance Rain. Not that long ago, and yet it feels like ages. So much has happened between then and now, and still, Izza hasn't been released from her self-imposed isolation.

"This is my fault," I say and spin in a slow circle, taking in the changes since last I visited. "Had I stayed, fought the monster haunting you—"

"Had you stayed and done the deed," she says. "We would not have been freed in the way that we have been. Look." She throws her arms high and wide, indicating the surrounding walls of Gaea's cathedral.

The location is the same as when first I found her, a sanctuary made of earthen elements, but now the pillar-*esque* trees lining the walls of the space, like age-old sentries, are healthier and more vibrant. The floor is no longer cluttered with dried twigs, browning leaves, or dying grass, and is instead covered in a patchwork of varied green mosses. And bright, golden sunlight shimmers through the breaks in the canopy, chasing away the darkest of shadows.

At the far back, the elements have even worked together to create a rather comfy looking bed. A proper place for Izza to lay her head. Everything is healthier and happier, the space feeling less like a prison, or a long-forgotten relic, and more like a magical home.

"How?" I push the one word free, at a loss for what more to say, then blurt, "and you?"

Not the exact same girl I recall, petite and frail, Izza is now a tad taller and more filled out. Her curves more pronounced and her exuded aura no longer fearful but confident.

She weaves her fingers together, then flexes them flat. "Much time has passed since your last visit, sister."

She jerks a point to the center of the earthen cathedral and smokey images burst into form, revealing the scene when last I left her. A scene I lived close to a month ago.

I stand before the monster of darkened mist, crystal sword in hand, and then I vanish in an implosion of light, returning to my other sisters within the binding as the sword clamors to the ground. The monster roars and growls, and a shaky legged Izza slips from her place of hiding. She picks up the sword with trembling hands and points it at the monster's chest.

"In you, we found the strength to stand up for ourselves." A cut of her hand through the air and the image of the past event disintegrates.

"We did not defeat him that day," she continues. "But we have since. That wicked piece of Garrthmal has been vanquished." I raise my eyebrow, and she shrugs. "We are almost sixteen years of age. We have had plenty of time, practically three years since last we met, to find our inner self-assurance and ability to stand strong. We have successfully left that nightmare behind."

Her use of the plural pronoun when referring to herself does not go unnoticed by me, but I do not question her... yet. I choose to address the other question tipping off my tongue. "How could so much time have passed? It's been less than a month on my end."

"Time is a relative element. A day for you, a month for me. More or less, either direction, it holds little meaning. I have been much occupied—growing, learning, evolving—to notice the passing."

She swings her raised arm in an arc, awakening moving images between the standing trees. Between each set is a different image, as if projected on a movie screen. Snippets I recognize. Some from my life, from my sisters' Crystia or Kaia. Others from Deona, Estala, Fiona, and all the Balance Bringers that existed between. The many versions of me and my sisters utilize elements or abilities in the various representations.

All the players, previous Balance Bringers trios, look the same or similar, blonde hair and kaleidoscope eyes. All aside from Kaia. She was the only one whose appearance was magically altered to hide what she was. Unlike the others, she has dark hair and dark eyes. But her true form occasionally flickers through in the moving images.

My attention snags on a remembrance of a shy Balance Bringer sneaking peeks at a young, horned male. He's hard at work, his sun-darkened skin firm over fit muscles and his auburn streaked hair curling playfully around his horns. Horns that curve like a dancing wave away from his face. Her version of my Jaden or Deona's Jove. The tracer from Izza's own lifetime—Dhmaric. The two never officially connected, but if they had, would Izza's history have differed? I tend to believe so.

Izza moves across my view, breaking my regard. Small amongst the grand trees of the temple, everything she exudes is resplendent, and for a flicker of a moment, she appears every bit a deity.

She shifts closer to a captured memory of Deona wielding water in an unnatural way. "My sisters and I did not walk the world long enough to fully bloom into our gifts. Elementals did not respond to us as they did for the First." Deona and her sisters being the First.

She relocates between two other images, one of Kaia brandishing a sword and another of Crystia communicating with the big cats at the Preservation Center. "Our fighting technique and species communication was bereft."

She drops her hands and folds them at her waist. "But we discovered, together as one, something for which we appear to have a natural affinity. And we have you to thank for the awakening of that insight."

My hand flies to my chest. "Me?"

When I had previously made contact with her, I'd accidentally pulled my consciousness out of the interaction, thereby failing to defeat her tormentor and leaving her alone to defend herself. Yes, that may have forced her to find and embrace her inner strength, yet I fail to understand how that exchange led to any insight.

She nods. "Like I said, we are bonded, and you have successfully extracted my sword from where I hid it on more than one occasion." The crystal sword, a gift from Dharmic, said by Raundel to be hidden within Izza's heart.

The other Balance Bringers are unaware of the weapon's true source. *Still*, I wielded it more than once?

At the clear confusion on my face, she clarifies. "Like the other Balance Bringers before you, you extracted the sword during your binding. No other has wielded the weapon outside of the ritual. Unlike them, you found the blade a second time, pulling it free to defend me and defeat my monster. You may not have stayed to finish the action, but the power of your heart was made clear, and the sword will now answer to you when you are in need."

Both times mentioned were within the binding ritual, so... does that second wielding truly count? If so, then another step closer to fixing the Balance Bringer line and the balance of worlds, between worlds, has been realized.

"And this?" I ask, motioning between us, then her and the sanctuary. "How do we free you from this place? Reunite you and your sisters with the rest of us?" The ancestral line of Balance Bringers.

I glance around the space once more. "By the way, where *are* your sisters?"

Her hands lift to her heart. "They now reside within me."

I nod my understanding with a sad smile set in place. Izza and her sisters are connected as I was with Crystia and Kaia, before the Balance Bringer binding. They can feel and hear each other, but that connection could be stronger... if Izza were to unite with me as the others have.

"We would like to," she says, as if aware of my thoughts. "We are... you and us, after all, the same, only having lived different lives, in different worlds, with different experiences. Those differences bring beautiful new clarities to the whole of what we are and what we were always meant to be."

I whole-heartedly agree. I'm not sure I would have when the prophesied transition began for me, but I do now.

"How, then, do we make that happen?" I ask.

"Well..." She enunciates the word with extreme clarity. "Given that you are the only sister to ever discover us and our location during a binding ritual, my sisters and I were under the impression that your gift for the fifth element was on an equivalent level with our own. And, it is, quite possibly, through that element that we shall resolve this tiny predicament."

I wouldn't call being trapped in some pocket of space, forgotten by the rest of the worlds... mostly... a *tiny* predicament. But that opinion means little when faced with the suggestion I utilize a fifth element to help Izza escape her prison.

The known elements are those of nature, earth, wind, water, and fire. What else could there be?

"What element is that?" I ask.

The edge of her lips tug upward. "How about a small demonstration?"

Sure. I nod.

She reaches past me, her hand wrapping around a handle on a grandiose entrance that hadn't been there a moment before. One tug and the door swings open and deja vu slaps me across the face. The monster who chased her into hiding in the first place.

A thick and heavy mist billows in through the opening with a slithering hiss. Fingers of haze snake forward, searching. For her. For me. Unlike before, Izza doesn't cower or sprint for cover.

"*Izza*." Her name stretches across the seconds like a reptilian churr. "Let us stop with the games. They have drawn on far too long."

The eerily familiar voice sends a shiver through my system. I know this voice. Have had direct contact with its source. So has the First; Deona, Estala, and Fiona.

A hand whips free of the vaporous swells and clamps around my wrist. My feet freeze and my heart flips to panic-mode. All inflowing fog folds away revealing Garrthmal standing before me.

"Fiona?" His facial muscles slack.

"Garr?" I jerk back against his unrelenting hold.

The being in front of me is neither the friend to the first three sisters, nor the taller individual I met who was hiding his goat features and living amongst the Treeites, but some sort of metamorphosis between. To gaze at his face, the satyr is apparent, but the rest of him is an ugly distortion.

"Enough." Izza grabs my free hand, and the surrounding air sparks into a glimmer. Garr, any lingering mist, and the door at his back, vanish.

I spin on her, my mouth agape. "What did you do and how did you do it?"

"Connected with the space element," she replies. "Used intuition with the element to shift us through perceived temporal order."

"You moved us through time?" My voice pitches. Her

responding shrug is so slight it's hardly visible. "Time travel. You can time travel?"

She frowns. "It is not as simple as that, but yes. We are all capable. But after your first visit, I realized my sisters and I were instinctually using spatial displacement to hide. We hid so well we erased our existence from the minds of all. A most terrible error."

Which explains why everyone outside of Raundel and I don't recall Izza, or her sisters. Raundel had said Izza's tracer had gone mad after her disappearance. *Does Dhmaric remember her?* Given Jaden has merged with all his previous selves, Dhmaric included, I'll have to ask when we're next together.

"We may not excel at water, earth, air, or fire," Izza says. "But when it comes to the space element, we have a rather brilliantly reckless relationship."

And you have a handle on time travel.

If I could move through time and visit the past, then I would be able to correct the events and mistakes that ultimately resulted in where things now stand. I could make sure Dreya never becomes the evil that she is now. By doing so, I would save countless lives.

My brother Ry would no longer be missing his fingers, his leg; Dohlan would not have a clawed hole in his chest; Opal and Gitta wouldn't be infected; Mo's skin and eyes wouldn't be devoid of life; and maybe, just maybe, my father and sisters would still be alive.

Or...

My gaze wanders across the multitude of images playing all around us. A continuously running life view for each Balance Bringer sister to ever live. My roving gaze slows to a stop on three playing side by side. Life as experienced by Deona, Estala, and Fiona.

In the stories unfolding; darkness chasing Fiona, infecting an innocent, and eventually attaching to Garrthmal. In between... a lot of sadness. Too much turmoil.

Or... if I were to reach even further into our past, visit the start, I might set things right from the very beginning. Avoid many of the issues faced by my sisters through the ages.

I snap my attention to Izza. "You said we're all capable of time travel?"

She presses her steepled fingers to her lips. "That is not exactly what I said. The element is space and I do not recom—"

"If I were to stop the darkness when it made its first appearance," I point to the life visions of Deona, Fiona, and Estella, "I could erase the horrors Dreya has inflected upon Hiddenkel. I could also stop Garr's obsession before it ever began."

Izza shakes her head. "Garr's obsession started long before the darkness arrived." She swivels a point to Fiona's life display.

A memory unfolds between Fiona and the young satyr. They're settled at the edge of the homestead's outlining tree line, the family cottage in sight, cozy against the hill and shaded at the front by beasts of trees. Surrounding activity suggests preparation of some sort.

Music set free by the instrument in Garr's hands trills the air at Fiona's back, and she closes her eyes to better savor the melody. The song stops and a second later, something tugs at her hair. She spins to find Garr with an impish smile on his face and his hands held suspiciously behind his back.

"What did you do?" she asks.

His shoulder jumps and his hooved foot scuffs the ground. "Sorry," he says with a whimper. "I want to have a piece of you with me always. Doing so helps me feel stronger. Safer."

"Show me," she demands.

He pulls his hand from behind his back, revealing a thick lock of her hair. He frowns and dips his horned head.

Fiona tugs at her now uneven hair, a whirling windstorm giving birth in her chest. "Never again without my expressed consent. Understood?" He nods. "Good. Now, I must go, and think not my departure is due to what you did, but because I am late for laundry duty. Deona and Estala will surely chastise me for my tardiness."

Fiona jumps from her place on the ground and takes off at a run across the clearing, glancing back once, before heading straight for her sisters.

"That is the moment, then," I say, nodding to myself.

Garr's connection to the Baba Yaga had recently been uncovered, and I can't help but suspect Fiona's hair was what was used in the spell now linking him to the Balance Bringer line.

"No." Izza shakes her head. "Time and events are not something any of us should meddle in. The ramifications are unknown."

"Have you tried?" The question popped into my mind as a retort, but once spoken I'm honestly curious.

Izza drops her head, and I can't decide if her reaction warrants a yes or no response. "We heard you. Did you know that?" I'm not sure when or what she heard so I remain quiet. "You said you wanted to *straighten the path to balance.*"

My first thought when I found myself here with Izza after sitting on my grandmother's crystal throne. "Exactly right," I reply. "And that's why I need to go back to these moments."

I spin toward Fiona's life reel. The image is of the world flashing past her as she runs. I slam my hand to the memory. Wish to be there, in the time of the First.

Izza screams my name. "This is not the way."

Maybe not, but it's already too late and I'm going to give it my best try. My body and mind are already shifting through time.

For the briefest of moments, I am nothing and nowhere, and then...

My knees and palms hit the ground. I lift my head and blink. Trees and shrubbery, nothing distinguishable.

This is not where I saw Fiona running in Izza's projected image. Where the heck did I end up? When did I end up?

"Child." Something grips the back of my collar, yanks me to my feet. "What in all of Gaea are you doing this far from the homestead?"

I'm spun around and come face to face with my aunts Meira and Edna. Or, as they are now known in my time, Madame Marrouske and Opal, Mother to the Augur clan.

"Oh." Aunt Edna drops her hold upon me. "You are not ours. When exactly are you from, child?"

TWO

Well, *crap of a time travel landing.* Wiping the dirt from my palms as a stall tactic, I rattle my brain for an appropriate response, a reasonable action, to the question posed... *"When exactly are you from?"*

Yeah, I'm not so sure I should tell them the truth.

"Most clearly not a child of the now." Meira's hand darts forward and pulls my hair clear of my ear, exposing my pointy tip. She rubs my hair between her fingers then, with a soft huff, allows my gold-streaked tendrils to fall back over my shoulder, as her attention shifts to my attire.

Such a conundrum, one I hadn't considered in my unplanned jump to wherever *this* is: What to say when I run into those who see me for who I am.

Of course, my elven aunts would recognize the truth. Quite careless of me not to expect this encounter, given my intended time and place of destination. Both of their scrutinizing stares are cutting through my defenses and driving my intentions into a stupor. My search for a reasonable response comes up empty. In my time, they're forever old and knowledgeable, and quite possibly a little less than trustworthy, with their secrets and manipulations.

The versions of them now standing before me are younger. Skin mostly wrinkle free and glowing, hair soft and absent of gray, but their eyes are still bright with wisdom.

"Answer the question, child," Aunt Edea pushes. "When are you from?"

I'm too exhausted to create a clever lie. "Not now," I say. "Later."

"Speak not the obvious," Edea retorts. "How *much* later?"

My gaze drops over them, taking in their youthful... by comparison... appearance. "Much, much later, based on what I see."

Both elves jolt back as if affronted.

I take advantage of the moment to catch my bearings. Trees, trees, and more trees. In the sky above, a faint trail of smoke. Possibly... *hopefully*... coming from the family homestead, which I'm guessing is my aunts' intended destination.

Meira picks at my hair and, once again, gazes at my two-colored eyes. "Is this how our girls will someday look?"

"When three become one? Yes," I blurt.

Neither of them appears surprised by this reveal, and why should they be? If Deona's memory is correct, Edea is responsible for the three-way soul split that created my sisters to begin with.

Aunt Edea begins to circle me, shaking a reprimanding finger. "What have you done? You should not be here."

My hands fist. "I had to come. Things are a mess, and I need to set them right."

She releases a dubious laugh. "You cannot fix the future by changing the past. Do you not know that, child?" She leans in, bringing her face close to my own, her gaze searching my features. "You will only succeed in creating more problems. Have we not taught you such?"

I hold her gaze and say nothing. Whatever discord that eventually creates the rift between my aunts is not yet a glimmer in their lives.

"No." I cross my arms. "You have taught me little. Most of what I know I've learned on my own, from my many selves, or from others... who were not you."

They flinch, confusion and disbelief evident.

My words were an unnecessary jab, but the anger over what Opal, Edea, did to Dohlan and the way she manipulated his life, is a collection of burning coals, continuously heating my resentment. He deserves better than the treatment he has received, from Opal... and from Dreya. Even from me.

The memory of Dohlan cuffed and chained, his chest torn open from Dreya's attempt to claw out his heart, flashes to the forefront of my mind. My sister Kaia, dwelling within me, cringes.

Forcing that image away, I return my attention to my aunts. Deona, Estala, and Fiona's hearts swell with love and appreciation for both females. My many incarnations that followed have positive memories of Meira. Edea pointedly missing for the years between Deona's and my time. Can I hold the sins of their future selves against them now, when such thoughts are not even a consideration?

No, I can't.

"If you knew the truth of the situation," I say, "then you would understand why I need to do this. Or, at least, try to."

"Doubtful," both aunts say in unison, as if sharing the same brain.

The word sparks challenge, firing my mouth to spout things I ought to keep to myself. Or not share with them when they are separated by countless lifetimes from the situations I face.

"Everything you've built," I point at Aunt Meira, "your beloved home and centuries' old connections are in danger of destruction. And you." I swing my jab to Aunt Edea. "Your son has sacrificed his health and wellbeing, may very well die."

Edea crosses her arms. "I have no son and shall never bring offspring into this world."

I match her posture, crossing my arms, then pop my hip to the side. "Yeah. Don't place any bets on that stance."

Meira taps a finger to her lips. "If these things you speak are the truth..." She tilts her head. "Why choose now to implement your "fix." Why not return to the point of divergence?"

My forehead pinches. "The moment of divergence?" The moment when... *oh*. My mouth pulls into an 'o'. "The moment when Deona became three?"

"Not *that* divergence," she replies. "The one that transpired shortly before."

I jolt straight. *Before the soul split?* That would be... I suck back a breath... "The separation of species?"

"The creation of worlds," she corrects. Her steely gaze is tight on me, watching my every muscle twitch.

I bite the edge of my lower lip and shift my weight. "If I were to do that, then... well... the world I knew as my home would cease to exist."

Meira's eyes widen. "Curious," she says, at the same time Edea burst with, "Selfish."

"I'm not..." I don't finish my sentence because maybe I *am* selfish. "We're talking about worlds filled with lives. We can't simply obliterate worlds full of lives They're lives rich with hopes and dreams, family and friends—"

"If the worlds were never created," Edea says. "then their energies would have manifested in a different manner. They would not be *obliterated*, merely birthed into something other."

"And my life as I've known it would never have existed." My shoulders slump. "I just can't."

"Won't," Edea counters. I tilt my head in a noncommittal agreement.

Meira pushes in front of Edea. "Am I to understand you correctly? Were you not raised in this world?"

"Um." This conversation has dragged on too long. I glance around at the undeveloped terrain. Trees and trees and more trees. "I wasn't, but can you tell me where and when I've ended up?"

"You do not know?" she counters.

I shake my head. "Are we near Deona's place?"

Edea snaps, "Stay away from our girls," while Meira points to my left. "The homestead is our current destination."

Meira confirms my suspicions, only she has not pointed in the direction of the rising smoke trail.

"Is it close?" I ask. She nods and Edea frowns, deeply. "And *when* am I?"

Edea's frown grows even deeper. "Tomorrow, we celebrate the anniversary. The birth of the three."

The preparation for the celebration was what I saw in Fiona's memory with Garr. Maybe I'm not too late.

"I'm sorry, but I've got to run." I spin on my heels and bolt.

Edea raises a fist. "You cannot interfere—"

"Gotta run, I said." Not waiting for further argument, and ignoring their objection, I race through the woods in the direction Meira indicated. I swerve around trees and rocks, pulled by an inner need. The need to get to Garr and stop his deal with the Baba Yaga.

I run and run and run, and with each quick paced stride, I'm considering and calculating every possible action with Garr. I'm accessing Deona's and Estala's and Fiona's memories of Garr, knowledge of the area, and the events surrounding this time in their lives. And I'm searching for landmarks to orient myself.

My elven aunts were nowhere close to the original homestead, as I had assumed, and time is a passage that's difficult to track when racing through the woodlands. But my focus is unwavering, and I keep my feet in motion. I'm unsure how long I've been running when dead ahead and visible through the break in the trees, a plume of smoke rises into the sky. The sight, a signpost or beacon marking the family homestead.

Through Deona's memories I have a decent understanding of where I am and how much further I must run to reach the homestead. If memory serves, the three sisters would currently be at the stream, taking care of the laundry. That location is a bit of a distance to the right, and the place where I witnessed Fiona and Garr through her memory, slightly further in the same direction.

But where to find Garr now?

A shout and a holler snap my attention to my immediate left. The sounds of males, not fitting with Deona's family; the sisters and their father. Another bellow and I'm pivoting, dashing in a new direction. The sounds of a fight draw my charge to the ruins of a village being reclaimed by the elements, and straight into the grapple between two males and a monster.

I jump into the fray without a single thought.

Two Fae males swing and slam into a towering beast bulging with muscles and bad skin. He stinks of sweaty feet and looks like the worst-case scenario for an acne commercial. A plethora of bumps and wrinkles and grayish skin tinted with green. Troll.

A spiked tusk sails past at eye-level. The Fae males dive and duck, missing a strike from the primitive weapon by a hair.

"Female," the blond male yells.

Something about his features is vaguely familiar to me, but I can't place what.

"Run far from here," the brunette follows up in a voice that causes my heart to squeeze. A voice my memory recognizes.

I should get myself to Garr, stay on the mission that brought me to this time and place. Only, it isn't my style to turn my back on others in need. And these males, they're in need. The Fae males are back on their feet, coordinating, and instigating another assault.

I break into a hard run.

Both males shout at me to retreat yet I keep moving as if their words flew past my ears unheard. The troll's arms swing wide. He connects with the blond, knocking him sideways. Coming quick at his mate's back, the brunette receives a foot to the gut. A grunt and a whoosh, and the second Fae is flying backwards.

Something whispers in the back of my mind that I should be concerned for these males, that they mean something to Deona, Fiona, and Estala. But I can't allow myself to be distracted. Pushing all my strength into my legs, I dart straight for the troll. Leap and slam him in the side, feet first.

He topples and rolls, clear of the Fae males. I fall onto my side. Roll onto my back. Shove myself to my feet.

The troll is rolling back and forth, trying to find his balance, and the Fae males are yelling at me to run. Of course, I don't listen. I'm not a cowering female in need of protecting. Today, I shall be the one doing the saving.

I plant my feet firmly in the dirt, flare my hands at my side, and reach out to the elements. Wind answers, tossing the troll several feet back and pinning him against the wall of a long-forgotten building.

One of the males grabs me from behind, tries to pull me back and turn me away. Likely under the guise of chivalry. I shrug off the hold and communicate with Gaea's earth, lady green. Roots and vines explode from the ground, wrapping around and imprisoning the troll. The vegetation pulls him flush against the ground.

He roars and struggles against the binds.

"How. How did you do that?" The question is filled with tones of astonishment, confusion, disbelief.

I turn into the question and come eye to eye with Jove, Deona's love and Jaden's first incarnation. My breath catches in my throat, my gaze shifting from his soul striking green eyes to his leg. It's undamaged, but in history as Deona remembers, Jove had suffered a somewhat serious injury. One that had been a recent concern with Jaden. How much will the wound's absence affect future events?

"Are you both all right?" I glance past Jove to his companion.

Jove's attention to my attire appears to snag on my boots. "Humbled by our beating, but we shall recover." He presents his hand in waiting. "May I?" Reluctantly, I rest my hand in his and he places a soft kiss upon my skin. "It was our honor to be assisted by one as fair as you, my lady. I am Jove of Narfolk Bay. And you are?"

Unsure if my father's name holds any significance in this time and place, I decide to use the name I grew up with. "Anala Janssen."

Jove's green eyes swirl with a sea storm of blue. Chest tightening, I snap my hand from his touch. Displaced in time, as I am, can he still look into my future? What would happen to his timeline if he did?

The blond elbows Jove to the side. "Apologies. Sol, also from Narfolk Bay. What are you?" His delivery is rushed and weaved with clear strains of excitement. His hazel eyes alight with curiosity. "I have seen many things, but what you did here, it was simply..."

I toss a fleeting glance over the village ruins, the Fae males, and the bound troll, realization settling into my bones. This is where Deona and Jove first met. Have I...

My hand presses to my heart. No, no. I can't think that way. I'm here to set things right, not mess them up. I swivel my gaze between the males and come to rest upon Jove. There are so many things I want to say to him, but more than any words, I want to feel the flesh of his hand in mine once more. Feel his heartbeat and the tingle of our connection to confirm what we are, what we become is still strong and healthy.

But I can't allow that. Not with Jove. Not when he's destined for Deona, my first incarnation.

He reaches for me, the swirling blue mist in his eyes settling. "You—"

I step clear of his grasp. "I have to go," I blurt. "But the two of you should head north-east, around the waterways. You will find what you seek there." I turn and jog away, needing to put distance between us before I do something that will mess up my future.

"What is it we seek?" Sol calls after me.

Without offering a response, I glance over my shoulder to the males. Only, my gaze doesn't seek Sol, but Jove. His unwavering stare speaks volumes of confusion and loss and...

I snap my gaze away. Make haste for the homestead in search of Garr.

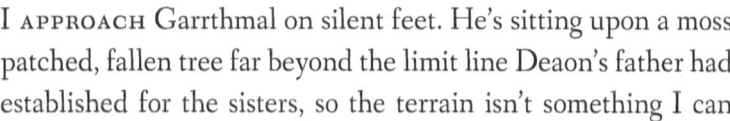

I APPROACH Garrthmal on silent feet. He's sitting upon a moss patched, fallen tree far beyond the limit line Deaon's father had established for the sisters, so the terrain isn't something I can access through their memories. In ages yet to come, other Balance Bringers have traveled through the area, but with much time between then and now, with changes, large and small to the land.

In other words, not easily recognizable.

The vegetation is thich and the trees dense. The resident bugs, a constant buzz in the background.

Had I been forced to rely on basic hearing and vision, even with elven, Fae, or Immortal warrior upgrades, I may not have located the satyr. But with the elements of earth and air lending their aid, I found my way directly to Garr. Although the first three sisters view him as a friend and relatively harmless, I have seen his future and I know differently.

My insides are tied into a forest full of knots. How do I behave? How do I talk to him? How do I keep my opinion of what he may become from tainting my every word and action?

Unaware of my approach, Garr's busy twisting Fiona's clump of cut hair around and around his finger, his thoughts appearing worlds away.

A soft chittering resides in the branches hanging overhead. I catch movement and tiny lights. Pixies? Not a threat... I don't think... so I refocus on the task at hand.

"Garrthmal," I say, shelving my disgust and taking a seat on the falling tree beside him.

He jerks sideways, clutching Fiona's hair to his heart. Shock blasts across his face as he soaks in the sight of me. "Who are you?"

I steel my resolve with a deep breath. "A better question than who I am is what do I know?"

"What do you know?" His goat eyes blink twice.

"I know your future and..." I swallow hard and drop my gaze to his hands clutched around Fiona's hair. "I think you should reconsider what you are planning."

"And what is it you think I am planning?"

I narrow a pointed stair on him. "You know, because, where I came from, you've already done it and it hasn't done you any benefits." I push away the desire to scoot farther away from him.

He sucks back a breath with a hiss, then lays his open hands before him, revealing the band of hair. He twined the ends, holding all the strands together, then decorated them with the tiniest of flowers.

"Will she ever love me?" he asks.

I sigh. "What's her love worth to you if it's forced? Only made to appear as true through magic's influence?"

He drops his gaze and silently contemplates. "Are you a seer?'

"In a manner of speaking." I tilt my head into my shoulder with a shrug.

"You must be, in order to see our futures." He glances between my face, the hair held in his hand, then back again. "Tell me, why do you look so much like them?"

We need not clarify that Deona and her sisters are of whom he speaks. "What do you know of *them*?" I ask.

He leans his upper body away. "They are a gift from the goddess Gaea, herself. Ultimate beauty and power and..." He sighs. "They are everything."

I slap a hand to my chest. "Wow. Thanks. A little stalker-ish, but a major compliment if I ever heard one." He blinks rapidly, his brow furrowing. I stand and tip my head. "A gift from the goddess Gaia herself." I curtsey.

"Are you suggesting..." He stands and stares at me. His fingers uncurl and Fiona's hair slips free, dropping to the ground.

I nod. Lift a meager smile to the edge of my lips. "Your path needs to change."

He drops back onto his rump on the fallen tree. "I am listening."

With a gentle swing of my hand, motioning to the hair now resting on the ground, I say, "Was that for the Baba Yaga?"

His expression pops wide.

"How about you and I pay her a visit?"

Because I'm not afraid of a little witch... or an evil, badass Baba Yaga.

THREE

Apples as large and hard as baseballs hit the ground all around us. Zip past our heads in near misses.

"Never return here," screams the Baba Yaga. "Or I shall have your head. Use your heart and spine for the darkest of spells."

Despite whatever tentative arrangement Garr had established with the ancient witch, to say she was not happy to see me would be an understatement. On the upside, I located the source of the rising smoke. Between her chimney, smoker, and bubbling cauldron, the Baba Yaga is expelling all kinds of gasses into the atmosphere.

A ripe red apple slams into a tree at my side, exploding into mush. Laughter bursts from my lungs, and I continue to run and leap free of the old witch's pitch range.

"How can you laugh at her?" Garr asks, panting in his effort to keep up with my escape. "And why did you not simply dispatch her with the power coursing through your veins?"

I slow to a walk, sensing that we are not only outside of the Baba Yaga's throwing range, but that she has also lost interest.

Outwardly, she may have deemed us unworthy of pursuit, but deep down I believe she is secretly afraid of what might come of a confrontation between us.

I link my hands behind my back and smile. "I laugh because she wasn't a threat."

"Maybe not to you." His hooves slam with a heavy thump to the packed earth. "But she could have ripped off one of my horns."

I toss him a sideways grin. "I had you protected." With a shield of hard air at our backs. "And I did not 'dispatch' her, as you so called it, because doing so would have been morally wrong."

"But she tried to kill us!"

"No, she didn't." I shake my head. "She was afraid and just wanted to scare us off."

He shoves his fisted hands into his armpits. "Nothing about that exchange left me with the impression that she was afraid. What I saw was anger, full out fury."

"Fear can hide behind many masks," I reply. "If we take harsh action against anyone for their fear or anger, then we only serve to justify their bad behavior."

Garr marches quietly forward with his head hung low, a few huffs matching his strides. He no longer carries Fiona's hair, having dropped the treasure at some point during his panicked run. A fact that supports my goal where Garr is concerned. But our conversation and his acceptance of my message holds more significance to me.

As leery as I was of Garr coming into this mission, I believe this early version of him really does have the best of intentions with regards to his relationship with the first three sisters. If I stop the darkness, prevent him from getting infected, I foresee events falling into place for a more balanced future.

My gaze shifts to the sun in the sky. I have around twenty-four hours or so until the darkness makes its appearance.

We come to the edge of the homestead clearing, and I stop, my gaze moving over the homestead. The desire to go investigate, compare the cottage to the one Dohlan took me to, is potent. And yet, an action I can't chance. My presence is best to go unnoticed by as many as possible. I've already interfered with too many, my aunts, Jove, Sol, and Garr.

At my side, the satyr continues forward beyond the line of trees, but I grab his wrist, tugging him to a halt. I try not to shiver at the feel of his skin beneath my own, but I can't allow him to continue forward.

As recalled by Deona, Garr is not seen by any of them until the evening at the celebration—tomorrow. Cognizant of the so-called butterfly effect, I don't want to drop any more changes into their history than I already have.

Garr glances down at my hold on his wrist. "Why are we stopping?" he asks. "I want to see the sisters."

I tow him backward into deeper tree cover. "We can't," I say with a slight shake of my head. "That's not the way things were scripted."

He turns to fully address me. "You mean in the future you've seen?"

I nod. "You don't see them until tomorrow, at the time of the celebration."

He huffs and drops to a crouch, arms resting on his bent knees. "How far into the future have you seen?" He tilts his head back to gaze up at me.

I don't know how to answer that question without either outright lying or giving too much of the truth away. And if Garr learns the truth, what could that translate into for the way history will unfold. My silence must speak a language of its own, for his shoulders square with something akin to resolve.

His lips purse. "Far, then. What have you seen of me? What do I become that made you come here now and intervene?"

Before I can formulate a response, laughs and uplifting chatter drag both our attention to the clearing. Deona, Estala, and Fiona step clear of the tree line near the stream. In their arms, clean and folded laundry. Not with them, Jove and Sol.

Shouldn't they have met by now?

Within a blink I am sifting through Deona's memories, her panic matching my own, and the answer is yes. Yes, they should have met before finishing the chore of washing the laundry.

My heart accelerates with the power and pound of a jack rabbit's quick leap. My attention darts from the sisters, to the tree line, to the homestead, and every space in between.

Where is Jove where is Jove where is Jove.

My breath becomes heavy and hard. I can't get enough.

Holy Gaea and god, please tell me I didn't change history. Didn't change something so significant as the first Balance Bringer meeting her Tracer.

I stumble backward. "Where are they?"

"Where is who?" Garr asks, his face narrowing with intense concern.

My hand slaps down on his shoulder. "I need to find them." Which means leaving Garr unattended. "Promise me you won't go and see the sisters until tomorrow."

He nods, tight lines casting from the corners of his eyes.

Nothing bothering with another word, I spin and race for the ruins of the abandoned village.

EVEN WITH THE wind at my back, my legs can't carry me fast enough across the terrain. Four words are stuck in a cycle, spinning around and around in my head, *what have I done?* I search my soul, the memories of my many incarnations for changes to my history.

If something has changed, will I feel it? Or do I exist outside of the current alterations to this new narrative branch?

Maybe I should fold space again, relocate myself at a time before I interfered with Jove and Sol's brawl with the troll. Stop myself from intervening. Only, my last—and only—attempt at time-space manipulation wasn't exactly a bullseye execution. My time and place arrival isn't guaranteed.

The rush of water, a river cutting through the village ruin, indicates my growing nearness. The outermost remnants of buildings meet me, beckons me forward. When I left the males, they were near the village center and the stone bridge connecting the two sides of the ancient settlement.

Deona remembers the location well, for she and her sisters fought a troll there, saved Jove and Sol at the location.

My breath hitches.

Not just one troll. Three of them.

Holy Gaea! Why had I not remembered that before? Had I been so rattled by coming into contact with Jove?

Crapcrapcrapcrap.

"Jove!" His name bursts from my lungs and clashes over the land, through the air like a tsunami. A guttural snarl is my response.

Not Jove but a troll.

A sea of panic borne emotions rumbles and cracks within me, and in that moment, I understand the frame of mind that caused a young Deona to rip the world into multitudes.

I round a corner, straight into the path of a troll, and skid to a harsh halt. This new monster is as ugly and hulking and stinky as the one I previously bested. That bested one several yards to my right, still trapped within my earthen binds, and appearing angry as ever. He's not getting free anytime soon.

I face off against the newest arrival.

An unmoving male with dark hair dangles from the troll's oversized hand.

Jove! My insides scream.

The troll sneers at me and tosses Jove aside, clearly freeing himself to better attack me.

But I could care less about the smelly brute. All I care about is Jove.

My gaze follows the toss and drop of my would-be Tracer. His limbs flail like a rag doll. And his destination drop... into the lap of a smaller troll. A troll already making a meal of... of... chomping down on the torn apart shape of...

Oh heavenly Gaea! The small troll is eating Sol!

I need to get to Jove before he, too, becomes a meal.

I break into action, racing straight for Jove, both trolls becoming obstacles that need to be removed. The larger of the two trolls stands between me and Jove, the smaller of the two has Jove in his lap. Engaging in a fight is time I refuse to waste. But physical prowess is not the only tool at my disposal.

Refusing to slow, and charging forward with the speed of an immortal, I beseech the blessed elements, requesting their assistance. And they answer. The ground cracks open and swallows the larger troll, dropping him in a too deep hole.

I leap over the gap without pausing.

Wind and water work together, raising waves from the river below, and curling them up and over the side of the bridge. The elemental force sweeps the small troll and all remnants of the now deceased Sol out of sight.

I collapse at Jove's side and pull him to me. My hands searching his entire body, my senses seeking his breath, his heartbeat. A simple eye flutter.

His entire body, internal systems, are silent and unmoving. He's nonresponsive to every plea I make. Every attempt to rouse him.

Blood leaks from his nose and mouth. His neck is broken, and the back of his skull crushed.

My chest compresses and I can't breathe. Can't think. My body falls numb, as my vision blurs and erupts into red. Everything is red. My vision, red. My temperature, red. My emotions, the bloodiest of red.

Jove is dead. No connection can be made between him and Deona. No eternal bond made. What does that mean for every Balance Bringer and her Tracer to come after this? Will there even be Tracers after this horrible end.

If Deona loses her Jove, do I lose my Jaden?

Every incarnation within me screams and I release a cry that sounds far more animal than anything else.

The red behind my eyes explodes into the purest of bright illumination and is then engulfed with an endless space of nothing. A free-floating darkness. Like I'm drifting in outer space without stars. Trapped in a black hole.

My heart and mind surely are. The true depths and devastation of what I've done are tearing me to pieces. Each shredding, dull knives lacerating my spirit and soul.

My insides are crying, even if a tear does not touch my cheek.

I'm not even certain I have physical form in this place I've transported myself. No longer feet on the ground in Hiddenkel, past, present, or future, wrapped in my grief, I have wrapped myself in the fifth element of space and now dwell within... or beyond... the tangible spaces.

I have destroyed everything.

Not only my many lives, but the chance for balance among

the many worlds. In my reckless need to fix things, I became the ultimate nuclear bomb.

Giving myself to the void, I wish the nothingness to absorb my pain and erase my existence.

I drift and float and...

No.

I will not lay down and accept defeat, no matter how dire. There is a way to fix this, I merely need to free my mind so that the answer may find me. A solution that will save Jove and Jaden, and every version of him in between.

Adrift in the empty space of the fifth element, a possible remedy takes form. I'll return to Izza's self-imposed prison, a space existing outside of time and thus likely unaffected by the changes.

I'll return to that place at an earlier time and stop myself from ever making this time jump.

I close my thoughts and sights, fold the fabric of time and space, and release myself to the moment when visiting this time and place became a real possibility in my mind.

FOUR

My consciousness slips through the folds of space, pulling me to the point where the act of divergence was taken. When I decided to jump to the beginning, to the first three sisters, and then proceeded to destroy that which I hold dear... my connection to Jaden.

Shifting closer to my destination, blurry images and words from the surrounding moments glide over me like silk on a soft wind.

The voice of my past self, inflected with both desperation and fragile hope, saying *"Have you tried?"* becomes my time target. Not long after that exchange with Izza, I made my first attempt at adjusting events in the past.

Like colored shadows cast into a room, Izza and I come into view, playing out a scene from my past. Izza dips her head and shakes, her disapproval... apprehension... evident. *"We heard you. Did you know that? You said you wanted to straighten the path to balance."*

I'm still focused on that goal. With my jump to the past, I may have failed to stop the darkness, but I *had* adjusted Garr's actions. If everything was left to unfold from that point, I believe his part in our history would be far different. But my meddling had other ramifications, something else Izza had warned me about. Now Jove is dead, had died instead of connecting with Deona, and that change to history cannot be allowed to stand.

Determined to fix my world-ending error, I zero in on my location in the proceeding moment.

"Exactly right." The voice of my past self echoes in my ears, my words and known intentions sparking a prickling sensation across my scalp. The me from my history isn't done. *"And that's why I need to go back to these moments,"* she says.

And I need to stop you, I think. *Or me. Stop myself.*

I release my shift through time and space and step into the moment. My past self is spinning toward Fiona's moving memory, hand reaching out. The plan, I remember well. I just lived it, and it unfolded in catastrophe.

I lurch forward and grab the hand of my past self, halting my action before I can follow through on the horrid mistake. My past self jerks and spins on me, stares, mouth dropping open

"You don't want to do this," I say to myself.

Her gaze travels over me, and I can see her reaching for understanding, trying to grasp what is unfurling between us.

Around the walls of Izza's hideaway, the moving memories of all the Balance Bringers shudder and turn staticky, as if in flux, their histories undecided, and awaiting the decision of my past-self. Will a domino effect of changes be reflected or not?

"Trust me," I continue. "This one will go poorly."

"How poorly?" My past self leans into me. "What do I do?" She studies my face. "Or have already done?"

Izza steps close. "We knew we shouldn't mess with time."

I spare her a quick glance, then return my attention to my

past self. "If you go, you will likely succeed in adjusting Garr's path, but you will also cause a..."

I close my eyes and swallow against the emotions lumping in my throat. *My actions led to Jove's death. Me, I'm at fault.*

My past self lowers her voice to a whisper. "What happened?"

I fortify my resolve, drag a deep breath, and pin my attention on my past-self. "Don't chance changes to the evolution of your bond with Jaden."

"Jaden?" Face paling, my past self gasps and yanks her hand free, grasps a clasped fist to her chest.

The horror in her expression is absolute. I don't need to reveal the truth for her to understand the results of our visit were fifteen shades past devastating.

The surrounding memory images sharpen and an odd, untethering sensation twinges through me. I become light and dizzy. My past self has solidified her decision not to repeat my mistake. As a result, my existence no longer belongs in this time and space.

I'm obsolete, a never-was, because the events that created this vision of me no longer exist. And, therefore, neither do I.

I'm fading and becoming nothing in this moment.

I STARE at the space where, moments ago, stood a version of myself from the future. Utterly surreal. Like something out of a science fiction movie. I came back to warn myself, correct my mistakes.

What had I done in the past that resulted in something horrible for Jaden?

Whatever I did, it had to involve Jove. He would have been there; at the time I had planned on targeting.

Izza settles onto a nearby bench. "What do you think happened?"

I can't answer her question with certainty, but my gut suggests something utterly ruinous happened to Jove, or Deona's relationship with him. But what?

I worry my lower lip. "Do you think a change to the past could have resulted in bodily mutilation or death to Jove?"

"Dhmaric," she murmurs, clearly recalling her own version of our lifetimes-bound Tracer. "We cannot allow harm to come to him. Time must be left alone."

"Yes. Maybe." I press my lips together in a firm line and scratch the back of my neck, turning away to study the memories of the previous Balance Bringers.

"Maybe?" she blurts.

"Okay. Hear me out." I spin back to face her. "The me from the future told me not to chance changes to Jaden, or in your case," I motion to her, "Dhmaric. She didn't say time travel was off the board."

Izza jerks back, her face pinching. "Off the board?"

"Not allowed," I clarify.

Izza rises to her feet, her head shaking adamantly. "Such antics are too dangerous. You saw the expression on the face of that future you." She flings her arm wide, as if to indicate the version of me that is no longer present. "Whatever she did..." She swings a harsh jab at me. "You did, was a grave error. One that you cannot duplicate, no matter the historical variations."

I nod and drop my gaze to the ground. "The future is still trapped in a dire situation."

I may have managed to get the old water god to remove Dreya's curse, and thus her power over the water elements, but she was still outrageously strong with the darkness. Had warped much of the landscape and occupants, casting her chains around them, forcing them into her service. And all for what? A grudge?

And, yes, maybe I was selfish in that I want to undo the damage done to my family and friends. Make it so that their physical inflections never happened. But those friends and family are the foundation of my own inner strength. And I need them.

"We will find a way," Izza consoles, suggesting all the Balance Bringers now residing within me will discover the answer and fix the worlds.

But what if they don't? It wouldn't be the first time the Balance Bringer had failed. Not all of them had developed a relationship with the fire element, and even fewer... possibly only Izza... had connected with the fifth element, space... and thereby time.

Lips pursed, decision firm, I raise my gaze to Izza's. "I think I should try again." She's already shaking her head. Swiveling back and forth again and again. "I'll stay far away from any Balance Bringer or Tracer lines. In fact, I'll target a time when neither are walking the world in physical form."

Izza stops shaking her head and considers me. "We are uncertain."

"It could work," I argue. "All I need to do is prevent one event from occurring and my timeline should be far more manageable." One pissed off and destructive Dreya being replaced with a far more amenable one.

She frowns. "And if your efforts fail?"

I shrug. "Then I'll hit the reset button, like I did this last time."

She returns to her seat and folds her hands in her lap. "We are still resistant and do not recommend the act, but..." She glances over me with a sigh. "It is your life, your choice, and your mistake or success to make. We suppose you will learn, one way or another."

"Thanks for those delightful words of encouragement." My voice drips with sarcasm.

She shrugs, a playful smile tipping her lips. "If we refuse to share the truth, what kind of sister would we be?"

"Cherish and loved." I tug her off the bench and enfold her in my embrace. "Always. No matter what."

Her squeeze around me tightens, communicating her appreciation. "If not during the life of a Balance Bringer, how will you know when and where to focus the fifth element's gift?"

How *will* I pinpoint my destination? I blink, the answer slipping into place as if pushed there by my grandmother—Her lingering power resonating through the crystal throne where my physical body was last located.

With my current time travel dally, does my physical self still exist in that place in time with Jaden, in my family's destroyed throne room?

A question for a later time, after I fix the larger concern—Dreya and the darkness.

What put Dreya on the path to the darkness? Her gift, later turned curse, from the old water god. And where did she receive that thoughtful gift? At the bottom of the small lake located behind the family's winter castle. A castle and lake I have recently visited. Depending on how you view things, I'm still physically there.

The where determined, I need to choose the when. Something my ancestral memory share can help me with. I haven't experienced any dream-walks from that time period, but my father was present. Which means, I have access to two relatives with front-row seats to the time-significant event, my father *and* Dreya.

"Well?" Izza pushes the question I've left unanswered.

"I know the where," I reply. "And my father and aunt will show me the when."

"How is that going to work?"

"Ancestral memories."

Her expression widens with comprehension, then shifts into a somber smile. "Do be careful."

I wouldn't consider being anything but, not with so much at risk. Jaden, my brother, the worlds. Closing my eyes, I give myself over to the fifth element. Infant, as I am, at working with space and time, the collaboration between me and the medium is almost second nature. A possible gift from Izza, given her ease with the connection.

No tingling thrills wrack my body. No rush of wind beats against my skin. I'm shifting in and through a void, an absence of senses. Nothing to see or hear or feel, within or without.

Complete emptiness. Nothing, nothing, nothing... *something.*

My eyes pop open. Goose bumps are exploding across my skin and my entire body is shivering. A landscape of ice and snow surrounds me, the temperature dropping with the setting sun, and I am *so* not dressed for the weather.

In one direction, an endless vision of a frost blessed terrain with a cluster of floating islands in the distance. In the other, a glistening white royal mansion—the old family castle. I'm positioned on a bluff, near a barren tree and overly large stone marker, with an unobstructed view of a frozen lake.

And on the lake, two people; one skating and one guiding. A far younger version of my father and aunt. *She looks so... innocent.*

Crap. I can't be seen.

Jolting into motion, I dive for cover behind the stone. Bump into another body.

"Pardon you." The voice is deep and rich and filled with a mischievous annoyance.

"Pardon, yourself." I twist onto my side and take in my unexpected companion. "Who are you and why are you hiding?"

He grins, a smile that draws a sparkle to his eyes. "I could ask you the same." He shifts and leans his back against the stone. "Seems we have something in common. Sneaking a peep on royalty." He lobs his head to the side and pins me with a pointed stare. "Must say, though, there is something about you that is oddly familiar."

"Really?" I narrow my eyes, scrutinizing his features. "I'm sort of thinking the same. You kind of remind me of a guy I once met. Only darker." I circle my hand before his face. "Darker hair, skin, and eyes."

He scratches his temple with a solitary finger. "Perhaps you met my brother. He is the brighter of our pair. Considers himself the better half."

"Hmhm." I frown and continue to consider his appearance. He looks an awful lot like Jove's friend. "You're the one, aren't you?" His eyes widen, a silent prompt for me to fill in the blank. "You're responsible for what becomes of Dreya. You're the one who breaks the ice, paving the way for her cursed state."

"The princess?" His head jerks back. "I take no issue with the princess. Why would I want to cause her harm?"

I shift to fully face him. "Maybe my father, the prince, was your target, but Dreya is the one who will end up paying the dearest of prices."

"Your father?" His mouth drops open and he sucks back a breath. "You're her, aren't you? You are the Balance Bringer. You're the one with whom I take issue." He lurches forward, grabs my upper arms, and shoves me flat on my back in the snow. "You ruined my life."

"Sorry?" My apology is weak, and my smile pretty much negates the sentiment, but I'm gaining perspective on the situation. "If your beef is with me, let's you and I work out our issue, and let them be." I shift my head to indicate the pair on the frozen lake.

His lips lift to the side in a crooked grin. One that tugs at Fiona's heart and memory. Memories of Sol's transformation after...

"Your word combination makes little sense," he says and presses more weight into his hold on me. "But I agree to her terms."

"Happy to have an agreement." I smirk and put no effort into fighting back. At least, not with physicality. "Sol's your brother, isn't he?"

"Brilliant deduction." His eyes fade to cold.

"I'm sorry I hurt you, Sol."

"Sol is not here right now."

The sun has fallen beyond the horizon, the sky now dark, and the temperature freezing. Plus, the male pinning me to the ground should have died ages ago, but is here instead, filled with a festering animosity, because of something that should never have happened to him. A misfortune he suffered because of his proximity to the Balance Bringer.

My heart clenches. If only I had been able to fix things properly with my last attempted time fix, then we wouldn't be here, facing this situation. I want to press my hand to the side of his face, communicate my understanding and sympathy through the touch. But alas, I can't move. So, I summon the wind to caress the skin of his cheek.

His head jerks an inch back and the dark of his dark eyes bleeds into the surrounding skin. "Sorry you got infected."

"I am not." His voice is close to a growl. "Had it not been for the infection, I would not be."

"That's one way to look at it." I open a channel to the elements.

The roots of the nearby tree explode from the ground, wrap around Sol's dark brother's limbs and yanks him free of me. He's thrust to the tree trunk, the binds winding around a multitude of times, securing him in place. He struggles against the constraints.

Pushing off the ground, I glance to the lake to verify our secrecy. The lake is deserted, Dreya and my father having returned to the castle home at sundown. Thank Gaea our presence went unnoticed.

And thank Gaea, I achieved my goal. No one fell through the ice and Dreya didn't get cursed. Take care of Sol's issues, make sure he doesn't return for a second attempt, and the purpose of this trip will be realized.

"Where should I send you that is safe for you and everyone else?" I search the horizon.

He bunts his shoulder against the confining tree roots. "What do you care of my safety?"

"I've always cared." I step before him and press my hand to his heart. "Fiona cared, Deona cared, Estala cared. I care. None of us wanted this for you, *ever*."

I press a slow, lingering kiss to his forehead. Count the seconds as I shift my forehead to his, whisper my apology once again. I breathe in his years and years of misery, then cup his face in my hands and pull away.

A lonely tear rolls down his face. "I have spent my entire existence hating you, planning to destroy you, time and time again. And for the first time, I am unsure how to feel."

"Living in anger is no way to exist," I say. "Might I suggest you spend some quality time working on forgiving me, forgiving yourself, and forgiving everyone else involved in your plight in life. Put the resentment behind you and find a way to live in contentment. Actually, enjoy your life for a change."

The darkness bleeding from his eyes recedes and his eyes lighten. I take his silence as reluctant acceptance of my recommendation.

"I'm glad we could come to an agreement." I wiggle a finger at the distant floating islands. Under the guidance of earth and air, the land masses begin to move, glide our direction. The binds around him separate from the tree, tighten around his body, and combine with ice and air to hold him immobile.

"I'm going to send you back home." I pull his secured body to mine in a hug. "I hope the next time we meet, if there is a next time, that we can agree to get along."

"We shall see," he says.

The elements shift him back, our gazes unwavering every moment of the movement. In the quiet of our exchange a thousand thoughts and feelings are exchanged.

Unless, of course, it's all my imagination.

The elements remove him from the castle's property, and maneuver him all the way to, and up onto the floating islands without hesitation.

I suck back and release a deep, cleansing breath.

I did it! Now to just verify the success reaped from saving Dreya. Then I can return to Izza, free her from her self-imprisonment, and then balance the worlds.

Easy peasy.

Closing my eyes and clearing my mind, I enter the void of space and focus on returning to the time in which I originally left—the throne room in my family's winter castle.

Within the absence of senses and the infinite nothing I whisper a promise to Izza, "I'll be along shortly, I just need to make sure what I did worked. Then I'm coming for you, coming to set you free."

Utter emptiness swaddles me, leaves me with nothing and nothing, until there is something.

The sound of birdsong outside a window and soft footsteps at my back. I open my eyes and...

This is not the throne room.

I'm pressed into a too-tight bodice gown with a low neck-line and billowing skirt, standing in front of a four-poster bed. To my side, a rounded wall set with a line of crystal cut windows. The textures and fabrics decorating the room are rich and vibrant, and definitely not left to ruin as the family's winter castle was when last I visited.

But this is definitely not the throne room, so am I in the winter castle or somewhere else?

A body, warm and inviting, presses to my backside. Hands slide around my waist, one drifting up and over my softest curve. A mouth lowers into the crook of my neck and nibbles, drags his teeth against my skin.

Everything inside of me is tingling with the connection of Balance Bringer and Tracer.

I spin into his embrace, his name a whisper on my lips. My fingers drag over his shoulders, up his neck and tangle into the silk of his hair.

"Jaden." I press a kiss to his lips.

He kisses me back, deep and luxurious, then pulls away slowly. "And here I thought you were an expert at telling us apart."

An expert at what?

I blink and gaze into his brilliant blue eyes. *Azure.*

FIVE

Yanking my hands free of his hair, I drop them to his chest and pat twice, then wiggle out of his hold. "Azure, you're here." *As in alive and not dead. What else is different?*

I hate that my voice pitches an octave in the delivery, but then this surprise is something I wasn't prepared for. Not only is Azure alive, but he's acting a tad too chummy for my comfort. I need to figure out what the dynamics are as soon as possible.

"I am." He grabs for my waist, attempting to pull me back into his hold. I step away and he advances again, his lips kicking up in a playful grin. His fingers curl in the folds of my skirt. "And we have a little time before either one of us is expected in any one place."

Ahhh... "And Jaden?" I take another retreating step and the back of my legs bump into the bed.

His hands slide between my curtain of hair and the side of my all-too-bare neck, gliding up to caress the space behind my ears. His gaze dips to the swell of my breasts. His tongue licking at his lower lip. "Jaden can join us later."

My body jerks back, attempting to create more space between us. "I don't believe he would appreciate what's happening here."

Azure pauses, then pulls his hands free of my body, clear puzzlement pinching his brow. "Since when would he be bothered?"

Um. Okay. Am I with Azure instead of Jaden in this new timeline?

He pauses for two breaths, regarding me, then continues. "If you would prefer to wait for his return and enjoy our three-some folly..."

My heart ricochets in my chest.

The three of us, together? How progressive of them. My mouth pops open. This new timeline, this other me, is so... so... I don't even know.

He holds me with a quizzical stare. "Are you all right, Ana?"

I don't know. "I never..." I don't even know where to begin finishing that sentence.

"You never?" he prompts.

Never expected to see Azure alive again. Never expected to be in this situation with Azure. Never been as close with a male as his advances are encouraging. Never anticipated returning to such a dramatically changed present.

"What of Ruby?" I blurt.

"Ruby?" His brow pinches. "Who is Ruby?"

I flinch. "You don't know Ruby? The fiery redhead with love connections graphed all over her skin?"

His eyes alight with understanding. "You speak of the queen's prisoner. I am not certain that is her name, but what about her?"

"Ruby is a prisoner?" Ruby and I were never friendly, but this path, I can't wish her imprisonment. "What did she do?"

His eyes narrow. "You know. You were there. It is not like you to forget."

Except when I didn't live the experience. And during this short time in this new present, so many things are different. My head is spinning and pounding with all the questions and issues.

"I..." I flatten a hand to my forehead. "*Gaea above*, my head hurts."

His eyebrows draw together, and he presses a tender touch to my temple. "Should I collect the royal healer?"

Royal? So I *am* in the castle. "I think..." I scoot away from him and around the edge of the bed, sit with a droop of my shoulders. "I merely need a nap." Some time alone to assess the current state of this world. Because, holy Gaea and god, I have an intimate relationship with both Jaden and Azure?

"Are you sure you would not like to consult the healer?" He brushes my hair from my face.

"Quite." I pull my legs and skirts to the bed's surface, then lay my head on the pillow, and close my eyes. "I just need a little quiet time."

The room falls silent, aside from the sound of our breaths. Azure has yet to turn and leave. And I do need him to leave, because... I just need him to leave. I crack my eyes open a slit. "Alone."

"Very well." He drops a kiss on my temple. "Should you need me, simply summon."

I nod and close my eyes, track the sound of his departure from the room. The moment the metal knob clicks shut, I bounce to my feet and, careful of the whisper of my skirt, dash across the room. Quietly turning the lock to ensure no one enters, I press my ear to the door and listen.

I should probably head back to Izza, but I'm living in the palace and Azure is alive! I need to know more before committing to this new now. The threesome change, although significant, is not enough to reject this timeline in favor of a reset.

So I listen. Collect more information.

On the other side of the door, Azure is talking with someone of the female persuasion.

"She says she needs a rest, but..." Azure hesitates.

"Yes? What is it?" The female voice is familiar, yet somehow different than what I inherently expect.

"I am uncertain," he replies. "She is speaking strangely and acting oddly."

"Oh, poor Azure." The female replies, clear teasing in her delivery. "Are your feelings hurt because my sister is not in the mood?"

I suck back a breath. One of my sisters is still alive? The revelation has me wanting to laugh. Could this new present have undone all the heart-breaking hurts? Significant changes, indeed, but changes I can most definitely live with.

"You know such things are not a worry of mine," Azure counters. "I am concerned about her."

"Then I shall retrieve the royal healer," my sister replies. I now understand the familiarity in the voice, but what I hear isn't quite right for either Crystia or Kaia. The tone and inflection sounds far more similar to my voice than either of theirs. So... what does that mean?

"She refused a visit from the healer."

My sister laughs. "Since when do you succumb to my sister's stubbornness?" Her question is followed by a male's grunt or groan. "I shall retrieve the healer."

Light footsteps move away. My sister, I assume. Several moments pass before a second departure follows beyond my range of hearing. What went through Azure's head that had him hesitating outside of my bedroom door?

Moving to the wall of windows, I take in the scene, and

attempt to gather my bearings, before venturing beyond my bedroom door.

My room boasts a view of a garden in full bloom and a glistening lake beyond the floral paradise. The view is in line with what I recall of the family's winter castle. Although, it's not currently winter, and everything is so alive and vibrant.

Maybe the seasonal use of the castle has been expanded.

When I drop my attention to the space directly below, the angle of the downward gaze is unexpected. I'm perched higher than I recall the castle being. Maybe this version of the palace received a few room additions.

Two people step into the garden below, drawing my eye. A couple decked in fine attire and bubbling with belly-deep chuckles. Realization washes over me and my breath catches in my throat. The couple I'm looking at are my father and aunt Dreya, happy and healthy and... well... the picture of an amiable ruling class.

My heart swells. The situation with Azure might be awkward, and the prospect of my sister, hopeful, but the vision of Aunt Dreya neither cursed nor infected with the darkness is... I lick my lips and press my had to my heart... is the optimistic sign I've been craving.

I press my hands to the window glass and call out to my elemental connections. The water, earth, and air can supply me with more knowledge than any visual inspection could ever do. Water responds with the roar of a rushing river across my soul. But earth and air... nothing. Like my request for connection was tossed into a dark room and abandoned.

My heart hiccups and I try again. And again. And again. Earth and air not only refuse to respond, but they are not even a whisper through my soul.

A sense of emptiness carves a hole in my chest.

Breath growing heavy, I push the panic away, refusing to yield to the emotion.

I lift my hand, palm up, and call to the fourth element of fire. Only, like earth and air, no sparks ignite in my blood. No fire bursts to life. No kernel of warmth stirs at all.

My eye begins to twitch, and my hands shake.

This. Can't. Be. Happening.

I close my empty palm—no fire, no wind, no earthen response. My stomach flops and I can barely hold myself upright on my weakening legs. What is wrong with me?

Please Gaea, tell me this isn't what I am in this new time-line. A yet to be realized Balance Bringer?

I need to get back to Izza, get her take on this situation.

Because, no matter how promising some of the other witnessed changes may be, an unrealized Balance Bringer has to be all kinds of bad.

As I have the three previous times, I close my eyes, and focus on the void of the fifth element. I can't sense it. Can't connect. If I no longer have access to three of the other four elements, maybe this fifth is beyond me, as well. Yet, if Izza is able to master space and time, while lacking the talent with the others, then I can do the same. We are, after all, versions of the same soul.

I can do this, I tell myself.

Still, try as I do, there's no moving through time and space for me.

I stumble backwards and fall to my butt on the floor, my breath coming too hard and too fast. My heart sinks as tears fill my eyes and wet my cheeks.

I'm trapped here... in this world of my making. What have I done?

For endless minutes, or possibly hours, I curl in on myself, the many folds of my skirt tangled around me. I've never felt so hopeless and so I give in to the overwhelming emotions. After what feels like not near enough time to breakdown and recover, a knock on the door pulls me from my pathetic self-indulgence. I sit straight with a jolt and wipe at my tears, sniffle.

I'm not ready for company, but I need to be. I need to pull myself together and gain a strong understanding of everything about this new world.

"Give me a minute." I push to my feet and clear all evidence of shaky emotions from my face. I smooth my skirt, fix my hair, and take a courage-inflating breath. "Who is it?"

The lock twists, as if assisted by magic, or an air elemental—my sister, I realize. The door opens and a girl who's almost the spitting image of myself steps into the room. A physical match, like Deona and her sisters had been... and so many Balance Bringer incarnations between. Thanks to my mom's immortal warrior's hibernating seed kicking into action during the gestation process, the age difference amongst me and my sisters granted us a sliver of individuality many of the others didn't have. Apparently, there was no hibernating in this timeline.

Kaia was the first of us to wield the air element. And it was clearly the air element that unlocked the door. So, am I looking at her now, without her mystic granted disguise?

She balances a cup of steaming liquid on a tray. "Azure suggested you are feeling a tad less, so Crystal has gone to fetch the healer. I brought you a proper cup of tea, thinking it might help."

"Crystal?" I follow her to the table and scrutinize the cup of tea.

"Yes, Crystal," she says. "You remember your sister, do you not?"

Is Crystal this world's version of Crystia? And if Crystal is fetching the healer and my sister is the one delivering the message, then both of my sisters are still alive? Which means...

I suck back a breath.

My sisters and I have yet to bind and that might be the reason why I can't access the elements beyond water.

Okay, I tell myself, *it's not so bad. At least, my sisters are alive.* And that, that's far better.

I raise my gaze from the tea and stare into her kaleidoscope eyes. They remind me of mine, before they changed, adopting a solid color. Her colorful eyes are dominant in shades of violet. Her hair a bright blonde, absent of the golden strands mine had recently grown.

I spin toward the mirror and study my reflection. No golden strands and my eyes are once again kaleidoscope in nature. Only mine are dominated in shades of blue.

Blue for water, violet for air. Are Crystia's—Crystal's—eyes dominated by green? I suspect they are.

I lean closer to my reflection. My hair and eyes are not the only thing different. The birthmark on my brow is gone. Warrior's mark, my mom called it.

Not a single sign suggests any marking ever existed. Guess that makes sense, given the lack of conflict between my father and aunt. My mom probably never had to run, and my birth took place under normal circumstances.

My sister steps beside me and places her hand to my forehead, as if feeling my temperature. "You do not look well. I suggest you have some tea and lie down until the healer arrives."

She returns to the table and drops a sugar cube into the cup of tea. I don't usually take sugar in my tea. Maybe this version of me is different in that way. I need to understand how this time thing works. Who I was in this world before, who I am dropping into this world, and what becomes of me by combining the two.

"Kaia?" I turn and follow her to the table.

She stops prepping the tea and turns to me. "Who is Kaia?"

I dip my head toward her. "Oh, Anaka, darling. You truly are unwell. You should lie down. The healer should be along shortly."

Anaka. My name isn't Anala but Anaka. Crystia is Crystal, and... "I'm sorry," I say and tilt my head in silent request for her name.

"Are you suggesting you have forgotten my name? Your own sister?"

I sigh and take a seat on the bed. "I may have forgotten more than your name," I admit. "Can you tell me what our situation is here?"

"Honestly, Anaka." She folds her hands at her waist. "You have me significantly worried. What is happening with you?"

Do I want to respond honestly? I don't know, but I'm saved from answering the question by the door opening and Crystal leading the royal healer into my room. Crystal is indeed a perfect look-alike, her eyes only brighter with green... as I expected. My attention travels past her to the healer and...

"Airmid?" I blurt. The royal healer is the same one I met at Madame Marrouske's sanctuary, the tree of life.

"Yes, dear," she replies and motions to my sisters. "Kayla and Crystal, you lovelies find a seat out of the way and allow me to get a good look at your sister."

From Anala, Crystia, and Kaia to Anaka, Crystal, and Kayla. At least the names are similar, making it easier for me to remember, and mistakes less obvious.

Airmid steps to my side and lifts my wrist, takes my pulse. "When did the unwell feeling begin?"

I tug my hand free of her hold. "No disrespect, Airmid, but

I don't need a healer so much as someone well versed in time travel." I lean into her. "You wouldn't happen to be knowledgeable in time travel, would you?"

"Time travel?" my sisters say in unison.

"Working the fifth element," I clarify. "Moving through space and time."

Kayla leaps to her feet. "Impossible."

Crystal frowns and crosses her arms. "We have yet to master the three we have."

Yes, a bit of a problem that is. "Is Zarah around? A time chronicler might be able to help me with my questions."

Airmid lifts an eyebrow. "A time chronicler in the palace?"

Kayla steps forward shaking her head. "Their kind are not allowed on the property."

Their kind? "Why not?"

"Is it not obvious?" Crystal answers. "Time chroniclers make excellent spies, and we cannot allow spies near the queen."

I stand and face my sisters. "Even Zarah, Ry's fiancé?"

Kayla's brow furrows. "We know nothing about a time chronicler named Zarah."

"And who is Ry?" Crystal adds.

My eyes widen, even as my heart accelerates. "Our brother, Ryland?"

"Anaka." Airmid places a gentle hand on mine, clearly meant to sooth. Sooth it does not. "You have no brother. No blood family, beyond the three of you, to speak off."

SIX

"I will send word to the madame." Airmid's parting words to me, regarding Madame Marrouske... or Meira... or whatever name my aunt is currently going by.

The royal healer had sent my sisters away, worried that whatever fever I might have would be catching. Although, she was able to identify no true fever, despite all the poking and prodding. She plied me with rubs, made me drink teas and tonics, and fed me a great deal of information, while closely watching and weighing my reactions.

I shove open a window and lean out, sucking back the early morning air. Fresh, rose scented air wafts up from the garden below. *Calm. Stay calm. I'll figure this out and somehow make everything all right.*

By the end of the previous night's conversation... or physical check-up... with Airmid, I *think* she had believed my need to talk with an expert on time travel, time distortion, and or time change effects.

Madame Marrouske, Meira, lacking a civil relationship

with the queen—*hard to believe*—isn't present at the palace. But she has well-placed agents to watch over and assist me when needed. One of them will get her a swift message. Airmid conveniently left out who those agents are. Said I knew of them, and would not expose them unnecessarily.

In her attempt to sooth, she'd drawn gentle circles on my back while delivering unwanted truths to my ear. "No set of Balance Bringer sisters have ever had other siblings."

I hadn't believed her. I still don't. I *do* have a brother; our connection has simply been kept silent. That's the only answer I'll accept. Mom and Ry kept our family relations a secret before, that has to be the case now.

Exhaustion had claimed me shortly after that discussion, one of Airmid's tonics suspect for the sudden oncoming of fatigue. In my original reality, I respected the healer, so I'm granting her the benefit of a doubt, believing my induced sleep came from a place of concern—for me and my wellbeing.

The sun having now risen on a new day, and opting for comfortable britches and a tunic over yesterday's too-confining dress, I set out in search of further answers, in addition to the information provided by Arimid.

My garden view bedroom is one of three set side-by-side, on the palace's highest level. Beyond my chamber, is a common room shared by my sisters and me. The furnishings, a sofa and two oversized chairs, with a low-lying table between them, are plush and inviting.

The room is vacant, and my sisters are still sleeping, their rooms quiet and doors closed. At the end of the farthest bedroom are stairs to the level below. And across the room...

I move there now—a large window providing a front view of the castle estate.

If the information provided by Airmid is to be believed, my sisters and I live at the castle estate as wards of the queen. Our parentage is either unknown or a closely guarded secret. We were born as traditional triples, in one birthing cycle, verses separated by an Immortal Warriors' fetal hibernation process—a fact I'd already deduced—which explains our practically identical appearances.

Pressing my fingers to the base of the window, I peer out the glass. The landscape is green and lush, even in the pre-dawn light. A far cry from the vision I experienced when last I gazed at this sight.

A vision of the land covered in snow and a chained, broken, bleeding Dohlan dropping to the path, floats through my thoughts. I close my eyes and shake the memory away. With the changes I influenced, that horrible event never befell Dohlan. Hopefully, he's out there somewhere, living his life, unaffected by all the manipulation.

In the distance, night torches are being extinguished along the palace property's protective wall. The gentle rising sun negating the need for additional lighting. A world awakening to a new day. The scene settles a sense of peace over me, even as my attention pivots to a cluster of floating landmasses on the horizon.

Many lifetimes ago, Estala imprisoned an infected Sol on those islands. I had returned a dark version of him to the holding location when I'd changed Dreya's past. Does he remember our exchange and is he still holding a grudge?

If he does, I'll likely find out soon enough.

I turn away from the view and stride down the stone steps, my destination, the throne room. If I can tap into the power of the crystals, maybe I can not only gain some perspective on my current situation but can reach Izza.

I marvel at most everything I see, my fingers needing to touch stone, and tapestries, furniture, and wall sconces, just to assure the items are real and not a prolonged dream. Staying on course with my intentions, my footfalls are soft, careful not to draw undue attention. Now that I'm a ward of the crown and no longer the rightful heir, I expect my access to the throne to be difficult, if not close to impossible.

Rule of the lands follows the females within the family line. In this adjusted history, that would be Dreya and her descendants. According to Airmid, my aunt has a king consort, along with an heir and spare already in training. Both children, and I'm told they *are* children, are said to behave well enough. Show promise to, one day, become good rulers. But then, they *are* young and there is a lot of time for change.

I spiral down the stairs, capturing glances out each window I pass. On the second level, I spy a small gathering near the main gate in the distant wall. Visitors have arrived... and so early. I need to hurry.

Quickening my steps, I descend the stairs, slink down the halls, and come to a pause across from the throne room doors, beside an alcove featuring a statue of my grandmother—Dreya's mother and the previous queen.

Funny. I don't remember this statue being here in my original timeline. I brush the thought away and refocus on my mission.

Of course, there are guards outside the throne room doors, even if the room is unoccupied. The chamber holds the seat of power, and the crystals are too powerful not to be protected.

If I attempt to talk to the guards, I'll likely only succeed in etching myself on their radar, making it even more difficult to sneak past them. I slip into the shadows of the alcove, attempting to disappear from all sight, and take measure of everything in sight.

Aside from the guards, the halls and corridors are relatively empty. The staff are busy, as always, but they use private passageways not visible to most.

The wall at my back creaks, the support slipping away. I stumble. Get caught and steadied in the hands of another.

"Worry not," Azure whispers at my ear. "I shall not reveal your hidden location, but can you tell me, why are you lurking the shadows?" His nose grazes the ridge of my ear and I shiver.

Again, alone with Azure. This time in a darkened alcove. Can I get used to this part of my new life?

"Jaden?" I ask, needing to push emotional distance between us.

"He should return today," Azure says. "As you know, he made a quick trip to visit our parents, and if he detected a fraction of what you have been experiencing since yesterday, he should be heading straight back."

Jaden and Azure's parents are alive? The boys had been orphans, raised by my aunt Edea, otherwise known as Opal.

Dreya isn't cursed or infected, my father and sisters are alive, Azure is alive, as are his parents. Already, so many lives saved. Positive changes to weigh against the awkward dynamics between me and Azure, or the differences in my sisters. I can work on acceptance of those relationships if this world I've created is better off, and to be my new reality.

My soul lightens at the thought.

But what I don't understand is, if things are now so much better, why was a new incarnation of the Balance Bringer born? Our birth tends to mark a coming need for balance, in the world, between the worlds. So... what's the coming big bad this life go-around?

The not-knowing and the lack of Balance Bringer preparedness twists gnarly knots in my belly.

"Ana." Azure tugs me to face him. "Let me help you. What is going on? What do you need?"

Snapping out of my internal thoughts, I glance back to the

males guarding the throne room doors. "I need to get to the throne and beg guidance from the crystals."

His brow furrows. "How will the crystals help you? Your element is water."

And if memory serves, water runs through the crystal caverns beneath the throne room. Hopefully, those crystals are super charging the water, and that combination will gift me the exact kind of umph I need to reestablish my connection with *all* the elements. And maybe my many incarnations, as well, because the Balance Bringer binding seems to have been reversed when did what I did.

"I just..." I bite my lower lip and glance between him and the throne room entrance. "I'm hopeful."

His chest heaves and his intense gaze suggests he's trying to decide if he'll help me or kiss me. I bite my lip.

"Very well," he says with a sigh. "Wait here and I shall clear the way for you." He stares at me a moment longer before tearing his gaze away and slipping free of the alcove.

I linger in the shadows, the statue of my grandmother acting as cover between me and anyone maneuvering through the halls and corridors. I press my hand against the smooth stone of the statue. Why was this gone in my original timeline? Had something happened to it?

Such a small, simple change, but one that could represent unexpected horrors.

Could it be Azure works quickly at enlisting help? A petite housemaid saunters past the two guards posted at the throne room door, catching both their eyes. They don't move from their posts, but their attention is no longer surveying anything other than her backside.

She disappears down a side hall. A couple moments later, a loud crash. The guards exchange a glance, then one of the males steps away from his post and rushes to the housemaid's aid.

One guard down and one to go.

Azure appears from another direction and engages the remaining guard. Their words are indistinct, but they nod and motion in the direction of the commotion. A second later, they vanish in the same direction. What mess could have been created?

Not wanting to waste a single gifted second, I dash to the throne room doors and slip into the room. Gently close and lean against the barrier at my back. The room before me is exquisite in grand detail—white marble with gold leaf trim. And no gapping hole to the cavern below. It's also beautifully quiet and empty and thrumming with power. The water beneath the floor is an energetic tingle vibrating over my skin, through my blood and bones.

I cross the round room moving toward the throne. The stone of the seat glistens in the morning light. Beams that shine through the stained-glass windows set in the ceiling. The cut of crystal captures those rays, and breathes color across every surface. The floor, the walls, my skin. I am mesmerized.

A sense summoning me forward, the power beneath my feet grows stronger with each advancing step toward the crystal throne. Energy generated below channels to the seat of power. Power not only to rule the land, but to grow within yourself and connect with *everything*.

I can almost envision how my grandmother must have appeared, seated there.

I step onto the dais and then next to the chair, my fingers reaching out and gliding across the smooth stone. A whirlwind of verve zings and sparks beneath my touch and a warmth blooms through me like a welcome home. Without further hesitation, I spin and sit.

I assume the same position in the throne as I had when I began my time and space adventure. Back straight, butt flush with the seat, and arms flat against the chair arms. For a flash of a second, the energy moves through me like it remembers me and our previous exchange. As if the elements exist in multiple timelines at once, sharing their awareness across all.

And as quickly as the power and connection is there, it's gone. Vanished as fast as flipping a light switch. A hand wraps around mine and yanks me to my feet.

"What do you think you are doing?"

I blink up and peer into my father's face. "Dad?" My pulse takes off like a spooked pixie.

"Royal Commander Marduk," he corrects, his frown immediate. "Tell me, child; are you confused? You have no known father, I have no children, and you most definitely should not be in this room unattended, much less sitting upon the throne."

O. Kay. My sisters and my paternity must have been kept a secret from him. *At least he's alive.*

I quickly school my expression. "You're right, I must be confused." I bow my head. "I'm really sorry. The elemental energies drew me to the throne." Not a complete lie. Once I was in this room the apex of power became a strong tug.

He grunts and narrows his gaze. "We shan't tell my sister about this little infraction." His sister, the queen.

He nods at me with a conspirator's grin on his mouth, then grips my upper arm, and leads me out the throne room's side door and into the back halls.

He releases me. "I expect better behavior from you in the future."

I swallow hard. "Yes, Royal Commander." I want to ask a thousand and ten questions of him, but he's unaware of our connection, so where could I begin and what could I possibly chance?

"I do appreciate your spirit," he says. "But... might we act in proper decorum when dealing with matters around our queen." He winks.

I blink wide, unsure how to respond. I get the distinct impression that he's sort of messing with me to relieve the tension, but he is the royal commander and prince, and I'm considered a ward of the queen. Though I suspect she isn't very involved in my life, or the lives of my sisters. So, a wardship that is less like family and more like an exchange student.

"Have I stunted your tongue?" he asks.

My heart squeezes at the playfulness in his voice. He could be a father kidding with his daughter, which he is, only he doesn't know it. And until this exchange, I don't think I realized how much I missed having a father in my life.

"Brother."

I jolt at the new, yet familiar voice, and my father and I both turn toward the approaching queen, Dreya. I try not to tense or shudder at the memory of the dark Dreya I knew, and instead, curtsey deep to camouflage any unfitting bodily reactions.

"Sister," my father says, dipping his head.

She motions for me to rise, without making eye contact. "Mardy, I was not expecting you this morning?"

"Am I not allowed to surprise you, Drey." He cracks a wide smile, and she replies in kind, then they both lurch forward, wrapping in a hug and laughing.

I'm a complete outsider and I'm clearly missing some joke between them. I take a step back. I barely put an extra foot between us when Dreya pulls away from my father and turns to me.

"Which one are you, dear?" she asks.

That question answers one or two of my own. She doesn't spend enough time with me or my sisters to notice the difference in our eyes.

"Ana," I reply.

Her eyebrow rises. "I had not realized we were on familiar standing."

"So sorry." I courtesy, again. "Anaka. I am Anaka."

"Ah." She lifts and drops her chin. "The pinnacle."

My father grabs my arm and nudges me down the hall. "She was just leaving." Releasing me, he guides Dreya in the opposite direction, chatting about a morning drink or something.

Rather than listening to their conversation, I make haste escaping the awkward company. I make it halfway down the hall when the queen calls me to a stop.

"Oh, Anaka," Dreya says, bidding me to turn back. "I have summoned Oriana Opal Edea Virrie to the palace. Expect her in three days' time. We are past the point of awakening your destiny."

My gut knots.

Aunt Edea, coming here, to combine me and my sisters? Yeah, that doesn't sound particularly fun. Of course, it is Aunt Edea's son who I last saw in the worst of ways, so maybe...

"Will her son be joining her? Sir Dohlan Marsoun?" I ask.

Dreya appears perplexed. "I do not believe Lady Oriana O. E. Virrie has any offspring. Who is this Dohlan male to you?"

"We've met a few times." Hopefully, my words don't scream *lie*. "I was just curious about his health."

My father's brow arches and Dreya's lips purse. Her head tilts. "Such an odd thing to say." She considers me for two breaths. "But if there is anyone in particular you wish to locate, you may consult the populace keeper."

"Thank you." I bow my head. "I will do that, and I will be

ready for Edea's arrival." I glance away, down the hallway, then back. "Now, with your permission?"

"Granted." She tips her head in a silent nod.

I turn away, my thoughts on escaping Dreya's company and visiting the populace keeper, yet make it less than seven long strides when I come face to face with a small child. She's peeking around a corner with her eyes as dark as coal. She steps three-quarters into view, keeping the wall as a partial hide, as if afraid to fully face me.

Her face shows no expression. "I will some day be queen, and you will not. For what you are to become, your sisters will die."

Well, that was dark.

"There you are." A royal nanny dashes into the hall. "I have been looking for you everywhere." She leads the child away.

One of Dreya's kids, I take it.

I watch their departure and shiver, then turn the opposite direction at the "T" intersection. I dash to the main hallway, burst through the dividing door, and run straight into a body. A familiar body.

Home and happiness wrap around me. Finally, a place in the palace, in this alternate life, where I feel like I belong.

I throw my arms around him. "Jaden."

SEVEN

"Jaden." I grab him, clutch at him like I feared I might never see him again. And maybe, on some level, I feared exactly that. Still do. Because I have yet to know *this* Jaden.

"I am here," he says, his arms pressing us as close to one as possible. "I felt your anxiety and rushed my return."

"Yes, I—" He halts my word with a finger to my lips.

"Not here," he whispers, and his lips press to mine. A hello in a most intimate way.

Soft and firm, perfect and pure, he *is* my Jaden, only acting upon different lifetime experiences. His heart and soul are the same, the truth translated through our kiss. No matter our incarnation or the spin of our reality, we find our hearts together.

He shifts back and strokes his thumb across my cheek. "Take a walk with me?"

I nod. "Wouldn't you rather talk in my room, or yours?"

"No." He places his hand on the small of my back and leads

me toward the garden. Tilts toward my ear and whispers, "The walls of the palace may have ears."

We move through rooms and past personnel, toward the oversized doors leading to the garden. Azure leans against the side wall, watching us but making no move to join. The guys exchange a look that suggests they previously agreed Azure would sit this one out.

Or maybe stand watch?

He waits beside the garden door as if to stop anyone else from entering.

At a bench located in the center of the garden, a handmaid waits. The same female from earlier, who distracted the throne room guards. A handmaid I now recognize as Gitta. The elf with the ghosting ability that I knew in my original timeline as being in Madame Marrouske's service. Is she one of the well-placed agents Airmid spoke of?

"Gitta?" I ask, stepping up to the bench and wrapping my arms around my middle.

"My lady?" She tilts her head. "Have we met?"

I bite my lower lip. "I suppose not."

Jaden rubs his hand up and down my back. "I suspect what Anaka meant to say is that she would like to know you."

Gitta gives me a closed mouth smile. "Yes, my lord, it would be an honor."

Why do I feel like I just received the brush off from the petite elf? She was cool with me before. Before I changed everything.

She turns to Jaden. "Everything within the garden is secure, and I shall continue to patrol to keep it so."

"Very good," Jaden says and motions for me to take a seat on the bench. No one else is sitting, so I continue to stand at his side. "And beyond the garden wall?" he asks.

Gitta nods. "Being taken care of."

This all feels very cloak and dagger. I grab Jaden's hand, tugging his gaze to mine. "What's going on?" I toss a glance around the garden. Nothing but bushes and flowers and peaceful silence.

"One moment." Jaden dashes to the back wall, jumps up and surveys the view beyond. After a moment, he drops down and returns to my side. Slides his hand along my waist and pulls me against him. "We are doing what we can to insure our privacy." His breath at my ear warms my skin.

"Is privacy a problem here?" I start to pull away, but he holds me to him.

"Yes," he replies, his fingers gliding along my waist., his lips moving along my temple. "The ears in and around the palace have been growing in sensitivity. If we act as an enamored couple, we are less likely to draw any interest."

My hand settles on his chest. "Must we act? Isn't that what we are? An enamored couple."

"Hmmm." His throat hums and he drops his face into the crook of my neck. "

Closing my eyes, I allow myself a moment to savor his nearness. No matter the living reality, his incarnation, or the alternate timeline version of him, I find myself fiercely addicted.

The sensation of his smile spreads against the skin at my neck. "I like to think so, but I received some distressing emotions from you yesterday and this morning regarding Azure."

He lifts his head and turns his attention to Gitta who is still standing beside us. "Thank you, Gitta. You may check the garden."

She jerks on her feet. "Of course," she says and speed-walks away.

"Alone at last." His words tickle my skin. "Now talk to me

and tell me what has you in such a state." He sits on the bench and pulls me into his lap.

Not sure what to do with my hands, I rest them on my thighs. "Can I trust you?" I ask.

His scrutinizing gaze devours my expression. "Was there ever a time when my trust has been in question?"

My heart jackhammers in response. I grab his shirt and drag him close. So close our lips are a hair's width from touching. "I can't answer that... because I don't remember my life in this timeline."

He wraps his arms around me, pulling us cheek to cheek. "What do you mean by that? What has happened?"

"I was living a different reality," I whisper. "Based on an event that has since been changed. After I changed that event, I was returned to this reality, but with the memories from my previous life, a life that... apparently... no longer exists."

"How is that possible?" The surprise is evident in his tone, yet not a single hint of disbelief.

"I accessed the fifth element," I say. "I moved space and time."

His hand clenches at my back. "You are only able to work with water."

"Maybe in this new reality, but that wasn't the case before. I was almost a fully realized Balance Bringer. I was able to wield all five elements, I had access to my ancestors through my Immortal Warrior memory share, and I was bonded with most of my incarnations. I was stocked and armed with information, experience, and power."

He pulls back and cups my face in his hands. "Then why chance any changes?"

"Because..." I groan and drop my forehead to his chest. His hands rub soothing circles against my skin, and he places a soft kiss on my crown.

"When you're ready." His murmur rumbles through me.

I make myself ready and unload all my burdens, about my experiences before the change, and my reaction to everything since. I tell him about Dreya, my aunts, his brother and clan. About my upbringing in another world and the family who raised me. He listens, never once interrupting.

"In that reality, the chances for success felt insurmountable." With a sigh, I rest my cheek on his chest. "But now, Dreya is a proper queen and is neither dark nor evil, and so many that had been lost are still alive. So..." I drag the word out. "This has to be better, right? I must merely get used to the new relationship dynamics."

"You are different."

At the sound of the child's voice, Jaden and I jerk apart. The young girl from the hallway, with her unusually dark eyes stands before the bench, staring at us.

"Your highness." Jaden rises to his feet and dips his head. "We did not hear your approach."

He nudges me, jolting my body into action. Leaping to my feet, I too bow. Being in the presence of royalty is new to me and something I must immediately adjust in my reactions.

The tiny royal frowns and gazes past Jaden to me. "No one ever does." Although young in appearance, the child's words are spoken with an air of experience and wisdom. "You may be different," her gaze shifts over me as if searching for something, "but you are in *my* world now and your queendom is no longer a consideration. It would do you well to remember that. Your life has been promised to the satyr but your fate was sealed long ago by the Sun and Moon."

My mouth drops open.

Before I can begin to gather my thoughts for a response, the same royal nanny I encountered in the hallway dashes into view.

"Your highness! Why am I always dashing about, trying to locate you?" She pauses at our side, her breath heaving.

The child casts a wicked smile in my direction, then turns away, leading her nanny from the garden saying, "Do not blame me that you cannot properly handle your job."

Jaden leans into my ear. "Still believe this is a better reality?"

"I may need to gather more information." I can barely hear my own voice. "Who was that?"

"Wibke, the queen's second born."

"Is she a seer?"

"What she is is unknown. But here is no longer the place in which to discuss such matters."

Of course, because our privacy was shattered... by a child. A child that appeared so unchildlike.

"Sorry, my lord." Gitta skids around one of the garden paths and comes to an abrupt halt. "The highness is a shifty one and she managed to get past my security efforts."

"Indeed." Jaden grimaces. "She is something else." Azure dashes into view and exchanges a look of knowing and understanding with his brother. They both turn their intense gazes on me. "What would you say to brunch?" he asks.

"I could eat."

"Good." Both brothers take my hands, Jaden on my right and Azure on my left.

"*Listen closely, Ana.*" Jaden's voice whispers through my thoughts. My eyes burst wide as his hand squeezes mine. "*I take it, by your expression, this is not something you experienced in your previous reality. As long as both Azure and I are connected to you, you'll be able to hear whatever messages we send your way, but we will not hear your response until your sisters join the connection.*"

Curious. And super handy!

*"There is something not right with the royal highness Wibke.
Try to avoid her if you can."*

PROVING difficult to eat and hold hands at the same time, we
enjoy small talk over brunch. Crystal and Kayla join us at the
excessively long table and even though we are a group of five,
my heart aches for my old gang: Jaden, Ry and Zarah, Mo and
Bree, Raundel, Lobrka, and Klarda, Shadow, Clef, Al, and even
Ruby. We are... were... quite the large family. And now, all but
Jaden are a churning hole of unknown in my gut.

I do have my sisters, though. And I find myself too often
grabbing their hands and holding them tight, as if they might
cease to exist at any second.

Crystal drops her head on my shoulder. "You are rather
clingy today."

"I just love you endlessly," I reply, and she giggles.

When we are collecting and stacking our dirty dishes, a
soldier steps up to our table, his body tense with formality.
"The royal commander has requested the presence of the
Balance Bringer on today's ride. Likely to be an overnighter.
Departure is at ten hundred hours."

"That is only an hour from now!" Crystal says.

The soldier tips his head in confirmation. "Then I recommend you get moving." He spins on his heels and marches
away.

I frown and mumble, "Darn. I was hoping to visit the populace keeper."

"You want to research a few old acquaintances?" Jaden asks
and I nod. "Write down the names, and I shall see that
someone trustworthy works on your list while we are away."

Agreeing to trust whomever he deems trustworthy, I

scribble down several names and hand him the list. Then all of us, the brothers, my sisters and I, head to our various rooms to quickly change for a day on horseback—leather riders and, in my case, hair braided to keep out of my face. We reconvene beside the stables for our ride assignment and mission objective.

The procession is organized five wide and countless soldiers long. The Balance Bringer sisters and Tracer brothers are situated somewhere around the middle point of the long line, broken up to ride three and two, with soldiers placed at the end of our rows. Jaden and Azure flank my sides and my sisters ride at my back.

The show of force has less to do with our destination and pertains to the fact the Balance Bringer rides amongst them. No one sees fit to inform us where we're going, and when I ask, I'm ignored. Still, despite the journey being relatively boring, the sites are new and that keeps me entertained.

When the sun is high in the sky, we stop for personal needs and lunch. The food is bland but the drink refreshing and the opportunity to stretch my legs glorious. I walk a circle around the camp before settling down with my group. Jaden, Azure, my sisters, and I sit with the soldiers that flanked us, or rode before or behind us. Azure brought a deck of cards, and we engage in a game or two, then my sisters and I step to the side and practice... or play... with our elements.

"Balance Bringer." The Royal Commander, my father, approaches. Everyone in our circle jumps to their feet and bows. "Quite all right," he says, waving the show of respect away. "I thought you might be curious about our objective."

I nod, a tad too enthusiastically. "Yes. Curious indeed."

He glances around the circle, focusing on me and my sisters. "We are making way for the floating islands."

I blink. I remember shoving an infected Sol on the floating

islands, as Estala had first done so very long ago. In my previous reality, the floating islands were no more... or, at least, no one talked about them, and I never saw them.

He rubs the scuff along his chin. "The last sighting of the islands anywhere near the center of rule was around the time of Princess Malke's birthday. Since then, they have primarily stayed to the rim of Hiddenkel. As of yesterday, that status changed, and they have begun to float up the center of the territory."

My back straightens. I popped into this reality yesterday. I'd seen them. This morning, on the horizon. Surely, the timing is a coincidence.

"Additionally, an increase in weeping has been reported."

"Weeping?" I blurt and automatically glance at Jaden. His lips are pressed tight and fists are clenched.

"You know, sister." Kayla leans to better see me. "The precipitation falling off the islands like rain."

"Oh, yes." I bite my lip. "Sorry." Were my memories of this timeline in place, I wouldn't embarrass myself with questioning the obvious. I reach over to Kayla and squeeze her arm.

A flash of concern filters across the Royal Commanders face. "I would like you three," he yanks a quick point to each of us Balance Bringer sisters, "to assess the water and anything else you may find concerning about the moving land masses."

"Consider it done, Royal Commander," Crystal says on our behalf.

Without further decorum, he turns and leaves.

I spin on Jaden. "Why did you look so upset when you heard where we are going?"

He steers me off to the side. Soldiers move all around us, cleaning and packing up, preparing for our departure, but they don't appear to be paying us any mind... hopefully.

"Do you not know this in your version of reality?" he asks. "The floating islands are home to The Sun and The Moon."

"Sol and his other half are The Sun and The Moon?" Sol sealed my fate?

That can't be good. Not that anything about Princess Malke's delivery sounded remotely above grim.

"Who is Sol?" Azure asks, and I spin to find not only him, but my sisters also listening at my back.

I turn back to Jaden. "You don't remember him?" He shakes his head. "Of course, you wouldn't." The realization is an anchor tugging at my gut. "The other Jaden, he merged with his many incarnations, just as the Balance Bringer is meant to do," I glance back at my sisters, "eventually. Anyway," I continue with a shake of my head. "He could remember anything from any of his incarnations. So could I. Sol was a friend, best friend really, to your first incarnation known as Jove. Estala, one of the first Balance Bringer sisters created the floating islands and vanquished Sol and his darker half there. Maybe, because Sol is blond, and the meaning of his name, he is the sun, and his darker half is the moon?"

Jaden and Azure suck back synced breaths and Crystal grabs my arm, jerking me to face her. "What are you talking about?" Kayla is at Crystal's shoulder, her peer narrowed.

Jaden's hand presses to the small of my back. "They should know... about you."

"Of course, they should." I just haven't had a lot... or any... private downtime.

Crystal and Kayla link hands and offer their free hands to me. I accept, believing I'll be able to talk to them as Jaden and Azure had spoken to me. A sharp zap rockets through me and a maelstrom of information from my life downloads from me to them, through the connection.

The sensation is a rush. Like rocketing down a monster slide made of memories.

My sisters gasp, release my grasp, and step away. Crystal's hands are pressed to her mouth, whereas Kayla's jump to her chest. "Inconceivable," she murmurs.

Crystal leans toward me. "Did you really live in one of the outerworlds? See all those wild and foreign things?"

"I did." And now, at the mention, I rather miss it.

"Gaea have mercy," she whispers. The wonder on her face is a thumbnail short of magical.

"Come." I wave my sisters forward and yank them into a tight hug. Arms wrapped around one another, our connection is heavy with emotion, and growing rapidly with deep understand—of what we are to one another, and what we can be. These beautiful sisters of mine, they may not be the ones I've always known, but they are now tethered tight to my heart.

Horns blare and we all startle. The call to move ends any further conversation at that moment. We rush to our horses and climb on with moments to spare before the forward motion reaches our position in the procession.

The second half of our journey is strikingly different. Now that all the secrets between us have been revealed my sisters and I are full of spirited whispers, like a group of excited middle schoolers. Just being near them exhilarates me.

Until ruminations of our next stop, the floating islands and whatever awaits us there, begins to press upon my shoulders.

Sol should remember me since this version of him existed at the nexus of the timeline split. Has he learned to forgive and find peace, as I suggested? Or only festered in his hatred all the more?

Guess I'll know soon enough.

We ride for hours, my muscles and bones discovering new places to ache. My physical body in this life has clearly spent far fewer hours on horseback than the one in my previous reality. My skin also burns, additionally indicating I've had less sun exposure.

Have I been living like a pampered royal ward all my life? Have I even learned to fight? I remember all the maneuvers, but what of the muscle conditioning? What kind of Balance Bringer have I been raised to be?

We crest a hill and the floating islands come into view in the valley below. The land masses hover over a wide square of maturing crops, dripping water like rain, from the island to the soil. The vision is as my sister described it.

To the edge of the field is an Immortal Warrior encampment, awaiting our arrival.

We descend the hill and join the warrior ranks. Dismount and stretch. My legs might as well be rubber for as sturdy a stride they provide.

I've barely had time to orient myself when an officer appears before me. He's filthy, likely from having been on the road for too long. His fingers, ears, and the tip of his nose are a blackish brown.

"My ladies," he says to me and my sisters with a tip of his head. "The Royal Commander and Warrior Commander have gathered in the war tent and request your presence."

"Surely we may call it something other than a war tent," Crystal says, reminding me of the version of her I grew up with, Crystia. "It is not war we now go to, but a proper investigation of the elements."

"I shall pass along your suggestion," he replies, sounding uninterested in debating the tent's name. "Now, if you will follow me."

The three of us fall in line, following the officer through a camp filled with equally filthy warriors. Jaden and Azure also tag along, bringing up the rear.

If I'm to be taken to the royal commander *and* the warrior commander, then I'm going to see my mom and dad together, in the flesh, for the first time... ever.

She'll know who I am. Rather hard to keep that a secret from the female giving the birth.

Ready or not, Mom, here I come!

EIGHT

I step into the tent and find two burly males of commanding stature. One is my father and the other... is *so* not my mother. The bubble of hope that had grown since the idea I'd been seeing my mom was introduced bursts. "Who are you?" I blurt.

My sisters file into the tent at my back, bumping into me, as the royal commander turns toward me, eyebrow lifted, and face twisted in an expression somewhere between horror and humor.

"I see our little chat on proper decorum has already been forgotten." My father grins, his eyes crinkling at the edges. "Commander," He turns to the other man. "Let me introduce you to the Balance Bringer trio, Anaka, Kayla, and Crystal." He motions to each of us as he says our name.

The commander presses his blackened hand to the metal of his breast plate and bows. "Warrior Commander Usoff Cale at your service." His sharp eyes are the same color as Ry's.

My eyes widen. Usoff Cale? That was the name of

Ryland's father—the warrior commander who died in battle. But if he didn't die... Ryland still has his father. *Great news!*

But what of Mom... or me and my sisters?

The conundrum clouds my head, but I can't obsess about those questions right now. The group of us, my sisters, Jaden and Azure follow the commander's request for us to have a seat at the table. Laid flat across the surface are several maps that appear to track the progress of the floating islands.

"Royal Commander?" Someone calls from the tent flat.

"Yes." My father waves the male in. "Join us. And if you could..."

"Consider it done."

I recognize that voice, but here among the immortal warriors and royal regiment is not where I would expect to find him. I spin around in my seat and stare at the tall, dark, pointy eared elf, Lobrka. I want to jump out of my seat and toss myself at him. Hug him forever tight. But I've already embarrassed myself in this meeting.

I gaze at him, hoping to catch his eye, but he shows no outward signs of knowing me on a personal level.

He takes a stance against the tent wall, legs shoulder width apart and his arms clasped behind his back. "The patch is in place. You are now secure."

The patch had been used at the tree sanctuary by Klarda and Madame Marrouske. It works like a bubble, preventing sound from escaping the immediate space. Within the security of our magically protected privacy, discussion begins regarding the floating islands and the lands they have traveled above.

Almost two decades worth of tracking is evident on the maps present. Supporting documents cover any abnormalities noted in the land touched by the weeping. To date, nothing overtly harmful has been detected as a result of the islands sweeping overhead or the water falling from its side or underside.

But, being present and being detected are not the same thing. I know Sol to be infected with the darkness, and Sol is on the islands. So, if the islands are weeping, I consider that concerning. Possibly concerning enough to spark the rebirth of the Balance Bringer into this generation, answering my earlier question of "why are my sisters and I here, now in this time."

Tomorrow morning, at first light, by the commanders' orders, we shall take a more magical approach to assessing the elements and any possible effects.

Commander Usoff Cale knocks his fist to the table. "Tomorrow, my son will lead a small platoon to protect and support you in your investigation."

Unless Usoff has another son I don't know about, I will get to see Ryland tomorrow. I shouldn't get my hopes up that he will remember me, but I can't help myself.

I bounce my leg and bite my lip and... Gaea above, I hope he remembers me.

"Are there any questions?" The royal commander asks. With no questions, we're dismissed with orders to get a fine meal in our bellies and a good night's sleep. At a hand motion from my father, Lobrka releases the sound patch and we all file out of the tent.

No sooner are we outside of the tent than Jaden finds my hand and links his fingers with mine. "What do you say to dinner by the campfire?"

I glance back to the war tent. Azure walks with my sisters, the three of them chatting and heading to who-knows-where. The commanders and Lobrka have yet to exit the space.

"I'll tell you what." I slip my hand free of his hold. "Why don't you go on ahead and I'll catch up in a few minutes."

His gaze shifts between me and the tent, a frown pulling to his lips. "What are you up to?"

"Trust me." I drop a kiss on his cheek and then jolt, realizing that's the first kiss I've given him in my new reality. He makes a long face at my reaction.

His hand brushes my jawbone. "Hey, no worries," he whispers in a clear attempt to comfort. "We will always move at a speed comfortable for you. Tell you what, Azure and I will get the tent set up for you and your sisters, if it has not already been erected, and then you join us for that dinner by the campfire."

My tension relaxes. "Wonderful. Thank you, Jaden." I press another kiss to his cheek.

"Happy to be of service." He heads off through the rabble of soldiers, glancing back over his shoulder at least once.

I watch him until he is swallowed by the activity of the camp, a baseball sized rock resting in my chest the entire time. When he's gone, I turn back to the tent and spy Lobrka's retreating a row of tents away, moving in the opposite direction of Jaden. I jog after him, calling his name.

He stops and spins to me, an eyebrow racing up his forehead. "Bringer." His voice is as surly as I recall and that fact makes my heart squeeze.

"Lobrka." I race to him and grab his arms. "Patch."

He sighs and drops his head in a side nod. "Done."

"I remember!" I blurt.

"Sorry?"

"I remember every incarnation of the Balance Bringer I have ever been, and their interaction with you."

His shoulders jerk straight. "Well. That is both curious and unexpected. Tell me, how did this come about, given the fact, I know you have yet to undergo the binding."

"True," I reply. "But I sort of did a thing."

"What kind of thing?" He grimaces.

"I changed the timeline."

His grimace grows. "Explain."

I do just that, telling him all about my experiences before I changed Dreya's fate, the discovery of Izza in her spatial safe zone, and my ability to utilize the fifth element, thereby changing the timeline.

He crosses his arms and narrows his gaze. "You were one incarnation short of becoming a fully realized Balance Bringer, something we have never before succeeded in achieving, and you decided to change the past, resulting in this." He jabs his hands toward me in reference.

"Gee, thanks. Am I so horrible?"

"Not at all." He sighs. "But you have left this world and all of us within it at a disadvantage."

"Actually, I left more than this world at a disadvantage. But from what I've seen so far, this reality is in better shape than the one I left behind." I may not be, but the world is, and that's what's most important. "In fact, I have yet to see the type of significant imbalance that would spark the reincarnation of the Balance Bringer. So, I have yet to understand why I'm here." I tip my head to the side and pucker my lips. "Unless, of course, it would have something to do with the weeping islands."

"Truthfully? I think we need to look closer at the people surrounding the queen," he replies. "Her king consort, her children, her closest advisors and confidants."

Like the freaky young princess?

"Ana." I jerk at the sound of Jaden's voice, then spin to face him. He swings his attention between me and Lobrka. "I can see your mouths moving but I cannot hear what you are saying. I need to talk to you."

"The patch has been removed," Lobrka says. "I shall leave you two to talk."

Jaden reaches for the dark elf. "You may want to stay. This involves you, as well."

"Is that so?" Lobrka brushes Jaden's touch away. "Speak on, then."

"Very well." Jaden steps back, raking his hands through his hair. "I received a glimpse of tomorrow."

My head snaps up and I catch the diminishing remnants of the blue swirling through his green eyes.

He continues. "I think you should stay away from the floating islands."

My innards twist and tangle. Yeah, that's not going to happen.

First Sol, and now the weeping. There's no way I'm not going to try and figure out what's going on with the traveling landmasses.

JADEN HAD no option but to accept the fact that there would be no talking me out of investigating the floating islands. I need to know what happened to Sol, how he's involved in this timeline, and how he supposedly sealed my fate. The not-knowing will irritate my insides endlessly.

And, who knows, be quite detrimental to my *life*.

We sat around the campfire in silence, Jaden, no doubt, festering in his irritation over the inability to change my mind.

We filled our bellies with tasteless camp food. No, not tasteless. Odd tasting. Definitely not the fare I enjoyed at the palace last night and this morning.

And when ready to crash for the night and I crawled into the tent shared with my sisters, I laid back, held Crystal and Kayla's hands and asked about the queen's history.

The king consort is a male named Theon. Father to

Princess Quirina, and the queen's second husband. The first king consort and father to the royal heir, Princess Malke, a male named Price, died of mysterious circumstances a couple years into the marriage. Neither marriage was believed to be a love match, but arrangements for political reasons. A cupian fae attempted to convince the queen of her true love match with a known monster and enemy of the realm. This cupian fae was Ruby, and not only was her advice ignored, but she was tossed in the dungeon for her attempt.

I fall asleep with my brain still working out what factors in Dreya's life should be seen as warning signs and which are simply bad luck.

Quirina *has* to be one of the concerning factors.

THE RIDE from the camp to where the company of warriors stopped our horses was between ten and fifteen minutes. We could have been here yesterday, dealt with the issue and already had it behind us. But the powers that be... my father... wanted to wait until daylight hours. So, now, here we are at first morning's light, the islands float a hundred or so feet away. Not yet close enough for me to capture the weeping in my palm.

Crystal jumps off her horse and grazes her fingers through the tall grass. "Something is not proper. The dirt and plant life are unnatural here."

I climb off my own horse and join her, kneel at her side. She isn't wrong, the water in the soil is less than healthy.

Kayla sniffs the air. "The spores in the air have been unwell for the last few minutes of our travel. The closer to the islands we get, the larger the ratio of unwell to well becomes."

I stare up at the islands and recall Estala's memory of lifting the chunks of earth from the land, sending them afloat. They have stayed in flight for so terribly long. In my previous timeline, they were no more, but here they are, still going and going and weeping black water.

Maybe I really am looking at the reason from the current incarnation of the Balance Bringer.

Although, I'm still not going to discount Princess Quirina. Because she's not right.

"My lady." Ryland's booted feet step into my view, drawing my gaze up to his face. "Do you think it wise for you and your sisters to dismount?" He offers me his hand and I accept, allowing him to lift me from my kneel upon the ground.

His fingertips are dark, like every other Immortal Warrior in the camp. Every bit of exposed skin is dark with dirt. Are they conserving time or water by forgoing baths? Tips of fingers, ears, and noses are the darkest, next followed by the outer edges of the eyes and lips.

"We appreciate your concern, Captain Ryland," I say. "But you can't very well expect my sisters and me to properly do our job without connecting with the elements. And that is easier done when not trapped on the back of a horse."

"Of course." He grins and dips his head in a clear attempt to hide his laughter.

I met this version of Ry, shortly after breakfast, when we mounted the horses to make the ride to the floating islands. And since that first meeting, I've caught a humored expression on his face multiple times. As if he finds something about me and my sisters funny. Maybe he does. Whatever the case, I won't let his reaction build hope in me that he might remember who I am to him.

"Captain Ryland," I ask, "Have we ever met? You seem oddly familiar to me." I bite my lip to prevent a too-wide smile. I've been wanting to tackle him with a hug all morning and holding myself back has been an exercise in willpower.

He tosses me a sideways grin. "I would remember if we had, so I will have to say no."

Jaden appears from behind me, linking his arm with mine. "Do I detect flirting taking place?"

"No." I jolt. "Definitely not."

Ry's brow lifts. "I shall try not to be offended."

"Enough of this." Azure steps between us, his hands waving further conversation to a stop. "Shall we get to business, ladies?" He swings his gaze over me and my sisters. "The sooner we get this situation evaluated, the sooner we may return to the palace. And I would very much like to leave this place."

Crystal presses her hand to Azure's bicep. "Your wish is our command, sweet thing." She tilts her head, suggesting they move closer to the islands.

I roll my eyes and swing my attention to Jaden, laughter lighting my face. From what I've witnessed or learned from previous incarnations' memories, every version of Crystia shares a similar personality, and I love that.

I grab Jaden's hand and drag him closer to the weeping falling off the side of the floating landmass above. Lobrka appears at my side. His narrowed gaze telling me, quite firmly, to be careful.

Kayla stays at Ryland's side. "Whatever is affecting the air, it has a tainted organic flavor to it. I suggest a closer look at earth and water."

"On it," Crystal and I say in unison.

I extend my arm, sliding my open palm into the stream of falling gray liquid. The water cascades over my skin, its silvery song singing of a great beyond. Of a darkness void of life and love...

I suck back my hand and hiss, "tainted."

"With what?" Jaden says a moment before Lobrka asks,

"How badly?"

"I'm uncertain." I rest my hand upon the land and reach down and down until I connect with the groundwater. There too, slight but present, *taint*.

"Sisters," Crystal calls to me and Kayla. "The plant life is not well, the soil within which it grows, as well. I suspect it starts with the water and is also carried on the wind, spreading the infection."

It starts with the water. My first element.

My gaze travels to the edge of the closest island and the water spilling over the side. My memories tumble back to the day of Sol turning dark and being tossed into the sky on a suspended landmass. Fast forwards to him on the snow-covered hill above a frozen lake, when he came up against me, and not any of my previous incarnations. The day I stopped him from changing the world.

But did I?

Because whatever is happening now is likely changing the world. And equally related to Sol and his darker side.

I straighten my back and push my hands into my hips, stare upward. *I need to get up there.*

Need to identify the water source and verify Sol's situation or involvement.

Decision made, I suck back a steadying breath and steel my determination. "Don't follow me," I say to the males around me; Jaden and Lobrka, and anyone else too foolish enough to try.

"Where are we not to follow?" Lobrka asks. Jaden doesn't bother because he likely already knows through our connection.

"It will be obvious in a moment." I break into a run before anyone can stop me.

I reach out to all the surrounding water particles, my only

option of elemental support. Water rises, the particles amassing and freezing into solid stepping stones. Solid footing ready for each forward step and then vanishing in my wake, preventing anyone from following.

"Ana, no!" Jaden's voice calls at my back. "Not this. Not alone."

He foresaw the possibilities of this moment the night before, and he's allowing his fear for me, and his fear of the possibilities, to stop him from action. After everything I changed to get to this moment, I won't let the possibilities define or decide me.

I ascend the free-standing steps of ice, connected only by a frozen stream in the shape of a ground-to-island pipeline. The ice grips the soles of my feet, holding me steady along the way. When my feet find purchase on the lowest hovering island, I discover little more than a small shack and walled-in garden. The source of the tainted water is flowing from somewhere above. One of the other islands. I must go higher.

I climb higher, and higher still, sloshing through an inch of chilly gray water covering each island along the way. The islands show signs of civilizations, or rather, a lonely, refined existence. I pass a house left to rot and a gazebo surrounded by brown roses. I try to imagine what it once looked like, when this place was as close to a home as it ever was. It had to have been beautiful. Beautiful and terribly isolated.

On the topmost island resides a tall-standing temple of white stone—steps leading to a domed roof supported by heaven-reaching columns—from which the gray water rushes.

Water slushes against my feet and ankles with each additional forward climb. My feet are turning to ice cubes, cold enough they burn, and tingle with promise of numbing. Each footfall within the icy element brings a translation of slow decay... and impending doom.

Careful not to slip on slick surfaces, my advance up the stairs is slow and steady. The temple awaits at the top. And within that temple, dark water billows like a fountain, spewing from a mass heaped on the ground at the temple's center. A mass that appeared oddly like...

I step closer, wading through the water.

On the temple floor, a bundle of clothing and flesh is pinned to the ground at three points. A blade through each wrist like a crucifixion, and a third pierced through the right shoulder blade. A thin layer of water covers the body, blurring the features, but I have no doubt who I'm gazing at—Sol. Or whatever constitutes Sol at this point in the timeline.

Dropping down on my knees, I lean over him and whisper his name. His eyes drag to a slow open. His mouth gapes and gray water bubbles with garbled sound.

"Sol?"

His searching gaze finds me, his mouth opening and closing like a fish.

"What happened to you?" I ask. "Why are you pinned to the ground? And why is all this dark water weeping from the islands?"

His head jerks as if beckoning me forward. I inch closer, careful yet reluctant. Water rises off his body, moving up and around me, encompassing me in a bubble of gray liquid.

Sol's message resonates in the element surrounding me. "Have you come to finish me off?"

"No. I came here to understand what's going on."

"Please?" His plea causes the water to move in harsh vibrations.

"Please what?" I ask, closing my eyes and reaching through the water for clearer understanding.

"Please end me."

NINE

I gasp. "Sol, please explain to me what happened."

"You happened."

My hands trace around the wound inflicted on his body, the daggers through the wrists and sword impaling his shoulder. "I didn't do this to you. How did *this* happen?"

"You made me curious about the princess, and that curiosity led to this. He could have killed me, but he refused. Needs me to control the islands."

I can't hold the grimace from my face. "Who did this and why does he want control of the islands?"

"Theon." An excess of water pops and fizzles from his lips. "I had only begun to know the princess, but he wanted me out of her life because he had plans for her station."

"When did this happen?" I pull the dagger free from his right wrist.

The f'n king. Could our luck get any worse? I just want to... ugh! Hit something.

He hollers, his body jerking. No new blood seeps from the

wound, but the flow of tainted water spilling free of the cut slows to a mere trickle.

His heavy, ragged breath steadies and he says, "He found me shortly after the untimely death of the princess' first husband. Dreya never cared for that male, and if he had not met unfortunate ends, I might have personally introduced Prince Price to death."

I blink at his admission. "Do you think Theon did something to Prince Price?" After all, Theon is Dreya's king consort. A relationship that could never have come to pass if Prince Price had lived.

"Possible." He coughs. "The bastard. He did this... to me. A true sign of... of his character, I would think."

I would have to agree. I pat Sol's shoulder and give him a grime smile, then drop my gaze to the next blade. "Hold on."

I wrap my hand around the handle of the dagger embedded in his left wrist and, with a fleshy *thwuak*, yank it free. He cries out and then relaxes, closing his eyes. So, I continue, allowing him to rest and merely listen.

"Let's say this Theon guy killed Price so that he might one day sit next to the throne of power. Why would he take issue with you and Dreya?"

His eyes crack open and despite the gray water filming his face, I spy emotional pain in his eyes. "I fancied her," he says. "And I believe she fancied me as well. The queen had made new marital arrangements for Princess Dreya, but with nothing official in motion, we gave the matter little thought...

"Until Theon showed up at the foot of my islands, seeking an audience under a falsehood. And, out of respect to Dreya, I foolishly invited him into my home. The results of that meeting are what you see before you."

I rise to my feet and straddle his limp form, grab the hilt

sword pinning him to the floor. "And he didn't simply kill you because he needed you—for the islands and the weeping."

"The weeping?" The question is a cough of a delivery.

"The floating islands are weeping dark water," I reply.

"Ah." His head tilts back, eyes fluttering closed then open. "I am the weeping," he says. "The darkness seeping from me in the form of my emotional and physical pain. In the form of tears, likely infecting everything it touches. Am I right?"

Infecting everything? How long have the islands been weeping? How much territory have they covered in that time? And how much of the land and inhabitants have been affected?

"I see the fear in your eyes, Balance Bringer. End me and the weeping should come to an end. At least you can have that."

A hard frown pulls to my lips and my gaze narrows. "Are you ready?"

He doesn't respond, but ready or not, this is happening.

Not allowing myself to give another moment to the thought of what I'm about to do, I yank the sword free from his shoulder. Sol's body bucks, a scream breaking free from his lips. The water leaking from his body slows but does not cease.

"I don't want to kill you Sol." I drop back at his side, resting one hand on his chest and wiping the water from his face with the other. "I want to save you."

"You cannot save me, Balance Bringer."

Memories of time spent between Fiona and Sol. Without my bound connection to my many incarnations, I cannot remember everything that transpired, but I remember enough. No part of me wants to dirty my hands with his blood.

"Think of it as a mercy," he continues. "Because that is exactly what my death would be. I have lived too long and suffered too much."

"Sol—"

"Deona." The mention of my first incarnation halts my words. "That is who you are, am I right? Or the equivalent of her." Liquid stops bubbling from his mouth.

"Correct."

He tilts his face toward mine, making no effort to lift his body from the ground. "I listened to you that day on the hill. It took me several years to get into a mental space where I was able to successfully apply the advice given, but once I did, my life changed for the better. I, in fact, lived some of my best years because of what you said to me that day.

"Now I request something from you."

I nod. "Anything I can do to help."

He lifts his hand in silent request. I slip my hand in his, lowering back at his side, once more.

"Show me the mercy of the Balance Bringer." He now uses a voice cracking from disuse, instead of the water to translate his message. "End my punishment."

"I will if I can."

He coughs up water. "You fail to understand. I am asking you to end my physical life."

"But—" He tugs on my hand, yanking me forward and cutting off my words once more.

"What I have become needs to be stopped, for the land, for the inhabitants, for her."

"For Dreya?" I ask, searching Sol's face. "You didn't simply fancy her, did you? You fell in love with her."

His eyes close and he swallows hard. "The truth is, Balance Bringer, I cannot stop the weeping. It has gone on for too long and has become part of who I am. So, if you are to save this world, then my end must come."

Has it truly come down to such a choice? In order to save the worlds, I must take a life? I may have previously been ready to destroy Dreya, but everything now settles differently in my heart and soul. I want to protect, not ruin.

And yet, I have no words, for he may very well be right. If he is the source of the weeping, a weeping that is infecting the realm with the darkness, and the weeping will continue as long as he lives...

I heave a weight-of-the-world breath.

Sol tightens his hold on my hand. "Deona." My gaze drops to meet his. "You know this must be done. And before my spirit leaves this world, I promise to bestow upon you all my memories spanning back to the day we last met."

In other words, all that he knows regarding Dreya and Theon and the islands' condition.

"Take the blade from my hip." He tilts his head in indication. "And use it to pierce my heart."

My heart freezes to a stop, even as my attention drops to the weapon. A weapon of fine steel forged in the fires of Guardoone, sure to deliver death to an immortal warrior. But will it do the same to whatever Sol has become? I shake my head.

Sol's hold softens, his fingers gliding over the back of my hand. "I forgive you," he says. "For then, and now, and what has yet to come. I forgive you. Now do it... for the realm, and for Dreya."

"If she loves you as you love her, she wouldn't want you to die."

"Nor would she want me to suffer."

I worry my lip and breathe deep and heavy. Can I take a life? Sol's life? Once best friend to Jaden's first incarnation, Jove.

His fingers work clumsily at the steel strapped to his hip. He drags it free, arm and hold shaking. I snatch the weapon from his clutch, but he repositions his grip, clamping his hands over the blade and centers it over his heart.

"You need not do this alone. I will help you." He pulls the blade downward, slicing into his skin.

"Sol!"

He grits his teeth and drags the steel deeper. "Do it. You know you need to."

"What will happen to the darkness in you, if I kill you? Will it end with you?" Because it surely didn't in my original reality.

He groans, his body shifting with apparent pain. "It will likely migrate to you."

Exactly the kind of crap answer I was expecting.

I purse my lips and nod. It wouldn't be the first time I'd been infected by the darkness. The cure, for me, at least, has primarily been water directly from the goddess Gaea, and thankfully, water is my element in this current reality. So... I should be able to handle the infection.

"The longer you wait," he says. "The more infection will be spread." The more potential damage to the worlds, in a realm without a fully realized Balance Bringer.

I drop my gaze to his and we stare at each other for endless minutes, a silent argument waged between us. If I don't grant his wish, I'm likely dooming us all. And if I do, am I dooming my soul.

But what is my soul compared to the realm, all the worlds, and the endless inhabitants?

Okay. I can do this. I will do this. I must do this. "I'm sorry," I whisper.

"I am the one who is sorry," he counters. "Sorry to bring this lesson of hard choices and consequences upon you. But you are strong, Balance Bringer, and you shall persevere."

I'm not as confident, but I must put the needs of the worlds ahead of my own.

My white knuckled grip upon the hilt shakes, and my breath, its heavy and harsh. "I'm so very sorry, Sol." My words are choppy and choked.

I sound like I'm crying. Am I crying?

"Already forgiven. Now do it, I am ready." He closes his eyes and sucks back a deep breath.

Memories slam into my consciousness, all memories owned by Sol. I gasp and react, plunging the steel into Sol's heart. His head jerks back, his mouth dropping wide open, no sound or breath escaping.

"*Forgiven,*" whispers around me, and through the water at my feet.

I gasp and yank my hands away from the knife. I stare at my offending hands, as my entire body shakes.

Sol's chest stills and his lifeforce blinks out, then dark water explodes from him like a geyser.

The blast slams into me, thrusts me backward, out of the temple and onto the steps. My body rolls to the ground. The rush of water pushes me across the landmass and... with a whoosh and a tumble... caries me straight over the island's edge.

I plunge into the open air and fall like a stone for the ground far, far below.

Somewhere behind the chaos I hear someone calling my name. Actually, several someones—Jaden and Azure, my sisters, maybe even Lobrka. They scream because I'm dropping, too fast, through open air, toward an unforgiving surface.

I should care but... *I took a life.* An action which has torn a hole through my soul. Regret and anger and sorrow shredding at everything I am like cat claws to a sofa arm.

Then there's Sol's memories crowding my mind. And the

darkness slushing through my veins. I'm falling in more than a physical way.

Wind rushes at my back, pushes against my skin, and slows my descent.

Though, not slow enough.

And a torrent of tears leak from my eyes, creating a streaked veil around my senses. Pain rises up to meet me, breaking free of the ground in an elemental gusher. Choking sobs wreck my body and I struggle against the desire to give in and allow this fall to be the end of me. I have far more to do, worlds to save, and I am far from done.

I hit the ground, not with a thud, but with a splash. Water rising from the ground and pulling from the weeping in order to create a pool to soften my fall. I crash into the water, and no sooner does my body stabilize than the water returns to the ground from whence it came.

I'm not dead, I live to fight another day, possibly—hopefully—to fulfill my destiny. But for the moment, I want to give in and allow my body to breakdown and wallow, if only momentarily.

Only, the land above me grumbles, sending a spray of dirt and rock onto my head. Cracks, like the shattering of a mirrored surface erupt across the underside of the various floating islands. As if preparing to crumble apart.

"Ana!" Jaden grabs my arm, practically drags me to my feet. "We need to move. Your sisters may not be able to hold the islands for much longer."

"What?" I drag my arm across my face, wiping away the remnants of my tears, then glance from the rumbling islands overhead to my sisters. The effort they press into their elemental connections is evident in the stress upon their faces. A trickle of sweat glides down the side of Kayla's face.

Right. The islands are coming down, and likely doing so soon.

I take one shaky step followed by another. And with each additional step, my strength recovers, my actions becoming sturdy once more.

Jaden and I run past my sister, Kayla and as we do, she faints. Azure is there to stop her from hitting the ground. As her head lulls to the side, her body unconscious, large chunks of rock fall free from the underside of the islands. Crystia sways, as well, and Lobrka steps to her side, providing support. She leans into him. Closes her eyes.

The floating ground grumbles and earth begins to fall. Big massive hunks of land crash to the ground. The islands float no more and collapse to the land below. Earth explodes all around us.

Jaden and I break into a run, sprays of dirt and pebble rocketing past us. Something heavy slams into my back and I stumble forward. Jaden braces my arm, helps me recover my steps. Blasts and booms fill my ears, drowning out all other sounds. And my vision is lost in a cloud of thick dust.

I cover my mouth against the oncoming sputtering coughs and keep running. The ground beneath our feet rolls and shudders. And I find myself too often struggling for balance. Immortal Warriors appear in the fray, guiding us toward the camp.

We race out of the valley of destruction and collapse to our hands and knees. I count my raspy breaths as the dust settles around us, revealing massive mounds of broken earth and shattered building bits cluttering a once untouched valley.

I may have made it clear of the falling landmasses, but I have not yet cleansed myself of the darkness. And there's only one way I know to purge the infection. I collapse onto my butt and flip my hands, palms splayed to the sky. Beseech the elements and the elemental goddess, Gaea.

"Please, Gaea, cleanse me and mine, body and soul, of the dark infection now making our blood and bones its home."

The sky cracks open and releases a downpour upon us, drenching us straight through our clothes. Lurching forward and dropping to my hands, I gag and expel plums of dark gas and tarry splatters. I hack on repeat until the rain stops and I'm coughing only clear air.

With a sigh, I collapse in on myself.

Jaden grabs my upper arms and lifts me, shifting me to the left and right, checking my body as if in search of injuries. "Are you infected? Injured?"

"No. That was a cleansing rain and I'm fine." I lie... because, inside, I'm a tangled mess.

"Why, Ana." He shakes my arms. "Why did you do something so careless? Taking on the islands alone. You could have died. I could have lost you."

"Could have. Should have." The world is spinning and my head pounding. The edges of my vision are fading to a complete black. "Jaden, I..." I. Can't. Breathe.

"Ana." He pulls me close, his hands finding the side of my face. "What happened?"

"I... I took a life." And I can't breathe. "How do I live with that?" The world goes dark and my body limp.

I AWAKE ON HORSEBACK, held in place between Jaden's arms, my back leaning against his chest. My head jerks up, and I swallow against my dry throat, then wet my lips.

"Welcome back to the land of the living." Jaden's words rumble through his chest and vibrate against my back. "The royal commander wanted to talk to you about what transpired, but you and your sisters passed out. Which, after all the energy the three of you expelled, your exhaustion was to be expected."

A dose of the power I had in my previous reality would have come in useful when dealing with Sol and the floating islands, but the deed was done and the only person that died was Sol. At least, I think he was the only one who died.

"Sorry about that." I quickly survey the company around us. Our party is smaller than the one we had when we set out. "Was anyone hurt? Killed?"

Jaden rests his chin on my shoulder. "Everyone is fine. The royal commander assigned several of the guards to stay back and help with the situation. In trade, the warrior commander lent us his two best males.

My chest compresses. No doubt Ry is among those two. He would most certainly be one of the best warriors among them. "And my sisters?" I ask.

"They are exhausted and sleeping," he replies.

"Why did the islands collapse?" I gaze at our path ahead. The palace is already visible in the distance. How long have I been asleep?

He takes the reins in one hand and wraps the other across me, hugging me tight against him. His nose and forehead brush through the back of my hair. He murmurs, "You told me you took a life." I swallow a stone-sized lump. "I assume the life was that of the Sun and the Moon. It is said that the life of the monster and the existence of the islands are tied together. Destruction of the one equals destruction of the other."

Holy Gaea and god! I not only took a life but destroyed a magical landmass all with one act.

I'm kicking things off to a great start here in my new reality, I think sarcastically, and hold back against the dam of tears wanting to flow.

The quick trot of horse hooves approaches from the front. The royal commander and Lobrka come our way, others quick to move out of the path. They swing their horses around and come to a measured stride on either side of us.

"Lady Anaka," my father says. "I understand the recovery sleep of a Balance Bringer is a hard thing to wake one from and has been known to take a long time. I am pleased to see you awake relatively quickly."

"Thank you, Royal Commander." I dip my head. "Your concern is appreciated."

The edge of his eyes crinkle. "You owe me a debriefing." His attention shifts past me to Lobrka.

Lobrka nods, a barely perceivable motion of the head. "Already in place, Royal Commander." Meaning the patch, trapping the sound in the space around us and granting us full privacy.

"Very good," my father replies, returning his gaze to me. "You may speak freely, Anaka. Tell me everything that happened, and you learned. Leave out no detail, no matter how small. You never know what may turn out to be significant."

I tell them everything my sisters and I discovered—the tainted water flowing from the islands, tainting the land, and spreading tainted spores in the air. I tell them what I found upon the island, about Sol bleeding the tainted water, and me being forced to end him in order to end the flow.

I choke on those last words and Jaden holds me tighter, wrapping his arm firmly around my waist. Pressing his face against my cheek.

My father's jaw is tense, but he doesn't say a word. He's listening, thinking, calculating.

I don't need to be a genius to deduce his thoughts are similar to the ones I had upon discovering these facts. If the islands had been weeping tainted water for years, sailing over large portions of the realm during that time, much of the groundwater and soil have likely become infected. That translates to water supplies and crops for livestock and inhabitants, alike. All of Hiddenkel has slowly been introduced to the darkness.

Which also means... I suck back a breath... I may not have been noticing filth on the immortal warriors, but the signs of infection. I glance down at my own hands. They appear clean, but then I did just invoke the cleansing waters.

What of the others showered upon?

I tilt my head toward Jaden but pin my gaze on Lobrka. "When it rained, did anyone else cough up a dark substance?"

"Several," Lobrka says.

Okay. Good. But was it enough? "That would be the infection being purged from their system."

Lobrka's gaze shifts past me to the royal commander, then returns to me. "Good to know."

On the other side, my father coughs. I spin to face him. "Did the monster..." Sol. "...tell you who was responsible for his state?"

"He did," I mumble and glance around at the surrounding soldiers. Even with the patch in place I'm leery of speaking the truth in front of so many. What if one of them can read lips?

Noting my apperception, he guides his horse closer. My heart is pounding like a stampeding horse. Anything I have to say regarding the mastermind behind Sol's condition could be considered not only deeply personal to the royal commander but possibly seditious.

I cup my hands around my mouth and whisper the traitorous words, "King Theon."

TEN

The queen has fallen ill. The whispers move through our returning party with the speed of wildfire. My stomach is churning on an endless loop, and my chest is squeezed too tight. I saw Dreya only a day before, and she appeared perfectly healthy.

My father had cantered away from our conversation and then galloped ahead of our party to the palace. The message regarding the queen caught fire shortly after.

Weaving my fingers with Jaden's, I cling to him like a life preserver and allow his calming effect to wash over me, but it has little impact. Our shared unease creates a battleground for his soothing ability. He's as tense as I am about what may have befallen the queen.

"You don't think..." The king did something to the queen? Maybe because of the fall of the islands, because of Sol.

"I cannot say," Jaden murmurs in my ear. "Whatever has happened, we shall weather the storm together." I squeeze his hand in response.

Our horse carries us through the gate in the outer palace

wall and proceeds to take us to the side where the stables are located beyond the far end of the main structure. When we come to a stop, Jaden dismounts first and then offers his hand to assist me.

I accept his offer, even though I can dismount a horse fine on my own. But... I am still tired, and this body is far more achy.

As soon as I am on my feet, I'm pushed backward into Jaden, Azure pressing into me, taking my face in his palms. "My heart has been bludgeoned with agony, fearing for your life when you rushed up to those dangerous islands." His voice increases in volume. "And then you tumbled off the side..." He sucks back a ragged breath. "Gaea above, I could murder you, if I were not so deeply in love with you."

My mouth pops open.

In shock, not as the invitation he took my action to mean. His mouth descends on mine faster than I can react. Using his hands, he tilts my face into the motion and kisses me deeply. Deeply, but quickly. Stopped by Jaden's cough.

"She is not yet ready, brother," Jaden says.

Azure steps back, his expression pained. "I cannot understand how we were not something more in this other reality of yours. My brother and I, we are two parts of the same soul." His arms fall lax at his side.

"True." I move clear of Jaden's touch, convinced that seeing me with him only causes Azure more pain. And though I may not choose to kiss him, I don't want to hurt him.

I reach out and take his hand in my own. "In the other reality, I grew up a world apart from the two of you. Jaden came and found me, brought me home." I smile at him then return my attention to Azure. "You were unable to come for... *reasons*." Reasons too complicated and now inessential to get into. "When we finally did meet, you were in a relationship with another.

"She held your heart and you never looked at me in that kind of way. So this..." I wave a hand between us. "Takes some getting used to." Not to mention the two guys at the same time bit.

Yeah, I'm not sure that kind of thing is for me. The other me, maybe, but who I feel to be inside grew up with different conditioning.

"Who was this other female?" he asks.

I step forward, taking his hand once more, and meld my other palm to the curve of his cheek. "Does it matter?" I ask. "That was a different lifetime that no longer exists."

"Call it curiosity. I would like to know."

Our horses are led away by an attendant as a soldier steps into view, his unwavering stare demanding our attention. "Lady Anaka, you and your entourage are to come with me."

I assume Jaden and Azure are my *entourage*. "What about my sisters?"

"They still sleep and are being taken to their rooms as we speak. Royal Commander requested your presence, not theirs."

My father must want to talk further on what I learned from Sol. "Lead the way."

I follow the soldier, and the brothers link hands with me, walk at my side. We're led away from the palace and deeper into the guts of the on-premises military life. We move past a commissary, bathing rooms, and barracks to a steel door set in a thick brick wall.

The soldier pushes open the door. "For your protection, this is the most fortified room on the property."

For our protection? Or for our imprisonment? "Protection from what?" I ask.

"Royal Commander did not say, only that he wanted you to wait here."

I purse my lips and start to step forward, only Jaden grabs my arm and holds me back. Instead, Azure slips through the door first.

Jaden relaxes his grip and lifts his chin indicating Azure. "Let him verify the space is clear."

"Okay." That's a level of security I'm not fully used to. I sigh and shift my weight.

"My lady! Lady Anaka." Gitta's breath is heavy and she stumbles to a slow, then stops and hands me a folded sheet. "Lady Oriana Opal Edea Virrie awaits you at the palace, but I believe it unwise to see her."

Edea, Opal, is here a day early. "Why shouldn't I see her?"

"She is unwell in an ungodly way."

"And she is in the palace?" Jaden asks, moving closer to the conversation. Gitta nods. "Then, might I suggest you stay with us?"

"Oh, I am not sure..." She shakes her head.

Insides twisting over Dreya's possible state, I grab Gitta's hand. "Until we know what is going on." Glancing to Azure and receiving the all-clear, I lead Gitta into the room.

Stone walls are softened by humongous tapestry, and gray stone covers the space beneath our feet. Set into the floor pattern, large circular designs, like family crests, are inset at equal distances around the space's perimeter. Fires burn in two hearths, set on opposite sides of the room, a collection of over-stuffed red and gold furniture set between them. Sofas and chairs, and a long table cutting down the center of the room. A place to gather, strategize and plan, safe behind barriers of forti-fied stone and steel.

"What now?" I ask the soldier.

"Hopefully, the royal commander will be along shortly," he

replies. "Until then, make yourself comfortable. I shall be just outside the door." He steps out and closes the impenetrable barrier.

"Sit with me." I tug Gitta to the nearest sofa.

She pulls against my hold, her head shaking. "My lady, 'tis not proper."

"Listen, Gitta." I spin to her and smile. "I know who you are, you know who I am, and titles hold no meaning here between us."

A stunned expression pops onto her face, but before she can respond, Azure steps up to us and pins his gaze tight on me. "Please tell me who she was?"

My responding sigh is automatic. "What good will it do?"

He grabs my arms, demanding my focus. "I need to understand how I could ever feel for another when Jaden and I are of the same soul, and our soul belongs to you."

I bite my lip. He has a valid point. What is it about Ruby that snared Azure in the other reality, and would she have the same effect on him in this one? If she's locked up here, in the palace dungeon, we might be able to get an answer to that last question.

I scratch the back of my neck. "I'll tell you what. I understand that there's a woman locked up somewhere around here. Fiery redhead with red markings on her body."

"The cupian fae?" He blurts.

"That's the one." I strike a sharp finger through the air. "She may be able to illuminate the answer you seek, as well as add to the information I expect the royal commander wishes to discuss." He stares at me, contemplative. "Do you think they would release her to our care for a little chat?"

"No idea." Azure frowns. "But you want me to find out, am I right?" I nod and smile wide. He stares at me in a moment of evaluation before continuing, "And you want me to find out now." I can't decide if the tone of his voice is disappointment, disapproval, or irritation. I nod again, regardless.

"Right." He heads for the door. "I shall return shortly... or so I hope." He leaves the room.

Jaden touches my elbow. "What do you hope will come of this?"

I shrug. "We shall see." I swing my gaze over Gitta, and she quickly attempts to smooth her confused expression. Confusion likely born from my conversation with Azure. Grinning inwardly, I start unfolding the slip of paper she handed me. "What do we have here?"

She glances over my shoulder. "It is the list Jaden asked me to run past the populace keeper."

"Awesome. Let's have a seat and take a look." I lift my gaze and catch both Gitta and Jaden staring at me. Bewilderment turns to understanding a millisecond later. No one in this reality is used to my modern day, California way of speaking. "Sorry for the confusing otherworld language."

"First." Jaden punches a pointed finger to the air. "You need to hydrate. You have not drunk enough water after everything you went through." He turns his attention. "Gitta?"

She shifts on her feet, as if intending to handle the task, but Jaden stops her. "I was not asking you to get us water. I was asking if you would like some."

"Oh, but—" He waves away her dispute.

The steel entry door bangs open, and someone stumbles in, as if shoved. He catches himself and spins back toward the opening. "Let me help." He marches forward.

The soldier in the doorway... not the one who led us here... shakes his head. Blocks the newcomers exit. "Royal Commanders orders. You are to remain here until further notice." The door slams and locks.

My body jolts and beyond the door, thunder cracks. Did we

just become prisoners? I shove the list from Gitta into my pocket. "What's going on?"

The newcomer turns to us, and I find myself looking into the eyes of my brother Ry.

"I cannot be sure," he says. "But I think a power play is currently taking place and military force is involved. There are too many engaged, and too much going on, to be a skirmish. Whatever it is, it is big."

I wrap my arms around my middle in a self-hug. "Is this coming from the top?" As in the king or the queen. Or maybe the princess, because I wouldn't discount the idea of Quirina being a demon.

He shakes his head and shrugs. "I am not familiar enough with who is who here at the palace and no one has taken the time to explain anything to me. Too quickly I was grabbed and tossed in here." He grabs the door handle and yanks, then slams his fist into the metal. "I can handle my own. Let me fight." He slams his fist to the door a second time. I spy blood left on the surface.

"Warrior Ryland," Jaden approaches my brother and rests his hand on Ry's fist, gentles it away from the door. "You are the only son of Warrior Commander Usoff, am I right?"

Ry lowers his hand and turns back to face us before focusing on Jaden. "Correct."

"He's protecting you," I murmur. Whatever is going on outside of these walls, my father is trying to keep Ry safe.

Ry's gaze snaps to me. "I need no protection."

"We're quite sure you don't," I assure, and then note Gitta backing across the room.

"Look at it this way, warrior." Jaden slaps Ry on the back, causing Ry to stiffen and scowl. "You have been trusted to protect one of the most important inhabitants of the palace." He tilts his head to indicate me.

"Yeah?" Ry removes Jaden's hand from his body. "Except you are all in here, safe from whatever is transpiring beyond these walls."

"Safe from what?" I ask. "What exactly is going on out there?"

"Destruction, bloodshed, and black magic."

"Oh crap." My hand flies to my mouth. "My sisters. Azure."

A crash at the back of the room has me spinning to Gitta. She has backed into a table, jiggling and knocking things over. Her eyes are wide and blinking in a too-pale face, her shaking hands raking up and down her thighs.

"It has begun," she says and cringes. She turns her head and focuses on me. "I am sorry, but I must go to her. Find out what I should do next."

My hand flies out, as if to calm a scared animal. "You should stay, Gitta. She would want you to stay with me. We may need your—"

The door behind me bangs open, again... and Gitta whispers, "Sorry," then vanishes in a cloud of vanishing smoke.

"Gitta!" Lobrka barks from behind me, his voice filled with venom. Too late, she vanished. Undoubtedly, gone to Madame Marrouske. "Skittish elf," he grumbles.

I turn to him, the question already leaping from my lips. "How bad is it?"

"Bad." He takes quick stock of the bodies in the room. "Where is the other one?" He raises his chin toward Jaden.

"Running an errand," Jaden replies. "Should we be worried?"

Lobrka scruffs the hair at the back of his head. This version of him keeps his hair cut closer to the scalp than the one in my previous reality. Likely to better fit in with the whole royal guard role.

"I cannot say," he finally admits. "The situation is not good."

I lurch forward and grab his arm. "My sisters?"

He shakes his head. "They are unattainable, out of our reach. They have been locked in their rooms and are heavily guarded. I believe they are safe from harm, because the individual behind this will not chance empowering your Balance Bringer abilities."

In other words, they'll be kept alive. The good and the bad in that sentence crushes my heart. Because, if we are all kept alive and separate, a fully realized Balance Bringer cannot be actualized.

"I will take the lead," Lobrka says, then points to Jaden. "Jaden, you stay next to Anaka and protect her with your life."

"Of course," Jaden says and tugs me flush to his side.

Lobrka swings his attention past Jaden and me. "Warrior Ryland, you cover our backs."

He grabs the door handle and pauses. "If we are quick and quiet, we might manage to get out of this without direct incident."

I push free of Jaden's hold. "You expect us to leave the palace? Without Kayla, Crystal, and Azure? And go where exactly?"

"Away from here," he fires back, shoving his face in mine, answering my last question first. "And yes I do. You are the priority here. You know that." He grabs my shoulder and squeezes. "As hard as it is to hear, you and Jaden are the primaries. If either of you die, that is it for this life. But if your siblings pass, their souls will find their way home to you." He presses his fingers to my heart.

"I hate that." I glower.

"I would expect nothing less." He pats my upper arm. "But Edea is here, and she is not the Edea you remember." I drop my head. My aunt is infected, and based on how Gitta and him are acting, the infection is beyond concerning.

He starts to open the door and I grab his hand, drawing his eye. "Is Edea the real issue here, or is it the king?" At my back, I discern Ry's surprised reaction.

Lobrka grins. "Oh, the king and his little prodigy are very much an issue."

Of course they are.

He leans close and whispers, "Still satisfied with the change you made?" ...to the timeline.

The jury is out, but I can't think about that now. Apparently, an internal war has broken out in the palace, and I need to concentrate on getting out alive.

Pressing my lips into a tight line, I shove him in a silent lets-go.

"Oh, we shan't be exiting this way." He grabs my shoulders and spins me around. "You three shuffle off to the other side of the room and I will join you in a moment."

He opens the door and leans his head out. "I need one of you to come with me and the other to lock and guard the door. I will let you two decide which shall do which job, but you have only a second to decide."

Less than a second passes before the soldier who led me to this room slips through the entry. The door starts to close and then stops, the words "Hold on" calling from the other side. A breath later, the door pushes open wider, and Azure drags a scowling Ruby into the room.

The moment they are out of the rain, she yanks free of his hold and shoves him away. "Were you raised by goblins? You have all the tact and decorum of on raised by barn rats." She rings rainwater from her hair and brushes splatters from her shoulders and chest.

"Honestly." He shakes his head. "You are the most unrea-

sonable female I have ever had the displeasure of dealing with."
He turns away.

Behind his back, she makes a childish face and murmurs a
derogatory term. I'm too shocked by their exchange to react to
the humor found at the sight.

Azure, likely aware of her behavior but choosing to ignore
it, scours the room, his gaze landing on me. "Why do I feel like I
just committed a jailbreak?"

The steel door slams shut and the sounds of locks on the
exterior slide into place. Lobrka engages the interior locks and
ushers us to the far side of the room.

Jaden moves to his brother's side. "How did you get her out
so fast?"

Ruby laughs. "No one is paying any attention in the keep.
No one has been watching us down there since sometime last
night."

Azure swings his gaze over the people in the room. "That
says a thing or two about the situation, doesn't it?"

"Sure does." I fold my arms across my chest. "And none of
it is good."

Lobrka jogs past us and kicks a square stone in the far wall.
Something pops, followed by a hiss of air.

One of the floor crests, the one closest to him, is now raised.
Lobrka spins the circle design to the side, exposing a staircase
winding down into the darkness.

"Ready?" Lobrka asks and motions for us to get moving.

Ruby sighs. "Let me guess. We either face the darkness
down there," She cuts an arm toward the descending staircase,
then swings her directional point to the steel door, "or the darkness out there."

"That is correct," Lobrka says at the same time as Azure
knocks her in the back and says, "Get moving."

Shouts and bangs start echoing beyond the stone walls of

our room. Something sounding too much like an explosion goes off.

I jump and snap my gaze toward the steel door, just as something crashes against the other side.

"Go!" Jaden orders and we all start rushing down the steps.

Lobrka seals the latch behind us, joins us at the base of the stares, and ignites a string of lights running the length of our foreseeable path.

"This way to freedom," he quips, and takes the lead in our attempted escape.

ELEVEN

My feet drag forward, exhaustion creeping into my bones. I haven't yet fully recovered from all the energy I exerted yesterday, and my wobbly knees are a constant reminder of that fact. Yet, I push myself fast and hard, and ignore the fact that a meek part of me wants to cry. Beneath the scrape of my fingers, the rock walls are rough and unforgiving and a constant reminder to keep going, keep the drive until fresh air kisses my face once again.

The tight tunnels flicker with soft illumination provided by fairy lights that could be considered distant cousins to an electric light bulb. Each glowing beam spaced within sight of each other, they are yet distant enough that small pockets of thick shadows live in and around the midway point.

The tunnels continue to extend endlessly, and we move with haste and motivation. And though no sounds promise followers at our back, we refuse to lower our guard. Lobrka leads our group, at a quick and cautious pace, with Azure at his side. Ry along with the other soldier bring up the rear, and the rest of us, Jaden, Ruby, and I advance within the cushion between.

Ruby keeps grabbing at my clothing, her hand shaking. No doubt, seeking some sort of comfort that she's not alone in the dark abyss. And each time she seizes onto me, I clutch her firmly and pray it helps her continue onward. So far, she hasn't broken down.

My mouth grows ever drier with each further step away from the palace. *My sisters, my sisters, my sisters.* I swallow once, twice, ten times against the desert in my throat. Then press the heel of my palm to dull the constant ache crackling in my chest.

Needing to redirect my thoughts, I turn my attention to Ruby. "Why did the queen have you locked up?"

Ruby huffs a nervous laugh. "Not the queen. It was the king who issued the order."

My eyebrows lift. "Why would he do that?"

She rubs her arms. "Because he hated what I had to say."

"And what was that?" Chills race over my skin and, like Ruby, I rub my arms against the dropping temperature. Although, I'm not certain if the growing cold is a hundred percent due to our location, or if my mood is a factor.

"I shared my gift with her," she says, jaw clenching. "I told the queen what that feces of a being never wanted her to hear. Though, truth be told, I believe the queen's heart was already well aware."

I pucker my lower lip and let the jigsaw puzzle of King Theon slide closer toward complete clarification. "You told the queen her soul's lovemate was someone other than the king, didn't you?"

Her jaw clenches. "I did, and look where it got me." She trips and stumbles.

Azure spins and catches her arms, preventing her from falling to her knees.

She steadies herself and shoves him away, her muscles taunt and face flaming red. "Get off me."

"Hey." He fans his hands wide, feigned disfavor in his expression. "I was only helping you avoid scrapes and cuts from a fall. I meant nothing more by it."

She hugs her arms across her chest and thrusts her fists into her armpits. "Sure you didn't." Clear sarcasm is evident in her tone.

Azure shakes his head and turns away, steps into the shadows between illuminations, mumbling, "Next time, I promise not to save you."

Their exchange is rife with irritation, and scrutinize it as I do, I'm not sure if I can identify the Azure and Ruby from my previous reality. Are their heated exchanges their form of flirtation? Or a denial of sexual tension?

Curiosity getting the best of me, and finding the distraction helpful in masking my unease, I lean toward Ruby and say, "Did you feel or get anything off him just now?"

"Are you seriously asking about my gift?" She grimaces. "From the moment he ushered me into that room above, I knew his match was you. As you are his... and his." She points from Azure to Jaden. Azure has his back to me, but Jaden tips his temple to mine.

"Never came across a split soul match before," she adds and scrunches her nose.

Jaden weaves his fingers with mine and squeezes my hand. I turn my attention to him, and within the dim light of the tunnel, my anxiety melts and we share a moment of harmony through our exchanged gaze.

Returning my focus forward, and the curve of the tunnel ahead, I pause momentarily on Lobrka and Azure's backs. If

Azure is not Ruby's match in this reality, how could the two of them been a match in my previous timeline?

My lips press into a twisted frown. "What about you, Ruby?" I ask. "As a seer of love connections, do you get one of your own?"

Her nose wrinkles and forehead pinches, even as she continues to stare at the ground, watchful of her footing. "Who are you calling Ruby?"

I jerk. "Isn't your name Ruby?" The idea that her name might be different hadn't occurred to me, but the possibility should have been near the front of my mind considering my own name.

"No." She bursts with a healthy laugh and Lobrka tosses us a tight glare, then hushes her. "Whatever gave you that idea? *Hmm?*" she murmurs. "My name is and always has been Scarlett."

"Oh." I wince and drag my fingers against the stonewall of the tunnel as if to help center myself. Even if I end up spending the rest of my days in this alternate timeline, I don't think I'll ever get used to all the differences. "I didn't realize. Sorry."

My fingers catch a sharp shard with a stabbing prick. With a jolt, I yank my hand away and suck the tiny trickle of blood from my finger.

Behind me, Ryland snickers. I ignore him. And as Lobrka hushes the group *again* I press the question on *Scarlett* a second time. "The question still stands. Do you get your own love connection?"

The difference of love connections between the two realities is now a feverous itch I need to scratch. It's also an excellent distraction from our situation and surroundings. If Scarlett and Azure are not a match, what change made Ruby the one for Azure?

She sighs, the sound heavy with akin to longing. "I have a

beautiful love whom I have not seen since that fecal matter tossed me into the palace dungeon. Another cupian fae like myself."

Curious, and a mystery I may never solve, given I'm now living a new reality.

"And I may *never* see him," she continues, her voice growing with what... fear, anger, frustration? "If our doom is to be forever trapped in this goddess awful dank labyrinth."

Lobrka spins back and growls, showing his canines. "Enough with the chatter. Keep it quiet and keep it stealthy. I would like us all to make it out of this unscathed. Right now, none of us can be certain exactly what we are dealing with or how widespread it is. The two of you are not helping with all the blather." He uses his hands to crudely mimic us talking.

As stoic as the dark elf tends to be, his displeasure now seeps from him in volumes. And his form of cooping is clearly far different from mine or Scarlet's.

"Jerk," I murmur, even though he isn't wrong.

We push on and on and I'm beginning to believe the tunnels will never end. "Do you even know where this goes?" I ask Lobrka, my thoughts feeding the seed of despair growing all-too-healthily inside of me. "This tunnel is starting to feel like a trap."

"We have passed a few exits," he replies. "All of them are too close to the palace to chance." I glance over the uninter-rupted stone walls. "All the exit passages are camouflaged as added protection."

In case the enemy is inside the tunnels. I nod and keep my feet moving. After all I've been through, I will live through this *inconvenience.* No other option exists.

Scarlett presses into the side wall with a wheeze. "Any chances we might take a break soon?" She breathes heavily and presses her palm to her ribcage.

Lobrka turns and scrutinizes her, then me. He appraises the entire group. "Five minutes. No more." Despite being accommodating, he appears less than pleased.

"Wow." Scarlett throws out her hip and crosses her arms. She kind of looks like she wants to punch him. "Your compassion is overwhelming." She leans against the wall and starts to lower herself to the ground, clearly exhausted and trying to hide how much so.

Lobrka pitches forward and stops her mid-action. Hauls her to her feet. "Not here. In the darkest of the shadows between the spread of light."

Smart, I think as Scarlett huffs, yanks her arm free of his touch, and moves out of the light. Drops to a sit.

Lobrka remains standing, studying the tunnel in both directions. Everyone else takes the opportunity to catch their breath and get off their feet. The soldier takes a place next to Scarlett and Ry sits on the opposite side of the tunnel, produces a water bladder from somewhere and takes a swig.

I watch him, my heart clenching. I miss my brother... deeply, and even though this version of Ry is whole and healthy, all his limbs and fingers intact, he's not and never will be the male I knew and loved. Our shared experiences... our history... no longer exists.

For a moment, that thought creates a vacuum in my soul... and then I stamp it closed.

My gaze flickers over Jaden and Azure, then I sit next to Ry. He offers me his water bladder and I accept. The water is more than refreshing, it awakens and revitalizes the elemental side of me. A much-needed recharge.

"Thanks." I pass the bladder back to him.

He nods and remains quiet. If I am to read his face as I would the Ry I previously knew, I would guess he's considering everything currently known about what is happening. Something we should all probably discuss. But another topic of interest clawed its way to the top slot when I had my first contact with the Immortal Warriors.

I fold my knees into my chest and wrap my arms around my legs, hugging them to me. "Your father seems like an intense kind of male. I bet you take after him, don't you?"

He chuckles. "He can be rather intense, yes. And you may be right. I too can be intense from time to time."

Or... a lot of the time. I grin. "What's your mother like?"

His expression turns somber and my chest crushes inward. *No. Don't say it. No, no.*

"She was strong, inside and out. Decisive and steadfast—"

"Was?" I mumble.

I press the heel of my hand to my chest, pushing against the building pain. She can't be gone. Not when so many who were deceased in my previous reality are now alive.

"She passed close to eighteen years ago."

I open my mouth to rudely ask how, when a trickle of stone echoes in the distance. My attention darts down the tunnel in the direction we'd come from and focuses on the darkest shadows at the farthest end.

I thrust my newly discovered heartache to the back of my thoughts where it will be dealt with later, and align my full focus on whatever threat may be unfolding before me.

A hand on my shoulder causes me to jump. The males have gathered around me. Jaden tugs me to my feet, Lobrka in our faces, his finger to his lips needlessly reminding us to keep quiet. Azure takes hold of my other arm, the two brothers working in tandem to move me away from the unidentified noise.

And Ry, he positions himself at my back.

I've never been one to easily accept help, much less protection. And I'm definitely not a girl in need of protecting *or* saving. Or, at least, I didn't use to be. This new-to-me, transformed life is mind-warping.

Lobrka yanks Scarlett off the ground and shoves into action. The soldier grabs her arm and rushes her down the tunnel in our wake. I note the way she clutches her chest, then turn my attention forward. I imagine her heart is racing as mine is. And my heart may be running faster than I am.

Gaea and god, please don't let us all die in the dark of these tunnels.

Racing through the tunnels, following every curve and turn, I search the walls attempting to identify any hidden exits. A way out of this hell.

We pass beneath wooden reinforcements and break into a space roughly the size of my bedroom back in California. Behind us is the tunnel from which we came, and ahead, the tunnel splits. Two options to choose from.

"Which way?" Jaden asks.

Lobrka spins back toward the sounds at our back and Ry steps to his side. "Are you thinking what I am thinking?" he asks the dark elf.

Lobrka tilts his head toward Ry. "If it involves the wood beams, then yes."

They exchange smirks, then attack the wood supports. Each taking opposite sides with powerhouse kicks. They kick and smack and knock the supports free. The upper beam crashes to the ground, bringing with it a ton of rock and dirt and clouds of dust.

But, if their intention was to block the passage, the objective isn't achieved. Plenty of space is open for someone to climb through. And the shuffle and scatter of pebbles in the darkness beyond promises that something is indeed coming that will likely choose to do exactly that.

Lobrka curses, then motions us to keep running. Only I

don't move. I need to prove to myself and others that I'm a useful team member and capable of something other than being protected.

"I can close the gap," I say. "That's the goal, right?"

"Do it," Jaden and Azure say in unison.

In the tunnel beyond the collapsed rubble, three black-veined faces advance. Their eyes are like obsidian and, when they hiss, their canines are too-long and too-pointy. All I can think is, *vampire.*

My soul grows cold.

Are these the infected? They look nothing like the monstrosities Dreya created.

"Do it already," Scarlett yells, her voice winded.

I hadn't realized I'd frozen in place, staring at the coming threat. Scarlett's yell jolts me into action. Blinking away my dark reflection, I slam both my hands to the stone of the tunnel.

My fingers tingle, my senses seeking connection with the groundwater. The element is on the outskirts of my reach, and I stretch and ache for the link. Working with water was easier *before...* before I landed in this lifetime... and I need the working relationship to be like it was before—to move smoother and faster.

The infected are too close and the tunnel is not yet blocked. The soldier jumps away from us and through the opening, his sword swinging. He cuts down one of the infected, clearing its head from the shoulders, then cuts his blade through the chest of the second.

Before he can withdraw, the third infected is on the soldier, sinking its teeth into his exposed neck.

My heart hiccups. Holy god and Gaea, it *is* a vampire.

Scarlett hollers, clear panic in her inflection. "Do it already."

Jaden and Azure cover my hands with their own and

awareness bolts through me. The water element responds, shifting through the soil, and destabilizing the stone surrounding the partially collapsed tunnel entrance.

The grumble and thunder of shifting rock resonates in the space before me.

The remaining infected snap toward me, and a breath later, the soldier rises from the ground, spinning to us, fully infected. They reach forward and rush.

"Close it," I whisper to the water. "Don't let them pass."

The elemental caress glides over my skin and through my blood.

The tunnel rattles with a boom, and the ceiling falls. Sound, and debris blasts us with the force of an explosion, throwing us across the space and slamming us onto our backs.

I cough against the field of dust clouding the air and filling my lungs. The hacks and wheezes of other group members compete to be heard over the ringing in my ears. I roll onto my side and spit the filth from my mouth, then press onto my knees and cough up more.

Lobrka slides his arms beneath my armpits and lifts me to my feet. "We need to keep moving."

"You could at least say thank you." I weakly shove him.

"Thank you." He doesn't sound remotely grateful. I decide not to hold that fact against him. Instead, I ineffectively brush the dirt from my clothing and shake it from my hair. "Okay. Which way?"

The dust is starting to settle enough to distinguish shadowed shapes. Lobrka is the tallest and easiest to distinguish, after Scarlett's curves and flow of hair.

She coughs into her fist. "Is anyone going to say anything about what just happened?" She swings a hard point toward the collapsed tunnel. "That guy..." the soldier, "...just died! And the things chasing us are unnatural." She makes no effort to mask her horror.

"*Highly* unnatural," Lobrka deadpans. "An excellent reason to keep moving."

"Agreed." Ry steps into view holding his shirt over his mouth, using it to filter the air he's breathing. "We should head south and rendezvous with my father's battalion."

I clench my jaw. Elves and immortal warriors, so devoid of compassionate emotion in times of turmoil.

My gaze drops to Ry's exposed abdomen, noting the tattoos marking his skin. There are fewer on this version. Fewer battles likely equals fewer deaths. Except... I recall the immortal warriors I met at the floating islands. They had all shown long term, slow exposure to the infection. What does that mean for their condition now that things have clearly escalated?

I'm debating whether I should say something or not when Lobrka says, "We should go north and make way for Palinot Woodlands and the Balance Bringer's mystic."

Joining the immortal warriors could be bad, considering what I witnessed. If they turn, that's a whole lot of trained killers to be in the midst of. As for Meira or Madame Marrouske, whichever name she chooses, will likely have protected the tearman, the tree of life, from the infection spread by the weeping, but beyond that, what does he have to offer the situation? Can I undergo the binding without my sisters, while they still live? Can she offer me the answers to clearing the infection that has likely touched every inhabitant of the realm: animals, plants, and more complex beings?

I shake my head and stare at the ground, considering the options available in our situation.

Jaden clears his throat. "I believe Anaka has another idea."

"I do?" My head snaps up.

Jaden taps his temple and then his heart. *What does my heart say?*

An idea develops around a kernel of thought I had two days ago. "Can we go to the Time Keep?" I ask, believing a place filled with Time Chroniclers is my best chance at finding someone who might be able to help me understand the time changes I have affected.

"The Time Keep?" Lines press into Lobrka's brow. "Why there?"

I cover my mouth against a cough. "I need to consult a Time Chronicler."

"The Time Keep works for me," Scarlett says. "That area is far more appealing to me than the woodlands or a bunch of warriors who answer to the king."

Lobrka's gaze narrows. "Still think you made the right decision?" *Changing the timeline.*

I press my lips together and shake my head. I can't answer that question. Too many unknowns still exist.

A clatter of rocks snaps everyone's attention to the collapsed tunnel.

Azure grabs my hand. "We need to go." He pulls me toward the open tunnel on our left.

Jaden is right behind us. "We go north," he says, his tone allowing no room for argument. "Not to the mystic, but to catch a ship. We will go by sea, round the southern cape and come at the Time Keep from the water. In so doing, we avoid as much of the populace as possible."

Jaden captures my free hand and my tracers and I move down the northern tunnel.

From my previous reality, I can recall the time it took to travel from the port village to the palace. This time, the travel takes longer. Though, my thoughts could be responsible for dragging out the feeling of time. Adding weight to my feet.

My guilt is on repeat: My mom is dead, my sisters are locked up, my dad may be dead, injured, or worse, my aunt is married to a mad fae and is mother to a demon child, Opal is infected, and the entirety of the realms is either infected or endanger of being so soon.

I can no longer believe the lives saved—my father, my sisters, Azure, Usoff, Ry's physical health, and Dreya's mental state—out weight the damage reaped upon Hiddenkel.

We push through without sleep, and we're all exhausted and starving by the time Lobrka reveals a side tunnel leading to an exit. We climb into the pre-dawn air, thick with mist, in what appears to be the middle of nowhere.

I drop onto my butt, close my eyes, and breathe deep, willing the fresh air to clean my lungs and remorseful thoughts.

Have I done the worlds a disservice?

The tingle of Jaden's fingers glide across my cheek. "How are you doing?"

My eyes slowly peel open. "I could eat and then sleep for days."

He grins and then pulls me forward and places a kiss on my forehead.

Azure steps up to us. "We can eat and sleep after we are safely onboard that ship currently docked in the port."

I rise to my feet, and both Jaden and I turn in the direction of Azure's attention. Several kilometers away a village is settled seaside, and tied up at the dock, a large seafaring vessel.

Staying hidden and within the shadows as much as possible, we make our way toward the dock.

"Hopefully, it is too early for news of what is happening at the palace to have made it all the way here," says Lobrka, and leads us behind a building where the rest of us wait while he secures our passage.

In the quiet moments while we wait, growing colder and

more damp, my mind can't stop returning to the negative space, spinning everything around and around. The island weeping infecting the realm, the food and drink supply. Something put into motion by King Theon who is now enacting some sort of play for control. Who even knows what has now happened to Dreya. And then there is my mom. Can she truly be deceased? Ry has no reason to lie to me.

"I secured us passage and two cabins." Lobrka's announcement draws me back to the now. He's gazing at the changing color of the sky. Dark blues lightening with faint hints of pink. "Departure is at sunrise so we should get moving."

We do exactly that, Scarlett grumbling much of the way. "Why am I staying with you losers?" she says.

Ry grunts. "Because these losers are your best chance of staying alive and uninfected."

"Whatever," she mumbles, and climbs the gangway.

We're handed towels to dry the clinging mist from our clothes and skin, and then are divided into two groups of three. My Tracer brothers with me in one cabin, and Lobrka, Ry, and Scarlett, in the other. Lobrka arranged for jugs of water, porridge, grapes, and bread to be awaiting our arrival. I'm barely through the door before a chunk of bread is in my hand.

I take a bite, drop into one of the two wooden chairs, and avert my gaze from the bed because... ugh, I'm so tired. If I look at it, I'll be crawling into it. But there's something I need to do.

I pull Gitta's list from my front pocket.

I should probably sleep first, but after the news about my mom, I can't wait. I need to know whatever information Gitta has found.

I unfold the slip and read the first name provided; *Dohlan*.

TWELVE

I gasp for breath, unable to tear my eyes from the list. I tell myself that the information provided is not definitive. After all, Ruby and I are both known by different names in this reality. The same could apply to the others listed in the negative. I hope.

I silently read the list for the hundredth time.

Dohlan Marsoun: *No record of existence*
Zarah of house Chronos: *Last known location – Season's Cape Time Keep*
Yuromo of Loreitta Village: *No record of existence*
Satyr Garrthmal: *Last known location – Ivey City*
Augur Clan Members: *No record of Augur Clan existence*
Alabaster (White Ghost): *Last known location – City of Palinot*
Shadow: *No record of existence*
Clef: *No record of existence*

What if changing Dreya's history, also significantly

changed Opal... Aunt Edea's history? As Dohlan's mother and founder of the Augur Clan in my reality, maybe saving Dreya changed those two things here.

I press my hands to my heart and breathe... breathe.

Could it be Dohlan was never born? Without the clan, would the members have different names or not survived?

Possible, I guess.

Breathe, breathe, breathe.

But that doesn't explain Alabaster being searchable and found under the same name, if the one on the list is the same white ghost. *And what of Mo?*

Crushing. The weight of the realm is crushing my chest, making breath difficult to attain.

"Shh." Azure takes my hand and guides me from the chair to the bed. "It does you no good to obsess over these things."

How does he know what I am and am not obsessing over? I don't ask.

Jaden joins Azure and the two of them help me out of my damp outer layers, wrap me in a fuzzy blanket, and then guide me to sit on the edge of the bottom bunk. Jaden messages my temples and whispers for me to eat and sleep. With his ability washing over me, my body wants to obey.

Azure holds a glass of water in my hand, helping lead the drink to my lips. He does the same with the food, feeding me grapes, spoonfuls of porridge, and nibbles of bread. He works patiently to fill my belly and get me hydrated. All the while, Jaden holds my anxiety at bay.

If I weren't so physically and mentally exhausted, I could care for myself, but I am those things, emotionally spent, as well. And... well... I enjoy their loving attention.

I grow drowsy, my eyelids heavy. Jaden's ability on top of my already worn condition likely speeding my fall towards sleep. I close my eyes and release the tension in my muscles.

Azure washes my hands and face with gentle wipes of a damp cloth, and then Jaden lowers my head to the pillow. He kisses me goodnight... even though day is dawning outside the portal window... and I let the darkness swallow me.

THE GROUND ROCKS and sways and sloshes with water. My feet slip and slide, finding it difficult to find balance. The ocean spray is everywhere and covering everything, matting my hair to my face, my clothing to my skin.

I'm on a ship, but not the one I boarded earlier today with Jaden and Azure. No, I'm on one of many ships at war on the water. Two armadas going head-to-head. And my body is getting tossed around like a bingo ball in a spinning cage.

Night blankets the sky and in the distance, a city built into the rocky rise of a hill is exploding with fireworks. The city of Palinot's warnings to its citizens, because of the attack coming from the sea. I remember this night, but that was in a different reality, and I was in the city, not on a boat on the water.

The dragon wall around the city is uncoiling, and water is pouring onto the ship, taking the form of an ice queen—Dreya. People are screaming and yelling and racing all around me. I spin around, trying to understand where I am... or *when* I am. Everything around me has the makings of a dream-walk, except what I'm experiencing seems to be pulled from my previous history, only from a drastically different angle.

"Madame Mystic," someone yells. The call is corrected by a female yelling, "Bree is fine."

Bree is here?

I turn and spy my mom through a window to the control room. *And my mom?*

My heart jumps. *Am I dreaming? Having a nightmare?*

The ship rocks and my feet slip out from under me. I tumble sideways and catch myself against a barrel. I pull myself to my feet and Bree is within reaching distance, but she doesn't see me. No one sees me.

I stretch my arm and try to tap Bree, snag her arm, but I can't touch her. My hand doesn't move through her but is repelled, pushed away like opposing magnets. I attempt to tag someone else and meet the same results.

What is this? What is going on?

Grabbing the side rail, I scrutinize every detail. The armada, the city, the uncoiling wall, and light show in the sky. If this was an ancestral dream-walk, I would be in the control room as my mom, but I'm a free agent in the scene. And this reality now ceases to exist, so...

I turn around and face the ice sculpted image of Dreya standing on the ship's forward. She's glaring down at Bree.

"...now it's just you and me," she says. "And I will never stop until I obtain what I want..." Her icy stare swings to me. "And you took everything from me, twice. So, I shall take everything from her."

I gasp. Did she just talk to me? In this dream, projected memory, or whatever this is.

I need to understand what this all means. Is this some sort of message for the universe, or from Gaea?

"Or possibly me." Dreya's ice hand grabs my wrist. "You had no right rewriting my history."

I scream. Scream for Gaea, scream for my mom, scream at Dreya.

My body jolts, a strangled yelp struggling to break free from my mouth. An arm tightens around me and pulls me into a soothing warmth.

"You are all right," Jaden says. "Wherever you were, you are back with us now."

I crack my eyes open and stare up at the underside of the top bunk. The sway of the ship is a rocking lullaby, attempting to lure me back to sleep. But returning to that dream... or whatever it was... is not something I want to do.

All three of us are on the bottom bunk together, Jaden and Azure cuddling at my sides. I fold my hands over my waist and the brothers add their hands to mine, weaving their fingers with mine. They nuzzle the curve of my neck, their breaths on the tip of deep sleep.

"Ana," Azure half groans. "Your body is still in need of more rest."

I respond with a moan.

Jaden's hand on mine tightens. "I promise not to let you return to that place." The place I experienced moments ago before awakening. "I will keep you in safe, relaxing zones."

"Promise?"

"Always."

I release myself to the peace I pray further sleep will bring. Jaden and Azure's presence warms me, soothes me, and reenergizes my elemental side. And then everything around us is transforming and melting into something new.

Jaden, Azure, and I are intertwined, floating in an ever-expanding ocean. Water serving as a conductor through space and time. We drift in the midst of everything all at once, a fluidity of events and timelines.

Images of my previous dream flitter into view and vanish. Morphing into visions from my previous reality of our trip to the city of Palinot on Zarah's flatboat. Visions that relax my senses into a state of calm.

In that acquired calm state, our shared awareness—me with my elemental water relationship and now linked, fueled, with the soul split embodiments of my bonded Tracer, Jaden and Azure—I become one with the mist. The precipitation covers the realm and carries my sight throughout, moving with the wild grace of a slipstream.

My observation settles over the winter palace, drawn to the tower housing my bedchamber. All the windows of my sisters' adjacent rooms are thrown open. Crystal leans out one, closing her eyes to the fall of mist on her face. Her eyes pop open, and she lurches further out the opening, angling her upper body as if to see the next window over.

She calls out to our sister Kayla, "I think she is present in the water. Can you sense her?"

Kayla pops her head out. I stretch forward as if to place a palm of mist upon her cheek. She shivers and replies, "She is."

"Kayla. Crystal." My thoughts reach out to them. *"I miss you. Are you safe?"*

"Anaka," Kayla whispers. "Worry not about us, we are not the concern. Get yourself far from here. Find a place that is somehow safe. We will eventually join you, one way or another."

Her message is clear, and it twists my heart into a tangle, but I have no other answers on how to fully realize the power of the Balance Bringer without our binding. And under the circumstances, the binding... their necessary passing... is secondary.

Only... Gaea above, I don't want it to be so. Kayla and Crystal may not be *exactly* the sisters I grew up knowing, their upbringing and experiences having made them different in some ways, but at their core, they are the same beautiful souls... and I love those souls.

"Let's pretend for a minute," I muse. "That we were not the prophesied Balance Bringer, but just normal sisters with a normal life."

"What are you doing?" Kayla queries.

"Just indulge me a moment," I reply, my sentiment slipping over them with every droplet of water. "If no one expected anything from us, and you could do anything, be anything, what would you make of your life?"

Kayla laughs. "If only. But I would surely find me a tantalizing member of the male species that I would never have to share with *you*, and would make him beg for me, every minute of the day and night."

Wow. That explains her relationship with Dohlan in my original timeline.

"A worthy goal, Kayla." I allow a touch of humor to coat my response and she hums in response "And what of you, Crystal?"

She sighs. "Truth? I have always wondered what it would be like to open a candle making shop. I think I would like to try such a thing. Maybe, someday I will... in my next life."

Candle making? Is that something Crystia used to consider? Maybe as a possible hobby? If so, she never shared those thoughts with me. That possibility is a tightening noose around my internal organs.

"Someone is coming," Crystal says, her whisper urgent. "You need to go. Fulfill our destiny."

I'm not ready to go. But then, I'll never be ready. Not truly. All I can really do is be steadfast in my love for my sisters and always be prepared to do right by them.

My chest swells with responding promise, my view already swirling down and around the castle, moving within the walls as clinging mist on the shoulders of staff and soldiers. My view moves with an officer striding as if on a mission straight into the throne room.

He halts in the middle of the room and stands at attention. "My King," he says and bows.

"You may rise." The king stands beside the crystal throne and waves a hand in the air. "Inform."

"The Royal Commander was injured but has escaped. We are currently taking measures to recapture."

The right tip of the king's lips tilt toward the ground. "And the other?"

"The girl is on the run. The room has been cleared, and the tunnels beneath have collapsed. We are currently working to clear the rubble."

The king grumbles and starts to turn away, then comes face to face with Princess Quirina. He spins back around and addresses the male, "Find them both and do not stop until that goal has been accomplished."

He dismisses the soldier with a halfhearted wave, his attention snapping to the entrance. A couple of males are dragging an unconscious Dreya into the throne room. The king glances at the princess, as if seeking her advice. She points to the crystal throne.

"Place the queen on the throne," the king orders the males.

They do as told and then vacate the premises under the king's command, thus leaving the royals alone in the room. The king remains in place, staring at the entrance doors. Princess Quirina moves around to the front of the queen and adjusts Dreya's hands on the chair arms, then glances at her father.

"Father." She sighs. "Go find that old Oriana Opal elf and tell her to find the Balance Bringer. Bring her to me."

He strides across the room without question or hesitation, like he is Quirine's puppet.

Understanding swells around me. *Maybe he is exactly that.*

The sound of the door slamming close bounced off the walls and Princess Quirine drops her hands on top of Dreya's. "Mother love," Quirine says with wicked sweetness. "Thank you for being my conduit."

First understanding, now realization. Quirine is attempting to access the power of the crystal cavern beneath the throne room, and she is using Dreya to do so.

My awareness swirls around Dreya, Quirine, and myself. *"What are you?"*

The princess hisses.

The surroundings shatter into a completely different scene. Dreya and Quirine are gone, and the throne room floor is broken, exposing the cavern. My unresponsive body now sits in the chair.

A sudden shift from one reality to another.

The element sweeps me out of the room altogether. My view instantly focusing on the lake beyond the garden wall. The feature morphs from the now to a day covered in snow. A young Dreya is skating on the ice, my father standing to the side. On the tree topped hill at the side, out of the view of the two royals, Sol and I argue.

I'm witnessing the moment I changed the timeline by stopping Dreya from becoming cursed.

Fog mists over the vision, and suddenly I'm watching Dreya fall through the ice, my father unconscious beside the lake, and a darkened version of Sol slipping away.

I gasp and slip back into an endless stream of water elementals. Jaden and Azure are wound around me, speaking straight to my mind.

Did you understand everything you saw? Azure asks.

I did.

And do you understand the message the elements are trying to send? Jaden says.

I believe so.

My connection with the water elementals has acted like a looking glass without limit, not only through space, but across timelines. And I'm fairly certain they are telling me I need to figure out a way to reverse my mistake.

I AWAKEN to the day coming to an end and the ship docked at the northern tip of the volcanic island that houses the Fires of Guardoone. No new travelers nor any stories of the infected board, but crates are loaded, and the males and females helping to load the inventory display darkened fingertips and hints of shadows on the edges of their noses.

After we depart, I lean against the ship's siding and watch the island slip into the distance. Lobrka steps up beside me and gazes out over the water.

"The floating islands never crossed the water," he says. "But those working places untouched by the weeping still had food and drink imported, among other things."

I suck my lips back and nod. "Hiddenkel's in serious trouble, isn't it?" I turn to weigh his expression.

He sighs and leans forward, clasping his hands and leaning his forearms on the railing. His mouth works but words don't come instead, after a moment, he nods.

"While I slept," I continue, "The elements showed me things. Princess Quirine is beyond infected and totally evil. I think she's puppeting the king and attempting to use the queen to access the crystal energy humming under the palace."

He shifts to face me, resting his weight on one arm.

"And my father... he's injured but still alive."

"You know of your father?" he asks. "Few individuals know of your parentage."

"Lived a different reality or timeline, remember?" I smirk. "He may be the royal commander here, but he was the king in my previous life."

"Even he does not know he is your father."

My mouth drops open. "How can that be?"

He shrugs. "He was not present for the birth and was told mother and child perished in the process. The queen had the records sealed for everyone's protection."

"So." I shift and press my hip to the side rail. "He doesn't know but you do?"

"Madame shared the information with me."

Of course, she did. "Did she tell you about my mother, too?"

He grins. "She did. Your mother did pass during childbirth. Her sister died that same night protecting you and your sisters from Edea. Edea was forced to retreat, but because of the abduction attempt, the queen ordered the birth records seals and the truth of your parentage kept secret."

"Even from my father?"

He shrugs. "I suspect the queen was unaware of who your father was, other than he had to have been fae. And she must have been unaware of Edea's involvement or fooled by her shapeshifting, given she invited her to the palace in order to work with you."

"Shapeshifting?" My head jerks back.

He turns back toward the ocean view, leaning against the railing. "In the past few centuries, she has found a way to significantly adjust her appearance."

Wow. "The evil princess sent her on a mission to find me." He nods, absentmindedly.

"We have to make sure she cannot find you."

I frown. "I think, what I need to do is undo the change I made to the timeline."

A bright grin slips across his lips. "So... you no longer believe you made the right decision?"

I release a heavy sigh. "The elementals sent me a message while I slept. I got the distinct impression they think I shouldn't have done what I did. So... I want to try and fix that."

His responding body language shows silent agreement.

"Will you help me?" I ask.

He turns and rests his palm on my upper arm. "Of course."

I start by imploring his help attempting to awaken muscle memory from a lifetime never lived, my previous reality. If I could access whatever I did through my dream, then maybe I can do this too. And if not, a little weapons training wouldn't hurt.

Lobrka agrees. Taking blades in hand, we spar and then shift to drills, practicing moves with sword in hand. When the night turns fully dark, we agree to revisit the activity the next day. I return to the cabin every muscle in my body aching.

The next morning, Ry's waiting to be a part of the exercises. Jaden and Azure join the efforts shortly after. All of us, minus Ruby, work on swings and strikes, blocks and jabs—defenses and attacks with equal attention. Ruby meanders nearby, picking at her nails, and appearing a hundred percent bored.

We continue on and off throughout the day, pausing for meals, water breaks, and too-often needed breathers... because *this* body of mine is not used to the constant activity. My senses instinctively reach out to my water element. It's everywhere around us, fierce and vivacious. And it answers, filling me with energy and knowledge.

Since I first found myself in this new reality, my connection with water has grown in strength and conductivity. My knowledge and experience from my previous reality helping this version of myself to improve my elemental connection.

I'm not nearly as strong and fast as I had been *before*, but I'm connected enough to get the water to move our ship at a quicker pace... at least while I'm awake and focused. Whenever I lose myself in thought or conversation, our speed decreases. So, I try to maintain focus, my intention to cut as much travel time off our trip as possible.

None of us know if the king's forces or Opal/Edea will already be waiting for us when we reach shore, but I'm implementing every skill available to me to better our chances of getting in and out of the Time Keep before they show. The ship is a day ahead of schedule when we round the southernmost edge of territory in the dark of night.

The sea is still as glass, the night a void of sound, and the first sight of Season's Cape, home of the Time Keep, complete shadow. Not a single light of any kind flickers within the awaiting city.

The brothers take a stance on either side of me, studying the sight. "That sight is less than desirable," Jaden murmurs.

THIRTEEN

Adock worker jogs at our side. "You should stay on the ship and sail back out to sea."

The male is skittish and appears ready to bolt at the first unexpected sound. All lights are extinguished, and the dock workers are waiting in the dark for our ship's arrival. They are anxious to get their hands on the inventory being delivered. Likely weapons imbued with the power gifted by the Fires of Gaurdoone.

Scarlett scoffs. "If only that were an option. By the looks of things, this is one of the last places I care to be."

Azure snorts. "Would you rather still be locked up in the keep?"

"Shut up," she snaps, and increases her pace, walking ahead of our group.

"Stay at your own risk," the dock worker says. "But a darkness is descending."

"What's going on?" I ask at the same time Lobrka says, "What have you been experiencing?"

He scratches his jawbone. "We had some unhealthy and dangerous visitors. Almost immediately, a few of our citizens started acting out of character. By orders from the Time Keep, all who were acting questionable were dispatched." *Killed.* "We were then told to remain indoors with lights off, no fires in the hearths, and window coverings closed."

He scratches his chin. Glances past us to the ship. "Only the dock crew was requested to be here to receive today's goods. Although, we were not expecting you for another day or so."

"We got lucky with the tailwinds," I say.

"Well." The worker scratches his chest. "You will be hard pressed to find hospitality. Everything is locked up and everyone is in hiding... so to speak."

Jaden drops his hand on the male's shoulder. "All good. Our destination should be accommodating."

The worker shifts his weight, his fingers fiddling. "Well. Good luck to you." He dashes off to join those finishing with unloading the ship. All the dock workers appear anxious to wrap up the process and get behind closed doors.

The Time Keep is located several blocks inland. We make the trip with quiet steps through empty streets. Streets so silent and absent of life, the city would appear abandoned, if not betrayed by the pristine condition of the many buildings' colorful paint, the maintained architectural accents, intact and ornate windows, and clean iron work.

Flowered vines soften sharp lines, and intricate time symbols add unique interest. Twirling time pieces are found at intersections mounted atop ten-foot pillars or hanging off the side of businesses. Bubbling fountains, likely once a draw for social gatherings, now glimmer in the moonlight, the water undisturbed.

Even the Time Keep gives the impression of being deserted. A structure built to touch the heavens and likely meant to shimmer with the reflection of a million stars, now looms over us like a depressed death deity, bent and buried in shadows.

Every surface of the monstrous structure appears to have been designed to reflect and refract light. From the highly polished stone, and the countless, larger-than-life crystal cut and colored glass windows, to the smooth surface of the water circling the place. Waters of time, Lobrka says.

The bronze ten-person wide door, offering no handles and covered in a series of elaborate locks, is set in the center of a many-paned, circular glass window. Clearly designed to be the centerpiece of attention, the window is taller and wider than my school gym, doubled and twice stacked, and decorated with depictions of the various ways to track time. The most dominant of those being the overall circle of the window itself, mimicking the face of a clock.

On a normal evening, when all the lights are burning, both inside and out, I have no doubt the design glows with the illumination. But now, in this time of fear and everyone hiding, no shadows move on the other side of the glass, and no one is present to release the multitude of locks set upon the door.

My fingers trace one of the locks—a bar to which several winding gizmos are attached. "Do you think they'll answer if we knock?"

Ry steps up beside me, hand fisted. "Only one way to find out."

"You cannot be serious." Scarlett steps between us, her arms sweeping wide, shoving me and Ry back from the door. She glances over her shoulder at our group. "I guess it is a good thing you decided to bring me along." She smirks and turns back to face the many locks.

She leans her face within an inch of one of the metal gizmos and whispers a word softer than my hearing can decipher. With that one word and a soft exhale, the gizmos across the surface start to spin and the bars to slide. The double doors unseal with a hiss of air and slowly swing open.

"Easy as breathing," Scarlett says and strides through the opening into the grand... and very empty... receiving room.

The rest of us follow, and when we have all crossed over the entrance, the massive doors automatically begin to close.

No one is present to greet us.

Lobrka scans the many spaces visible from our location. "I take it they are familiar with you here?" he asks of Scarlett.

Scarlett responses with a cackle. "Do you honestly think that the keepers only collect histories? They want everything. They collect love connections made as well as the ones never realized."

Everyone in our group spins to her, and my eyes pop wide.

She laughs. "Wow. You are all rather naive."

Lobrka blows out a breath. "As concerning as that information is, I would say we have more pressing matters to address. Matters that are likely making their way here as we speak."

"Right." She pops her fists on her hips. "You are here now. What more do you need?"

"I need to see a time keeper named Zarah," I say.

"Cannot say I know her." Scarlett spins on her heel. "I shall see if one of the hags is around to help you." She strides away, vanishing into the shadows of a hallway at the back of the room.

Now what? My gaze wanders upward.

The center of the building is open all the way to the extreme top. It's like staring into an alternate universe, the top floor being so far away I can't even make it out. The front wall is nothing but windows running the full height of the structure. A gangway swings around the interior, connecting the other sides, and opening each floor to a view of the center, and the lobby below.

If we are forced to search for Zarah on our own, we could die of old age before ever finding her.

"Who are you?" A female in a full hooded cloak comes from the same hallway through which Scarlett disappeared. Using gloved hands, the female draws back her hood, revealing her aged complexion, wrinkled skin, and white streaked gray hair. "Who let you in here at such a time?"

My back bolts straight. "Time of night, or time within an unfolding situation?"

Jaden presses a soft finger to my lips and shakes his head. The action draws a smirk to the old woman's face.

Lobrka steps forward as if our declared spokesperson. "We are here under the direction of the queen."

The female waves the sentence away. "We do not recognize her authority here."

"In this time of unrest..." Ry takes a step forward. "How about the authority of the royal commander, or the warrior commander?"

The female raises a hand to stop any further words. "Do not waste your breath. There is no authority we recognize and only occasionally entertain such self-important parties."

Jaden grabs Azure's wrist as if to hold him back from the action he foresees coming, but Azure breaks free, shoving Jaden away. "What would it take to secure your help?"

"What is it you want?" she fires back.

"I need to consult one of your time chroniclers. I'd—"

Jaden abruptly tugs me to his side as Azure spins back at me with a sharp, demanding stare, stopping my words before I can say more. Jaden kisses my temple, sending me a sliver of calm.

"Consult a time chronicler, you say?" she verifies.

I nod and we all fall silent awaiting her response. Her eyebrows rise and her gaze combs over Azure, then shifts to each male in our group, ignoring me altogether.

Her expression turns smug, and her eye contact turns tight on Azure. "Surrender one of your males to the Time Keep."

I gasp. She speaks of us as if we are "things," "items" to be traded. Not living creatures with thoughts and desires of our own. How can any being treat another in such a manner?

"No," I blurt.

My response is lost to Azure's firm response. "Done."

"What? No." I grab him and force him to look at me. He smiles at me, the expression lost to sadness and resolution.

Jaden grabs his brother's arm. "Do not do this. We will find another way."

Azure swings his arms wide, clasping his hands on Jaden and my upper arms, pinning the three of us in a close-knit circle. "The time to find another option does not exist and you both know that to be true."

"But." I shake my head, my insides churning with acid. "But you can't just hand yourself over to this..." I shake my hand toward the ceiling. "Whatever this is."

"This..." He raises his hands and, ignoring Jaden, shifts his attention to me, pressing his palms to my shoulders demanding my own focus. His fixed gaze is soul searing. "This is my chance to help you in working toward your destiny. Let me do this."

"But—"

He presses a sole finger to my lips, his eyes begging for my compliance. "There is nothing... *nothing*... I would not do for you. Jaden knows that to be true, because he feels the same, as well. And you need to accept that from both of us." His hand glides over my check bone, shifting stray hairs away. His face inches closer to mine, his voice softening. "You always have been and always will be our everything. What I do now, I do because of my love for you."

"But—"

He shakes his head and whispers, "Only love."

His lips descend on mine, soft as silk but with a firmness that promises pleasure. Only, this feels like a goodbye, and I can find no pleasure in that. His tongue sweeps through me and for the first time since my reality changed, I welcome him without guilt or misgivings. I clutch him closer and return his kiss without reservation, everyone else around us forgotten... except for the essence of Jaden I taste and feel within our exchange.

A forced cough echoes off the walls, the clink of heels marking Scarlett's return. "First, why are you two tangling tongues in front of an audience, *and* at a time like this?" she asks in pure Ruby style. "And secondly, why is everyone else simply standing around and watching like this is some sort of theatrical performance?"

Azure and I pull away, but I can't bring myself to release the caress of his face. I don't know what it means to be given to the Time Keep order, but I can't believe it will be anything fun or fulfilling. After all, in my previous reality, Zarah had run away from this place and the individuals in control.

My heart is screaming not to let this happen, but my head is saying it must be done.

"Try to show some respect," Ry reprimands Scarlett.

She huffs. "I thought you would want to know that not only has the ship officially left the port, taking with it our only escape option, but the light of several torches approaches from the north."

All attention snaps to her. "So, what is the plan?" she pushes.

Lobrka and Ry shift their angle to better face her. "How do you know this?" Ry asks.

"Tower windows."

Jaden draws me into his hold, and I realize the reason too late. Azure has already shifted beyond arm's reach from the group.

He addresses the female keeper, "Help my friends and I agree to your terms."

The female smirks, her eyes sparkling with apparent triumph and greed. I break free of Jaden's hold and lurch for Azure. Lobrka, Ry, and Scarlett swivel toward the action.

Smoke explodes like a bomb in the spot where Azure and the female keeper stand. The smoke billows and expands, blinding my vision. I dash forward, coughing and attempting to disperse the hovering cloud.

Azure is gone!

"Where is he?" I scream, waving more of the smoke to scatter. "Where did he go?"

Ry jumps forward. "What kind of magic is this?"

"Not magic," Scarlett supplies. "A trick to give the illusion of magic. There is obviously a hidden passage in the floor near where they stood. The smoke was used to camouflage their exit."

"Great," I blurt. "How do we find him now?"

Scarlett shrugs, appearing less than interested in the answer. "They will not hurt him. As the Keep's new stud, they will take special care to keep him physically and mentally healthy. He is, after all, of prime age and condition."

My mouth drops open. *What in all of God and Gaea's fallen Hell?*

Jaden pulls me into his embrace, his arms around me firm and failing to comfort. "He knew what he was doing, and this was his choice," he whispers.

"But. But." *Stud?* How could he? How can I allow him?

Lobrka scratches the back of his neck then flings his hand into the air at the side of his head as if in frustration. "How has his sacrifice advanced our efforts?"

"The agreement made shall be honored." We all spin toward the approaching voice. A cloaked figure moves in our direction, dropping their hood to reveal another female keeper. This one slightly younger with fewer wrinkles and brassy hair, but eyes void on any contentment. "And I am to see that it is so."

"I want to barter a new agreement," I say, curling my hands into fists.

"The keeper shifts her gaze to me, her expression flat. "I am unauthorized to make any changes or additions to the agreement."

I grit my teeth, all my muscles tensing.

"Anaka." Lobrka places his hand on my shoulder. "Do what you came here to do, and his fate will be changed by default."

Instead, he'll be dead. I suck back a breath and focus on my breathing.

The keeper turns toward the back hallway. "Follow me and I shall take you to one of our time chroniclers."

Jaden turns to follow, dragging me with him, but I force myself to stop, needing to clarify something. "Not just any time chronicler," I say. "It needs to be time chronicler Zarah."

The keeper stiffens and glares at me. "Why?"

Something about her expression and inflection raises my defenses. I lift my chin. "Because she is the only one I will trust."

"She is not for public readings." Her jaw tightens.

I cross my arms, but before I can respond, Lobrka steps in. "We never said a reading was what we seek."

The keeper tenses and remains silent.

Ry's gaze narrows. "Is this not the terms you are bound to? You took one of ours, now you must grant us an audience with Time Chronicler Zarah." He jabs his fists into his hips.

I blink at him. Will he see Zarah with the same love-tinted view he did in my original reality?

Moments of silence tick by like pregnant pauses in the turning of time. We all glare at the keeper expectantly, and after wordless seconds that felt like minutes, the keeper's shoulders slump.

"You are correct, of course." She frowns. "Follow me and say nothing. Lest you rouse the others."

Ominous. I exchange a glance with Jaden, then Lobrka and Ry.

"This should be good," Scarlett murmurs, clearly sarcastic, and we all quietly follow the keeper down the hall and down a narrow set of stairs several levels to a labyrinth of tunnels carved out of the ground.

The spaces are cold and damp and lit only by flaming torches mounted along the passage walls. Whimpers and whines carry from behind the many closed doors we pass.

"Is this a prison?" I ask, my restless fingers scratching at my thighs.

"Containment." The keeper doesn't turn her head to make eye contact but continues striding toward the largest door in the passage. The one set straight ahead. "Sometimes chroniclers are too dangerous to be allowed unsupervised practice."

At my side, Jaden's muscles tense. "This takes matters far beyond supervision."

She releases a humorless laugh. "You have no idea how dangerous some of these time chroniclers can be."

"Then explain it to us," Lobrka says.

"Not part of the agreement." She slams her hand against

the large door at the end of the passage and shoves it open. Steps inside.

Scarlett's hand flies to her mouth and my breath catches in my throat, the accompanying gasp audible.

Lobrka bursts, "What in all the realms kind of treatment is this?"

FOURTEEN

"Horrific." Jaden's voice is a vicious whisper. He squeezes my hand, granting me strength. "Is this her?" he asks.

I nod confirmation, then wrinkle my nose against the odors of weeks-old filth, rotting food, and other things I don't want to consider. In the space before us, in the center of a dark stone cell, Zarah is crumbled on the ground. Her head bent; a curtain of tangled red hair hides her face. Her exposed bare feet are grimy and marred with scabs, and her hands are covered in wool, wrists bound with shackles and chains.

Zarah is a petite thing. So many chains and heavy shackles can't possibly be necessary. Not to mention everything else that's savage about the way she's being held.

"Answer me," Lobrka snaps at the keeper. "Why is this female being treated in such a manner?"

"As I said," the keeper replies, "she is dangerous. Possibly the most dangerous time chronicler in recent history."

"Zarah, dangerous?" My brow creases and I start shaking

my head. *Lie, the keeper speaks lies.* "She's never been anything but sweet."

Zarah's head snaps up, one eye visible through the greasy strands of her hair. Her gaze narrows, clearly assessing me, attempting placement. "You know nothing of me."

The keeper grabs a bucket from beside the door and tosses its contents at Zarah. Water splashes over her. She shrieks and cowers away from us, moving as far as the chains will allow.

"For the smell," the keeper says, regarding the dousing. "This is the best I can offer."

Ry whirls to her, shoving her toward the door. "You are finished here." He pushes the keeper into the outer passageway and then blocks the door against her reentry. Stands like a guard in the opening with his gaze pinned on Zarah.

Four words of complaint from the ousted keeper... *head keeper will not...* and Ry is spinning away, vanishing into the outer hall. The keeper falls silent.

Jaden approaches Zarah, his hands pressing the air between them, as if attempting to calm her with the gesture. "We are not here to harm you."

She flips her wet hair from her face. "Why have you come?" Her body shakes as she pushes to her feet. "Nobody comes to see me. I am not safe. See." She presents her wool covered hands.

The keepers clearly don't want Zarah touching anyone, skin to skin, and collecting memories for the magical well where all of history is stored—the Urn of All. But what makes Zarah so different from the others? And what could *possibly* warrant keeping her here... like this?

Jaden opens his mouth to respond to Zarah's question, but I step forward and speak first. "Why have they bound your hands?"

"You do not know?" She tilts her head. "It is dangerous to

visit one like myself without understanding what you are dealing with." She grins and the expression appears half mad.

And maybe she is—mad. Who's to say what this kind of imprisonment would do to one's mind.

Lobrka leans against the stone wall, shoving his hands into his pockets and crossing his legs at the ankles. "Is she as you remembered?" He turns his attention toward me.

I shake my head. "She is, but she isn't."

"Then maybe she is not the one we need," he replies.

"No," I start, to which Jaden finishes, "She is the one."

"I understand why Anaka would think so," Lobrka says to Jaden. "But what makes you certain?"

Jaden taps the edge of his eye in an unspoken indication of his seer's sight. The gesture appears to satisfy the large elf.

Zarah scrutinizes our every word but chooses to add nothing to the exchange.

Ry appears in the doorway, silently taking up his stance. No sight or sound of the keeper in the passageway. He wouldn't have hurt her... would he? My heart quickens and I try not to compare this Ry with the one I knew before.

"Oh!" Scarlett jolts and walks deeper into the cell, her attention fixed on Zarah. After a moment, her gaze shifts to Ry, then back to Zarah. I suspect I already know what Scarlett is realizing.

"Wow," she says. "Never known a Time Chronicler... or whatever you are... to have a love connection. Much less one as strong as you do. Most of your kind, like the one in the hall, purge all their positive emotions at an early age, leaving them a big black pit of nothing when it comes to my gift."

"What are you talking about?" Zarah assumes a defensive stance and her gaze swings over all of us. "Time Chroniclers are not allowed love relationships. You should know that, cupian fae."

"Oh, I do," Scarlett tugs her neckline to the side and glances down at something on her skin. "Maybe the gods are having a laugh." She sneers and swings her peer between Zarah and Ry.

Ry lifts his chin. "What is she suggesting?" he asks regarding Scarlett's comment.

A sad smile drags on my face at the memory of what Ry and Zarah had been, could potentially be. Another topic I can't presently allow myself to consider. "Nothing we need to discuss right now. We have more pressing matters."

"Well, get on with it then." Zarah tugs on her chains. "Why have you come? Why me?"

All eyes turn to me, awaiting an explanation.

Where do I begin? "I realize you don't know me. And I may not know *this* version of you. But I *did* know you, and so I'm more comfortable trying to work with you, than with some other member of the Time Keep, a group you once ran away from."

She wrinkles her nose and tilts her head, studying me as if she is expecting to find insanity dancing beneath my skin. "You make little sense."

She's not the only one giving me the odd eye. Ry and Scarlett also stare at me like I'm crazy. But Jaden gives me a nod of encouragement, and Lobrka merely looks tired of waiting.

"I imagine, from where you sit, I would make little sense." I frown and cross the space, coming to stand mere feet in front of her. "The truth is, I'm looking for a time chronicler who can advise me on time displacement or timeline changes."

"Why?" she interjects.

"Because..." My shoulders lift, in reluctance, in shame. "I might have made a minor change to history, and when I did that, I awoke to a new world all around me."

Her entire body jolts to attention, her eyes widening and

sparkling, as a smile creeps into place across her face. "What did you change?" Her gaze sweeps over me with renewed interest.

I sigh. "I saved a life."

"And?" she prompts.

"And I woke up to a new life with everything being different," I reply. "I thought it would be better... not for me so much as for the realm... but I can't say that it is."

She gazes straight into my eyes, as if she can find the truth of my words in my irises. "And you remember the life you had before you changed the course of history? The life that is no longer?"

"I do." I frown.

She leans closer and tilts her head, studying me from both sides. "Are you like me?"

"If you mean a Time Chronicler, no." I shake my head. "But I was hoping you could help me understand how I might fix what I did."

Scarlett shifts into my peripheral view. "I don't understand. What did she do?"

Lobrka shushes her and suspecting Ry has a similar confused expression, I don't chance turning my gaze from Zarah. Likewise, Zarah does not move her focus from me.

"You are not pleased with the ripple effect you have found yourself within?" she asks.

I take her question as rhetorical, because I wouldn't be here if I was *pleased* with the way things are.

She grins, an I-know-more-than-you kind of smirk. "You may think changing one thing would be simple, but it never is. If you saved a life, then that change ripples outward, affecting every being that individual comes into contact with after the new adjustment. That might result in different choices made, not just by the person you saved, but by others around them, and around others twice and thrice removed. Events will be altered, lives different. Some might never be, others that never were, could come into existence. The possibilities are endless."

"So, I have learned." I rub my arms. "I thought saving a life would be a good thing, but everything has gone horribly wrong. This world is horribly wrong. Can you help me figure this out?"

She lifts her wool covered hands. "Can you give me access?"

I pull a dagger from my leathers and step forward, reaching to take hold of her wrapped hand.

"Anaka!" Lobrka barks, halting me mid-action. "You let one of us remove the coverings."

I turn back to where they're all positioned near the door. "She'll have to touch me eventually, if we're going to try and get any answers."

Zarah leans as far as her chains will allow, her body held at an unnatural angle. The chains upon her neck and wrists are the only things preventing her from face planting. "Scared I will hurt your girl, dark elf?"

He hisses, causing me to jump. "You would forever regret doing so."

She laughs.

And, yeah, I'm thinking this version of Zarah has a few screws loose.

Lobrka rips his gaze away from her and returns his focus to me. "Let one of us be the first to make physical contact, before you make any such attempt."

Jaden starts to step forward, but Ry beats him to the move. "I will do it."

Behind him, Scarlett smirks. No one but I notice.

Ry pulls his blade from his belt and lifts it with both his palms splayed as he approaches Zarah. She watches him with a keen sense of curiosity I had yet to witness. She thrusts her hands forward, giving him access to the coverings and shackles. The wool is bound tight beneath the shackles and chains around her wrist, making the quickest and easiest option to be cutting the wool away.

At least, for now.

Ry lifts the fabric away from her enclosed hand and lowers the blade, taking care to be precise with his placement. His face is a solid mask of concentration.

"Do not cut me," she whispers.

His gaze flickers up to meet hers. "I have no intention of doing so."

The small cell falls silent as if there is a collective inhaling and then holding of breath. Ry slips the tip of the blade through the wool and slices. He repeats the process again and again until the fabric falls away from her left hand.

She blows out a slow breath and holds her freed palm before her, ogling. "I cannot recall the last time I felt the unfiltered air upon the skin of my hand."

She appears frozen in place, savoring her small freedom. Possibly startled by it. Ry folds his hands over her newly uncovered one and she gasps, her gaze snapping to his face. Time Chronicler writing swims over the skin of her arms and the side of her face, marking her collection of his history.

Something about the way they are gazing into each other's eyes burns a desire for me to turn away and grant them privacy. But the notion is silly. These versions of my brother and his fiancé met for the first time only minutes ago.

His hands caresses hers in a semi-affectionate manner. "Do I have your permission to remove the covering of the hand?"

"Yes." Her voice is a squeak.

A grin cracks his façade, and he repeats the process of cutting away the wool on her right hand. He collects the discarded wool and steps back to the perimeter of the room.

Zarah examines her freed hands. Or maybe, she's simply taking several moments of appreciation.

After those several moments, she presents her hands to me. "Thank you," she says. "Now let me return the favor and see if I cannot determine what you did and how you might resolve matters."

I glance over my shoulder to Lobrka. "Happy?"

He grunts in response. My gaze shifts to an apprehensive-looking Jaden. He gives me a go-ahead nod. Ry is still watching Zarah and Scarlett merely looks like she's attempting to figure out a puzzle. I wish Azure were here, but maybe I can readjust the timeline once Zarah gives me some insight. Assuming she can.

I give her a no-nonsense stare. "Prepare yourself," I warn and clasp my hands over hers.

A shock of static electricity sparks between us, appears to rocket through her body. Her head knocks back, her mouth open and gasping, as a flood of chronicler writing moves over her skin—covering all her visible skin. So much writing, shimmering in whites, golds, and blues.

Behind me, Scarlett chokes. "So unlike any chronicling I have seen," she murmurs.

"So much," Zarah says, her eyes trance-like, staring into a world unseen by the rest of us. "Never before have I experienced anything like this."

Her eyes flutter shut, and she continues to absorb the history of my lifetime. Possibly multiple lifetimes. Unfamiliar with *this* Zarah's ability, for all I know she might be accessing the information from my previous incarnations.

Like a succubus, she keeps pulling and pulling, drawing endless information from within me. Her eyes move rapidly behind her closed lids, but the sensation for me is nothing more than a mere tickle.

"Is it supposed to go on for this long?" Ry asks.

"Maybe we should stop her," Scarlett adds.

"Patience," Jaden says. "There is a lot of information to absorb from Anaka." Lobrka grunts in agreement.

Zarah cuts through their exchange with a loud gasp, her eyes springing open and her gaze momentarily finding Ry before snapping to me. "You are the Balance Bringer."

No news there. "Guilty."

The writing across her skin is still in flux, but is slowing, as if losing momentum. "I find your alternative history quite curious."

"I'm sure you do." With snippets of your life outside of the Time Keep and a romance entanglement with an Immortal Warrior.

Her gaze wanders back to Ry, her face contorting into some mixture of pain and sadness. "You have, indeed, traded one messy situation for another far worse. And if I help you reverse what you have done, some things will return to as they were. They cannot be altered."

In other words, Ry will once again be maimed. My heart aches with the punch to my system, and my lungs struggle to find air... again. But what I now face is greater than any one person. Or even several.

The inscription that once ran down the side of Kaia's blade comes to mind; *Take no action without heart.*

I like to think my original action to change history came from a good place and was not born out of a selfish desire to restore my immediate family... at the cost of all else. But after all I have experienced, can I be sure?

My mind races, tallying the changes between realities. My father and sisters are alive, Ryland's father is alive, Jaden's brother and parents are alive. Dreya was never cursed and went on to have a family. But now, none of their futures look bright. In fact, they appear downright grim.

Plus, my mother is dead, and I can't find any information on Dohlan or Mo, Shadow or Clef. According to Gitta, Opal/Edea is infected, and Dreya's husband and child are the worst kind of monsters. Then there is Sol and the weeping... the realm's full exposure to a slow building darkness, orchestrated by King Theon and his devil spawn Quirine who are working to do Gaea-knows-what with their infection and the crystal cavern, using Dreya as a conduit.

Yes. Any positive to this reality is buried in the mountains of destruction befalling the realm.

"They never were," Zarah whispers, bringing my thoughts back to the present.

"What?" My chin pushes forward.

"The ones you were thinking about, Dohlan and Yuromo, they never were," she replies.

Now she's not only collecting my history, but my questions? My gaze drops to our clasped hands. Shaking my head, I slip free of the hold. She can't know. Can't be speaking the truth.

She continues. "Through the Urn of All, I can see across the countless memories within the realm, and those two friends never existed. The others, Shadow and Clef, they live or lived with different names. I see their faces and they are the same. One passed beyond the veil some time ago, and the other was sold into slavery."

I take several shallow breaths, desperately clinging to an inner calm that is disintegrating like centuries old leaves. She's providing me with more crap to shove toward the con list. In fact, I'm deeply falling into the belief that most every result from the change I made now leans, if not tumbles, into the list of negatives.

"Sometimes," Zarah says, "the only choices you have are bad ones, but a choice must still be made, and once made, we should always try to make the best of what we have."

She stares at her uncovered hands, flexing and folding her fingers. "Do you know why they locked me up?"

I glance over my shoulder to the others. No one speaks. None of us have an answer.

Her head lifts and her gaze washes over everyone before settling on me. "Because I *can* help you sort your bad choices and that scares them." Them no doubt being the Time Keepers. "They fear what they cannot control. And I am exactly that."

Her attention drifts to Ry once more. Is she imagining the life she could have had with him, the one hinted at in my memories?

She doesn't turn her gaze from him as she speaks. "I can mold time or rewrite it, and that scares them more than the wrath of the gods."

I gasp, stumbling back a step. The reaction of the others is muffled at my back.

"I see it scares you, as well." She drops her hands at her side and rubs the side of her thighs. "They likely would have killed me had they not worried they might have need for me. Or feared my father's fury."

"Your father?" I ask.

She hums. "She never told you," Zarah says regarding herself from the other reality. "Nor has she shared the full extent of her gift. Or, quite possibly, she has not yet realized her full potential. 'Tis curious. But I must say..." Her hands stop fidgeting. "I do prefer this alternative life you have shown me. And so, I shall help you."

Ry clears his throat. "What does she mean by an alternative life?" Scarlett seconds his question with a "yeah?"

"Worry not." Zarah's attention swings to them. Glides over

all four of them; Ry, Scarlett, Jaden, and Lobrka. "You all live in the Balance Bringer's alternative life."

"What is that supposed to mean?" Scarlett bursts. Jaden drops his hand on her shoulder telling her to calm down, and she immediately does so. Can this version of Jaden use his wave of serenity on others? I tuck that tidbit in the back of my mind to revisit later.

Lobrka uncrosses his arms and steps away from the wall. "How about we waste no more time and get to it then. What do you need to get started?"

Her grin sharpens. "Water, for one. It makes for an excellent conduit, as you know." She turns to me and gives me a knowing smile. "And to properly hone the adjustment you wish to make, I need access to someone who was there."

I start to open my mouth to offer myself. After all, I was there when I changed the history of things.

She lifts a finger, halting me before I even begin. "Someone who was present for both possible outcomes. Someone who lived the consequences."

My shoulders drop. Sol is dead. That only leaves my father or Aunt Dreya. One with unknown whereabouts and another in the heart of an infected ruled palace.

This could get ugly.

FIFTEEN

J aden grabs my hands and wraps them in the warmth of
his own. He raises one eyebrow, silently asking the question that doesn't need saying: *Are we really doing this?
Going back to the palace?*

If my father or Dreya are required to fix my timeline
fallacy, what choice do I have? I lift my shoulder and tip my
head.

Zarah raises her arms and jangles her chains. "You will
need to get me out of these if we are to travel."

Scarlett crosses her arms and scowls. "Who says we are
going anywhere?"

"Stupid child." Lobrka drops his hand on his sword and
pushes away from the wall. "It goes without saying."

"He understands," Zarah lifts her chin in Lobrka's direc-
tion, then says to Scarlett, "Maybe you shan't be joining us, but
I read the need for travel quite clearly in their silent exchange."
She gestures to me and Jaden.

Scarlett shakes her head. "After what we went through to
get here?" She barks a laugh. "I am staying right here in the

safety of the keep. I have seen what is out there, and I want no part of it. This place is a fortress. One of the most secure locations to presently be."

Ry bulldozes between Scarlett and Lobrka, slamming her out of his path with the bump of his shoulder. "We are quite content to leave you here," he says to Scarlett, as he pulls a thin blade from his boot and makes straight for Zarah. "Let me see your shackles." She obliges, a semi-shy smile playing at her lips and her eyes batting as her gaze devours his features. He wiggles and twists the tip of the blade in the lock.

A scream in the outer passage shatters our ridiculously unrushed behavior. Even with the agreement made with the time keeper, we shouldn't linger. Especially since we now intend to abuse that agreement.

One scream turns into several, and I dash from the room to investigate. The screams come from the cells lining the tunnel. The keeper silenced by Ry is bound and slumped on the floor to the side of the door. I squat and take her pulse. She's asleep and breathing softly.

From one of the cells farther down the passageway someone starts yelling, "They come. They come. They come." And from the door across the way, "Darkness descends, and they will bring our end."

"This cannot be good," Jaden says at my back, having followed me into the outer hall.

I leap to my feet. "No, it can't." I race back into the cell housing Zarah and screech to a halt. "Did you hear?"

"Yes." Lobrka unsheathes his sword. "We need to go. Now."

He directs Ry, pointing to Zarah's chains. Picking up on the silent warrior to warrior language, my brother stretches the chain taut, clear of Zarah's person. The dark elf raises his sword high and swings down hard.

The crash of steel and iron clang like a mighty bell, the sound echoing off the surrounding stone walls. Sparks spray from the collision, and Lobrka slices through the chain bound to the shackle around Zarah's right wrist. A touch of elven magic in the blade, if I recall from my previous incarnations. Without hesitation, he repeats the process two more times, freeing her from the chain at her left wrist and the chain hanging from her neck.

"Free at last." Zarah spins in a circle, the chains flying wide in the air. Ry and Lobrka leap from the path, avoiding getting hit by a mere smidgen.

Jaden snags one of the swinging chains, tugging Zarah to stop. "There will be time for dancing later. First, we need to get out of here." He glances from Zarah to Scarlett. "Are there any exits out of here, besides the way we came?"

Scarlett balks. "How would I know? I do not make it a habit of spending time down here amongst the crazy and locked up."

Zarah giggles and swings a limp point at Scarlett. "Because you are afraid you will end up locked up with the rest of us."

"Not likely." Scarlett crosses her arms and glowers. "I am not crazy."

"Ladies," Jaden admonishes.

Lobrka grabs Scarlett's elbow and directs her toward the outer passage. "Enough of the bickering. We have not the time, nor the tolerance for such behaviors."

We file into the passageway, two wide and three deep—Lobrka and Scarlett at the front and Ry with Zarah bringing up the rear. At our appearance, the calls from the surrounding cells change, the forsaken time chroniclers speaking in unison, as if organized. "She comes for you, Balance Bringer. She comes for you."

Zarah's breath raises the hairs on the back of my neck. "And all who stand in her way shall perish," she adds.

Nothing like starting the next phase of one's escape with a heavy dose of doom and gloom.

Except...

"Let them out," Jaden says. We all turn to him in question, and he continues. "As cover. As chaos. As a necessary distraction."

"Yes. Yes," Zarah chimes. "Wise, wise man. She has the keys to the cells." She points to the time keeper slumped against the wall.

Sure enough, the keys are visible, hanging from a large ring clipped to her belt. Ry snatches the collection free and riffles through them, seeking one for Zarah's shackles. Plenty of keys to unlock cell doors, but none to free the imprisoned from their chains.

"Makes sense," he murmurs. "Not to trust any one person with the keys to both the doors and the shackles. It's a smart safety measure."

I scoff. "It's irritating, is what it is."

"You get the doors," Lobrka directs Ry. "And I will set them free."

The males work in quick order, opening cells and releasing time chroniclers. Jaden directs them toward the stairs leading to the main hall. They dance, hackle, and skip, singing of a descending darkness as they climb their way free from the prison level.

Jaden links his arm with mine and leans into my side. "I fear it may not be enough."

I turn my head, meeting his gaze. "We work with what we have."

"Always." He squeezes me into his side. "And we shall do so together."

Again... always. Unlinking our arms, I slide my hand to his and hold tight. Our feet slap off the stone as we race up the stairs behind Lobrka and Scarlett and an unhinged band of time chroniclers. We break into the upper entry, expecting angry, high level time keepers to descend on us, only to find their attention on something far more imperative than us, or the released time chroniclers.

Infected soldiers and civilians repeatedly slam their bodies against the outer doors, trying to break through the barrier. The many locks remain engaged, holding the barricade firm, but every able body within the Time Keep's entry is gathered, a second line of defense, should the locks or hinges of the doors give way.

But I'm not worried about the locks failing or the doors bursting open. My gaze shifts to the sides and the many pounding hands visible through the transparent, artistic design depicting time. The surrounding wall of glass is where my concern lies.

As if triggered by my thoughts, a fist slams to the surface and fissures pop to life, snaking across the colored-glass surface. Scarlett yelps as both Lobrka and Ry curse under their breaths. The time chroniclers we freed start chanting about darkness descending and the end unfolding.

Behind me, Zarah giggles. I turn to her, and her expression falls flat. "This has ruin carved all over it," she whispers.

Jaden stumbles into my side, his eyes clouded and swirling. "Something is not right," he mumbles and staggers back a step.

My hand darts out, grabbing his arm and steading his stance.

"We need to find another way." He swivels, his hands grabbing at his hair and his gaze scanning the paths and possible exits opposite the front entrance. "Zarah. Scarlett. Show us another way out. *And quick.*" Urgency courses through his words. His heightened nerves are evident in his tensing muscles and clenching fists.

Having picked up on Jaden's request, the chants from the surrounding freed time chroniclers morph to *"quick, quick, quick."* Lobrka and Scarlett spin back to our group and they're saying something, something I should be listening to, but a whoosh thunders through my eardrums, filling my head with windstorm and a thundering beat.

My vision becomes fuzzy, the colorful glass wall before me is blurring into bleeding splotches of black and the surrounding time keepers breaking into furious motion.

A stab of pain punctures my lungs, and I can't breathe. Can't capture oxygen. The aching sensation explodes into utter agony, attacking every aspect of my body. My knees buckle and I start to fall, but someone catches me. Only, I don't see who has saved me from hitting the ground. My eyesight is a burst of white and red and pink. And my hearing, nothing beyond a shattering, a crashing, a plethora of hollers, and screams.

I'm tingling all over and the chaos of the world around me fades into the background.

I lurch forward, falling away from myself into an out-of-body experience.

My entire focus, my everything, zeroes in on my sister Crystal standing before me.

"They tried to stop us," she says, "but they cannot stop what we are, what we are destined to become. They locked us in our rooms, Kayla and me, thinking they could keep us contained, keep us from becoming. But we found a way. And our gifts..." She swings her hand in a circle as if to reference the three of us. "...shall be the powers now at work within you. Wield them with might and undo the damage brought upon our world." She casts a slight smile, then gazes down at herself and the blood spreading wide across her chest.

Kayla appears at her side, their hands weaving together in a firm grip. Kayla is also covered in blood, the blooming wound growing outward from her stomach.

I pitch forward, reaching for them, but my arm is heavy and refuses to move. "What have you done?" Panic dominates my delivery.

"What needed to be done." Crystal presses her palm to my cheek and Kayla mirrors the action, pressing her palm to my other cheek. "But worry not. You can never lose us, for we three are one."

Kayla's gaze shifts over my shoulder for a blink. "You need to wake up now and get yourself out of your situation."

My situation. The cracking glass. The descending darkness.

My awareness sharpens. I'm no longer standing in the over-sized entry of the Time Keep, but being held in Jaden's arms, carried at a quick clip. The space is dark, and the passage narrow. I blink to clear and focus my vision.

"This way. This way," Zarah says. "I saw it in the mind of one of my fellow time sisters."

I catch sight of shackle-encased hand flailing in the air, wildly directing our group. She leads us down an unlit hallway. Where are we and how did we get here so quickly?

I tap Jaden's shoulder. "I'm okay now. I can walk."

"Are you certain?" He keeps moving, making no motion to set me down. "You need not be strong in this moment. What you experienced would take a toll on anyone."

"You know—"

"About your sisters?" he says. "I do. And I can feel how this change has torn you up inside."

"Then you should also be able to feel that the loss of my sisters is not new to me, and my need to follow through with what must be done outweighs my desire to mourn." Because, if I am successful in adjusting the timeline... *again*... my sisters will be lost to me in the physical sense once more. "Now put me down."

Jaden follows Zarah and Ry down the dark passage, spins us around a corner, and then sets me on my feet. I sway a smidgeon and reach out to the wall. Jaden takes hold of my free hand, making sure I'm steady.

Ry glances back at us, his gaze sweeping over me as if evaluating my condition. "Is everyone now with us?" he asks.

I nod that I am physically and mentally alert.

Zarah tosses me a quick glance before returning to her forward rush. She has gathered and clutched the chains dangling from the wrist shackles to prevent them from swinging at her side. "The way out is just around the corner ahead. I saw the location in sister Janelle's mind several months ago."

Lobrka grunts behind me. "Convenient."

"She was angry at me for the extraction," Zarah mumbles, a statement I take to mean Zarah somehow managed to touch sister Janelle with her bare hand and likely extracted more information than just the location of the exit we now seek.

"No doubt," Lobrka replies from behind me, then gently nudges my shoulder. "Glad you managed to return to this side of the veil and are no longer baggage for Jaden to lug around."

If the situation were different, I probably would have rolled my eyes, granted him a sarcastic laugh, and playfully hit him. But our situation is serious, and time is of the essence. No one needs the added complication of me timing out. Something that is now a solid worry scratching at my thoughts. If my sisters have truly passed, and their elemental gifts are coming my way...or are already with me... need I worry about collapsing for days as I had in my previous timeline, before Dohlan's magical rub? I don't even want to consider the possibility.

"Me too." I say to Lobrka and toss Jaden a guilty grimace.

How long had he carried me? "What happened back at the entrance and how long was I out?"

"Besides you swooning?" Lobrka retorts.

I grit my teeth. "I didn't swoon."

"It was horrible," Scarlett interrupts and jabs a point at me. "You collapsing was incredibly irritating, dealing with your prone body when the glass wall was shattering and those horrible creatures were slipping into the Keep."

I jolt. "They got in?" I recall the bleeding black that filled my vision right before Crystal appeared.

"Oh, they got in," Ry says, to which Jaden adds, "And their infected state started spreading like wildfire."

"Was there biting involved?" I whisper.

Ry glances over his shoulder at me. "There was, indeed, biting."

I shudder. *So very vampire.*

"Here," Zarah squeals and disappears into a shadowed alcove, a heavy rattling and pounding immediately following. "Locked," she seethes.

Her head pops free from the shadows, her gaze seeking Lobrka. "Can your sword recreate the magic that cut through these chains?" She rattles the links hanging from the shackles still secured around her wrists.

"Move aside." Oozing confidence, Lobrka strides toward the door, unsheathing his sword along the way.

Zarah and Ry move out of the way, and we all take several steps back, allowing Lobrka ample room for his swing. Jaden tugs me aside, one hand grabbing at my hip and the other wrapping around the nap of my neck, tangling in my hair.

He lowers his face to mine, his breath washing over me. "How are you really?"

"I'm fine. I'll be fine." I have no other choice but to be. "You saw my sisters, didn't you? When your vision swirled and clouded."

The sound of Lobrka's sword slamming against the lock clangs through the cavern. Jaden raises his hand from my hip and drifts his fingers in a wavy line down my back. "I did... among other things."

I open my mouth to ask what other things, but he continues. "I am also receiving overwhelming awareness from Azure."

I gasp. "Oh my gosh! Of course, you're still connected. Is he all right?"

He heaves a breath. "Depends on your definition of all right. His head is ready to explode from all the infection bearing down on us and the..."

"And the what?" Good Gaea, how much does he glean from Azure? If I am correct about their intentions where he's concerned..." I can't finish the thought.

The clang of Lobrka's sword echoes through the chamber once more as Jaden's arm slips around my waist and hauls me closer. "I need you to listen to me." His words are a hum against my skin. "No matter what happens once we break free of this keep, you keep going until you succeed."

I push against his chest. "What are you—"

"Promise me." His nose rubs against mine, and his need, his want for me to comply, translates through his every tense muscle. "No matter what. You keep Zarah at your side, do not let anyone separate the two of you. And together, you set things right."

Lobrka's sword slamming into the lock sounds for a third time, followed by a crash and rumble, and Zarah's squeal. The door is now open. I shift to exit with the group, but Jaden holds me hostage.

"Anaka." He grips my chin and forces my gaze to meet his. He scrutinizes my face, as if seeking answers to questions he hasn't asked. He drops his head back to mine and closes his eyes, his lips whispering across my cheek, the edge of my lip like the flutter of butterfly wings. "Promise me," he repeats.

I close my eyes and inhale the scent of him. Dropping my hand to his chest, I savor the beat of his heart. "I promise."

His stress and worry are palatable. I want nothing more to ease all the negative emotions from his system... with my hands, my lips... because I have no words.

"Are you coming or not?" Scarlett's brassy delivery jars me back to the urgency of the moment.

Jaden's hands slide down my arms to my hands, his gaze never leaving my face as he replies, "Right behind you."

She turns and heads out with the others, Lobrka, Ry, and Zarah.

"Do not forget your promise," Jaden says and heads for the exit, pulling me behind him. He glances over his shoulder. "Make sure no one can separate you from Zarah."

"I understand," I say as I follow him toward the night beyond the door.

Before we can step into the open air, a horde of footsteps sounds in the tunnel at our back. A crowd of infected makes its way in our direction. Jaden yanks me outside and slams the door shut. We step onto a crumbling walk that gives way to an expanse of tall grass.

"They are coming," he announces to the others.

"Can we barricade it?" Ry asks at the same time Lobrka says, "We need to move." Meaning, move a hell of a lot faster than we have so far.

But... Ry's question about a barricade strikes a chord with me. Using the element of water, I could block the door with a wall of ice, preventing anyone from following until the frozen barrier melted.

"I've got this." I wave them off with a swing of my hand and summon the water up from the ground. Not as strong of a Balance Bringer as I was in my previous timeline, I still have significant control of my primary element. It responds... as does something else.

Dirt and rock also rise, and an impenetrable wall of ice and rock and packed earth forms in front of the opening. I sway with the exertion, but at least the infected within the keep won't be following us through this door anytime soon.

Earth. I controlled earth. Which only confirms a truth I've pushed to the back of my mind. My sister Crystal is gone. Kayla, too, even if I have yet to wield wind.

Lobrka steps toward me. "Anaka, you mastered more than water."

"Yeah," I say. "Crystal and Kayla are gone."

The world sways, and my body weights. I stumble back a step and Jaden captures my elbows, holding me steady. My back is pressed to his chest, his warmth easing my aches even as exhaustion plagues me. Slackens and slows my ability to respond.

The newly acquired elements ruin my muscle control and energy reserves. I sense them raging through me, exploring and familiarizing themselves with all the bits and pieces of me. Claiming their new home... and the process is draining. I want to lie down right here in the grass and go to sleep.

Crap. I can't afford to pass out for an hour, much less a day or more, like I had before when I came into a new element.

I clutch Jaden's arm. "Jaden. I—"

His hold tightens, and he throws me to the ground, covering my body with his own. A hiss zips past us. Ryland yells and Scarlett screams. A blink later, a handful of infected steps into view all around us.

"Hold!" Aunt Edea, a.k.a. Opal, fully veined with darkness, steps free from the shadows. "No one is to be hurt... *yet.*"

SIXTEEN

"**O**pal?" Despite my growing exhaustion, the question bursts from my lips before I can stop it.

I'm conflicted between Deona's memories of a loving aunt, my memories of her torturing me while also helping me to realize my greater potential, my unsettling knowledge of how she manipulated Dohlan, and then this vision before me of an apparent in-control yet infected individual.

Her gaze snaps to me. "Greetings, Anaka. We have not yet had the pleasure of meeting."

I grit my teeth. "And yet, I once knew you well."

Her brow lifts at my admission.

Lobrka and Ry assume fighting stances and Jaden quickly leaps to his feet, doing the same. Although, forever my protector, he does not leave my side.

Surrounding us are dark infected beings from various stations in life, all sporting blackened eyes and veins, as well as enlarged canines. I note citizens and soldiers, time keepers and farmers, and a rather difficult chance of escaping unscathed.

Scarlett shifts toward the center of our group, leaving the males as a barrier between her and the enemy, while Zarah swings the chains hanging from her wrists as if she's planning to strike, using them as her weapon.

I push up to my knees, and Jaden grabs my shoulder, leans close, and whispers for me to be careful. Although left unspoken, I know he is referring to my actions and word choices regarding our surrounding company. My silent smile promises I'll try. Then I return my attention to my infected aunt.

"Opal." I shake my head. "I would expect better from you." A partial lie. "This might be the first time we're meeting in this life, but there's nothing about this encounter that I'd consider pleasurable."

"Your words are curious to me," she replies, "but first tell me, who is this Opal?"

"Is that not your name?" I ask. "Or the one you have more recently chosen to go by?"

A humored grin lifts the edge of her lips. "I have never gone by any name other than Edea, the one given to me by my mother."

The light of my inner understanding brightens—another timeline change. No Opal, and thus, no Augur clan. No bringing the members together or possibly helping select their names. Hence Ruby now going by Scarlett. And then there's Dohlan... could his lack of existence be part of the reason Edea never took on the persona of Opal?

She huffs. "And why would I use any name other than my own?"

To hide your identity. A thought I don't commit to speaking. Instead, I merely stare back.

One of the darkened beings moves forward, and all the males in our group shift accordingly. My aunt lifts her hand and shoots the infected a sharp glare, halting him from any further motion. "I have not yet given the word," she reprimands.

Her scrutinizing gaze shifts over the members of our group, taking each of us in with careful detail. She tilts her head toward her accompanying infected. "I want the Balance Bringer brought unharmed. If you can wrangle the male beside her without great bodily injury, he could prove useful."

I gasp but she ignores me and continues surveying the group, her attention pointedly drawn to Lobrka. "Same for the dark elf. He, too, may come in handy when we must deal with my elven sister." Aunt Meira, also known as Madame Marrouske. "The rest are expendable." The rest being Ry, Zarah, and Scarlett... my brother, the time chronicler, and... well... this timelines version of Ruby.

"What?" Scarlett yells. "I am not expendable! I am a cupian fae," she declares.

"Like I said," Aunt Edea replies, no emotion evident in her expression. "Expendable."

Jaden grabs my arm, pulling my attention to him. "Zarah," he murmurs with a nod in her direction. "Remember your promise." My promise to keep the time chronicler at my side, let no one separate us, and together, set things right. But how exactly do I accomplish that feat under the current circumstances?

Before I can unscramble the thought into an actionable plain, an infected soldier to Edea's left throws a spear. It cuts through the air with barely a whisper, deadly accuracy in the aim. A fraction of a second later, a deathblow pierces through Scarlett's abdomen. The force sends her toppling backward, silencing the scream attempting to break free from her lungs.

Jaden lurches forward, catching her head and saving it from hitting the ground. She gurgles and spits up blood, the life in her eyes blinking out and her head lulling to the side.

"She was one of yours!" I scream. One of your children from another timeline. But this time around, no connections have been made and my aunt is unaware. And for that, Scarlett's life has been forfeited.

Scarlett is dead. Of Clef or Shadow, one is dead and the other a slave. My mom and sisters are dead. Dohlan and Yoromo were likely never born. Azure has been traded as a stud, a prisoner to the reproduction needs of the time keepers... should he survive the ensuing darkness. Ry and Zarah never discovered love, and Zarah has quite possibly been driven a bit insane from her captivity. Aunt Dreya has become a tool to be used by her infected and evil daughter. My father... I have no clue. The realm is falling into a nightmare of malevolent vampire-like creatures. And me, well, I'm less than what I was prior to my timeline change. Less powerful. Less realized.

I really screwed up.

"One of mine?" Aunt Edea questions. "One released from existence by me and mine, you mean. As, too, your other companions shall soon be."

Oh no you won't.

I may be exhausted, every muscle and bone in my body wishing for a long nap, but I still have power at my fingertips. The gift of wind from Kayla billows and churns within my blood... and I am angry. *So very angry.* And that anger, at present, is directed at Edea. Edea and the other dark infected.

With a primal shriek, I release the element, coupled with my rage. A windstorm explodes from my core, sweeping over the landscape, and skimming around my friends. They spin and slip on the grass, grappling for purchase, as the elemental hurricane slams into our adversaries, sending them toppling to a bump and slide or tumbling feet overhead.

I drop to my hands and knees, wind wildly wiping the hair around my face and pulling from my core, obliterating my energy reserves. Little is left within me. My muscles weight, and breath labors. My sides are squeezed too tight, and I feel as if I may have broken a few ribs.

I need to protect my friends but I can't... I suck back a deep, painful breath... can't pull myself to a stand, much less strike out with my questionable fighting skills or yet-developing elemental abilities.

My fingers are digging into the dirt and grass, but everyone around me, my friends and foes, are already on their feet and shifting into action. Both sides with weapons ready to clash. My vision blurs and I can't zero in on a proper count, but I don't need to know the totals to understand we are deeply outnumbered.

Especially with my newly acquired elemental gifts attempting to drag me into some sort of coma.

The enemy charges forward and the males from our group, Lobrka, Ry, and Jaden rush to meet them. Within the action, Ry shoves Zarah behind him, using his body as a protective shield. Jaden grabs her wrist and shoves her father back, pushing her toward me. She stumbles and reaches out, grappling for contact. My hand flops outward in a weak response.

"Get up, Anaka," Jaden yells, drawing my gaze up to him. "Hone your focus, and hold your promise."

My promise to protect Zarah, keep her with me, and change the timeline. But how? And with what strength?

My fingers strain for contact with Zarah. Grunts and groans, and the clash of steel reach my ears, but I hold my gaze on her, needing to maintain my focus if I am to have a chance at succeeding. Although, I am yet to formulate a plan, any idea or inking of hope as to how I might have a chance at achieving my goal.

A shuffle of movement and color swarms beyond her. She stumbles and falls, having tripped or pushed, and now crawls my direction. Someone yells and blood splatters, droplets hitting me in the face.

My heart clenches, then hammers. I haven't a clue who has been hurt—one of ours or one of theirs—but I can't afford a peek. Zarah is our only hope for fixing the mess I've made. I need to somehow protect her and keep her with me until we can get to my father or aunt.

But my energy is rapidly diminishing, as if my lifeforce is waning. No doubt, the elements of wind and earth are attempting to pull me into a hibernating state so that they may fully integrate with my body and soul.

Worst timing *ever*.

"Gracious Gaea, please," I beg, extending my reach for Zarah's outstretched hand. "Bring Zarah to my side. Keep her with me, bind her to me, protecting her wellbeing for as long as it takes to us to see our mission through."

My head drops, cheek to the ground, and my words are a mumble against the grass. An intimate request from earth itself. But an instantaneous drag upon my everything, one that chokes my oxygen supply, signals the response of not only earth, but water and wind as well.

My body glides forward, propelled by the motion of the grass blades, like I'm belly flat on a bed of rollers. My fingers touch, then intertwine with Zarah's, and an elemental coating slithers over us. Covers us, like a second skin. Connecting us in a fine layer of pulsating water, wind, and earth. Linking us, at least for now, as one.

Vines stronger than steel spring from the ground, twining around our wrists and physically binding us together. The remnants of my power surge through the connection—the tether of combined elements joining us, both internally and externally. I feel uncomfortably stretched, but no one will separate us until I will it so.

I fold to unfathomable fatigue, my body falls flush against the ground, and my eyes drift closed. The screams and hollers around me are fading into an all-consuming sea of black. With a sigh, I concede my fight for consciousness. Allow sleep to swallow my pain.

A millisecond later... or possibly hours or day after... I jolt awake with a scream, agony splicing across my side. Zarah's cry rings in my ear. And in my surrounding mind-fog, I distinguish Aunt Edea's call to stop. But stop what, I do not know. I don't expect I'll find out. My agony morphing into a burning sting is not strong enough to hold me in a state of awareness.

My desire... my need... to assist my friends cannot hold me in the fight. Nor does the panic over what may be transpiring. I haven't the strength to hold the emotions, the awareness.

The elements claim me for their newly brewing becoming, awakening, empowering... and I black out.

THE WORLD IS bumping and rolling like a ride on wooden wheels traveling across a harsh, rocky terrain. Voices and surrounding sounds are a mesh of noise, and when my eyes flutter open a mere crack, for that is all I can manage; everything is an indistinguishable blur. I'm aware only long enough to understand I'm being moved and the world smells like sweat and horse manure, then I slip down the long, dark tunnel leading to the void.

And the void is all that I know, for seconds and minutes and hours and days and months... and Gaea-knows-how-long. The vaguest sense of water, wind, and earth flowing through my heart and soul divorces me from thoughts and concerns about the reality of this timeline—the fate of my friends or the worlds.

For the briefest of moments, a strong sense of dread rises through me. The sense that I missed something wholly important. And wholly gut wrenching. But then fire burns the feeling into ash and wind whisks all evidence away.

My entire state of consciousness folds into a rendered refrain dedicated to and in wonder of the domain of Gaea. Only, after an unmeasured amount of time, memories of past experiences infiltrate the natural wonders commanding my senses and thoughts.

Memories layer upon one another, events taking place at the same chronicled moment in time, yet in different timelines. Recollections of moments I, Anala, spent with my mom and Crystia, at school with my best friend in freshmen and sophomore year, dating Jeremy, and finally time spent with the swim team, and training with Ry. Meeting Jaden and making the trip to Hiddenkel.

All things transpired in conjunction with opposing happenings belonging to Anaka. Schooling, meals, and quality sister time with Kayla and Crystal. Braiding each other's hair. Sharing palace gossip and giggling over awkward interactions with guards and soldiers. Private, personable meetings with Dreya that are almost warm and loving. Plus, countless occasions—sweet, intimate, steamy even—with Jaden and Azure.

I'm recalling them all, all the memories from both versions of myself—accompanied with associated emotions, thoughts, and knowledge. I'm chilled to the bone, flushed with heat, and everything in between. And something else settles into place on a subconscious level. Something I can't quite bring into focus, but I can sense it pressing against the walls of my mental capacity.

The not-knowing makes me uncomfortable and nervous.

Maybe I should push my comprehension ability regarding that something *other* into sharper shape. Only I already feel mentally and emotionally too full, busting at the seams, and I'm utterly distracted by knowledge gained from conversations with Dreya—another uncovered change between the timelines.

My sisters and I have long been aware of our parentage. The fact that Prince Marduk is our father has not been kept a secret from us, but he remains unaware—for his protection and ours. And our mother... she was *not* the mother I grew up knowing, but her sister.

I'm a cyclone of confusion and I don't know how this information makes me feel. These truths will take time to wrap my thoughts around. But... since the Balance Bringer soul is basically the same, reborn time and time again, I guess who our mother or father is doesn't change who my sisters and I are.

Not only did our mother pass away in childbirth, many present at the birth were also killed in an attempt to get to the Balance Bringer three. Kayla, Crystal, and I were narrowly saved. Where we were placed, and who we are related to, became a well-held secret for the first decade or more of our lives. Our presence at the palace was only revealed a handful of years ago.

The queen has always been honest with us, if not a smidgeon removed... and given her position and the Balance Bringer's intended destiny, her personal distance is understandable. Even if the lack of a parental figure in this life leaves me burning without and rather hallow within.

In my conThe layers of Anala and Anaka's memories, the flow of elemental connections, and that hidden something other owns me in the darkness behind my closed eyelids. Beyond those things, nothing else exists.

When awareness once more tugs at my thoughts, I have no concept of how much time has passed, but the world is no longer in motion. And it's both unnaturally quiet and ripe with excreting unease. The cushion under my head bounces lightly, even as the surface beneath the rest of me is hard and chilly and stationary. Stationary, yet possessing a somewhat familiar vibrational hum. Like static electricity popping in the air all around me.

I sense power and feel... *home.*

The cushion beneath my head stops bouncing, and a body behind me presses against the side of my head, then pulls away, and then presses in again. Press, release, press, release. A soft whimper drops close to my ear and morphs into a somber hum. A mix between crooning and crying.

My heart pulses in my throat and my stomach churns, the smell of fear clawing its way up my nose.

Is Zarah the one I hear? Am I propped in her lap? And is she rocking?

Crap. That can't mean anything good.

"Wake up, sister," Kayla and Crystal's voices whisper in unison. "You have work to do."

I moan against their urging. They aren't wrong, I have much... so very much... to do. My senses of sound and smell suggested as such the second I became half aware. And I want to wake up, get up. I really do. Only my thoughts are rather sluggish, and my muscles aren't prepared to respond to my commands.

Crappity crap.

My breath accelerates. I really need my physical self to speed up my recovery and be ready. My gut is telling me a threat sits nearby waiting for me to wake. I can't lay dormant when that is the case.

My scalp prickles and my mind begins to imagine every possible ugly scenario.

The weight of my sisters on my right and Zarah's morose presence on my left is the emotional pressure that finally helps catapult me into action. Slight as it may be. I try to lift my head but it's too heavy and my protesting groan rather weak.

The desire... the burning desire... is present, but the follow through is still lacking.

Come on body. Whatever drug they used on us, burn it off. Burn it off *now*. Fire element, do your thing and cleanse our system.

The shuffle of a foot sounds from several feet away. "She is finally starting to stir," someone says. "Nudge her and wake her up."

I don't care for the inflection used in the message delivery, and I think I'll have the desire to punch someone when I finally manage to yank my eyes open.

"No." Zarah's voice peals in my ear, her body shifting around me. "You... all of you." Her arm jerks as if she's jabbing a strong point. "Stay away," she continues. "If anyone is to wake her, I shall be the one."

My insides warm at her protectiveness and I find a sliver of my strength. Manage to hold onto it.

"Zarah?" My voice cracks, and my eyes resist any efforts to peel back my eyelids. I attempt to lift my hand, but a tug holds my arm wrapped across my chest. The earthen vine around my wrist and tied to her, has my limb held captive in place.

Calm. Remain calm, I remind myself.

She sniffles. "I am here with you. You made sure of that, did you not?" A flash of guilt rockets through me. She pats one hand to my shoulder and tugs the other against our connecting bind. The vine chafes my wrist. "Although, I am rethinking my decision to help you."

A laugh croaks free of my lungs. It rattles against the headache building at the base of my skull. I want to tell her she speaks a fib, but I can't be sure. This Zarah beside me isn't the same one I previously knew.

Nearby, someone coughs and the sound echoes around whatever space we're in. The reverberation suggests our holding cell is large and rather absent of absorbing materials.

Zarah's voice drops so close to my ear her breath is warm against my skin. "I would like to experience the life I have seen through you... the other you."

Not the life from this timeline where she's been held a prisoner by the time keepers, but the one where she is engaged to my brother. I, too, would like that. Would like to get back to that.

"And maybe I can," she continues. "Now that we are close to our goal. I hope you are strong enough to close the necessary distance."

At her declaration, my eyes pop open and snag upon the stained-glass ceiling. A familiar sight. Also recognizable is the energetic tingle thrumming over my skin—the water and crystal cavern beneath the floor. Zarah and I are sprawled out in the center of the throne room. . Realizing the source of the power I felt, my insides thrill.

Maybe, just maybe, all of our chances are not lost.

My head swivels from side to side, taking measure of our situation. Opal and a host of infected soldiers stand in lines blocking the double-doored exit. Unless the elemental powers within me rev to life, we won't be getting out that way as free civilians.

And in the other direction, the crystal throne. Dreya sits in the chair, appearing very much like a doll with her gaze partially glazed. Standing on either side of her, King Theon, and Princess Quirina. My insides turn to ice.

The eldest princess is nowhere in sight. As the daughter of Dreya and not Theon, has something possibly befallen her?

My attention scans both sides of the dais, seeking verification of Princess Malke's absence. In so doing, my gaze swings past a blur, something my mind resists recognizing. My chest tightens, even in spite of my lack of comprehension. I focus on sharpening my vision, understanding and accepting what I'm looking at.

Pikes flank the throne, slammed into the floor and standing upright. And on those pikes, severed heads, dripping blood onto the floor. Two of the faces I know all too well. Too, too well.

My body jolts upright and a scream rips free from my throat, full volume, full horror.

SEVENTEEN

I can't breathe... and I can't tear my gaze from Ry's severed, blood dripping, head on the spike. They killed my brother.

They killed my brother!

I press the edge of my fist into my chest, attempting to squash the pain.

Ry may not be my brother from this timeline, but the brother I knew from before. All our shared moments and adventures, blood or not, he is my brother of heart and soul.

I scream. Lurch forward to my knees. Then shriek and shout, drop butt to my heels, and continue to cry. My hands cradle my head in a losing attempt to hold my composure. Not only did they kill Ryland... and Scarlett, because her head is displayed on one of the other spikes... but they displayed their horrid death like some kind of sickening trophy.

Behind me, Zarah leaps to her feet and sways back and forth, screeching and shaking her chains. I can't tell if she's reacting to me or to the situation, Ry's demise, or a combination of all the above.

"Gone-gone-gone," she wails, then grabs and shakes my shoulders, leans near my ear and whispers, "But he need not be so." *Ry need not be dead, if we manage to change the timeline.*

I wipe my eyes and inhale deeply. Steel my shaking bones. Things are bad. They're really, really bad, but I can still—hopefully, possibly—change them for the better. Or, at least, to something better than this. A world not nearly as deeply consumed by the darkness. And a world where Zarah isn't insane, Mo and Dohlan are alive, Aunt Edea is slightly less wicked, Azure isn't a sex slave, and Ry, although horribly injured, is still alive.

I simply need to get Zarah and myself to the queen... close enough for the time chronicler to touch her.

And then what? I don't know, but I will let Zarah take the lead.

A wind whips around me, lifting my tendrils as I focus my full attention on Dreya and her seated position upon the throne. The elements will draw us together, even as they push everyone out of our way.

Everything is building and building and—

Zarah spins around to the front of me and drops into my lap, straddling me. Our connected wrists lift as she wraps her arms around my neck.

Pressing her lips to the rim of my ear, she whispers, "They are afraid of me. Want me dead. Even tried to kill me. But whatever you did caused them to stop."

She pulls back and shifts to the side, exposing her blood-soaked attire. She sustained a serious cut in the same location that I felt the pain in my side before passing out. How long ago had that been? Days, I think.

"When they tried to kill me," she continues. "You reacted, and since they want you alive, I was spared. But now they are afraid to get too close because of my touch."

I nod. "They don't want their histories collected," I murmur.

She snickers. "Possibly, but what they really fear is my ability to alter their history. Make them something other than what they currently are. Make them less threatening and more vulnerable."

I gasp. "You can do that?"

A smile teases the edge of her lips. "'Tis the reason the time keepers had me locked up. They matched my parents in order to make me, and then feared what they had created." She continues to keep her voice low for only us to hear.

"But the Zarah I know, or knew..." I don't know how to word my connection with the version from my previous timeline.

She shakes her head. "From what I have seen in your history collection, she succeeded when she ran away from the Time Keep. I was captured and returned, after which I trained in the abilities gifted to me by my father. I mastered the gifts, surpassed the keepers expectations, and then I was locked up for learning to use what they have given me... done to me."

A post pokes me in the side, rocking me back an inch. "Break it up," says the bearer of the long wooden post. "And stop talking amongst you. You are not to leave our sovereign waiting."

"You sovereign," I quip, "but not mine. Not even close to mine."

The male shifts to poke us with the pole once more, only Zarah lurches in his direction and he stumbles back several steps.

"See," she says. "They fear me."

"Let's use that to our advantage." I shove her off me, grab her hand, and drag her to her feet.

The elements have sprung to life in my blood and are electrifying the air around us. The ground beneath our feet grumbles, the walls sweat, and the air shoves us forward, even as it presses others in the room against the walls.

"Make way for the queen," I say and, dragging Zarah at my side, break into a run for the crystal throne.

Chunks of the tile floor rupture around the perimeter of the room and a rush of water explodes into the space from the crystal cavern below. Wind and water work together, spinning around and around, creating an elemental wall separating the queen, Zarah, and me from everyone else.

Zarah and I take three long strides forward, then Princess Quirine's wicked voice carries through the whirl of elements. "You might not want to do that," she says.

The wall of water thins, or possibly translates the image, granting me a sharper view of the princess and those around her. I immediately slide to a stop, Zarah bumping into my back, and the warring elements evaporate. Standing between Quirine and Theon is a darkened guard, but he isn't what captures my attention, sends my heart into overdrive. It's the male the guard has on his knees, a blade pressed to his throat.

They have Jaden!

Of course, they do. And to the side, I now note Lobrka also being held at a disadvantage.

"Emotions," Quirine says. "They are such a crutch, are they not? We would all strive much better without them."

I take a step toward Jaden. The blade held to his throat presses and a line of blood begins dribbling down his throat.

I suck back a hiss through my teeth and Quirine *tsks*. Admonishes me with a wagging finger.

Straightening my shoulders, I pin a tight glare on her. "Emotions," I say, "can fuel us and enforce our internal strength."

"Or drain us. Mislead us," she counters. "Best to carve them out and turn them to ash."

"Do you not feel for anyone or anything? Your sister and parents, for example." My gaze darts to Jaden, a dagger still pressed to his neck. The sight evokes a hard swallow in my throat.

Quirine smirks, her attention momentarily following my line of sight to Jaden, then darts back to me.

"Oh, I have feelings," she says, her voice edged with wickedness. "I simply choose which ones I will allow in."

Her head snaps back to Jaden and she erases the distance between him and her, captures his chin in her hand, leans forward, and drags her tongue in a long lick from the tip of his nose to his forehead.

My sight turns red, anger whipping through my blood. The sense of elementals leaping to the ready, preparing to respond to my emotions in kind, builds to the point of a too-tight balloon. The elements and my emotions are poised to explode at any moment in an uncontrollable tempest. I reign in my feelings and tap down the mounting elements. I can't afford an outburst of any kind.

I lurch forward, the connection between me and the time chronicler snapping taut, hindering my attempt. Quirine jumps in front of me, blocking my view of Jaden. And with a screech, she bares her teeth. A clear threat to bite. Bite me.

Zarah grabs my shoulder and yanks me back against her. "You want her power. I heard you," she says to the princess. "If you bite her, you will infect her and quite possibly, the power thrumming in her blood."

The edge of Quirine's lip lifts in a snarl, but she doesn't advance.

Behind us, beyond the throne room, in the spaces on the other side of the surrounding walls, noises rise. Crashes and bangs and the surge of yells. Quirine lifts her chin toward the back of the room, an unspoken command that sends her infected minions into action. They move into position, blocking the oversized, double doors.

A harsh, humorless laugh crackles at the left of the throne. There, Lobrka is held at bay by six of Quirine's soldiers. They press him into the ground, their hands heavy upon his shoulders, holding him on his knees, and twisting his arms behind his back.

Lobrka twists the angle of his head toward the princess. "They are coming for you."

Quirine's hands fist, the color bleeding from her knuckles. "Shut up!"

Before Lobrka and respond, Queen Dreya, who's been sitting silent like a vacant vessel in the throne, gasps and tips forward, her hands slipping free from the chair arms and powerful carved stone.

Quirine spins toward her mother. "Get your hands back in place in that chair and spear the power at whatever is going on outside." The power being the energy thrumming through the crystals beneath the floor. She swings a harsh point toward the doors. "Put a stop to whatever is causing that ruckus, and do so now!"

"My strength is drained," Dreya says with a wheeze.

"Do so or I have no need for you, your life no longer necessary."

I can't let Quirine take Dreya's life. Not when I'm so close to the physical contact needed to adjust the timeline.

"I can help," I blurt, jerking a step forward. Quirine barks a laugh, suggesting she finds my offer ridiculous. "No, seriously, I can." My gaze sweeps to Jaden, then Lobrka. "Free my friends. Allow them to leave here unharmed, and I will help you. Given what I am," *the Balance Bringer*, "...the elements powered here should respond better to me than to any other."

Sarcastic humor slips from her lips in a broken laugh. "Even if I believed you... which I do not... you cannot harness the power of the throne. It will only respond to the blood running through my family line."

Okay. I didn't know that. Can the same be said for the throne from my original timeline? Either way, either timeline, that restriction isn't an issue.

"Shouldn't be a problem," I retort and take another step forward. Zarah moves tentatively at my side.

Clearly noting my movement and direction, Theon shifts to Dreya's side, his gaze narrowing tight on me. Quirine eyes me. And even with the distance between us, the doubt is evident in her gaze.

Her fingers flare and feather, curl back inward. "You think your Balance Bringer status will nullify the bloodline safeguards?"

Something crashes heavily into the throne room's doors causing me to jolt. But Quirine does not allow the disturbance to draw her attention so neither do I. My focus remains on the darkest threat in the room, the princess and her father, King Theon.

I suck back a deep breath, centering my resolve. "I couldn't say, but I still know I can succeed with the throne. I already have."

"What does that mean?" she seethes.

Dreya's back bolts straight, drawing everyone's attention. "It is true," she says. "Anaka shares blood with my brother. She is the offspring of Prince Marduk."

"Really?" Quirine tilts her head, regarding me. Her reaction appears neither shocked or angered, but rather, delighted. The tips of her mouth kick up.

Something in my chest rolls and roils, and my determination momentarily falters. But I can't allow my resolve to wane. I haven't the time nor the leisure to dither.

"All right, then," Quirine says, with an upward wave to her father.

Theon grabs Dreya by the arm and drags her from the throne. She stumbles to the side with a yelp. Then falls to butt and thigh, hands pressed to the dais floor. She glances at me, then drops her gaze to the stone beneath her.

At the back of the room, many things continue to bang against the barrier. Bang and bump and slam.

The princess continues to ignore the commotion and motions to the now open seat. "Show us what you are capable of."

"Ana," Jaden calls to me.

I turn my gaze to him. "It will be all right," I assure, and I pray to Gaea and god I haven't just spoken a lie.

His expression betrays no fear, only faith in my and my ability to succeed. "Remember your promise."

"I haven't forgotten."

"No secret messages," Quirine barks and darts forward, grabbing my wrist. "You want your friends to go free, get in the chair and prove yourself." She yanks me up the dais steps and shoves me toward the throne, a too-wicked and thrilled smile brimming across her face.

What am I missing? Why does she look so happy?

At my side, Zarah scampers onto the dais, placing herself between me and Dreya. Even as I hold my attention on Quirine, I sense Zarah positioning herself for our mission.

The princess is less than half my age and half my size, and yet, when she pushes and pulls at me, she packs powerful strength. She jerks me around and punches me in the stomach, aggressively driving me into the throne.

I unceremoniously drop onto my butt into the seat of power, my hands grabbing at the chair arms to steady myself. The cut crystal beneath my touch flares to life, warm and bright. The elements within the crystal chamber beneath our feet rally and rush forth to meet my request.

Strength blooms in my chest, in my blood and muscles. Quirine was foolish to let me sit here. If my command of the elements was a threat to her before, now that is even more so the case. In my current position, the added aid of the crystals is compensating for my weaker grasp this version of me has on my gifts.

My gaze shifts to Jaden, and he nods, encouraging me to do whatever it takes to bring the timeline change to fruition. I suck back a breath and steady my heart. My mind is ready, my body is humming...

The doors at the back of the throne room burst open, and in the bat of an eye, a horde of armor-covered bodies spilling into the room, and the clash of battle explodes into the large space. My focus shudders from the throne to the room, my brain scrambling to keep up... even as Quirine screams and releases a cloud of dark-Gaea-only-knows-what.

The cloud moves against the glass ceiling like a swarm of locus, descending upon the fight. And, to the opposite side of the evil princess, Zarah lunges for the queen—reaching out her hand for the needed touch to change *everything*.

King Theon swinging arm is in action before the time chronicler can make contact.

Zarah is suddenly toppling backwards, the vine connection between us snapping stiff and pulling at my place upon the throne. The slam of her hip and shoulder against the stone floor reverberates through my bones, our link causing me to share in her experience... her pain.

Turning her back upon the exploding chaos in the room, as

if completely unphased and unconcerned by the uprising, Quirine spins in front of me and leans in close, stopping mere inches from my face.

"You thought you could betray me?" she says with a snarl. "What could you possibly gain by getting to my mother?" Her eyes narrow, silently probing for an answer. One I refuse to speak. Clearly noting my refusal, she continues, "Guess we may never know." Her head tilts toward her father, her gaze sending a silent communication.

In a flash, a blade—one forged in the Fires of Guardoone—cuts a line of red across Dreya's throat sending a spray of blood across the floor. My aunts garbled gasp for breath is lost in Zarah's screams.

My body falls numb, my mind blank. How will I fix anything without Dreya?

My gaze drops to my position upon the crystal seat. I'm now connected to air and earth, in addition to my already realized element, water, and I am in the seat of power. Maybe, just maybe, I can access time as space as I had done in my original timeline.

My grip upon the chair arms tightens and I throw my concentration into the task. When I had previously managed to move through the element, it had been like slipping through pool water. Now, my attempt feels like I am trying to climb uphill in the midst of an avalanche. I can't hear a whisper of the ability within my soul, much less locate it and utilize it.

I have yet to realize the element of fire. I guess it makes sense this version of me isn't yet ready to move beyond the basic four.

A slap against the top of my hand pops my eyes wide. Quirine's face is in mine, her grin wide. "Now you and all that you can do belong to me."

Her gaze drops to our connected hands. Inky black lines

are spreading across my skin, covering my hand and snaking up my arm. And with it, a deep penetrating coldness.

And something else. Something I can't quite...

Quirine's hand is ripped from mine, inciting a gasp to jump up my throat. Jaden is before me, somehow having managed to get free from the soldiers who had been holding him. The fighting in the throne room is all consuming, flowing up and onto the dais, likely aiding in Jaden's escape. Everywhere I look, fully armored warriors are engaging Quirine's infected soldiers.

A yelp draws my attention to the left of the throne. Lobrka has also managed to get free and is confronting Theon, dominating the infected king's attention. The now-slain queen has become nothing more than a heap of silk and too-pale skin, with a river of red pooling and spreading from where she has fallen.

Zarah pops up at my side and both she and Jaden grab my hands, tugging me out of the crystal carved seat. I stumble forward and throw my arms around Jaden, pull his body flush against mine. I'm trembling inside and out. Things are far worse than they were before I sought to change events in my original timeline, and now I've lost Dreya—my chance to undo the damage I've done.

"Jaden," I whimper, half-weep. "She's gone. Our ability to change things is gone." I don't need to clarify who the 'she' is I am referring to. He knows. I know he knows.

Zarah is pulling on my arm, saying "we have to go," over and over again. I mentally will her to understand that I need a minute, just a minute, to wrap my mind around this change in circumstance.

Jaden leans back and brushes his fingers along the side of my face, from my temple to my chin, his thumb drawing a soft line beneath my lower lip. "No," he whispers. His eyes are a swirl of blue and green, a sign that his Tracer ability is actively seeing beyond the now. "All is not..."

His words drop away and he starts to turn his head, as if to scan the battle scene owning every space of the throne room. Quirine's swarming darkness is falling from the ceiling like dripping tar, falling on warriors and sticking to their armor. The blackness moves as if alive, seeking breaks and joints through which the warriors' skin. If the substance succeeds, things will get progressively worse, and fast.

I avert my gaze from the scene and search Jaden for a clue to his unfinished thought. From behind him, a small hand folds over his shoulder, drawing his attention. Before he can finish his blink, he's falling backward into Quirine's awaiting arms.

She grins at me... thrusts me backward with a wave of black energy... and then sinks her teeth into Jaden's neck.

EIGHTEEN

My mind is screaming before the sound explodes from my lips.

That evil little princess is infecting Jaden, possibly draining him at the same time. I jolt free of the throne and dash toward his rescue. Toward my attack on Quirine.

"I will destroy you," I yell, my attention tight on her unwavering returned stare.

Her eyes are lifted to mine, even as her teeth are buried in my Tracer's skin, his body jerking, shuddering, webbing with black from the point of connection. The jerk of his limbs is slowing, his fight clearly weakening. I reach out with my infected, black shaded hand, and as I do, my darkened skin, plus the blood and bones beneath, throb with a weak ache. A throb that increases as I draw closer to Quirine.

The darkness now in me perhaps recognizes the darkness in her.

My fingers are within a foot of reaching my goal... pulling Jaden free and wrapping a tight chokehold around Quirine's neck. But before I can connect, something large and heavy plows into me, knocking me off course. An over-sized hand shoves into my chest, sending me flying backwards. Somewhere in the mess of my mind and the song of chaos, I detect Zarah's howl, feel her discomfort through our connection.

I bump, slam, and tumble with two other bodies also thrown into motion. One of the bodies—Zarah, likely yanked into action by our binding. And the other... Jaden. Tossed by the same force that shoved me. Falling on my side, I skid across the surface of the dais, coming to a stop with Zarah moaning and Jaden convulsing at my side.

Quirine is trapped within Lobrka's stranglehold. The dark elf is growling, teeth bared, muscles bulging, pressing his thumbs into the center of her throat. And Quirine, she's... she's...

Her hand bursts out through his back, his heart held firmly in her bloody grasp. My breath lodges like a stone in my throat and Lobrka... he tips to the side. Falls over dead.

I. Can't. Breathe.

Jaden is shuddering at my side, and I can't breathe. Can't move. Can't think beyond everything that has gone so terribly wrong in this horrible, ugly timeline.

In my peripheral vision, I note Zarah leaning over Jaden, pressing her hand to his cheek, and murmuring words to him. My gaze swivels to them as Jaden responds to her with words I don't hear.

Zarah's gaze snaps to me. Darts over the scene, the evil princess, then back to me. "We need to go," she says, with a clear urgency in her tone.

Quirine straightens tall and takes a step toward me. "You need to get yourself—"

A white ghost of a body slams into her, tossing her sideways. Her landing blocked by the location of the thrones.

Zarah crawls to my side and grabs my hand. "We need to go."

I know we do, but...

My gaze slips to Jaden. His body trembles, his throat working, and eyes focused on the ceiling. A mesh of darkening veins spread over his chin and reach up the side of his face. A messy knot grows thick and heavy in my chest.

"You're right," I reply, "I just need a moment."

I pull myself to Jaden's side. Undaunted by the infection spreading throughout him, my hands caress his arms, his face. "I'm so sorry." My words are muffled with tears. No matter the timeline, he's still my Jaden. With all that has transpired on the wrong side of what we wanted, what he hoped for; I don't know if I'll ever see a healthy version of him again. "I love you." I press a lingering kiss to his forehead.

"Don't..." He swallows hard, his head not moving but his gaze seeking mine. "Don't you give up. Hope is not lost."

Movement flickers beyond the throne and Quirine's howl rises over the sound of the din, vibrating at my ear. A crash silences her wail and resonates through the floor and surrounding walls.

"Go," Jaden says, the word a watery garble in his throat. "Get far from me. I cannot hold on much longer." He's succumbing to the infecting darkness.

Zarah tugs on our connection. "Come on."

My gaze doesn't wander from Jaden. I have so little time left with him and I don't want to miss a single breath. I'm afraid to blink.

He nods. "You can still make things right," he says, voice hoarse. "What you seek is near. Remember your promise and fix this." He coughs, a wet, sputtering cough. "Fix me. And restore us."

Zarah pulls at me once more and Jaden lifts his chin, be it

barely, urging me to heed her beseeching and move. Sniffling, I drop a too-quick kiss to his lips, and then I'm moving... or, in reality... Zarah drags me down the dais' steps and into the clashing chaos.

"Fix me. Restore us." Jaden's parting words are a trapped and jumbled repetitive cycle in my thoughts. *"What you seek is near."* I want little more than to fix him and restore us, but what I now seek... the only thing that can help me repair the timeline, repair him and us... is my father, Royal Commander Marduk.

Zarah leads me through the crowd like water through cracks, fluidly and without pause. She moves us unseen between those fighting as if we are a pair of ghosts. And when she spies someone with skin exposed, she reaches out, touching them. Words and symbols slip over her skin as she absorbs their history. Each touch is quick and, I imagine, the collected information short. Occasionally, Zarah adjusts our path after one such touch.

I swipe a couple of abandoned shields from the floor, passing one to Zarah to protect us from the dark goop occasionally dropping from the ceiling. I also grab a dagger from the loosened grip of a dead male.

"What are you looking for?" I ask, because she's clearly searching through peoples' memories for something of interest. "What is your goal?"

A nearby struggle sends a sword swinging wide. I brace my hand on her back, edging her forward and down, avoiding a hit. A breath wheezes through her teeth, her eyes wide as she tracks the weapon's continued path.

"That was close," she chokes out, her attention snapping forward, searching for something. Something she has yet to confess.

Remaining crouched, she leads me between moving bodies.

"There. Just up ahead." She turns back to me and tilts her head in the direction her gaze had been a second ago. "I *believe* that is what we need."

Bodies are moving all around us and, although they don't appear to take notice of us, they are knocking into us left and right while engaged in their individual battles. A thick thigh bumps into my side, and I grunt. Steadying my stance, I follow Zarah's directional nod to a warrior distinguished from all the others by his golden armor.

Golden for the royal commander. My father. And our answer to restoring the original timeline.

"What you seek is near."

Jaden knew. He saw my father's presence with his seer ability and he knew.

Taking the lead, I tighten my hold on Zarah's hand and weave us through the many fighting bodies toward the Royal Commander Marduk. As we draw nearer, I wave my hand to snag his attention, but he's too focused on the fight before him to take note of Zarah and me creeping through the holes in the chaos.

"Father," I scream, the title bursting from my lips before I can stop myself.

His actions hiccup, as if he has heard me and my word has caused him to fumble. Drops of darkness from above drop onto his armor.

His armor, I remind myself. *He is still protected within.*

Two warriors slip free from the fray, fighting their way to their commander.

"The queen is dead," one of them calls out. "As is commander Lobrka and a Tracer. The other Tracer brother is unaccounted for."

Between the two newly arrived warriors and Commander Marduk, the current enemy opponent is quickly dispatched.

My father shoves his sword through the chest of another, taking him down for the count. He pulls his sword free and swings back to the informative warriors. "And the Balance Bringer?"

One shakes his head. "Unknown," the other replies.

"I'm here!" I push a body out of the way to get closer.

Zarah stumbles, dragging me down with her. With a grunt, I pull myself back to my feet and...

A hand drops on my shoulder.

I spin around and come face to face with Aunt Edea... Opal. Her eyes and lips are rimmed in black. Every wrinkle and scar is pitch black or bruised in shadows. "You are coming with me," she says, her gray teeth exposed. "It is time to take your place as a tool upon the throne."

"A tool to be used by Princess Quirine?" I ask, not bothering to soften the venom in my voice. Her smile widens by way of an answer. "What happened to you?"

For a split second, I believe I detect remorse. But then, just as quick or quicker, the emotion vanishes. "Many mistakes, starting at the very beginning." She tugs me away from my father and moves in the direction of the dais, turning her back on me to emphasize how little fear she feels in my presence.

The darkness in her touch is colder than any ice block. It pulses and pushes against my elemental power and strength, attempting to shove my responses into an unwanted slumber.

I yank against her hold. "I'm sorry," I whisper.

"What for, child?" She doesn't deign to grant me a glance with her question.

"Sorry for the way this life has treated you. Sorry that I made it more of a mess than it already was." Because, as much as I disapproved of her actions in my original timeline, that version of her was easier to wrap my thoughts around than this dark, infected one.

"What are you talking about?" She turns back to face me. "I am not, sorry."

"Well... I still am." I shove my dagger with an upward swing into her heart. She gasps, expelling a drudge of dark liquid from her mouth and falls forward, crashing into me.

Behind me, Zarah is screaming for Commander Marduk, but I am in the moment, saying a silent goodbye... for now (hopefully)... to my aunt. One of my sergeant mothers from my first life as Deona.

Lowering to my knees, I lay her gently upon the ground, the surrounding fighters bumping into her prone body. One even stumbling and falling to his side.

"Over here. Over here," Zarah is yelling, but I'm not paying her any mind. I stepped into the timeline to make things better and all I've managed to do is make things worse. Incredibly, astronomically worse.

Almost everyone who mattered to me is dead.

Almost everyone.

Zarah tugs at our binding. I release a sigh. We can't afford this pause I've taken with my aunt, and yet I am slow to return to action. My gaze drifts over the infection spreading from my fingers up my arms.

The darkness, whatever it is, doesn't affect me in the same manner as it appears to do with others, and I wonder if that is because of the infection I previously weathered during my trip to find Madame Marrouske. That was a different timeline, but could some part of me somehow remember?

The darkness is cold, on my skin and in my blood, but I have no urge to report to evil Quirine. Do her bidding.

I lower my lips to Aunt Edea's ear. "I will undo this terrible mistake of mine and give you back the life you had before."

Golden armored hands grab my shoulders and lift me from the ground. Spin me around. "Anaka?"

"Dad?" I whisper. Even through the slit in his face cover I detect the confusion in his expression. I shake my head. "Sorry," I mumble and correct my greeting. "Royal Commander." I loosely straighten my shoulders.

"Are you all right?" He lifts his face shield to better scrutinize me. I nod my head, because delving into the truth would be a waste of precious time. "We need to get you to safety."

At our side, Zarah is jumping up and down, her eyes wide and lips curving into a tentative smile. Her gaze is darting between me and my father. Or, to be exact, my father's exposed face. Bared skin for Zarah to touch and use her ability.

Two immortal warriors move to either side of me, clearly intending to protect me from the surrounding battle.

"This way," Commander Marduk says with a tilt of his head, indicating the direction in which he intends to move us. He turns away, taking the lead.

Zarah's hand clasps mine. Her jaw is tight and her eyes expressive with her unspoken command. *"Now. Do it now."*

I lurch forward and grab his gauntlet covered forearm. "Wait." He turns his gaze back to meet mine. "Do you trust me?"

The side of his eyes crinkle. "In theory."

"Well..." I toss Zarah a quick glance before returning my attention to my dad. "I really need you to trust me now."

His brow hikes up, but before he can respond, the room rattles with a reverberating bang. A small group all clad in black stand at the top of the entry steps.

"Death to the royals!" One streams and lifts a hand high in the air. Within his grasp is a large ball with a flaming wick.

My chest squeezes as an unwelcome shudder rolls over me. *Bomb.*

Several things unfold at once. A wave of Quirine's infected minions descend upon the new arrivals. Marduk's warriors tighten their stance around me. The male holding the bomb cranks his arm back and then shoots forward, and Zarah launches herself, arm outstretched, at my father.

The destructive projectile is flying overhead as the royal commander's arm snaps up to block Zarah.

The world is screams and pops and bangs at my ears. Bodies pushing and shoving, jerking at my linked hand with Zarah.

The scene explodes in an all-encompassing white light and in the midst of it I imagine I see Zarah pinching my father's nose, and then that too is gone.

Everything is white static.

I FEEL INTANGIBLE. My body floating amongst clouds of mist and mesh. Was I hit by an explosive blast? Knocked unconscious or near death? Or am I tangled in my elemental connection, dragged into some in-between state like that time in the competition pool with Jaden and Dohlan?

A shiver of energy races from my fingers up my arm. The essence of Zarah in accompaniment. If she's been injured or killed, then the same can be said for me.

"Anaka." Her voice whispers along the elemental line binding us, holding us together, and keeping her alive until we accomplish our mission... or die in the process. "The attainment of our goal is uncertain. I touched him, but I cannot yet say if the contact was long enough or strong enough. Either way, should you awake in another timeline or in this one, I have both advice and a gift to bestow upon you.

"First, my advice, and something you have already suffered a hard lesson in... you should not mess with changes in long established history. The ripple effects are unpredictable and dangerous. Do not, by any means, take what I have done as an example." Energy dances along our connection.

"As for my gift to you," she continues. "The queen's life was fleeting when I reached her, but I still managed to collect several bits and pieces that... given what I glimpsed of your alternative timeline... may provide you valuable insight and help you in your endeavor."

She gasps and I mirror her grunt, a sharp, hot pain slicing through my chest and radiating with ice. If I could see my body or Zarah's, I would expect to see a sword cutting through one of us.

"This is my end," she says. "They have killed me. I pray they do not take you down with me. And should you survive, succeed, find yourself back where you started, tell the other me that with regards to my... our... extra gift, our father showed me the way."

She groans, intense aching lightning across my nerves. The surrounding whiteness throbs, beating, beating, like something bouncing around in a tumbling drum. The pain drops into a numbness, and then explodes into flashing images from Dreya's life—ice coated rooms, locked doors, long term isolation. And then Sol. Thoughts of Sol, waiting for Sol, dreaming of Sol, dancing and more unfolding with Sol.

Holy Gaea and god. Sol was a catalyst in creating the villainous Dreya I faced before my timeline change.

My thoughts spin back to witnessing Sol bleeding out black on the crashed floating island. That was this time around. The Sol that never connected with Dreya. But in my original time-line, they had a history. A rather long and heartbreaking one.

My heart is bruised and crushed by the clear, unrealized relationship between them. If Jaden were ripped from me in a similar manner, what would I become? Could I turn into another dark Dreya?

My chest squeezes, oxygen unavailable to fill my lungs. The flashes from Dreya's life become enveloped in the now-familiar, all-encompassing white. And the white bleeds to black... every muscle and nerve in my body awakening with a scream.

NINETEEN

I'm vaguely aware of laying on a hard floor, curling in on myself. I can't control the tears spilling from my eyes or the shaking taking command of my body. If I'm not dying, then I'm crumbling beneath the catastrophic results of my choices.

Since stepping into the first attempted time change, I've been holding myself together with little more than sheer will. Now that will is shattered. My attempts to improve the presented problem—Dreya and her infection of darkness—have only managed to make things unimaginably worse.

I clutch at the growing wetness spreading across my belly. The wound is not mine and yet it is, through the connection I established between me and the time chronicler Zarah. She's dying. Maybe she's already dead because I no longer feel her life energy buzzing along the bond. And if she had died, what does that mean for me and my intended destiny?

What does that mean for my brother's fiancée... my friend.

My friend, my brother, my tracer, my sisters, my mother, all my intense and crazy friends...

My body shudders with a deep sob.

Who's left? Have I managed to see everyone I care about killed, destroyed, wiped from existence? Am I the worst kind of monster?

"You cannot fix the future by changing the past. You will only succeed in creating more problems." I should have listened to Aunt Edea when she told me that. I'd been too blind and eager to see the truth in her words. Never, never, never shall I ever try to change an event in the past. Never again.

A shared exchange of murmurs sounds near my side, the voices are too soft to decipher. I consider investigating the source, but my muscles ache, refusing motion, and my eyes are too swollen to tear open against the weight and crust gluing them closed.

Though, what I can detect gives me clues to where I am not. Absent is the nickel scent of spilled blood, no smoke assaults lungs, and the only cries of pain are my own. I am no longer in the devastated throne room.

Did Zarah or I manage to move my physical form through space and time? Or did I pass out and somebody else relocated me?

A gentle hand brushes along the length of my arm. "Anala? Are you all right?" The voice belongs to Izza.

Izza!

Did we succeed? "Am I back?" I force my eyes open and, finding strength in this new blooming revelation, push my upper body upright, turning to face her.

I *am* back, and situated in Izza's self-imposed prison. Her home and private-dimension safe haven.

She worries her lower lip between her teeth. "As far as I can tell, you never actually left."

She glances to the projected life images from our many Balance Bringer sisters... the various versions of me... of us...

that surround the room. The moving images are her connection to our many lives from which she has been removed. Moments experienced by our many versions displayed like movies.

"You started to go," she continues, then narrows her gaze, giving me a stern expression. "Completely ignoring my objection, I might add. But then you bounced back like you had walked into an invisible wall or something. A second later, your entire body flickered, and the surrounding images flew past too quickly to absorb. It was too much information moving way too quickly. Then... in the blink of an eye... you were on the floor, curled in on yourself, whimpering, and wearing different clothes."

Bounced back? Is that what Zarah's time manipulation had done? Had she somehow kept me from interfering in the incident at the frozen lake, preventing me from stopping Sol and saving Dreya as I had previously?

If that's what happened, then thank our gracious Gaea.

Of course, that lands me back where I started. With a dark Dreya to contend with.

But better than where I was a moment ago.

Still... I glance down at my belly, moving my hands to view the blood staining my clothing.

Izza gasps. "Oh, my Gaea! What happened?"

Forcing a small clearing within the fog of exhaustion and anguish clouding my brain, I sniffle and wipe the tears from my eyes. "The blood isn't mine. Not really. I'm okay." And if we have managed to correct the timeline, then so is Zarah, the actual receiver of the wound.

The reassuring smile I attempt to pull to my lips fails miserably. "I messed up, Izza. I messed up bad. And I was so afraid that this time there would be no fixing what I'd done. I thought I'd never get back to this place. To you."

"But you did," she placates. "You found a way and now you are safe."

"I did." I bow my head with a nod. "And thank the goddess Gaea. Because my safety was not the concern." I shake my head. "I managed to hurt our Tracer *again*, plus so many others."

A muffled cough draws my gaze away from Izza. I blink at the sight of the male standing several feet away. My breath hitches, lodging like a stone in my chest.

"Oh, yeah." Izza sighs and tilts her head toward the third-party present. "Literally seconds after you flickered into a heap on the floor, Dharmic appeared." She leans closer to my ear and lowers her voice. "Did you have something to do with that?"

Not that I'm aware of.

As I watch, Dharmic transforms into the Tracer from my current life. *Jaden.*

My heart swells and I scramble onto my knees, sobs already racking my body. Sobs birthed from elation at the sight of him, as well as from the devastation from having lost him—*twice.* I fumble forward on my knees, arms outstretched and greedily reaching. His name squeaks from my lips, both a plea and a prayer.

"Ana." He sweeps past Izza and meets me where I'm kneeled, enclosing me in his much wanted, much needed embrace. "I'm here and whatever the trouble is, we'll face it together." He presses a kiss to my temple. "I've got you," he whispers, "and you've got me."

My fingers dig into his shoulders, half afraid he's an illusion and will disappear at any moment. "How are you here?"

He pulls back a smidgeon and turns his face toward mine. "After you sat on the throne and went into a meditational state, I heard a voice telling me to follow you. At first, I thought it was you beckoning me, but even though the voice was familiar, it wasn't a proper fit to be you. Still..." A shrug. "The message instilled a need in me, and I followed."

A voice... in his head? When last I laid eyes on a version of him, Zarah had her hands on his face and was murmuring something in his ear. Had she somehow sent a message to the version of him from my original timeline? And if not her, then what other explanation exists?

Movement shifts at our side. "Um." Hesitation dominates Izza's tone. "What happened to Dharmic?"

"I'm sorry, Izza. I told you I wasn't him," Jaden replies, making no effort to move or loosen his hold on me. "You matter to me, but our time is in the past. I'm here for Ana."

Here for me. Those words hug my heart.

I, too, don't release my embrace. I haven't had nearly enough time in Jaden's arms to heal my recent emotional wounds. In fact, no amount of time may ever be enough. Not when it comes to moments spent with him—healing required or not.

But right now, I'm a wreck and if anyone can help piece me back together, it's him. I need him as much as I want him. I need him to know and to understand.

"I lost you," I whisper, as silent tears streak the length of my cheeks. "I basically watched you die... twice."

"I'm here now." He erases one of my tears with a soft kiss. "And I have no plans to go anywhere." He kisses away another tear, then gently presses his lips to my closed eyelid.

I clutch the front of his shirt and hold him to me. Press my forehead against his... and breathe him in. The scent of him, the warmth of him, the energy of his life essence. "I can't ever live through losing you. Never again. Understand me?"

"We'll make sure you never have to." His lips brush against my nose, my cheek, my lips. A barely-there feather touch.

Beyond our focus, Izza makes a funny noise communicating her clear discomfort. "I think I shall make myself scarce," she says and turns away. "Take your time." She vanishes from sight. The clatter of a closing door marking her departure.

Jaden scoops me into his arms and carries me to the bed. "I'm detecting an avalanche of emotions, cascading through you, off you."

He gently sets me on the bed, removes my boots... and his, then stretches out next to me, and tucks me against his side. He guides my head to his chest and holds me there, his fingers stroking through my hair, along my arm, tracing my jawline.

Silent tears continue to stream down my cheeks. I don't want to keep crying and yet, at this point, I can't seem to stop myself. It's as if all my strength has crumbled and I am turning into nothing more than a mess of dust and pebbles.

He kisses the top of my head. "Lifetime after lifetime, you have carried more weight upon your shoulders than any one being should be forced to undertake. And time and time again, you have met the challenge with grace and dignity. I have every faith that you will find your way this time, as well. I believe in you. In fact, I believe you will perform better this time around than you ever have before."

His thumb draws a soft line across my upper arm, and he drops another kiss upon my forehead. "But every living thing... Fae, elf, immortal, or goddess blessed... is allowed moments of doubt and confusion. Down time to find and rebuild their resolve."

His fingers glide up my arm, traveling a line over my shoulders, up my neck, and along the curve of my chin into a fine feathered curve along my cheek. "What I am saying, Ana, is that your tears do not signify weakness, defeat, or failure. They are markers of how much you care. How vested you are in the well-being of the lives you touch. So, my love, cry as much as you need to and I shall stay here with you through every last drop.

"But if you might allow me..." He hooks his finger under my chin and raises my gaze to meet his. "Let me help you navigate those emotions."

As much as I'm often reluctant to his mood soothing, I don't want to continue feeling the extreme ache. If he can soften the edge... With a sniffle and a nod, I close my eyes and grant him permission.

The tease of his calming magic immediately dances along my skin, and I sink deeper into his side, welcoming the wave washing over me. Clearly understanding my desire, he does not remove the pain, only eases the pain inflicted. My tears do not cease, but soften.

I don't know how much time passes with us stretched out across the bed, but our silence, my body molded to him, his arms wrapped around me, holding me close, our bodies warming one another... the feeling can only be explained as coming home after a too long absence—happy, sad, beautiful, and perfectly imperfect.

Beneath the press of my ear, the thrumming of his heart in his chest moves in time with my own. A sound I shall never tire of.

I almost lost this, lost us, never to feel it again in this lifetime—*this us*. Jaden and Ana.

I tilt my head up, taking in the view of his stubble covered chin and lush, lowered lashes. Even through my tear blurred vision, his outward calm appearance is betrayed by the bob of his larynx and the tightness at the edge of his eyes.

Shifting onto my elbow, I reach up with my free hand and drag my fingertips gently across his cheek. His eyes snap open, his intense, green gaze immediately finding me.

"Ana," he whispers and dips his head, swiping the tears

from my face with his lips. His hand draws soft designs across the skin of my back and arms, the brush of his touch leaving a hum of electric tingles in its wake.

"Jaden," I reply, lifting my face to his, my mouth skating a mere breath over his before bestowing a feather light kiss. I tasted my vested emotions in my salty tears lingering on his lips. "I almost lost you this time around without letting you know what you mean to me."

His fingers slide across the back of my scalp. "You don't need to do this to yourself, Ana. I know how you feel. After all this time, how could I not?"

I heave a deep breath. "You have the benefit of remembering all our times together." All the lifetimes. All the versions of us.

"As do you." His finger traces a small circle at my temple. "You have joined with your sisters... with one exception." Izza. "You remember."

"Yeah, but..." His hand flattens against the side of my face, and I lean into the touch. "For you, the memories are like chapters in a book, whereas for me, they are volumes in a too-long series."

His lips lift in a silent laugh, the hard edge of his eyes softening. "Memories never compare to living in the moment. Our many experiences, our firsts in this version of us, are my favorite memories being made."

I suck back a breath. "Then let us make another first memory this time around. Let me share with you how much you matter to me." I pull his lips to mine, my kiss both tender and demanding.

One of his hands slips to my hip, squeezing, while the other moves to the nape of my neck, holding me to him. The kiss is languorous, brimming with passion, and when lips finally separate, if only a mere centimeter, I spill my desire.

"I want us connected in every way physically and emotionally possible." My hand slides into position over his heart, his shirt no barrier against the beating hum within his chest.

His hand drapes over mine, joining them with the weave of our fingers. "This has and will always be yours." He presses our hold over his heart. It pounds faster than it was a few moments ago.

Mine. His words wrap around my own heart like a heated blanket.

Slipping my hand free of our hold, and gaze dipping to his chest, I work the ties of his shirt, exposing his chest. His gaze is steady on me as I replace my hand with my mouth, closing my lips over his heart. His chest rises with a deep inhale, his skin burning beneath my touch.

His chest is a sculpted work of art—hard muscular lines stretched beneath silky soft skin. My fingers glide over the perfect ripples, my gaze shifting to watch my hand travel from his heart to his navel.

My attention snags on my hand, the dirt and dried blood crusted around and under my fingernails. With a gasp, I pull away. My hands beginning to shake. Everything that happened in the alternate timeline is my fault. None of it would have been a possibility if not for me and my interference. So many died or worse.

"Ana?" Jaden sits, following my retreat. "What's wrong?"

"I'm a mess." I fan my trembling hands wide before me, my gaze taking in my state. Not just the filth on my hands and arms, but the blood spread across my blouse. I can only imagine how my hair and face look.

Which part of me is the larger disaster—my physical or emotional state? At least my tears have finally stopped.

"Well then," he says, his gaze not leaving mine. "Let's do something about that."

Jaden clasps his hands around mine, stilling my quivers. He can sense my emotions, always has. He obviously knows the mess to which I refer extends beyond my clothes, skin, and hair. The edges of his lips lift, and he shifts, rising from the bed. He turns back and scoops me into his arms before I can protest. "You might benefit from a warm bath in more ways than one."

He carries me toward a bath I'd previously paid little attention to when taking in Izza's dimensional space. Situated behind a curtained screen is a large copper tub already filling with water, as if magically sensing our intention.

Um. My gaze bounces from Jaden to the tub and back again. "Will you be joining me?" My brain might be short circuiting. I can't believe I asked that. I bite my lip to prevent myself from saying anything else embarrassing and focus on allowing the warmth of his body to calm my anxiety.

His head dips, his gaze colliding with mine. "If I did that, I doubt much cleaning would take place."

My neck and cheeks warm, and his gaze heats as his focus drifts over my flushed skin.

My chest heaves. "But emotion soothing and messy knot untangling?" So much for biting my lip against word vomit.

A sound rumbles in the back of Jaden's throat and I can't tell if it is a groan or a strangled laugh. Possibly a mix between the two. He sets me on my feet beside the tub and, avoiding eye contact, takes a quick survey of the space. He grabs a towel from a far shelf and places it on a tub-side stool. Tests the water temperature with the dip of his fingers.

I wrap my arms around myself, hugging against the light tremble owning my limbs.

Jaden lifts his chin, indicating a thin shelf beside the tub. "Looks like there are plenty of additives for your bath, so I'll leave you to it."

His focus shifts back to me and his brow wrinkles, his

eyebrows drawing together. "Ana." His voice is laced with concern, and he drags his teeth over his lower lip as his gaze tightens. "You're shaking."

I am, and I'm no longer certain if the trembling is because of what I recently went through, or because of the situation presented before me.

His hands clasp my upper arms and gingerly glide to my palms. With a gentle tug, he encourages me to release my body hug. He then folds our hands together and presses our intertwined hands to his chest.

"There's no shame in needing more time," he says. "If that's what you need. You can save the bath for later."

"No." I shake my head. "I want the blood and filth of my mistakes and failures washed from my body." He nods, his gaze dropping to the rug beneath our feet. "Maybe..."

His lashes lift and his regard drifts over my face. "Maybe?" he presses.

I worry my lip. "Maybe you could help me?" My voice hitches, and I close my eyes against the burn scorching my face.

"You want me to help you undress and get in the tub?"

I'm not sure what I hear in his voice, be it shock, uncertainty, desire, or other, but I don't open my eyes seeking confirmation. I simply nod and squeeze an unsteady "yes".

"Ana." His voice is a mere whisper as his fingers trace a line from my temple to my jaw. "It would be my honor."

My eyes flutter open and meet his return stare. A plethora of emotion stirs behind his eyes. If only I could read him in the same manner he is able to read me.

Gaea above, when he looks at me this way, I want to give him anything and everything. I want to give him all of me.

His hands skim the curve of my neck, over my shoulders, and along the top edge of top. His fingers stilling and curling around the top tie.

"With your permission?" His green eyes pierce through me as I grant my consent.

He tugs and the knot slips free. I shudder as the fabric loosens, slides from my shoulders, and for the first time in this lifetime, I stand bare before him. My upper body completely exposed.

TWENTY

J aden removes my grimy clothing and guides me into the awaiting bath, his hands gentle and movements respectful. Ample bubbles float on the water's surface, granting me a trace of modesty. Aside from his heated eyes and roaming gaze, his assistance is nothing outside of virtuous.

The warmth of the water seeps through my skin, loosening my muscles, and ebbing my troubled thoughts. Of course, those effects... and others... may also be the direct result of Jaden's attention to my cleansing. The fact that I am naked in his presence.

He rolls up his sleeves and glides the sponge, slow and easy, over my skin. "You realize, in this dimension, this form you're in is a representation of yourself. We experience all the senses, all the emotions, but... you needn't be dirty. The filth upon your skin and clothes is how you choose to see yourself. I suspect your appearance is the result of the guilt you harbor."

I frown. He's right, of course, but as awkward and shy as I might be in this situation, I'm not going to complain about his help with my cleanup process... no matter how intimate the process may be. Or maybe because of it.

He massages the shampoo into my hair and rinses it clear, then pronounces me clean. For a moment I think he's going to climb into the tub with me. The look in his eyes suggests he wants to. But then he unfolds the towel and holds it wide, inviting me to step out of the bath and dry off.

I accept his invitation. Allow him to dry my skin and wrap the towel firmly around me.

He takes a step back. "Feel better?"

"I do," I say, summoning boldness into my words and actions. "And I'm ready for more." His brow pinches. "I don't want to take chances waiting for a tomorrow that may or may not come. I want to share my love for you in all the ways. I want..."

I let the towel drop to the floor. He sucks in a sharp breath between his teeth. He's already seen me naked, but never this bold. At least, not in this lifetime.

In case my display isn't communicative enough, I step forward, grab his shirt and tug. Understanding my desire, he helps me pull the shirt over his head, toss it aside. I reach for his buckle, but before I can unfasten it, his hands capture mine, stilling my actions.

"Are you sure?" He holds his gaze high, avoiding the temptation I've unveiled for him.

I lean forward and place a kiss upon his heart. "Utterly and completely."

A low groan vibrates at the back of his throat. A sound that's brimming with lust and desire. My body responds, growing heavy and heated in all my sensitive areas.

With his hands firm at my hips, he pulls me flush against his body. Leaving no space between the press of our bare flesh. His mouth drops over mine, and he ravishes me with his kiss.

His tongue sweeps through me, leaving me dizzy and featherlight.

His fingers skim a line up the center of my back, finding a steady home at the nape of my neck. Every cell in my body trembles at his touch. Holding my lips to his with the clasp of his hand at the back of my skull, he lifts me with his other hand, and I wrap my legs around his waist. He moves us to the bed, settling me softly on the surface. And when he stands over me, his wolf gaze consumes me.

Hand trembling, I reach for his belt and lift my gaze to his.

His hand clamps over mine, stopping me yet again. "No." He shakes his head once, and then smooths his thumb over my jaw, drags it across my lower lip.

"But I want—"

"Let me start." Using his leg, he nudges my knees apart. "Allow me to first worship you as the goddess given gift that you are." He kneels between my legs, his hands coasting over my thighs. "The one who has, time and time again, put the realms before themselves. The one who asks for so little in comparison to what they sacrifice. And the one who owns my heart and soul, wholly and sincerely."

Those words alone bathe me in a riot of tingling sensations. And when his fingers graze my sensitive skin, sliding upward, I concede with a strangled squeak. He proceeds to cherish my body with his mouth, hands, and tongue, showing me all the things he learned in our many lives together, and exploring new ones.

Every touch and kiss is a drug to my system, obliterating my ability to think beyond us... beyond *this*. My heart is pounding, back bowing, fingers clutching, tearing at the sheets. Electricity skates over my skin, fire courses through my veins, my body coming alive like never before. The elements respond, whipping into a frenzy all around us, as our hearts synchronize.

His devotion is patient and perfect. Coaxing away my shyness and eliciting a melody of breathy moans. The graze of his hair against my skin, every nip, pull, plunge, tease, and taste thrusts me into a maddening rush. Heat is growing and churning inside of me. I'm going to ignite into flames.

And then I do, figuratively, as I tip over the edge in wave after wave of glorious release. Jaden holds me through each delicious aftershock, adorning me with butterfly kisses in a plethora of locations.

He settles beside me, kisses the tip of my nose. "You are the most beautiful soul I've ever known." He nips at my earlobe. "All my years and lives belong to you, Ana. You are everything to me."

His kisses trail down my throat, his hands drifting over the swells of my body. With a groan, he returns his lips to mine. "I loved you yesterday. I love you now, today, tomorrow, always and forever. Magically bonded or not, I will always find my way to you, offer you my heart, and make you mine."

He speaks of the magical bond held between us since Deona and Jove. The bond I recently broke. And yet, even without that magic connecting us, he's still here, with me. Loving me. Thoroughly.

Gaea above, he is the earth below my feet and the sun, moon, and stars over my head.

My mouth crashes into his, devouring his words, his sentiments. "I love you," I say and then repay the honor of his worship, exploring and loving him in the manner he showed to me.

And when we finally join, our bodies fitting together in beautiful perfection, I discover deliciously wild and raw sensations I never imagined possible.

Together, we find fantastical bliss, blending and moving with the elements, with our lifetimes of love and passion. No place feels more like home than the comfort of Jaden's embrace... and in his arms, the warmth of his skin around me, beneath my touch, the steady thrum of his heart against my ear, is my everything... my world.

Wrapped around him I find the most peaceful sleep I've ever known.

The bed beneath me jostles, causing me to drag my eyes open with a disgruntled whimper. Jaden's arm tightens around my waist, holding me to his side. One of my legs is tucked between his and my arm is sprawled across his chest. The arm of his that isn't wrapped under and around me shifts into action, drawing lazy images on the back of my shoulder. My body hums with delight.

The distress that pressed upon me, strangling and splintering me, when I first made my way back here now feels like a distant memory. Yes, the experiences and ramifications still hurt... in all kinds of terrible ways... but rest and Jaden have brought me back to a place of reason.

With regards to everything I have gone through, I shall acknowledge my mistakes and misfortunes, do my best to understand what happened and why, learn from the unfolding and outcome, and strive to do better going forward.

"You certainly made yourself at home. And you took your sweet time doing so."

I jolt at Izza's statement, hugging the sheets to my chest and rising to a sit.

Jaden rubs his face. "Thank you for granting us time and your hospitality, Izza." His voice is gravely with sleep.

She smirks. "Did I have a choice?"

Jaden sits, the sheets pooling in his lap. Izza's eyes widen as her gaze snags on his bare chest.

Is it Jaden she sees, or Dharmic? Her relationship experience is likely nil, as she was so young when her time came to an end, and she never got so much as a meet and greet with her Tracer. They only had admiration from afar.

"Anyway..." She clears her throat and averts her gaze. "Time may hold a different meaning here than in the outer realms, but I think I'm ready to join the sisters in the Balance Bringer bond and vacate this place."

Jaden tips his gaze to me and I give him a silent nod. "Very well," he says. "Let's get this thing underway."

Izza grants us privacy so Jaden and I can get dressed. Wanting nothing to do with my soiled and bloody apparel, I make do with what Izza provides—less warrior approved and more maiden appeal. Not that what I wear will matter for long. When I pull my consciousness from this place, I'll return to my physical self, clad in what I was wearing when I first took a seat on the crystal throne.

When Izza returns, Jaden and I are both dressed and ready to go. She strolls across the old cathedral turned private hideaway and plops onto the bed.

"So, how do we do this?" She straightens her skirt and continues to brush her hands across the fabric, avoiding eye contact with Jaden. A hint of blush colors her cheeks.

Jaden pretends not to notice as crosses his arms and turns toward me. "Your brother told me what Madame Marrouske said about the Balance Bringer bonding, and I actually think welcoming Izza into the fold won't be that difficult."

"How so?" I take a seat next to Izza.

"Well..." He rubs the stubble shadowing his chin. "From what I understand, all the ceremonial stuff was less out of necessity and more to help mentally prepare you. The actual bonding itself is a choice. An intention you set here." He leans forward and taps both my and Izza's forehead.

He crouches, bringing his gaze level to ours. "The two of you are essentially the same soul, correct?" I bite my lip and glance at Izza. She's staring back. We both nod. "And you are both immensely gifted by the goddess. You have the power to accomplish this goal. You simply need to embrace the intention and then believe in yourselves as I believe in you."

I lean forward, bracing my forearms on my thighs. "And how do you suppose we do that?"

He pushes his arms out, his flat palms directed at Izza and me. "You are the ones with the ability, and it is you... both of you... who must decide upon the how."

"And you?" Izza asks, nodding to Jaden.

He blinks and presses his hand to his chest. "I piggybacked on Ana to be here. When she returns to the throne room at the palace, I'll return with her."

I reach forward and squeeze his shoulder, and he shoots me a bright-eyed smile.

"So, uh..." He stands. "I'll remove this distraction." He indicates himself. "And let the two of you determine how to bond and return to our friends." With a nod to Izza and a wink in my direction, he turns and walks away.

I watch him leave then turn to Izza. She's already staring at me, waiting. "What do we do first?"

"Not sure." I pull my feet up onto the bed and shift my body to fully face her. "But we're going to figure it out."

She matches my posture, pulling her legs up and turning toward me. "Shall we physically connect?" She presents her palms and I accept. Then begin to tell her how things played out when I bonded with our other sisters... the other versions of us.

We sit facing one another, legs crisscrossed, hands

connected, and heads bowed. We concentrate and chant. Call
the elements to our aid. Nothing happens for a span of what
feels like forever, until I'm too tired to maintain proper thought.
And when my brain can no longer interfere with the process,
things begin to unfold.

WATER AND AIR flow between us. Fire races through my blood,
jumping from me to Izza and back again. Trees lining the walls
of the aging cathedral bend toward us, while vines punch
through the ground, rising and wrapping, creating a cocoon
around us. My body is a frenzy of electricity, popping and
snapping.

"Join us, sister." Deona's voice whispers across our sisterly
bond, her words directed at Izza. "Be one with us. All of us.
You must simply visualize it, believe it is so, and allow it to
become."

Izza's responding unspoken question murmurs in my
thoughts and over my skin. She seeks hand holding, direct guidance... and the bound Balance Bringers within me rise to the
request. My head tips, mind spins, and muscles surrender.

Humming in every cell of my body is the magic responsible
for our creation. The verve sends me reeling. I'm falling out of
space, out of Izza's personally imposed prison, and slipping into
the domain of the Balance Bringer's binding.

Izza is still at my side, clutching my hand, and when the
world stops rushing past us, we're standing in the middle of a
thick mist, cloudy fingers nipping and curling around us. As if
queued by our arrival, wind spawns, brushing away the cover
revealing a polished lake.

I've been here before. I recognize the location from my
Balance Bringer binding rite.

We stand in the middle of the glossy lake, the liquid solid beneath our feet, and its surface as smooth and reflective as a black mirror.

Around the perimeter, cyclones drop from above. They spin into position, taking on the shape of individuals. And as transformation takes place, the whipping wind whispers Izza and my names. The world brightens to a squint-worthy glare and when I blink away the flare, the cyclones are gone, and our many sisters surround us. Izza's hold on my hand tightens.

"Welcome lost sister," Deona says. "We are pleased you are finished hiding and have returned to our collective memory. Please, join us. For you are us and we are you, and we are meant to be one."

Our sisters crowd forward, pushing in tight around Izza and me, placing their hands on our arms and shoulders. Each point of connection electric.

Earth and water pulse at my feet, air vibrates in my ear, and fire sparks against my skin, within the connection of all my many selves. The pressure upon my body gives me the sense of time and space folding in on itself.

The voice of countless Balance Bringers speaks in unison. "Just as the one became three and the three returned to one, the many sisters incarnated in the lifetimes after, once their time is done, willingly merge to reinforce *the one*."

"Yes," Izza says, her response little more than a whisper. "Bring me home."

A sensation pours over me like steaming rain, each droplet packing aspects of Izza. And those aspects—memories and thoughts, a plethora of emotions—seep into my skin... and deeper... into my soul. At my side, Izza's appearance flickers akin to a glitching video.

My connection with Izza intensifies and then settles into a comfortable place among the other sisters bound to me, bound within me. She's no longer at my side but stands among the many previous Balance Bringers surrounding me. Warmth blooms within me, and I've never felt so... so... complete?

Do I feel complete?

Nah, that's not really the word I'm looking for. Something is still missing, something I have yet to discover before I can claim such a state.

Maybe a more appropriate word would be united. My many selves are uniting. Becoming as close as we can to being one... without the magic that Madame Marrouske used on Jaden when, combating Garr's curse, she fused Jaden's many past selves with his current incarnation.

He suggested I do the same—magically fuse my many personifications—and maybe I will. But that's not something to be done here. And this, here and now, feels pretty damn good.

I stretch my shoulders and release a deep sigh.

One by one, my many past versions disappear, funneling into the one chosen avatar for all, Deona. Beyond the two of us, all definition along the horizon blurs, the gray of the sky gradually blending into the inky lake. Sound ceases to exist, the space where Deona and I stand mirroring the properties of a deprivation tank.

"What happens now?" I ask.

Deona shrugs, a hint of a smile on her lips. "You go forth and fulfill our destiny. Now, with the added benefit of Izza's knowledge and experiences in our well of resources."

I was hoping for a more structured answer. Ideally, a bullet point list of what I must do to achieve said destiny. But then, no Balance Bringer before me had to deal with Dreya.

I nod. "And what will become of Izza's created space?" I ask.

Deona shrugs yet again. "Izza's haven was created with

Balance Bringer gifts. You may preserve it or choose to let it fade. What becomes of the space is up to you."

I nod at that, unable to think of any reason to conserve the space. Izza no longer needs it.

"Your Tracer anchors your physical form." Deona says of Jaden. "The connection between the two of you working like a tether to lead you home. Should you still *require* a line to lead you."

I shake my head. "Jaden is no longer *my* Tracer. I released him from his magical bond."

A heaviness settles into my heart with those words, and I drop my gaze to my feet, stare at our reflection in the water for a heartbeat before returning my attention to Deona.

"So wise and yet so blind." Appearing to be holding back a laugh, Deona fiddles with her braid. "He never needed a magical bond to be our Tracer. He chose to be at our side. Not forced, but a choice of the heart."

My jaw slackens as I consider Jaden, Jove, and every Tracer in between. Jove, the first Tracer made the choice of his own accord, but would the others have chosen the same had magic not been involved? I don't know about all the others, but after what we shared hours ago, I can't help but believe those words are true of Jaden.

My heart thumps a heavy beat. I want to return to him, the true, physical version of him.

"Go to him," Deona whispers. "Your reason to be here is no longer."

Yes, it is. My messed-up timeline alteration has been corrected and Izza has been found, saved, united with all of the Balance Bringer sister incarnations. Our surroundings brighten in color and glow to match my current lift in mood.

I brush the wild hairs from my face and close my eyes, picture the throne room as it was when I settled on the seat of power. I envision the massive hole in the floor and the ginormous crystal labyrinth in the exposed cavern below. Taking a deep centering breath, I visualize returning in the moments after I sat down, and Jaden anchored himself to me.

The light behind my eyes is shifting and softening, my consciousness shifting back through space to my physical self.

"Ana." Deona's voice hums in my ear. "Since the first Balance Bringer, the original three sisters, no other incarnation has had the full unification of all." All Balance Bringer versions throughout the ages. "That is bound to mean something... make a difference. But..." She pauses. "You are not yet fully realized. One of the elements has constantly managed to evade us."

I'm missing an element?

My eyes pop open, but there is nothing but utter darkness and Deona is gone.

TWENTY-ONE

A hard slap against my cheek snaps my head to the side. A blinding light speckled with silver spots explode across my vision.

Ouch.

"Wha..." My voice is a tiny wisp, chalky with disuse, and my delivery sounds less like an attempted word and more like an escape of air.

I blink away my visual discomfort, bringing my surroundings into view.

Deona, and the place of the Balance Bringer binding—the conductive layer of water or shallow lake, where I stood a mere second ago, is gone. I have successfully returned to my intended destination—the decimated throne room within my original timeline. Every point of connection between my body and the crystal seat beneath me buzzes with energy. And, unexpectedly, my mom is in my face, doing I-don't-know-what. Trying to break me free from a trance? Rather harshly, too.

She swings her hand back, preparing to deliver a second slap. "Wake up, Ana!" Her arm shoots forward.

I raise a hand to stop her action and, in my peripheral view, catch the hint of movement—a palm lifting from my shoulder. A breath later, a masculine arm punches forward, working in tandem with mine to halt my mom's next strike.

Jaden. My heart flutters at the confirmation of his presence.

Our connection, both physical and emotional, allowed him to follow me to Izza's dimensional hideaway, so it makes sense that he returned at the same time as me.

"Mom?" My voice cracks. Lifting my free hand, I rub the side of my face, my skin burning at the point of her slap's harsh contact.

Mom, the immortal warrior commander, jerks straight, her arm relaxing, and attention sharpening. "Finally." The word is a sigh of relief. "I've been trying to break you out of your trance for far too long."

What is *far too long*? I don't vocalize the question. Instead, I address her clear sense of urgency. "What's going on?"

I push to my feet, breaking my electric connection with the crystal throne. My body aches with exhaustion and from too much time spent sedentary because, even though Jaden and I were active in Izza's private dimensional hideaway, it was our spiritual or soul selves that made the journey. Our physical forms remained here, in the throne room, unmoving.

Mom's chest heaves, her gaze drifting over me. "We depart soon. You" —Her attention shifts over my shoulder to Jaden— "both of you, must ready yourselves for travel. Your brother needs immediate medical attention, and I want to avoid delay. I presently have the healers loading him onto one of the transport wagons."

At the mention of Ryland, my thoughts become sodden with my last vision of him—deceased, his head on a spike. I shake the images away and remind myself that was in a life that no longer exists. Now that I have returned to my original time-line, my brother may be in dire need of medical assistance, but he is still alive. And, right now, that is everything.

Memories of the battle against Dreya, the cyclone of water exploding up through the massive hole in the floor and whirling through the room, consume me for half a second. The god Proteus retracted the gift of water and ice he'd granted Dreya so many years ago, and now, she can no longer wield the element. Unfortunately, the god did not act before Ryland lost several fingers, crushed a leg, fractured his ribs, and damaged his arm. How much can an immortal warrior recover from?

"Will the healers be able to help him?" I can't even imagine what that physical cost will do to his mental state. "Some of my magic now courses through his veins so maybe—"

Her head shakes sharply. "Based on what we've observed, your magic hasn't granted him any regenerative properties with regards to limbs lost." She falls silent for a moment, appearing to compose herself. "His ribs and arm are healing quicker than usual, which is good. As for his fingers and leg..." She sucks back a breath. "The healers are keeping him in a deep sleep, and I intend to have them work with the Gaurdoone black-smiths to fashion Ry a passable fix."

Like prosthetic limbs made of steel?

"Mom..." I blink back a tear threatening to escape the corner of my eye and nibble on my lower lip. My gaze flickers past her shoulder for half a second, as I attempt to picture Ry in an induced slumber with Zarah vigilant at his side. "Do you really think that will work?"

"It must," she replies. "He's too young of a warrior to lose his fight now."

I clamp my mouth shut. By the standards I grew up with in the outer world and the United States, my brother would be considered an old man. But here, as a true-blooded immortal warrior, he's still young, and I'm not going to argue my mom's point.

"Now," she continues. "I understand that you may want to examine this space further..." With a slight gesture of her hand, she motions to the exposed cavern situated below the throne room. Fanning out in all directions beneath the palace floor is a forest of monstrous crystal columns thrumming with energy. "But I would prefer not to leave you here, no matter the number of warriors I end up assigning to safeguard this discovery."

I cross my arms. "You're right. I would like to explore some more." I suspect that it was because of the generated power within the crystal cavern, and the throne's connection to that power, that I was able to move my consciousness through time and space to the location of Izza's hideaway.

"As I expected." She heaves a sigh. "But I want you with me, as we not only need to discuss what transpired here but must also decide upon how we will handle Dreya and her influence across the realm."

Another thing I can't argue with, deciding on a plan on how to best deal with Dreya. I nod and stifle a stubborn yawn.

The god Proteus intended to banish Dreya to a millennium of solitude, but she was quick, supernaturally quick. Within the swirl of darkness she created, I suspect she managed to avoid his entrapment and somehow slipped away. The yank on Dohlan's chain and his subsequent disappearance tends to support that theory.

Dreya may actually be more obsessed with Dohlan than Kaia is.

Jaden steps forward and wraps an arm around my shoulders, pulling me from my tangled thoughts. "We'll be ready," he says and tips his head at my mom.

She glances between us, nods, then turns and strides away.

I watch her depart through the open throne room doors. She walks right past Mo, who's leaning against the doorframe, her pale-eyed gaze steady on me. Her new, pallid appearance is a shocking reminder of my magic's unknown capability.

Dreya had turned Mo's heart to ice, and she practically died. Maybe she did. And I'm not exactly certain what I did, or how I did it, but now Mo lives. Even if her revived self is drained of pigmentation.

I press my palm against the stabbing pain splintering though my chest. My actions have unintentionally hurt so many people. Staring straight ahead, I focus on my breathing.

"Hey." Jaden's fingers trail a line along the length of my arm. "Do you want to talk about what happened in the other timeline you experienced?"

"Eventually. But"—I nod toward Mo—"I think there's something I must see to first."

He dips his head into the crook of my neck, his nose and breath grazing my skin. I shiver and flash through memories of the intimate things we did only hours before. "You do what you need to do, and I'll be here for you. Just don't overexert yourself. You used a lot of energy taking us to the other dimension and back, and I can see that you're tired."

God and Gaea, I hope I don't look *too* tired. Absentmindedly, I pat my fingertips to the underside of my eyes, as if I might be able to feel bags or dark circles.

"Don't worry. Nothing can dim your loveliness," Jaden whispers.

His words suggest he can still read my emotions. Maybe he can. When I destroyed the magic binding him to me, I'm not sure exactly what changed with his ability, and that's a conversation we should probably have... eventually.

He places a featherlight kiss against my temple. "To me, you will always be the loveliest sight in all of creation."

Weaving my fingers with his, I squeeze his hand, and plant my lips on his. Kiss him soft and quick but with undying gratitude for him being in my life. "You are too good for me."

"Not even remotely," he replies. "We're ideal for each other. Always have been. Always will be. Now, go mend what is bruised."

What is bruised is my relationship with Mo, and I'm not sure how to mend that, but I'll give it my best try.

I circumvent the cavity consuming the center of the room, and as I do, a chilled updraft from the hole plays with strands of my hair and fills the throne room with the scent of damp earth. My gaze flickers from Mo for a mere second, only once or twice, to verify my footing and take in the host of gemstone pillars below. Although the water that previously flooded the cavern has fully retreated, droplets glisten on all the stone surfaces.

Broken shards cascade around several of the massive crystals, marking the locations of where my family members were entombed. But I can't think about that right now. Mo deserves all my focus.

She pushes away from the doorframe, uncrossing her arms, and straightening her back. Her chest rises, yet her expression gives no indication of her mood. I swallow hard against my indecision. Indecision regarding how to best apologize and bare my heart.

I hate that I'm the cause of her condition. Had it not been for me, she never would have been here. Never would have found herself going toe to toe with wicked Aunt Dreya. And never would have been transformed into whatever she is now... albino or something more? Whatever I did to her, it's clearly different from what I did to Ry when I saved him from the poison coursing through his system.

"Mo. I'm..." I bite down on my lower lip. "I..." My shoulders droop. Why is finding the words so hard?

Her eyes tighten. "You changed me. I feel different." Her delivery is a statement of fact rather than an accusation.

My eyes burn with the sensation of tears once again threatening to break free. Is my reaction born of grief for Mo... possibly aided by my exhaustion? Or am I threatening to fold beneath a coalescence of everything? The countless deaths and losses, the endless ramifications of my actions and the impossible tasks awaiting me.

Gaea above, some part of me wants to crawl into a bed, curl up in a ball, and hide under the covers for a millennium. Only, today, I'm not giving in to that side of myself.

"I'm so, so sorry." I bow my head and shake. "I don't know what I did, but I was afraid I was losing you, and"—I raise my gaze—"I couldn't stand the thought of it. Losing you. But I didn't mean... Did I... Can you...?"

"Shift?" she offers. Yeah, that... to begin with. I nod, to which she shrugs in response. "I have yet to try. Regardless, I am thankful you did whatever it was you did. I was not prepared to die, and you still need me to keep you on the proper path when it comes to Sir Dohlan."

The desire to laugh cuts to the pool of emotions sloshing through my soul, warming my chest.

"You like him," I tease, even as something inside of me stiffens at the mere mention of Dohlan's name. My legs shift as if I mean to turn and walk away. But to where and why?

As if in response to my internal question, Kaia whispers into my thoughts, *"We need to get to Dohlan. We must help him."*

I shiver, recalling the last time I saw him—weak and chained, a clawed hole in his chest. The image cracks something inside of me, and I take a step back, but I manage to stop myself before I move farther away from Mo. I *do* ache for Dohaln's state, and I *do* want to help him, but Kaia is the one who is filled with desire to race to his rescue and once again fights for control of my physical form. She has me wavering between immediately chasing after Dreya, versus waiting to draft a proper plan.

I wobble, yanking all control of my body and mind far from my sister's interference. My internal struggle leaves me momentarily lightheaded. And in my moment of frailty, a yawn escapes.

Mo reaches forward and grabs my upper arm, her analytical stare intense. "Are you all right?"

My head bobs in an uncommitted nod as I wheeze a strangled cough.

Her eyes soften. "You are worried about him," she laments, her voice soothing. "So am I."

I frown. Sure, I have concerns, major concerns, regarding Dohlan, but I suspect Mo is picking up on my exhaustion, coupled with Kaia's attempted takeover. And maybe I would speak frankly, but...

Footsteps behind me mark someone's approaching path around the side of the throne room. The advance captures my attention even as Mo's gaze shifts to a point beyond me. What she sees draws a smirk to her face. A second later, Jaden's fingers trail a soft line across my lower back.

"Is everything good here?" he asks, his voice low. He dips his face toward my temple, and I automatically lean into him. "You appeared momentarily unsettled, extraordinarily weary, and..." He tilts his head. "And I got the feeling that..."

I was going to run?

Jaden doesn't finish his statement, nor am I given the opportunity to respond. Mo interrupts our exchange.

"Holy Gaea." Her eyebrows shoot up and her mouth drops open. "You finally did the deed. Consummated your relationship."

Heat flashes up my neck and blooms out across my cheeks. No doubt accompanied by a vivid shade of pink.

She bites her lower lip attempting, and failing, to hide a wild grin. For one not involved in the "consummating," she appears far too excited at the prospect of confirming her suspicion.

But is it mere suspicion? Maybe something shows on my face, or in my eyes, possibly a we-did-it glow between Jaden and me, that gives away the truth of our recent connection?

Jaden chokes a laugh. "Oh, Mo." He shakes his head. "What kind of gentleman would ever entertain responding to such a question?"

Her smile brightens, eyes twinkling.

Oh, yeah. She totally knows.

"Well, then... I guess congratulations are in order. And this is a good thing, right?" she says. "After all, you two are meant to be. You have always been destined."

Although her words are a spoken truth, I awkwardly shift my body weight and clear my throat. A flush of heat across my skin suggests I may possibly be blushing. I've never been good at this type of open communication and I'm definitely not ready to talk about the done deed or the change in Jaden and my relationship status with anyone other than Jaden. Plus, internally, Kaia still seeks to drag me toward Dohlan. If she were to succeed, that could create all kinds of complications.

Jaden's attention swings from Mo to me, but anything he's about to say is halted by a troop of warriors streaming past us into the throne room. They move in a line, taking up positions around the perimeter of the room.

I don't know what it is about the appearance of the warriors that triggers more concerns for Dohlan, but Kaia gains a tiny ounce of control and I reflexively take yet another step away.

I close my eyes and take a deep, settling breath. "Stop it," I murmur to her impulses. "We need to be smart, not impulsive. And... preferably... be much more rested when we eventually implement whatever action we decide upon."

When I open my eyes, Jaden and Mo are staring at me, their expressions filled with questions and concern.

"Come on," I say to them and move past the overflow of warriors, making my way out of the throne room and into the outer hall. Come into direct eye contact with Raundel.

"Deona," he says, once again calling me by the name of my first incarnation.

"Ana," I correct. *Again.*

He scoffs, as if to infer which name he uses is inconsequential. "We plan to depart in twenty to thirty minutes, and this time you will not sneak off on your own."

"Twenty minutes you say?" I glance at Jaden and Mo. Mo stares at me expectantly, but Jaden merely tips his head as if he knows what's going through my mind and he's silently adding his support to my intentions. "I'll be ready," I assure the large white elf.

I move to step around him, heading not toward the main entrance, but in the opposite direction.

He grabs my arm, halting my retreat. "Where are you going?"

I meet his gaze. "I have twenty minutes, right?" I don't wait for his response before continuing. "I'll be ready, I just need to verify something first."

I grab Jaden's hand, making sure he is with me... as if that fact was ever in question... then tug my other arm, attempting to free myself from Raundel's hold.

His grip tightens, refusing to let me go. "What must you verify?"

"That there's truth in the memories I now harbor."

"You doubt your memories?" he asks.

"They're not mine," I reply. "The memories were gifted to me and belong to another." Memories supplied by another Zarah but belonging to Dreya.

Raundel's brow furrows. "How?"

"The extraordinary gifts of a gifted time chronicler." I turn my attention to Jaden. "I'll tell you all about it later," I swear, then glance at Mo. "You, too."

Raundel grunts and releases my arm. "I shall go with you on whatever this errand of yours may be."

Of course, he will. I take off with purpose and don't look back. Merely jerk my chin over my shoulder in acknowledgement. "You really don't need to. I told I'd be ready, and I have no plans to skip out on my mom." Or my brother.

Jaden squeezes my hand. "And I'll hold her to that promise."

"Me, too," Mo chimes.

"Be that as it may," Raundel retorts, his tone filled with cynicism. "I prefer not to take chances while Dreya's location is unverified, and you've proven time and time again to be challenged when it comes to following orders or making safe choices."

Jerk. I don't bother to argue that Dreya is likely far from here, licking her wounded ego and coming to terms with the loss of her water and ice magic. Even though she's far from feeble, as she still controls the darkness... a power I now understand she got from Sol.

Not for one second am I going to make the mistake of assuming Proteus successfully banished Dreya.

As a parting gift from the *other* Zarah, I remember much of the castle's layout from my alternative timeline. Only, as I navigate down halls and around corners, I'm not guided by those particular memories, but by recollections of a young Dreya... before she became the evil villain we now know.

When Dreya's elemental ability was rescinded, the snow and frost that covered the many palace surfaces began to liquify. Everything around us is now damp, wet with melted ice. Walls, floors, fixtures, and furnishings. Yet, as I drive forward, the surrounding conditions aren't what I see.

I'm witnessing moments from Dreya's past. Moments that played out in the palace corridors. Casual conversations with her handmaidens, as they push her along the path in her wheelchair. Tense confrontations with her parents, or her brother... my father. She calls him Mardy, just like she had in the alternate timeline. I recall the memories as if they're my own.

At a wide junction, I glance down a hallway leading to the library. I recall the ice encrusted location from a previous, out-of-body encounter with Dreya. Turning my gaze up the stairs, I envision the bedroom where we faced an infected version of Gitta, the young elf from Madame Marrouske's sanctuary. That room once belonged to Dreya, before she was *gifted* by Proteus.

I turn away and head toward the Finvarra wing and the High Lady's chamber—home to countless years of Dreya's torment. When I reach the double doors to the once opulent room, Dreya's gilded cage, I hesitate. For a moment I'm unsure if I want to follow through on my original intention. The more I know about these years of Dreya's history, the harder it is for me to divorce that part of her from the monster I must vanquish.

"What are we doing?" Mo asks.

Jaden shoots her a pointed look and shakes his head, then says to me. "You are strong enough."

Strong enough for what? To set my guilt aside when facing off against Dreya? I don't believe that's what he means, but I don't ask for clarification. I suck back a deep breath and shove open the doors.

The past immediately slams into me.

TWENTY-TWO

I stumble back a step, a waterfall of Dreya's memories cascading over me. Dreya visiting with family, interacting with handmaidens, and meeting with... with...

My gaze darts from point to point around the room, images from the past flaring to life in my mind's eye. Young Dreya curled up on the bed, crying. Taking meals at the table, alone, so often alone, while staring out the large picture window to the world beyond. A world made inaccessible to her. Her uncontained emotions blasting the room with an explosion of ice. And her finding refuge in a hidden cabinet in the far wall.

Bolting into action, I dash across the room and yank the dusty curtains to the side exposing the small door with a broken handle.

"It's real," I whisper, my heart quickening. The hidden cabinet is real... the memories are real.

But of course they are.

Discovering newborn energy in an adrenaline spike, I spin back to the room.

Jaden, Mo, and Raundel stand in the doorway watching me.

My gaze swings from my friends to the massive canopy bed. Something warm and fluttery swells within me, and I move to the bed's side as if on automatic pilot. My fingers drag a delicate line across the aged and fraying fabric.

A male covertly visited me... I mean, visited Dreya... here in this room. My heart flutters at the recollection. Was Sol the visitor? *No.* I shake my head absentmindedly. If Sol is the Sun in the Sun and Moon, then it was the Moon who secreted into this chamber in the middle of the night. The dark-haired male I, Ana, met when I stepped through time and made the misguided adjustment of that particular event. The adjustment that led to a timeline I hope to never revisit.

For a flash of a second, I recall Sol skewered and bleeding out on the floating island. The darkened infection raining from the landmass and spreading the contagion across the realm. The vision is immediately replaced with a bright-eyed version of him sitting on a wall, his legs dangling over the side. He tosses me a devilish grin.

My heart squeezes.

Am I experiencing the emotions attached to *her* memories? Memories heady with curiosity, loneliness, desire, need.

I suck back a harsh breath. Nothing about being here, experiencing Dreya's past through her eyes, helps prepare my mind for successfully vanquishing her.

I can't reconcile the version of Dreya that lived in this room with the one who now hunts me, subjugates Dohlan with such cruelty, and is actively destroying the land with infection. Even cursed by Proteus, I witness kindness in her interactions.

Where did everything go so incredibly wrong?

My head swivels to the window.

The room hosts a view of the lake. The very one where she

had first met the water god and received his *gift*. But that land-mark is not what has drawn my gaze. I seek the palace garden located a level below, between this room and the lake.

When Mo, Bree, Gitta and I came to this place in search of Proteus, during my race to the lake I'd run through the garden and jumped over the surrounding wall. I now suspect...

Yeah. The more I consider the possibility, the more certain I become.

My muscles tense, preparing for my next action before I realize what I intend to do. Then my feet are shifting and, despite my looming burnout, I'm rushing from the room. I tear past my friends—Mo's confused expression, Raundel's scruti-nizing gaze, and Jaden's patient peer. Their quick footfalls affirm their continued follow.

"What are you doing?" Mo asks from behind me. "What am I missing?"

Not responding, I leave each of them to their own specula-tions... for now. I'll likely share my thoughts soon enough.

I hurry down halls and around corners, sliding on the wet floor and bracing myself against walls to maintain my upright stature. When I burst through the double doors and into the garden, once vibrant with color but now brown and barren, I skid to a halt... a new punch of adrenaline fueling me.

At a rusted table and chairs situated several feet into the long-ago oasis I momentarily envision Dreya's handmaidens gossiping over tea. The two females spent time out here with Dreya on a regular basis, but Dreya tended to occupy herself elsewhere within the garden. Somewhere along the back wall.

I scan the length of the structure, my gaze snagging on a location beside a tree growing too close to the barrier. My mind immediately overlays the memory of Sol sitting atop the brick partition, legs dangling over the side, with the current visual before me. Closing the distance, I brush my fingers against the rough surface.

This is it, the place where Sol and Dreya met. Where...

My thoughts fill with memories of Dreya's exile and my gaze turns south.

I suck back a sharp breath and spin back to the garden doors, to my patiently waiting friends.

"Sol," I declare. "He's the key to Dreya's shift into darkness. And I think I know where Dreya may have gone."

WE RETURN to the grand entrance with minutes to spare. Two, by my estimation. A few warriors move through the immense space with purpose, but the vast majority are found when we step outside. The masses are... for the most part... ready and waiting to head out.

Raundel marches past Mo, Jaden, and me and proceeds toward the back of the convoy.

Noting our arrival, Bree breaks away from the formation and jogs toward me. "There you are," she says. "I've been wondering where you were."

I throw my arms around her and hug her tight. "I missed you." More than I expected, given how little we knew each other before the day Jaden showed up at the Farmer's market.

Our quest to get to the lake here, planning to fight and stop Dreya, has been the most intense and relationship-bonding of our time spent together. Until this moment, I hadn't realized how much I had come to appreciate her camaraderie.

Bree snickers. "You missed me already?" She pulls back, a humored smile tugging to her lips. "What's it been... an hour, maybe two? I wasn't aware I'd made such a huge impression."

"Ha. Ha." I pat her shoulders and step away. I don't bother

to tell her what was likely only hours for her was far longer for me. We'll find time for that conversation later. My gaze moves over the preparing procession—warriors on horses, in wagons, and on foot taking up positions behind the mounted troops.

"I'll get us some steeds," Jaden says and, with a reassuring smile, starts walking away.

"Jaden," Bree calls after him and he glances back. "I believe the commander has reserved positions for the two of you beside her at the front."

He nods his thanks and leaves. Makes his way toward the lead.

I rub the back of my neck and return my attention to Bree. "What can you quickly tell me about the others, Ry in particular?"

In an attempt to control my worry and anxiety, I casually tap my chest... or at least I hope my actions appear casual. Whether Bree or Mo notice or not, they show no reaction. Mo's gaze sweeps over the many warriors moving around us, her observation snagging somewhere to my right.

Bree motions in the opposite direction. "See that huge wagon over there?" She swings her arm and flicks a finger toward an enormous carriage. Large wheels in the back, slightly smaller wheels in the front, windows all the way around the mobile enclosure. A canopied driver seat on the roof already hosts two individuals, and six anxious horses are harnessed to the rig. "Ryland is being transported in that beast. Zarah and the head healer ride with him."

Probably the most comfortable accommodation available within the convoy. I clutch Bree's hand, zeroing her full focus on me. "You can now access Madame Marrouske's power, right?"

"Her power *is* my power," Bree corrects.

Good. Good good.

"Then I'd like you in the carriage with my brother, doing whatever you can to not only keep him comfortable, but... if possible... improve his state. Maybe even heal him."

"I don't think I can heal him, but all right," she agrees.

She turns as if to head for the carriage, but I don't release her hand, so she watches me expectantly. Ignoring her scrutiny, I nibble on my lower lip, stare at the wagon, and envision my brother waking from his induced coma only to discover he has artificial limbs made of metal.

At least, I think that is what my mom intends to have done.

My heart feels twelve times heavier than usual. And my limbs... they feel packed with sand.

Gaea above, I could use a nap.

I shake the notion away and heave a deep breath. "And how is Zarah, the others?"

Bree's lips pull tight. "Zarah is holding up rather well, all things considered. As for the others—"

"They are over there," Mo gestures in the direction I'd seen Raundel venture. Bree and I look to where Mo is pointing. Lobrka, Raundel, and Al are all gathered around a slumbering Gitta.

"Al?" I ask, recalling the spike that had been driven through her shoulder.

"Sore, but managing," Bree replies. "She said that Gitta is the closest to her kind she has ever met, and she wanted to be present for the young female in her time of need."

Because Gitta is infected, and Gitta, like Al, is a being with ghosting ability.

My muscles tighten. "I should help." I can't explain why, but a sense of responsibility for Gitta's condition weighs heavily upon me. I pivot and stride toward the infected elf. My newly found friend.

"But you can't," Bree says, reaching for me.

I slip from her grip and keep moving. "And why is that?" I toss her a glance over my shoulder.

It's Mo who answers. "Because we know what you intend to do. A process proven to be intense, physically, and mentally demanding. But you are already painfully fatigued."

I sigh. Stop. Drop my head, then turn to face her. She folds her arms across her chest and pins me with an edged glare.

"You need to rest," she pushes.

"Yeah, well... I can rest on the road."

Ignoring any further protest from Mo and Bree, I march directly to my intended destination. Stride past the attending guards and up to the stern-looking elves flanking Gritta's side—Raundel, Lobrka, and Al. Although, I have yet to confirm if Al is an elf or something other.

"Bringer," Al says by way of greeting, the look in her eyes weary. Lobrka and Raundel merely narrow their gazes and grace me with quick head dips.

My attention glances over all of them, then beyond them and the lines of warriors, to the once grand palace. "Can we move Gitta away from everyone else. To someplace where it's easier for me to isolate the elements? Because I intend to cleanse her of this ugly infection."

My fingers clench and release, wiggle restlessly. Previously, I've succeeded in cleansing myself, Mo, and Zarah of darkness, but I haven't tried to access any of my abilities since returning from the alternate timeline.

I am as I was, I remind myself. I don't need proof to know I'm not the unrealized Balance Bringer from the other timeline. I'm as skilled as I was before that now-corrected mistake.

Raundel grunts while Lobrka raises his chin toward Bree. "What do you think of this, mystic?" he asks, as if her opinion trumps mine.

Bree grimaces with a hint of a shrug. "I'm not wild about

the idea, but I'm not going to stop her. We would all benefit from Gitta's cleansing."

"Why are you not *wild* about the idea?" Raundel says.

Bree raises a hand, waving it over me. "Because she's clearly drained," she says, at the same time Mo blurts, "She is already too tired."

"Don't listen to them." I brush the comments aside. "I have enough energy to handle this task. So, let's move Gitta out of the way and get this done. After all, we are up against the clock." We're supposed to be hitting the road, like, now.

Al's shoulders loosen, and she drops her arms to her side. "It will make travel easier if Gitta is healed."

"That it will," Raundel agrees, to which Lobrka nods, an uncommitted frown pressed to his mouth.

The convoy has yet to show signs of forward movement, so my colleagues grudgingly agree to my request. Together we move an unconscious Gitta away from the poised troop. As an extra security, we place the walls of the palace between us and everyone else and situate ourselves several feet inside the depressing garden.

Gitta is laid out on the ground, and I kneel at her side, holding her hand in my own. Everyone else stands in a silent circle around us.

I take a swift survey of the many darkened veins webbing Gitta's skin, then raise my gaze to meet the others. "Unless you guys wish to get soaked, I recommend seeking cover inside."

Bree is the first to move, followed by Al, then Mo. Raundel and Lobrka hold their ground.

"Water from the sky does not concern us," Lobrka states.

"And we choose to stay close," Raundel adds. "Just in case—"

"Ana." Jaden rushes into the garden. "What are you doing?"

I give him a haggard smile. "I would think that would be obvious."

"Well, yes." He returns my smile with a knowing smirk, his approach slowing to a casual stride forward. "But why would you be doing this without me?"

A grunt of a laugh slips from my lips. A second later, my mom follows Jaden into the garden, and my expression falls. Any words fail me as a thick knot lodges at the base of my throat. If she is here, there's either something wrong with Ry, or it's likely time to go. But I can't go. Not until I first see to Gitta.

"Is Ry..." The words finally break free from my clogged throat.

"No change," she replies, her scrutinizing gaze taking in every detail. "I'm here for you. Whatever you are about to do, I don't want you doing it. We don't have the time."

"We have the time if we want to have the time," I retort and return my attention to Gitta. "But, for Ry's sake, you go ahead and head out. Our little group here will catch up before you know it."

Jaden settles at my side, showing complete confidence in my intentions and subsequent follow through. He rubs a soft hand up and down my arm and glances back at my mom. "We all want to see warrior Ryland receive the necessary care, but he is not the only warrior currently in need of a tending."

"Of course not," she retorts. "But—"

"Gaea above." I groan, drag a deep breath through my chest, and throw my free hand wide, palm to the sky. As in previous times, I beseech Gaea's help and guidance with Gitta's healing. "Bless us with your mending touch."

I don't entertain my mom's argument about placing my health above Gitta's. An argument playing out in the background, beyond my internal concentration. And an argument Mom insists is not based on any family favoritism, but due to the fact that I'm the Balance Bringer, and I mustn't be so relaxed with my personal care. She has not witnessed the Balance Bringer I have become, and it's time she understood I'm no longer just her little girl. I'm Gaea's proxy.

With one hand gripping the elf's sleeping form, and the other raised in earnest to the goddess above, I close my eyes and reach out with all the energetic strength I'm able to summon. Then I tap into the elements coursing through Gitta—the water in her body, the air flowing through her lungs, her blood.

I make the same requests as I did when I cleansed Zarah. *Take the infection from her and give it to me. Please, Gaea. Give. It. To me.*

Jaden squeezes my other arm in a mild show of support as rain falls from the sky in fat, heavy droplets, pleating my skin like hundreds of tiny stones.

"No, Ana." My mom lunges for me. "I said not—"

My raised hand swings toward my mom. Wind promptly responds, sailing through the garden, shoving her toward the double doors, thus putting distance between my mom and me. The element holds her back and prevents her from interfering further.

A cold and clammy sensation slithers from Gitta's skin onto mine. It sinks through to my blood, casting shadows over my soul. I shiver, start to shake, my body exploding with goose bumps.

Gitta wheezes, a darkened wisp expelling from her mouth. She doesn't wake. Doesn't even stir. But her form clears. The darkness that webbed across her body now creeps over my skin and, unlike previous times with the cleansing, the transfer carries impressions from a handful of Gitta's murkier memories. Most prominent among them, a too-young Gitta standing amongst the many trees of the woodlands, lost and alone, tears making tracks in the dirt covering her face.

I'm reminded of the time in the church parking lot, when a splatter of water element granted me momentarily access to the memories of my high school bully, Skylar. I don't want to experience that kind of intimate sharing again. Especially not with Gitta.

I shudder. Then my body sways, infection and exhaustion sweeping over me. Jaden's grip on me tightens, both supporting and holding me steady. I sense other helping hands anchoring me, as well—Mo and Bree.

My mom barks my name, her inflection firm with authority, and possibly a tad of concern. But after all I've been through, I've grown into my own and she no longer holds the same sway over me.

Still... I pull away from Gitta, breaking our connection, and terminating her memory share. As well as eliminating any chance the infection has of returning to her system.

My body is cold and weighted, my blood moving sluggishly through my veins. The infection has been cleansed from Gitta, but it's now making a new home within me. A situation I'll soon change. Because even in my exhausted state, my body knows what to do. Knows what it *must* do. The memory of the time the darkness lingered in my system is strong. How it affected me, the pain experienced when Azure attempted to purge it from me... yeah, I'm opting for no repeats.

I push away from Jaden, Mo, and Bree, and anyone else who stands nearby. Throwing my arms wide, I make it clear no one is to come close. Familiar with what happens next, Jaden helps keep others at a distance.

I stumble and fall, pick myself up. Stagger on heavy legs, creating more and more space between me and the people I care about. The fourth element is churning in my core. Its breath warming to life and ready to tackle the job.

"Okay," I mumble under my breath. The element thrums over my skin in response.

A heartbeat later, fire erupts in my veins.

I collapse forward, onto my hands and knees as the element races through my blood, spreading to my muscles, tendons, skin. The heat has my body ablaze, and everything burns. Burns like wildfire. Burns the infection at a cremation level until all that exists is miniscule dust particles, dissolved within the rain or carried away by the wind.

The ongoing downpour crashes over me, and the heat pouring off my body turns to steam. When the last of the steam dissipates, the rain dwindles to a trickle and the air element releases my mom.

Before I can express the need or want for help, Jaden is at my side and I'm leaning into him. "Thank you," I say, voice soft, my words of gratitude intended for him alone. I lift my gaze to Raundel and Lobrka who stand opposite me, on the other side of Gitta. "She's clean now. Once she wakes from the induced sleep she should be good."

Raundel scoops her into his arms like she's light as a rag doll. "You have our gratitude."

"And you? How are you?" The question comes from my mom.

With a heavy sigh working my chest, I turn my attention to her for the first time since I began the process of healing Gitta. "I'm fine, Mom."

Her wide gaze takes in Gitta as Raundel strides past her. She then rakes her attention over me. "But you're—"

"Tired. I know. Everyone keeps pointing that out to me," I say. "But that's nothing a little downtime won't fix. And since we're supposed be heading out any minute now"—I grin—"I expect I'll get *plenty* of downtime sitting on the back of my horse."

She frowns. "Sitting on the back of a horse is not the kind of regenerative rest you require."

A dull throb resonates across my frontal lobe. Because of her, because of what I just did for Gitta, because of my already existing exhaustion. I shake my head and sigh. "It will suffice," I reply.

The convoy's departure is already behind schedule, so any further combative words are shelved for later. We all make our way to our assigned mode of transportation in relative silence. Bree joins my brother and Zarah in the carriage, Raundel and Al take positions beside the horse drawn cart carrying Gitta, and the rest of us mount our horses.

By the time the mass of horses and warriors have traveled beyond the palace compound and are making their way along the weathered route leading toward the closest port, my thoughts have melted into the churning sound of squeaky wagon wheels and hooves on dirt. If anyone near me is talking, I don't hear them. There's only the hum and thrum of movement. Lots and lots of endless movement.

I don't know how far we've traveled when the light fades and the world around us dims. Nor do I have a clue how long it has been when my eyelids grow heavy or the surface beneath me begins to slide. And when a hand glides over my arm and wraps around my wrist, I know I should look, but I don't. The hold is torn from me too quickly. I fall away from the touch, tumble off my horse, and hit the hard ground.

TWENTY-THREE

With a disgruntled moan, I tug against the glue sealing my eyelids closed. The glue being a combination of weighted exhaustion and crusted sleep dust. I'm laid out on my back, and all around me are the sounds of endless hooved movement, squeaky and groaning wheeled carts, and the quiet chatter of tired warriors.

We're making our way to Maitias Garrison, an immortal warrior compound. I remember that being my mom's plan. And I had been riding horseback at her side, until...

My eyes tear open. I start to sit up. "What happ—" The spaces around me blur and whirl. Halting my sitting progress mid-lift, I suck back a sharp breath, and then release a whimper.

"Hey-hey," Bree's gentle voice murmurs from some point near or around my knees. A tender nudge of a hand against my midsection guides me to lying flat on my back. "You're not yet ready. Your body needs more rest."

Maybe, but I'm not going to concede to the command because when has my body *not* needed more rest. In a slow and careful movement, I prop myself up onto my elbows as my surroundings at last come into focus. "Where am I?"

Bree's brow lifts. "You don't remember?"

My gaze glances over the wooden walls and interrupting ring of windows. Before I can fashion a solid thought, much less voice a response, someone else interjects into the conversation.

"You passed out. Fell off your horse." I gingerly swivel my head to Zarah. She's sitting on a bench that runs the length of the carriage I've managed to end up in. "Good thing you are a quick healer," she says with a playful grin.

"Good thing, indeed," I mumble and recall Jaden reaching for me as I began to topple from the saddle. The memory is a bit blurry around the edges, but I'm certain I slipped through his grip and fell away from him. "Jaden, he tried..."

Tired to catch me, only our horses weren't close enough, his arm not long enough, and his attempted hold on my forearm not firm enough. And then I tumbled into the space between my horse and my mom's. Ha. I bet that took the mighty immortal commander by surprise.

Bree huffs a choked laugh. "Yeah. He was all kinds of not happy," she says, regarding Jaden. "Him and the others, Mo and Lobrka, are now riding directly behind the carriage." She tips her head back, indicating the space behind her. Or more specially, the space beyond the carriage.

I glance over her shoulder and attempt to see through the windows set in the upper half of the back door. A combination of dirt and imperfect glass distorts the images of the world beyond. Still, the fuzzy combination of colors matches what I would expect to see, with regards to those three.

"He wanted to stay at your side until you woke up," Bree continues. "But, um, yeah"—Her shoulders rise and pinch, as her hands spread wide—"I had to explain to him that this wasn't a luxury coach bus with ample space."

"He was less than happy," Zarah chimes in, a humored grin twitching her lips. "But he was accepting... eventually. And he remains close, should you need him."

I nod, my attention gliding over Bree, and Zarah, then the quiet individual sitting next to her—the master healer I presume. If I'm in the carriage with Zarah and Bree, then that would mean...

My gaze drops to the makeshift bed laid out on the floor a mere foot from me. "Ry!"

The sight of my brother, still peacefully deep in his induced sleep state, cuts through my exhaustion and heightens my awareness. I lurch sideways and, ignoring the throb in my skull the action elicits, press my palm to his chest as if needing to verify he's alive and breathing... still in this world with me. His pulse is shallow but steady.

No sooner has my skin brushed against his, than blue veins, alight with a spectral glow, web across his body.

"No!" Zarah leaps from her seat. She grabs my hand and yanks it from my brother's body.

In her haste, she doesn't slip on a glove to prevent direct contact, and instead grasps me with her bare, uncovered hand. Her time chronicler ability flares to life and recollections of experiences I've endured, both old and new, race across the connection.

Unlike the version of her I met in the alternate timeline, this Zarah is no longer affiliated with the time keepers. Still, affiliated or not, her talent is an innate part of who she is. It's like breathing to her, and it continues to work as the goddess designed—gathering my histories to be stored in the Urn of All. The ethereal urn where all memories collected by every time chronicler are preserved. A rather magically, unique way to document the realm's history.

"Sorry. So sorry." Zarah jerks her hands from me so fast her balance teeters. Bree and I both reach out and steady her, but she shrugs off our touch. "You should avoid touching me," she says. "At least, until I cover up."

Startled by her outburst, I clutch my own hands to my chest. "Why can't I touch him?" I bite my lower lip and study the unnatural glowing veins lacing his skin. "Did I do something wrong? Activate something?"

"Of course not," Bree quells. I appreciate her kindness, but it is Zarah I turn to because she was the one who leaped forward and stopped me.

She blows out a long breath. "Whatever you did to him when you previously healed him, it has changed him fundamentally. And I just feel"—she glances at the master healer, who has remained oddly quiet since I awoke—"we feel that any unknown healing magic, Balance Bringer or otherwise, should take place in a controlled environment."

In other words, not in the midst of a moving caravan.

"Plus..." Bree taps her fingers against my calf. "In your given state, we don't know what any attempt would do to you."

"To me?" My hand presses to my chest. "I..." My gaze flutters to Ry, then back to Bree. "I would be fine. I *am* fine. My *given* state is fine."

"You're not fine yet," Bree counters, to which Zarah adds, "You really are not."

I narrow my gaze. "How can you know that from this short interaction?"

Bree crosses her arms and drops them heavily against her chest. "The bags under your eyes, for one." She leans toward me. "You're not the energizer bunny, Ana. You need to occasionally recharge. And right now, is one of those times." Her muscles loosen and her expression softens. "Ry is stable and not in any immediate danger so why don't you take this opportunity to allow your energy reserves to restore. Not just the physical ones, but the mental and emotional ones, as well."

I frown and scrutinize all of them in the carriage with me.

Zarah leans forward, pressing her elbows into her thighs. "We have a fair amount of travel ahead of us before we reach the garrison. You might as well use the time wisely."

"But I..." My gaze wanders to my brother. "Ry..." Would I be foolish not to do as Zarah suggested? I am still tired, but how can I rest when my brother is in such a way?"

Bree taps my leg again. "You will be more helpful to *everyone*, Ry included, if you are at your full strength. And for that to happen, you need to rest." Zarah nods her head a tad too enthusiastically.

My lower lip juts out, and I release a heavy sigh. "Fine," I say, sounding like a pouting child.

I lay back and, continuing with the pouting child behavior, cross my arms, close my eyes. Surprisingly, not much time passes before I manage to fall back to sleep.

My body tosses and turns, a will, not fully mine, attempting to push to the forefront. There is somewhere I need to be and the company I travel with is going the wrong way. I need... I need to strike out on my own.

"I need to go to him," I mumble.

"You need to stay put," someone replies. "Tell Kaia to stop this nonsense."

"Nooo." I shake my head and pull at my neckline. Is it hot in here? I swear I'm sweating every ounce of water my body holds.

"I can help you with this, Ana." A damp cloth blots my

forehead. "When we reach the garrison, I can help you with Kaia."

"No," Kaia mumbles. "No. I need to go to him."

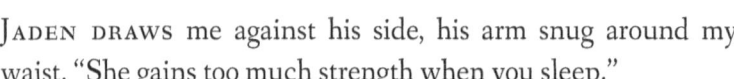

JADEN DRAWS me against his side, his arm snug around my waist. "She gains too much strength when you sleep."

A hum passes over my lips in response because, as much as I hate to admit it, she does. Kaia has for a while now and I'm not sure what to do about my sister and her Dohlan obsession. She had her life and this one is mine. Or should be, anyway.

I rest my palms against the wood railing and gaze out across the water. I awoke several hours ago to the troops loading horses, carts, and warriors onto the ships that now carry us toward the Maitias Garrison. It is there that I will meet with my mom and other clan officials to decide what will happen next regarding Dreya and the infecting darkness. Until then, everyone—Jaden, Bree, Zarah, Mo, Mom—has ordered me to take it easy.

Apparently, moving through space and time like I did is more draining on my energies than the other elements are.

Jaden's hand brushes over my hair as he drops a gentle kiss to my crown. "Have you given any more thought to our discussion?" Merging the many past life versions of myself in order to quiet all the voices and influences within me.

Earlier, when I was in the carriage and became overwhelmed by my sister's emotions and desires, Bree suggested she could help me with the merging process. I haven't decided against it, but... nor have I openly embraced the idea. What if the process ends up with me leaning more toward behaviors associated with Kaia?

I tilt my face up to meet his gaze. "What if I do that and start chasing after Dohlan all of the time?"

"Ouch." Jaden clutches his chest. "You wound my heart with the mere suggestion you might choose him over me after all we've been through."

I twist in his hold and lightly slap his arm. "You know what I mean."

"I do," he murmurs, his touch brushing a line up my arm, over the curve of my shoulder and into the arc of my neck.

A shiver races over me, more from his touch that sends exciting thrills through my system, than the chilled breeze that skips from the water and across the deck.

I press my forehead to his warm, firm chest, and he wraps his arms around me like a shield. "The idea scares me." Every day, I grow more and more comfortable making such admissions to him.

"It will never happen," he assures. "Our connection is true and pure. What your sister and Dohlan feel for each other was created from and amplified by elven magic."

He's right, of course. At least, I think, hope, pray he's correct on that fact. I overheard Aunt Edea... Opal... say things to Dohlan that support that line of thought. Still, magically induced or not, those emotions feel pretty damn real to Kaia. I'm certain the same can be said for Dohlan. He's a complicated mess, but, yeah, I've seen the commitment, an emotion beyond desire, in his eyes.

The remainder of our trek to the garrison passes rather uneventfully. I spend a lot of time at my brother's side. I also share my experiences in the alternate timeline with those closest to me.

In a little one-on-one session with Zarah, where she uses her time chronicler ability, I let her see firsthand everything that happened with her alternate self, as well as the added message she sent herself, using me as a conduit. Whatever that Zarah shared with this Zarah, the information was hidden away in my psyche for only her to unlock and collect. I'm not privy, unless she chooses to share the information with me.

For now, she doesn't.

"I need to let everything sink in," she says, before thanking me and hugging me fiercely.

By the time the ships docks at Maitias Garrison, Gitta has returned to her old self—healthy and uninfected. She, along with a bandaged Al and a quieter than usual Raundel... who was already fairly quiet... join Jaden, Lobrka, Mo, Bree, and me as we go ashore. I haven't seen my mom in some time, but I know she'll find me soon enough.

We still need to discuss the threat that is Dreya. But she also said she'd be attending to a few other matters first, so my friends and I would have a few hours to ourselves.

Because of Ry's condition, he and his entourage disembarked first. Zarah and the master healer are accompanying him to the infirmary, and the rest of us are left to catch up before they set out on the next leg of their journey. After briefly being attended to here, to make sure my brother is stable enough for the continued journey, he'll be sent by speed rail to Gaurdoone Point where he'll then be outfitted with prosthetic limbs.

My brother the cyborg.

My heart bellyflops into my chest.

I still need someone to explain to me how the prosthetics will work. Especially when weapons forged with the Fires of Gaurdoone are supposedly deadly to an immortal warrior.

The wharf is a frenzy of activity. Freight being reallocated. Escorted horses heading to nearby stables. Bodies moving every which way, with and without goods in hand. Navigating the crowd forces me to pay attention to my course so that I obsess a smidgeon less on my brother's situation.

"Pleased to see you are all still alive," says a familiar voice.

At the sound of Klarda's greeting, my back snaps straight and I search the surrounding crowd. The gray hobgoblin towers over many of the surrounding warriors and other beings. Her height comparable to that of Raundel and Lobrka. Her scrutiny glances off of each of us, her crooked grin faltering when her attention lands on Al.

"What happened?" She pushes past everyone to get to the injured clan member. Grabbing Al's lower arm, she inspects the bandage.

Al shrugs off Klarda's concern. "Lucky shot from that wicked water witch."

"Dreya?" Her gaze shifts to me. "Is that why you took that not-so-little unsanctioned trip?"

"She is—"

Klarda shoves me in the shoulder. "Do you realize someone could have been seriously hurt?"—she shoves me again—"Do you understand—"

Jaden grabs Klarda's wrist and removes her hand from my person. She shoots him a what-the-hell glare, but he doesn't flinch. "Ana understands and has already suffered enough. She doesn't need you pushing her around."

"Oh, I'm sorry," she says with a bucket load of snark and peels Jaden's hand free. "Wouldn't want to upset our precious Balance Bringer. But if she is going to live up to her title, she needs to be smarter than that."

He shoves forward, getting up in her personal space. "She's plenty smart."

My hand wraps around his arm, and I tug him back. He needn't get so worked up over another's opinion of me. It's a trivial matter, all things considered. "Jaden," I say softly. His gaze swivels to mine, and I shake my head. "It's fine." He starts to refute, but I repeat myself and stand firm, then turn my attention to Klarda. "If it's any consolation, Dreya has been stripped of her water magic."

"Well..." Klarda grumbles and crosses her arms. "That's something, at least." Her gaze flickers to Al. Al's lips kick up and she shrugs.

Raundel snorts, then moves past me, slaps his palm down on Klarda's shoulder, and gives her a nod. The lines on her face smooth, an unspoken exchange taking place between them. He pats her upper arm twice, then walks away, taking a path toward the garrison. Lobrka and Gitta follow him.

Klarda and Al linger, whispering between them. When Klarda drops her lips over Al's, my feet kick into motion. Jaden, Bree, and Mo stick to my side, and together we trail several feet behind the trio of Madame Marrouske's sanctuary elves.

A couple of familiar faces are waiting for us when we step through the garrison entrance.

"Ana." Shadow tackles me and I yelp. He swoops me into his arms and spins me around. "My spy and trespassing mate."

My yelp morphs into a giggle as Shadow sets me on my feet. Clef stands only a few feet away, a humored smirk curling his lips. Not a moment passes before he and Jaden are engaging in the male loose hug-pat greeting.

"Glad to see she did not get you killed," Clef says, stepping back from their embrace. Clearly holding back a laugh, Jaden simply shakes his head. "And you,"—Clef's attention snaps to me—"That was an extremely uncouth thing you did, sneaking off like that."

A wide grin blooms across my face. "You only feel that way because I didn't take you with me."

"True." He dips his head into his shoulder. A second later,

his grin matches my own. "Come here." He motions me forward for a hug.

Remembering all the looks he gave me back in Palinot City, the way I found him watching me while I slept, and the overt flirting he's been guilty of, I grimace and wave away the request. Not this time, corndog.

Clef frowns, but Jaden and Shadow burst into laughter. I turn to Mo and Bree, who are both rolling their eyes. "Males," Mo mumbles, then glances past me to Jaden's clan members. "Where's the red head?" she asks.

"Ruby is with our mother," Shadow says. The clan mother being Opal... my aunt Edea... and, as I understand it, Dohlan's actual mom.

"As you can imagine," Clef jumps in. "She has had a really hard time of it, lately." Dealing with Azure's death... obviously. "And one of the ways she has been coping, has been to visit with our clan mother. Although, from what I understand, Mother has not been saying much."

"Opal's here?" I ask.

"I want to see her," Bree and Mo say in unison.

My head jerks back. I'm not the only one taken by surprise. The males also stare at Bree and Mo with wide-eyed expressions.

"Awkward." Shadow clears his throat. "But if that is what you want, I will check with the powers that be and see if they will permit a visit. Now, come on." He motions us to follow him. "Let me show you where you can wash up and rest, before the demands start pressing heavily upon you."

"Wash up?" Mo blurts. "Goddess above, yes please. I am covered in filth for days."

"I could get down with that," Bree adds, then blinks and looks at Mo. "Not with you, I mean, but on my own."

Clef covers his laugh and inappropriate comment "happy to help" with a cough.

"Don't worry." Jaden tosses Clef a stern glare as we all turn and follow Shadow through the garrison. "I don't think any of us were confused by your comment."

"Maybe not, but definitely intrigued," Clef mumbles.

Jaden dips his head into the crock of my neck and whispers at my ear, "Must say, though, I wouldn't mind conserving water with you."

Oh my Gaea. Heat flushes up my neck and across my cheeks. "I'd be on board with that," I reply for only him to hear. And if I take my mom at her word, we'll have the time for a shared washup.

We climb stairs and turn corners, and each step of the way, I do my best to pay attention to the path, remember how we got to this point in the garrison. But Jaden's fingers are entwined with mine, the heat of his palm pressed to mine, making me decidedly distracted.

Still...

My brother, I remind myself. I shouldn't be thinking or feeling this way when Ry's physical state hangs in the balance. My thoughts are selfish. And when my mom said we'd have a few hours, I'm certain she didn't have intimate activities in mind, but rather eating, resting, and cleaning up, in no particular order.

And, well... my stomach grumbles... I am a bit on the hungry side.

Turning another corner, we plunge into a throng of bodies—immortal warriors and other beings moving in every which direction.

"In case this chaos fails to make it obvious," Shadow says. "This is always a hub of activity."

Movement comes at us, from behind us, and from either

side. I relinquish Jaden's hand to better move through the crowd.

"Stay close and keep up," Clef adds as we dodge bodily collisions.

But I can't dodge them all. Someone slams my shoulder from behind and walks briskly away, outfitted in such a manner they're unidentifiable. But their whispered words linger.

"Watch your back."

TWENTY-FOUR

J aden's fingers rub circles into my shoulder, slowly unraveling the knots that reside there. "It could have been nothing more than a snarky comment about being in their path," he says regarding the "watch your back" remark I received in the outer hall.

"But what if it's something more?" I don't know if I should be concerned with the whispered message or not, but I can't seem to stop my mind from rolling the possibilities around in my head time and time again. Do I have a target on my back?

Roughly twenty minutes have passed since Shadow deposited us in a private room. Mo and Bree are in the room next to ours. And ever since Jaden and I found ourselves alone together, I've been stressing and obsessing.

Jaden's hands slide up the back of my neck, massaging my tight muscles. "Either way, there is nothing to be done at this very moment. Try to relax and release all this tension. A healthier you will be in a better position to face any upcoming challenges."

"What if some of the warriors here blame me for what happened to Ry... one of their own?"

"Ana." His breath whispers over my skin, followed by a soft trail of kisses. "Let me help you."

He steers us from the front receiving room to the back bedchamber and proceeds to do exactly that... guide me into physically relaxing and mentally forgetting the many things plaguing my thoughts. I lose articles of clothing and lie with my belly on the bed as his hands knead and rub and stroke my skin, his lips adorning my body with endless, whisper-soft kisses. Everything about him is an aphrodisiac, and I willingly bend to his ministrations.

He is the artist, and I am his clay.

And when my muscles are as loose as cooked spaghetti, the change of his exploratory touches heats my skin and swells a pool of warmth between my hips. He flips me onto my back and hovers over me, one hand firm at my hip, his hooded gaze soaking me in.

"You are the most exquisite thing I've ever had the honor of experiencing." He places a kiss on the side of my neck. Whispers into my skin. "I never want to go another day without reminding you exactly how much you mean to me." His lips skim down and down, depositing another kiss on my collarbone.

My hand flattens along his cheek and sweeps back through his hair. "I feel the same. You keep me sane, and I would be nothing without you."

His hand glides up over the swell of my breast, and I become melted putty.

A knock sounds at the door.

We both groan and his gaze lifts to meet mine. "Should we ignore it?" I ask.

I'm immediately rewarded with a smile curving his lips.

"You guys in there?" Shadows voice calls from the hall. "Our mother, Opal, is requesting to see Ana, and the visit has been approved."

Sighing, Jaden draws a blanket over me and pulls away. "Take your time getting ready. I'll see to Shadow." He heads into the receiving room, closing the bedchamber door behind him.

I make quick efforts of tugging my clothes back into place while listening to the exchange in the next room. Shadow asks where I am and then makes a comment about Jaden's messy hair. Oops.

A beat of awkward silence. And then Jaden's reply, "She'll be out in a moment."

"Ah, huh." By the tone in Shadow's delivery, I can picture him giving Jaden an all-too-wide teasing grin.

Somewhere out in the hall, a door slams, the sound followed by rapid footfalls on the stone floor moving in the direction of Jaden and my room.

I straighten the front of my shirt and head for the bedchamber door, step into the receiving room.

"What is this?" Shadow says. He's standing in the hallway a foot outside the open door and his attention is focused on something down the corridor. Something that seems to be moving closer at the same rate as the thuds of quick footsteps.

"We heard you talking about Opal," Bree's voice replies to Shadow's query. "Can we also see her now?" Mo adds.

Shadow shakes his head, a frown pulling into place, as he dips his head and steps forward. Jaden steps out of the way and Shadow moves into the room without responding to Mo's question. A moment later, Mo and Bree appear in the vacant doorway and file into the room behind him.

"Well?" Mo pushes.

His gaze fixes on mine, quickly sweeps over me as if looking for something out of place, then swivels back to them. "Sorry, but no. Only one visitor at a time, under guard supervision, and the Balance Bringer is the one who has been requested and approved."

Mo's shoulders slump, her lower lip pushing out in a pout. "I want to ask her about something personal."

Bree pats her shoulder. "We could always file an official request, with..." She glances at me and grimaces. "The immortal commander, I guess."

Her statement pitches with the inflection of a question. A question to which I shrug, because, yeah, I don't know, but my mom sounds like the appropriate place to start.

"Do you think we have time?" she tacks on... because we still don't know who is going with Ry and who is going elsewhere, and when all these departures will begin to take place.

"I don't really know," I reply. "But there's no harm in asking."

Shadow waves his hands. "Enough time wasted." He shifts to face me. "You ready to go, Ana?"

Um...

Jaden moves to my side, and wraps his arm around me, his fingers gliding across the small of my back. "Am I allowed to escort her?"

"Sorry, bro." Shadow slaps Jaden's bicep. "Like I said, only one. And right now, that one is your girl."

Jaden shakes his head. "I don't know how I feel about this," he says. "My trust in Mother has fractured."

"Don't worry." I lean into his side and squeeze his hand. "No doubt, she's securely confined, and I'll be fine."

He dips his head, dropping his gaze to mine. "Of course, you will." He turns a steely glare on Shadow. A silent threat to ensure my safety.

"All right, then." Shadow grabs my hand and tugs me free from Jaden and my friends. "We should get moving."

"Wait." Bree jumps in front of us. "I made this for you. Here." She extends her open palm, presenting an imperfect circular pendant.

"Oh yeah," Mo quips. "She stunk up the room real good making that thing."

"What is it?" I understand it is a piece of jewelry, but coming from Bree, I highly doubt it's merely an ornamental trinket.

Shadow yanks on my arm. "We need to go."

"Hold on a second." I resist his pull and pluck the pendant from Bree's hand.

"It's magic," she answers. "Meant to help you with that "struggle". Wear it and when you are ready to unite your many incarnations, simply smash the stone. The unity will begin."

I twist Bree's gifted pendant between my fingers. The piece adds a lot of jingle hanging around my neck, even if the three pieces I wear hang at very different lengths.

The new piece sits just above my breasts, Dohlan's ring-on-a-string hangs low, between them, and Kaia's crystal necklace falls at my collar bone. I've worn Kaia's piece since Mom gave it to me the day of Skylar's birthday bash. That necklace, paired with my crystal wristbands—mine and Crystia's—already has me adorned in power gems. Now, with this added bit... I don't even know.

Why would I want the option to unite my many incarnations hanging around my neck?

Shadow comes to a stop at the bottom of a long descent. We're clearly deep beneath the garrison. He tosses me a resigned smirk, then knocks on a steel door set in the wall before us. "This is as far as I get to go, but the warriors stationed here will take good care of you."

"Thank you for walking me down here, Shadow." I wrap my arms around him and give him a tight hug.

"No problem, Bringer."

The steel door swings inward and a warrior in full body armor steps into the opening. Shadow shifts away from me and motions to the immortal male. "This is Ian. He's going to take over from here."

Ian and Shadow exchange a wicked grin and fist bump. "Good to see you, Shadow man," Ian says, then tips his head at me. "And Balance Bringer, this is a historic moment for me."

"You honor me." I flatten my hand against my chest.

"You are too kind." With a bow, Ian steps aside, granting me access to the room beyond.

Accepting the offer, I step through the doorway then turn back to Shadow. Give him a slight wave.

"You got nothing to worry about," Shadow says, leaning against the doorframe. "Mother would never hurt you. And as for these guys"—He lifts his chin indicating Ian and the other warriors situated deeper in the room.—"I have gotten to know them a bit these last two days and they are good males. They will watch your back."

I stiffen at the choice of words, but he doesn't seem to take notice. With a smile and a loose salute, he spins away, and the door is closed.

The phrasing is nothing more than a coincidence. I suck back a deep breath, fortifying my resolve and next step. I spin to the interior of the room, the warriors and the barred door separating the guards' station from the cells beyond.

"She has been rather docile," Ian says, leading me to the barred door at the other side of the room. "At times, she appears all but comatose. But, since she requested an audience with you, I suspect she will be receiving."

"Gosh. I hope so."

Ian unlocks the barred door and, without swinging it open, he turns to face me. "The inmate is in a cell behind three different confinement walls. Two walls of bars, and another of slotted crystal set between. You are not to attempt to cross or get around any. You are also to stand four feet away from the outermost enclosure. Do you understand these rules as I have stated them?"

I nod.

"Do you have any problem following the rules as stated?"

I shake my head.

His chest rises and falls. "There are presently only two inmates incarcerated here. The one you seek is in the second cell on your right. You are to ignore and go nowhere near the other inmate at the far end of the passage. Understand?"

The other inmate has got to be Garr. Despite the satyr once being a friend of Deona's and getting infected as a result of that relationship, I cannot bring myself to look at him after what he did to Jaden in the tree city, or to Azure in Palinot... took his life. I tell Ian that I understand and agree to the conditions, and he grants me entrance into the room.

"We will be watching you," he says, pausing my steps a mere foot into the room. "At no time will you have full privacy."

I glance over my shoulder. "Understood."

He assumes a guarded position on the inside of the barred door, with legs spread shoulder length and arms crossed over his chest. I turn away and walk to the second cell, my aunt Edea or Opal's confinement space. She's sitting on the cot of a bed watching my approach.

Her attention flickers to Ian for a heartbeat, then returns to me. "Nice of you to visit your old aunt."

"Did you not summon me?" I fold my arms across my chest and scrutinize her condition. Far more blackened veins than when I last saw her.

"Did I?" She weaves her fingers together and settles them in her lap. "I suppose I did. Nevertheless, I am pleased you came."

"How could I not?" I say, to which she raises an eyebrow. "There are a few things I need you to explain to me."

She rises to her feet and shuffles to the front of her barred cell. "Are there now?"

"You know there are." I too move forward, within inches of the row of bars on my side. Six feet still exist between us, with a slotted crystal wall situated midway between the two barred walls on either side. "I want to know what you've been doing since you walked away from Aunt Meira and me." So very many lifetimes ago. "You also need to tell me what you have done to Dohlan and why. And what you know about Mo and The Nethers. Those are my starting points, but I'm sure I'll add more."

She huffs a soft laugh, her gaze drifting down and to the side. "None of that really matters. Not if the end goal is achieved."

"Really?" I blurt, my inflection filled with incredulity.

"Really." She closes her eyes and shakes her head in a barely-there movement. "And I cannot believe it has taken me so many lifetimes to understand what must be done."

"What are you talking about?" I wrap my hands around the bars. "Does it have to do with achieving my destiny?"

"We should have seen it," she says, not answering my question, then slips her hand between the bars and rests her wrists on the crossbar.

With a metallic clunk vibrating through the walls, the lights dim and the room illuminates in a red glow. A low hum, accompanied by a shrieking alarm, erupts and echoes through the chamber.

What in the name of Gaea? I jolt back a foot.

"Step away from the bars," Ian demands, his arm extended in a sharp point toward Opal. "You are—"

Opal's head kicks back and mouth drops open. The infecting darkness seeps free from her fingers and palms in a searching wave—a flecked black against the luminating red all around us.

"Stop that! Stop it now!" Ian slams his hand against the wall, hitting a button mounted beside the door.

Buzzing vibrates through the ground beneath my feet and an electric charge from the crystal wall raises all the hairs on my body. Within a blink, an array of static lightning explodes to life, jumping off the crystal barrier and bouncing through the space between the wall and Opal's imprisoning bars. Jagged lines of light, in varied intensities, zip and zap in every direction.

The swell of darkness swirls through the chaos like dust on a wind, finding an unfettered path to the slots set in the wall-to-wall crystal divider. Whether the openings in the partition serve for the flow of air or sound, now they provide the infection access to move beyond Opal's confinement.

"Opal," I yell, taking a step back. From the bars, from Opal, from the approaching darkness. "What are you doing?"

She doesn't respond. Her head is back, and her eyes glued to the ceiling of her cell. Her body shudders uncontrollably as the affliction continues to bleed from her pores.

"Aunt Edea, stop!"

Nothing changes. Can she even hear me? Has her body been overtaken?"

The darkness hits the air in variegated clouds of contagion and, instead of attacking anything within reach, it moves in nebulous form toward me. Appearing unaffected by the energized lightning attack, it glides through the openings in the crystal wall.

"Nope." My hands fly up, flaring wide. The elements snap in response, racing to my command... or my defense.

Water dampens the walls, floor, and ceiling, moisture growing heavy in the air. Even as the condensation morphs to rain in the space before me, the atmospheric change fails to weight the airborne darkness, push it to the floor.

Earth erupts the ground with stone and vines, building a wall to block the path, but the wave is already moving through the cracks before the natural elements have fully taken form or shifted into place.

Air sends a tempest packed with strength and speed. The force slows the infection's advance but does not halt it. The haze of corruption merely dances on the wind, jumping up, spinning, and swirling wide... and still continues toward me.

Holy Gaea and God.

Ian is hollering something, only within the chaos of howling wind, crumbling and cracking earth, and the drum of falling rain in the chamber, I can't make out his words. The warriors behind Ian in the outer room are yelling, and somewhere down the corridor another is roaring and banging the bars—Garr?

"Bringer." Ian's voice grows in volume and my hearing zeroes in on him. "Do not let it touch you," he repeats, as if knowing I couldn't hear his first delivery.

The sarcastic side of me wants to laugh at his direction because... been there, done that.

I don't laugh. Instead, I press my focus to the threat moving all too close.

If water cannot weight the approaching threat, and earth cannot block it, nor can air push it back...

Fire ignites in me and spreads outward, flashing forward, and attacking the impending darkness.

I. Am. Burning.

Burning away the newly sprouted vines, raising the temperature of the continued wind, evaporating all the clinging moisture, and—

Beastly power, in the form of glacial blades, slam into my chest. My feet are knocked out from under me, and I'm airlifted. Weightless for a flash of a moment. Then I collide backside against the ungiving stone of the wall. Slump to the floor.

The red glowing lights, the sirens, the electric lightning, they all switch off. And the entire chamber swims in a thick black.

Somewhere in the gloom, a fleshing thump. A deafening silence.

TWENTY-FIVE

I ce spirals into the depths of my chest, and the world around me reels. My breath hitches, my head pounds, and confusion momentarily owns me.

Wowwa. What just happened?

Mist sprays from the ceiling comparable to a fire sprinkler system. Only, whatever substance is showering over me, it isn't water. I wipe my fingers across my cheek and the suspect substance. My fingertips tingle and numb, muscles ache and tire.

I glare at the dampness covering my hand. It's all over me. Is this stuff drugging me?

Somewhere far to my left, Garr is roaring from his cell at the end of the vault. His outbursts grow weaker by the moment.

My gaze swivels to Opal. She's prone on the floor, the shallow rise and fall of her chest the only visible movement.

All the guards from the outer room spill into the space. Their movements are sluggish, then quick, then sluggish again. Or maybe my perception is distorted, and their actions are consistent. They're clad in full cover, including face masks, protecting them from the stuff drizzling all over the chamber.

Keys jingle, preparing to be used, and weapons are at the ready. One of the warriors unlocks the doors leading to my elven aunt's cell and advances.

As if materializing from across the room, Ian appears at my side, crouching down to meet my gaze.

I jerk, my head bumping against the hard wall. How did he get so close without me noticing? I press my eyes in a hard blink and attempt to clear the fuzz taking hold of my brain.

"Did she infect you?" His voice is muffled through the face mask he wears.

They're all wearing protective breathing gear. Should I be concerned for myself? I am, after all, completely exposed.

"My lady." His clad hand drops onto my shoulder, and I lurch, my awareness sharpening. "Did she hurt you?" He studies my face intensely.

"I don't believe so," I say with a shake of my head, and push to a straighter sit.

"Good to hear." His gaze washes over everywhere my skin is exposed. "What about infection?" My brow pinches. "Did she infect you?" he clarifies.

"I..." My hand jumps to my chest. Presses. "I don't think so. I don't feel infected. Do I look infected?"

He pulls back a couple inches. "I can't say you do."

"That's good. Very, very good." I steeple my hands over my nose and then drag my palms down my face.

"Ian," one of the warriors calls from Opal's cell. "We need you for a moment."

Ian glances over his shoulder. "Be right there," he says with a lift of his chin.

I tilt my head and gaze past him to the warrior's grouped around Opal. "Is she all right?"

He swings his attention back to me. "How about I head over there and find out." He rises to a full stand and looks down at me. "I will be right back. Stay here."

I don't respond but simply watch him move through the series of open doors between me and Opal. Are they checking her for signs of life? She hasn't moved since I first checked on her after whatever went down transpired. Aside from the mild signs of breath.

My head loops to the side, my sight directed toward the cell at the very end. No movement is detectable, and Garr is suspiciously silent.

My gaze rises to the ceiling. The mist is little more than an occasional spit. Still...

I need to get out of here.

In clumsy form, I push to my feet and stumble free of the chamber. Keeping my eyes trained straight ahead on the steel door I know leads to the outer hall, I stagger, pressing my hand to the wall to steady me.

I reach the door where I remember saying goodbye to Shadow. Wrapping my hand around the handle, I yank. It's locked.

I pull harder, attempting to tap into my immortal warrior/Balance Bringer strength. Whatever might I may usually control, at this moment such forces choose not to show. And yet, I *need* to be able to breathe where that misty substance doesn't contaminate the atmosphere.

In the room behind me, Ian and the other warriors are still with Opal. From what I can tell, she still hasn't moved. And Garr, he's still quiet. The longer I stay in this environment, the higher the chance of me falling prey to whatever sprayed the entire chamber.

But how do I get clear when the door is locked, and my strength is subpar?

Muscles in my shoulders slump, and I drop my forehead against the steel barrier, let out a long breath.

My elemental gifts, weak but present, mingle with my breath, turning my exhale into a draft or gust. Air slips through the cracks and seams of the door. A series of clicks and slides promptly follows, and the door pops open. Grants me passage to the beyond. To freedom.

I stumble, wobble a moment, then drag in a deep, clean breath, and regain my composure. Leaning with my back against the wall, I gather my wits and aim my focus. I need to find out what exactly happened with Opal and the infecting darkness. Is she all right? Am I? What about Garr?

But I'm not going back into that chamber. Not yet. Not until that stuff in the air clears and I feel like my normal self once more.

I should... Yeah... I should tell my mom what happened. I turn toward the stairs, take two steps and stop. A fluff of orange fur trots down the descent, ears perched and tail swishing.

"Meow." The cat's paws hit the bottom landing and he saunters to my side. Circles my feet and rubs against my ankles.

I blink wide. "Oscar?"

I haven't seen the family feline since that disastrous night in Palinot City, when Dreya's search for me and subsequent attack on the community resulted in destruction of property and bodily injury. But I should have known he was here somewhere. After all, if I had taken the time to think about it, I would have remembered he came to Hiddenkel with my mom, and was traveling in her company.

"Meows. *Ahana, see* mom."

"You're talking. I can understand you." I knell and rub the top of his head. I've understood the words of other animals, but Oscar hasn't ever spoken anything but cat chatter to me.

"Meow."

"You're right. I do need to talk to my mom." I scratch under his chin. His raised head and closed eyes suggest he enjoys the attention. "You wouldn't happen to know where she is right now?"

"My lady?"

"Ian." I jolt to my feet, back board straight.

"You were supposed to sit still and wait for me," he says.

"Sorry." With a shake of my head, I turn to face the immortal warrior and prison guard. He's lost the face mask, no doubt not needing it in the hall. "I needed a taste of clean air," I add.

His lips pull into a taut line, and if I were to venture a guess, I'd say he's questioning my motives. About not sitting still and waiting for him, coming into the hall, and likely visiting Opal in the first place.

"We need to discuss what happened back there." He steps closer, eating up the space between us. "I saw what she did. She pushed the darkness into you."

"Um. No." I drop my fists onto my hips. "Look at me"—I motion to myself and physical state—"I'm not infected."

"Hmmm." He tilts his head and glances over me. "We are not as convinced as you are."

"We?" My gaze shifts past him to the warrior standing in the cell chamber's open doorway.

Ian lifts his chin as if indicating something behind me. I turn to see who or what he means to identify, as Oscar starts to yowl. I come face to face with another immortal and startle.

He winks and blows dust in my face.

What the—

Oscar hisses. Leaps on the warrior with claws extended.

The walls and floor teeter. My sight fuzzes, then fades.

A cat screeches and—

I crash backward to the ground, head slamming against the stone. Everything is gone, and I slip into the darkness.

A LOW MOAN vibrates in my throat. Rattles and clomps fill my ears, a cloying perfume clogs my nose, and the surface beneath me is riddled with endless jarring bumps. My eyelids refuse to lift, and a strong internal throbbing is rooting a headache deep in my skull.

Plus, the way I'm laid out... yeah... so not comfortable. I shift my arms and legs, attempting to find a more pleasing position, only... my limbs won't move and something scratchy is wrapped around me.

Am I tied up?

I groan. Gaea above, I'm too tired to think my situation through or react appropriately.

"Where am I?" I mumble, not recognizing my own craggy voice.

Someone nearby curses. "Jav, get the lullaby and dust her again." The male voice is somewhat familiar, but I can't quite place it.

"What...?" I grumble and force my eyes open. I want to ask *what is lullaby* and *why is it dusted*, but the name likely says it all. I'm being drugged. And by the male Shadow told me would watch my back. Looks like that "watching" isn't in any good way.

The reason for my unfinished question leers over me. Ian. We're in some sort of wagon-styled transport, and Gaea knows where we are. His intense hazel eyes meet mine for half a beat before he looks away, toward the flap in the side canvas wall.

"And Jav," he continues. "Since it failed to keep her down

nearly long enough, keep the powder close. We will douse her at regular intervals."

An arm reaches through the canvas flap, handing a large satchel to Ian. "Giving her continued doses could kill her," Jav says.

Ian smirks. "That would certainly solve a problem, would it not?"

They're going to drug me *again*. And they don't care if it may kill me?

Despite my weakened state, panic kicks my fight or flight mode into full gear. "You can't do this." I wiggle, buck, and kick, struggling against the binds holding my wrists and ankles. "Not only am I your commander's daughter, but I am also the realm's royal heir, and the Balance Bringer." I turn my head toward Jav, but he holds his attention elsewhere, avoiding my gaze. Coward.

Ian grabs my bound hands and straddles me, pressing me into reluctant submission with his weight. He then shoves a rag in my mouth and... overcoming my relentless head shakes... holds it in place with a band tied around my face.

Lurching my upper body forward, I growl at him and buck my lower body, attempting to knock him off. Wind rips at the wagon's canvas cover, swooping into the space, shoving at him and the dust he extracts from the satchel.

I will not allow him to blow that stuff in my—

His lullaby dust covered palm slaps over my nose and mouth and... well, crap... that stuff works fast.

One breath and I'm fading back into blissful darkness.

THE TOES of my boots are dragging in the dirt. *I'm* dragging—being dragged—across the dirt. My body is slumped between hands hooked under my arms. And my head... my aching, pounding head... weights from my neck like a wet sandbag.

I don't know where we are or what these warriors have planned, but whatever it is, it can't be good. Not if they felt the need to secret me away and keep me drugged the entire time. A dozen or so hazy memories suggest I awoke, or tried to wake, multiple times only to be forced under the blanket of sleep time and time again.

Wake up, wake up, wake up, my internal voice screams. But my body... it isn't ready to comply.

"We need to hurry," someone says. Someone I don't recognize. "They have been on our trail for at least a day now, and they are closing in fast."

A day, at least? How long have I been kept unconscious?

"All right." The voice sounds like Ian's, and it's practically in my ear. He has to be one of the males dragging me to Gaea-knows-where. "Can you get the big guy?"

Within the momentary silence, I image I'm missing some sort of nonverbal communication.

"Too heavy. We need more hands on him."

One of the captors holding me readjusts their grip, yanking my shoulder up, and... *Ouch.* Shocks of sharp stabs rock down my arm and across my back.

"We will take care of him last then," Ian says. "Go help Jav and Stev with the other one."

"On it." Footsteps move around and ahead of us and— "Shit!"

The hold on me releases, and I fall against the ground, dirt and grass scratching my skin. Muscles rebelling against the abuse.

"Hold her," a warrior yells, to which another replies, "I am trying."

Hold who? Who else has been subjected to this treatment with me? My mind immediately drops the answer into the forefront of my mind. The obvious and only reasonable response, Opal and Garr. The three of us were in the chamber when whatever Opal did unfolded. They are both infected and Ian asked me...

Yeah. He asked me if I was infected now too. Based on everything that has transpired since then, I'm guessing he didn't believe I was clean but touched by the darkness like the others.

"*Maybe you are,*" Kaia whispers within me. "*Touched.*"

"*Maybe you always have been,*" Fionna, one of the first three Balance Bringer sisters, adds, remembering the first time the darkness chased her down. It collided with and bonded to Sol instead. And, well, after too many years of him acclimating, all my incarnations now know how that ended. Loss and death.

"*Maybe...*" Deona muses. "*Maybe that is what Aunt Edea finally concluded.*" The image of Opal staring at me through the bars of her cell, telling me she should have seen it sooner flashes behind my eyes. Deona sighs. "*We never should have run in the first place.*"

Crystia clucks her tongue. "*Because the darkness was always meant to be balanced by us,*" she murmurs. "*The Balance Bringer.*"

For the first time, I see it. Me and my sisters, when we were Deona, Estella, and Fionna. The night of the ceremony, we had come into the rite with three of the elements already awake and active: earth, air, and water. During the rite, fire came to life. But that night, when I followed the call deep into the forest, maybe it was not what I thought. Maybe the tug, or part of the tug, was the appeal of the darkness.

Could that be what I had been missing all along? The

reason why all the Balance Bringers between Deona and now have come up short with regards to our destiny?

A tiny groan seeps between my lips. What a time for such an epiphany, while I'm drugged and bound, and about to be what? I don't know what, but I need to find out.

I need to open my eyes. I need to move. I *need* to bring the elements to my aid.

"Hold her legs." "Just lift, swing, and toss."

They're clearly talking about Opal, but what are these warriors trying to do?

Struggling against the ache to remain prone, I drag my eyes open. My vision is as if I'm seeing the world through a cloud—soft and fuzzy, faded around the edges. I wobble and shift onto my side to gain a better vantage point.

Opal is foaming at the mouth, and her body is convulsing. Her movements continuously jerk her free from the males attempted holds. Still, they don't give up, their attempts unyielding, as they try to—

I suck back a tight breath.

This place—my heart accelerates in my chest and strong, destructive memories tumble to the front of my thoughts—Deona remembers this place. Gradnar's Gourge. It's located far, so very far, from Maitias Garrison. The distance between the gorge and the garrison has to be four times that of the distance between the garrison and the palace where we recently fought Dreya.

My estimated of the number of days the warriors kept me drugged and unaware jumps. Quadruples.

Gradnar's Gourge was created when Deona contained the largest of infected trolls and forced it downward, into the Nethers. This place is a one-way passageway to the Nethers.

"Quickly, before she bucks free again." The warriors lift Opal and start to swing.

"No," I try to scream, but the sound coming from my lungs is weak and not even a whisper. My blood is warming, and my skin suddenly feels stretched too thin. This. This cannot happen.

Lightning cracks overhead, then slams into the ground. The clouds open with an immediate downpour. If I can't stop these males with my own hands, I will halt their actions through Gaea's blessed elements.

The earth shudders beneath me, be it from the pounding of the rain, the crash of thunder, the strike of lightning, or earth responding to my fury, I am uncertain.

Fire licks up the walls of the gorge, flashing before the group and their attempt to toss Opal into the massive crack in the world. One of warriors hollers. Another cusses. But be it rain or lightning, moving earth or fire, these misguided warriors refuse to be thwarted.

They toss Opal's body through the fire and into the gapping gorge beyond.

"No!" Everything inside of me is screaming.

I scream so loud I think I hear horns blaring.

"They found us," Jav yells.

My screaming ceases, and I try to twist my body to see the land behind me. I can't make out any troop of rescuing immortal warriors, but not that I am listening for the sound, I can identify the pounding of horse hooves.

I imagine my mom and Jaden at the forefront, leading the charge.

"Hurry. Get the freak," one of the warriors directs, regarding Garr. Three of the males run past me to the wagon used for prison transport. In less than a minute, they are dragging an unconscious Garr out and over the side.

Ian and another grab me under the arms once more. Begin moving me toward the gorge.

"It's too late," I say. "You might as well stand down."

The warrior, not Ian, huffs.

Lightning strikes the ground a few feet in front of us, but the males don't even slow. They keep closing the distance on the hole to another world.

"My mom's forces are here," I state the obvious. "And you will be prosecuted for your actions. No point in making it worse by adding an additional crime against me to the list."

"That may be so," Ian says without a lick of emotion on his face. "But it will all be worth it if our actions remove dark infected influences from our realm."

My heart squeezes to a stop.

These males have no intention of aborting their plan, no matter the consequences to them.

I spin in their grip, catch sight of the other males hauling Garr forward, and beyond them, the approaching rescue. The immortal warrior troop is close, but not close enough. If I don't do something to save myself first, nothing will remain for my mom's force to do when they arrive but arrest the traitors responsible.

The ground grumbles and rumbles, causing dirt and stone to give way, making the giant crack of the gorge larger.

Nope. Nope. Don't want that.

I yank against their hold, try to back up. We're getting too close.

The wall of fire jutting up from the hole, flashes brighter and higher. Definitely hotter. The males dragging me ever closer don't seem to care.

Ian grabs my shoulders, and the other guy pulls my feet out from under me. I jerk and buck, my actions similar to Opal's convulsions. And, as they had to Opal in the end, they hold tight to me. Swing me. Left to right and left to right. Release.

I'm airborne, my body careening through the wall of fire

and into the gorge. But even as I have lost the physical fight, the elements have not deserted me. Wind rushes up to greet me, hugging my skin, and lifting me. Rising on a cloud of air, I begin to drift away from the danger of toppling into the other world of the Nethers.

"Ana!" Jaden's voice carries over the surrounding chaos and the song of the wind. I can't see him... yet... but my soul warms knowing he came for me.

Before I can call back, a hard body, encased in armor slams into me, knocking the breath from my lungs. Ian grips my arms in a tight grip, holding his body to mine. His determined stare meets mine and in that moment, I understand he is willingly giving his life to try and end mine.

Shock ripples through my core. The air around us shifts... and with his surprise attack, his added weight, and my momentary mental lapse, we break through the protective cloud and plummet into Gradnar's Gourge.

TWENTY-SIX

Broken and craggy earth races by at our sides. Ian and I are falling and falling. Spinning and clinging in the gale.

"Why?" I scream against the rushing wind.

Ian's response is almost swallowed by the airstream, but I manage to recognize his faint words amongst the gust consuming us. "A water witch infected with the darkness has devastated the realm. We would not survive a darkened Balance Bringer."

"Unless the Balance Bringer was always meant to take the darkness, devour and balance it," I counter.

His arms wrapped around my body, his face in mine, his confused expression holds mine gaze captive. His mouth opens a fraction, but no thoughts emerge.

And still, we continue to plunge toward another world. A world an adolescent Deona created to hold all the beings she deemed unsafe to live amongst the Fae, elves, immortal warriors, and other humanoid type beings.

"That—"

"And you may have doomed yourself to death, or a life in the Nethers. And for what?" I say.

"No. What you say cannot—"

Our hips and shoulders slam into a stony outcrop. Ian's hold is torn away, and we're knocked in different directions. His body vanishes into the darkness of the ever-deep pit. A free fall into a world of trolls and Gaea-knows what else.

My back slams against another impeding shelf. Pain ratchets through my muscles and bones. I reach out for the side-wall, reach out to the air, both attempts to slow my descent. So much wind is rushing past me, I can't tell if it is the result of my circumstances or reacting to my call for help.

A strange question pops to my mind. A most inappropriate time, indeed, but I can't escape the thought. As I try to wield the element, would Ian view me as an air witch, as he deemed Dreya a water witch?

Dreya... poor Dreya... was a victim of her circumstances. And those circumstances made her what she is now.

My knee and thigh bang into the jagged ridge. I cry out and, with the lingering thought of Dreya on my mind, I pull myself out of the fall.

SPACE FOLDS AROUND ME, cocoons me, then releases. I drop, landing with a bounce. Back against softness and... an explosion of dirt encompasses me. It clogs my nose and throat. Sends me into sputtering of coughs.

Sitting up, I wave away the floating particles.

Not dirt, but dust. Dust for ages.

At least I'm no longer falling.

Blindly embracing the most dangerous of elements was a huge risk, but I couldn't allow myself to end up in the Nethers.

Not with the current state of things. And if Deona's memories serve, something in the Nethers dampens the Balance Bringers connection with our Gaea-given gifts.

Yeah. Couldn't chance that. Not right now. So...

I utilized the element of space and went where it took me. But Ian, he's likely dead or now trapped in a world completely foreign to him.

Not your fault, the voice in my head placates. *He made the choice to drug you, kidnap you, toss you in Gradnar's Gourge. So, dead or in the Nethers, the result is from his actions and of his own making.*

All true, but also not what I need to be thinking about right now. I need to get to the business at hand: figuring out where I am and what I need to do next. Because...

I'm now in a bedchamber. One clearly abandoned for years. Neglect and age mark every surface—furniture, fabrics, walls and windows. Including the bed beneath me. It's springs hiss and squeak, the sheets tear with the friction of my movement, and the dust... yuck.

I push to the side, move toward the center of the room and turn in a circle taking it all in. I know this place. Not from my personal experience or that of my many incarnations, but from memories I know hold.

This was once Dreya's bedroom. When she was exiled from the palace and sent to South Tower—a fortress at the water's edge.

I dash to the window. The frame is pushed open, and the glass is broken.

The inset seat before the window—my fingers drag gently over the deteriorating cushion—Dreya used to sit in this spot and stare out, watching and waiting from my father's not-nearly-enough visits.

And here—my hand moves up the side of the window frame—Sol had defended her honor in this very spot.

So many memories here. Some good. Many bad. And my heart—I press my hand to my chest—Dreya's heart—beat for those moments shared with the Sun and the Moon. Sol and his darker side.

When I dug deep within myself and used the element of space to pull me out of the fall into the gorge... or passageway to the Nethers... it was thoughts of Dreya that brought me to this place. The place where the last of her hope and kindness was shattered.

I lean out the window and recognize the scorched earth from a memory of my own. A dream-walk where Kaia and I stood on top of a fortress surrounded by angry water and *this*—fire razed land.

I mentally dive into Dreya's memories and... she didn't do this. Which means, someone else did after what went down here.

Gaea above. My chest tightens, ribs feeling like they might crack.

They made the monster she became, then they denied it and tried to cover up the evidence. *They* being my grandparents on my father's side. Because, who else would do this, and so thoroughly, to royal land? There may be some, I guess, but I just know my thought holds truth, even without the proof. Or the memory.

Tilting my head back, I stare at the ceiling. At the cracks and bubbles in the finish. This monument to loss, hopelessness, and depression is where I suspected Dreya may have retreated after losing her water affinity.

At the edges of my perception, I sense something. Something familiar and tugging at a tiny thread inside of me.

I leave the bedchamber and begin the climb to the roof.

The howl of the wind beyond the tower walls tears through the stairwell, whipping my hair wildly around my face. Bushing the tendrils aside, I hold them against the side of my head, halting their interference with my vision.

The tugged thread within me chills as if a sliver of ice has taken up residence in my core. The sensation grows colder with every step I take toward the roof, or battlement as I believe it is called in these old structures.

The door to the roof is open, wood splintered and broken off the hinges, allowing easy access for the elements to find their way inside. Explains the flow of wind along the climb.

The moment I step out onto the rooftop, I'm hit by a memory of Dreya and Sol's darker side dancing under the moonlight. A smile holds her lips and heart, as a lightness glows within her soul. The male responsible returns her smile and holds her steady so that she may forgo her cane. A tool she no longer requires.

This rooftop used to be an escape for Dreya. It used to host chairs and tables and lounges. None of those items are here now.

My attention swings from the center of the space, where royal prisoner Dreya once found a small semblance of joy and peace, to the side rail where the now villain Dreya stands. She's turned away from me, granting me a side view. But I know what I'd see if she were facing me—hard lines hiding her true emotions from the world.

Cementing my resolve, I take two steps in her direction. "I suspected I'd find you here."

"I am surprised it took you this long," she replies, not turning her gaze from the world beyond. "This is the spot where your father took everything from me." She spins around to face me and throws her arm out in a point to the open space at her left.

When I look to the side, I can see everything as it was in the moments before, the floating islands, Sol, my father. Empathy washes over me and... *great Gaea...* how am I supposed to do anything to stop Dreya when I feel sorry for her? Almost understand her?

In that moment, I'm speechless. My thoughts a messy knot of unknowing. Unknowing on how to proceed in dealing with my broken aunt. She must be stopped, I know that, but—

A labored wheeze derails my thoughts, and I pivot toward the sound. It came from the shadows collected beside the rooftop door. Someone is hunkered within the gloom and, when I arrived on the rooftop, I had walked right past them without notice. I'd been too focused on the memory from Dreya's past.

Somewhere inside of me, Kaia jolts. *"Dohlan,"* she whispers and drags me closer.

I don't stop my sister's forward drag on my body and neither does Dreya attempt to stop my approach. Although, she does leisurely meander in our direction.

The last time we saw Dohlan, his chest had been clawed and torn open. He was wounded and bloody and caged with chains. The chains are now gone.

I kneel at his side. He's wearing the same soiled clothing as before, his shirt in shreds exposing much of his skin. And his chest, well...

My breath hitches.

I touch gentle fingers to his skin, an inch below his collarbone. He shudders, his gaze jerking up to meet mine. Pain and sorrow linger in his dimmed blue irises and my heart aches at the sight. My palm flattens over the new, long and deep scar that centers over his heart. He raises a hand, presses it over mine.

"I'm sorry," I whisper, wishing I could heal him and remove

the scar marring his skin. But, even if I could, a scar like this one goes far deeper than skin. And that kind of wound I could never erase. Not fully.

He shakes his head. "This was always destined to be my fate." He leans close, as if a secret waits on the tip of his tongue.

Dreya appears in my peripheral, her hand curling into the fabric at the back of Dohlan's shirt. She yanks him away. Releasing him to stumble from me and collapse at her side. "This too your father took from me."

My brow pinches and my mind launches into a sprint. "He took Dohlan from you?"

Lowering a loving gaze over him, she trails a hand through Dohlan's hair, dragging across his temple, to caress his cheek. "The being at Dohlan's origin," she says.

"I don't understand."

She sighs and pulls her hand to her chest. Swings her attention to me. "At the beginning of what you see here"—she glances down at Dohlan, her gaze lingering, then turns back at me—"he was something other, something beautiful, something mine.

"But he was not well, the darkness I received from Sol affected my child's gestation. That damnable elven witch suggested she could help him, and foolish as I was, I trusted her. Trusted him to her. And then she took me from him, the parts of me that created him, and added something different. Something I still do not know. But when she was done, she had him believing *she* was his mother. Not me. And when I found him, told him the truth, he refused to believe me. Do you know what that does to a mother? To be forgotten and refused by your own blood?"

Dohlan shakes his bowed head.

On top of everything that was done to Dreya, all the

torments she suffered, there is now... has been... the loss of a child. Her and Sol's child.

I suck back a short breath. "Do you mean Opal?"

I knew she'd done some horrible things to Dohlan. Apparently, I barely knew the half of it. If that. Had the infecting darkness made Aunt Edea, Opal, that way? *Oh!* And holy Gaea and god! Dohlan and I are related. Which means him and Kaia— I shake my head, unable to finish that thought.

Dreya scoffs. "Oriana Opal Edea Virrie, at the time betrothed to Lord Donican Marsoun. I thought that made her trustworthy. I knew so little back then. Their eventual marriage was a farce. She used him to get to my family. And why? Because of you!" Her jaw tightens and face darkens.

These new revelations have me unsteady on my feet, yet I blink back my confusion and embrace a warrior's stance. I prepare myself for Dreya's attack, for I have little doubt one is coming. Not if her connect-the-dots thought process labels me with blame for the loss of her son.

But... "It seems to me that Opal is responsible for that loss and not my dad," I say.

She perches her hands on her hips. Walks away from me and Dohlan, then spins back. "If your father had not done what he did that day, the darkness would not have come to me, and my child would have been safe."

And you would have been different. Better. Had Sol lived and the last bit of your hope and joy had not been torn away from you.

Dreya moves to the edge of the rooftop and, turning her back on me, gazes out at the ruined landscape. "This may have once been my prison, but it also held some of my most fond memories. To be here now is bittersweet."

Great Gaea, my empathy for my broken aunt keeps expanding.

And if any truth exists in the new thought regarding the darkness, had Deona and her sisters... my sisters... not run from the first appearance of the element, none of this history would exist. Sol wouldn't have gotten infected, spent his life outcast and cursed, only to pass the baton to Dreya.

So, one could argue that everything bad that happened to Dreya stems from an action or inaction of mine. Because, had Sol not been infected, he wouldn't have been there to cause the accident that led to Dreya's water curse. She would have had a life more similar to the one she lived in the alternate timeline, but without the element of infecting darkness. Not if Deona had taken it at the start.

Only—I bite down on my lower lip—there were issues in the alternate timeline that had nothing to do with the infecting darkness. Issues born because it didn't infect Dreya. I worry my lower lip between my teeth.

Dohlan crawls to my side and grabs my hand. "Ana," he whispers. "Do you still have the ring?"

My attention drops to his own ring nestled on his index finger and dulled with dirt. My eyes flicker to Dreya, then back to him. "Deja vu," I whisper.

"What?" His brow furrows.

Remembering this moment from a vision Jaden shared with me, I now need to decide... Do I let things play out the way envisioned, or do I try to change things?

Dreya still stands at the roof's edge with her back to us. I get the sense she is mentally walking down memory lane. I'm not sure if that is a good or bad thing with concern to her intentions regarding Dohlan or me.

I drop to my knees beside Dohlan. "I do," I reply to his original question and pull the string and ring free from my neckline.

He tips his head toward mine. "Maybe you should put it on."

I should wear the ring because the ring wearer can counteract Dohlan's actions when under Dreya's command. Or maybe it's the ring in combination with my blood. The ring Dohlan wears and the one I hold in my hand are mate rings, the one dangling from the string originally belonging to my sister.

I nod and pull the string over my head. Take my teeth to the cord, bite and grind, break the twine. The ring slides free into my open palm.

"What do you have there?" Dohlan and I both snap our heads up at Dreya's sharp question. She's glaring at us with eyes black as onyx. "I do believe that does not belong to you."

My hand fists around the ring. "And you think it belongs to you? The ring was my sister's."

A wicked smirk lifts one edge of her lips, her face darkening to match her eyes. I realize what she intends to do a moment before she acts. A blast of the infecting darkness explodes from her palms and hurdles straight for me.

The cold thread residing in me since the incident with Opal sharpens and drops in temperature. It's as if that piece of me recognizes the force Dreya wields. Darkness calling to darkness. Clearly, Opal *did* infect me. And maybe that's a good thing.

Taking a chance that my sisters' earlier thoughts are correct, I throw my arms wide, preparing to accept the incoming dark. Before it connects, something slams into my side thrusting me to the ground. My hands scrape against the coarse stone, cutting scratches across my palms.

This isn't how I remember things playing out in the vision Jaden shared.

I raise my gaze to Dreya's quick approaching steps. A flash of a second later, a thought occurs to me, and, following it, I slip through the folds of space and time. When I return to the rooftop, my breath is heavy, all my bones and muscles are revolting, and I'm standing on the other side of my aunt. Now, for this to work, I need to move fast.

Slamming an elbow into her back, I shove her to the ground, and flip her over. Straddle her, holding her in place. I don't have any physical weapons since Ian and his buds made sure to relieve me of such pieces. But I always have me.

Holding her flat beneath me with the force of the wind, I slam my hands to her shoulders and... before I can follow through on my planned action, someone grabs Dreya's arm. The only other person present is Dohlan.

Is he trying to protect me, as he likely did when he pushed me out of the way in the previous attack?

He yanks Dreya's body toward the roof's edge as she growls her protest. Refusing to release my hold upon her, I'm hauled along with her. And when Dohlan lifts and tosses Dreya over the tower's side, I too get tossed.

I scream his name, but it's already too late. Once again, and all too soon, I am free falling.

TWENTY-SEVEN

The air rushes past and Dreya screams. Nothing like speeding toward the hard ground from far above to strike the fear in even the most evil of villains. But then, Dreya hasn't always been evil. Maybe our fall is her rude awakening.

With the help of the wind still at my command, I hold us together tight and slow our descent. And then, following through on my original plan, I reach out to another element and push us through time and space.

We materialize amongst green grass and shade trees. Dreya is on the ground, and I'm on top of her pressing her down, like I had been on the rooftop before Dohlan interfered. But then her gasp resounds in my ear, and I pull away, jump aside.

She lurches to her feet and, forgetting the fight with me, turns in a slow circle, taking in each detail, from every blooming flower to the floating island visible behind me. Her eyes are wide and wild. "What... What is this? Is this some kind of cruel joke? Where are we?"

"This is it, Dreya," I say, taking a step back and spreading my arms wide. "No jokes. No deceptions. You make the right choice right now and the dream you lost so long ago can be yours once more.

The sun casts a long shadow of someone approaching. Dreya's gaze flickers to the newcomer and her mouth pops open, as her hand flies to her chest.

I sense my win already blooming.

THE PLAN WASN'T EVEN *a consideration when I first found myself at South Tower. The idea simply popped into my head as if dropped there by some higher power. Maybe Gaea, herself. I was ready to receive the darkness. Or as ready as I would ever be. I'd thrown my arms wide, and I was waiting. Prepared to test the theory.*

Only, the darkness didn't come.

Shoved to the ground, out of the path of the darkened attack, I missed the connection. That was when the idea exploded in my mind. My body and my consciousness reacted. And once more, I embraced the most dangerous of elements. I stepped away from that moment and entered another.

This one. Dirt and loose hay are at my feet, the nickers, snorts, and huffs of horses are all around me, and my hands—I raise my scratched palms for inspection—sting. Plus, Dohlan's ring is gone.

My chest tightens.

I only allow a millisecond of panic, despair, whatever... then I steel my resolve. Just because the ring is gone, does not mean all hope is lost. I still have the mission that brought me here.

If the scenario on the rooftop with Dreya and Dohlan didn't play out as seen in Jaden's vision, maybe I can change things for the better. Nothing drastic, not like before. I learned that lesson, hard and true. But maybe a small change that will only affect things going forward from the point I just left.

I stand in the entrance of a horse stable, South Tower rising into the sky before me. And all but butted directly against the tall structure, a series of floating islands. Islands I'd seen resting on the ground in my alternate timeline. Sol's islands.

Floating stones, acting as steps, span from the lowest island to the tower roof, allowing three individuals to climb toward the magical landmasses.

At ground level, Immortal warriors are everywhere, filling the gap between the sables and towers. I doubt I could get to the tower unseen, but I don't have to. I slip back into the shadows of the stable building. The plan, avoid contact with anyone but the one for whom I came.

I have a little bit of time before I need to get to them... I think.

I lean deep into the corner, stifle a yawn, then curl in on myself, attempting to become one with the gloom like Shadow does, and wait.

As it turns out, I don't have to wait long.

Thunder booms in all directions vibrating the stable walls. The land quakes sending the corralled horses into a frenzy, kicking and bucking. Shouts and screams explode in the outer yard. Plumes of dirt billow in from outside, attacking every open space, showering the walls, the horses, me. And still, I wait.

I don't need to peek to know what is happening. The event it burned in Dreya's memory and summoning it to my mind burns my heart, and my eyes. My father has ended Sol, and with him, the magic of the islands. All the floating landmasses have fallen to the mainland. And in that fall, my father, Sol, and Dreya.

My aunt is hurt, grieving, and angry. Unmeasurably so.

My father took the love of Dreya's life, and yet unknown... her child. As horrific as this moment may be, I will not cry. Even if the tears want to burst free. Instead, I huddle in place and mark all the sounds from the world beyond the stable. No one has entered the building. In the chaos unfolding, the horses are all but forgotten.

The time for me to act is marked by the whispers that follow Dreya's departure and the hollers summoning aid for the prince and royal commander, my father. When my aunt said her peace and walked away, he was alive but unmoving. Aware enough to mumble.

Shifting out of the shadows to a position beside the large barn-type doors, I survey the situation outside. My father is laid out on his back in the dried mote surrounding the tower. A flurry of warriors and what appear to be healers rush around him. The other individual who fell from the sky is crumpled among the wreckage of what used to be a magical world. For the moment, that male is being ignored, because... well... he's dead.

As much as I yearn for the familial connection, would love to run to my dad, and check on his state, that's not what I'm here to do. Plus, seeing him would only complicate matters. At this point in his life, I'm not even a thought. So... Not knowing who I am, he'd likely sick his guards on me, have me detained, being that I'm in what's supposed to be a secured area.

I don't have time, or energy, for any such inconvenience.

And, honestly, I should get moving. I don't know how long the next step will take, or how much it will demand of me.

Glancing down at my attire, I contemplate stepping out in the open. Letting others see me. I'm not wearing an official immortal warrior uniform or armor, but my attire is dark and well fitted. Not so obviously different that I should turn eyes when moving amongst those working the scene.

I fix my gaze on Sol's prone body as I step free of the stable and make directly for his location. No one bothers or questions me, and I make it to Sol's side without incident. He is slumped amongst mounds of broken earth and jagged boulders, bloody and battered, his skin drained of life. His limbs have been laid straight; his arms crossed over his chest. Dreya's parting gift.

Crouching beside him, I check his pulse and feel for any breath. There is none. My father was quite successful in bringing an end to the monster of the floating islands. Had he known how his sister felt about said monster, would my father's actions have been different? Does the answer even matter?

Not sure what exactly I am going to do or how I am going to do it, I place one palm over his heart and press the other to his temple. It was a feeling, a knowing in my gut, that brought me to this place, here and now. As such, I'm counting on that same feeling to guide my actions.

I close my eyes and hand control of my thoughts and actions over to Gaea. My elemental gifts swell and warm my muscles and bones. Earth, wind, water, and fire become a cyclone in my chest. Space and time hold my current actions in a pocket of time. Whatever I do advances with the clock, but only for me and Sol. To anyone sparing us a glance, we are but a brief snapshot in time.

The cold sliver of darkness I possess explodes around us in a nebula speckled with dark stars. Sol called the darkness ether, and it dwelled in him longer than any one soul, so he should know. Ether is the fifth element, and I needn't fear it. I should bring it home. But first, Sol. Then Dreya for the ether.

With eyes closed, and my hand pressed to Sol's body, I concentrate on being nothing more than the hand of Gaea. May she guide my way.

Sol and I are hidden in time and space, within a nebula-ether cloud, with the natural elements of water, wind, earth, and fire moving in and around us with enough speed to charge the surrounding atmosphere. To create an energy spike.

A hand drops on my shoulder and I jolt. My eyes snap open

and, without moving my hands from Sol's body, I turn my head and lift my gaze. A woman surrounded by an inhuman glow stands over me, her smile bright. She kneels, bringing her face level with mine, and recognition ignites in me.

The woman before me is wearing the face of Deona's mother, Glynnii. She died in childbirth and was absorbed by the tree of life. The tree, thereafter, taking Glynnii's form when choosing to communicate in any elven or fae form. But the tree is under lockdown back at the sanctuary, so how can—

"Sweet child." She presses her palm to my cheek. "You must know the tree is only a part of what I am. I am the goddess to which I've heard you pray. I am the land and the sky, the trees and the flowers, the rocks and rivers. I am everything and everything is me. I cannot be contained by one elf's magic." She means Madame Marrouske's safety protocol to protect the tree of life from Dreya.

I swallow hard and try to dislodge the words trapped in my throat. She smiles as if she knows my tongue is tied. She probably does.

"You needn't talk. Simply listen." She removes her hand from me and her skin glows as if she has an internal light source trying to get out. "You have not been without your trials and tribulations, but I sense great potential in you. You may succeed where others have failed. But you travel in new and untested waters for the Balance Bringer, so tread lightly and with care.

"You have mastered water, wind, earth, and fire. Now you have a taste and basic feel for space." My brow pinches and her face lifts in a humored smile. "You call it infecting darkness or ether."

Right. Got it. I nod.

"Those five elements together spark the energies of creation. Of life and spirit."

I blink. And blink again. Is she saying what I think she is saying?

"You are not a goddess. You cannot create life at will. But you are goddess gifted, and I believe you already know what you are capable of. You have witnessed examples with your friends."

With my brother and Mo. I healed them both at different times. But when I healed Ry, I hadn't realized my air, fire, or space element.

"Sweet thing," she mollifies. "The elements have always been in you, through every cycle of your existence, physically manifested or not."

"So I could—"

"Anala." Her tone is sharp, as she abruptly stands and stares down at me. "I know what you intend to do. You know what you intend to do. But understand that this element, more than any other, will take a toll on you. Even more so than that of space."

"What exactly do I intend to do?" I ask, feeling ten shades deeper than dumb.

She traces her fingers through my hair and gives me a sad smile. "You know, even if you haven't admitted it to yourself yet. That knowing has brought you this far."

"But I thought—"

She vanishes. No bright or fading light. Just there one moment and gone the next.

"My actions were being guided by a higher being. By you," I mumble, then turn my attention back to Sol and gasp.

Electrical charge, in the form of thin, blue lightning, shoots from my hands into Sol's body. I'm reminded of a defibrillator. Or the time an all too similar energy expelled from my body when I pretended to fire a finger gun at kids playing in Ry's trailer park... and also at my home in Faredale, when everything was crumbling around Ry and me.

Is this another thing that has always been in me?

Sol's back arcs, his shoulders jerk, and his limbs begin to shake. Electricity runs from me, through him, and back to me again with a chorus of spits and hisses. Fire races through my veins and jumps to him. The same for water, wind, and earth. And the nebula of ether surrounding us soaks into his skin.

A minute passes. Maybe five or fifty, and then all falls silent. Deathly so.

His chest doesn't rise with breath, but his complexion is less ghostly.

Gaea and god I am death's door tired. I'm not sure I can do this again if needed.

His eyelids pop open, and hazel eyes snap to me.

My breath lodges in my chest. Holy goddess, it worked. Whatever I did worked.

"Hey, you there," a call comes from behind me.

All my elemental gifts took a breather after the workout on Sol. As a result, we're no longer hidden in time, and now we've been spotted.

I glance over my shoulder to the approaching warrior, then turn my attention back to Sol. "We need to get out of here," I say. "Come with me?"

He nods without hesitation.

He hasn't taken his eye off me since he reawakened. He's a beautiful creature, and I can see where Dohlan got his looks from. Not that Dreya isn't gorgeous, in whatever appearance she chooses to wear.

Clutching his hand firmly in mine, and sandwiching the connection between our bodies as I lay mine over his, I suck in a deep breath, rally my strength and, for the third time today, call on the fifth element. This time, with a side of fourth.

A blue blaze ignites all around us and, together, we slip through space.

CAN'T. *Catch. My breath.*

I roll off of Sol and lay flat on my back. Pressing a hand to my chest I focus on breathing in and out, in and out. Each inhale and exhale timed and steady.

"Hey." Sol appears hovering over me. I'm caged between his arms. "Are you all right?"

"Yeah." I close my eyes and envision a blanket of serenity draping over me. "I just need a moment." A moment to find the calm and power necessary to finish what is planned.

"Granted," he replies. The heat of his presence shifts away from me.

Water and fire glide over me, warming and loosening sore muscles. Earth weights me, bestowing comfort. And air wisps through the corridors of my mind, building a sense of tranquility. Space and spirit are notably absent in my moment of mental rejuvenation.

"Thank you for coming with me," I say, voice labored. Eyes still closed. "It was a bold move, trusting a total stranger. Especially given the circumstances."

The sound of him shifting scrapes across the floor beside me. "The circumstances being that I died, and you somehow brought me back?"

He returned with full awareness of what happened. That's good, I guess. "Yes," I reply.

"Hmm." A moment of silence drops between us, and I imagine the wheels of his mind churning. "It has been many lifetimes. So many I have lost count. But you are no stranger to me, Deona."

Of course, he would remember me as Deona. Our incarnations do look eerily similar, minus the length of our pointed ears. Hers are definitely longer.

My eyes pop open and, ignoring my body's objection, I sit up. "I am Deona no longer. Well... I am, but I'm not. It can all get rather confusing." I wave my hands as if to dismiss all the words that just spilled out of my mouth.

His eyebrows arch, and a tiny laugh bubbles up my throat. My shoulders relax, and I extend my hand in greeting. "You can call me Ana."

He takes my hand and shakes. "Ana, it then is. Pleasure to meet you. And thank you for..." He glances around us. We're in Izza's cathedral-converted-home inside her private pocket dimension. "Whatever this is. Oh." His brow pinches, and he lifts his chin at me, then taps a finger to his nostril.

Taking the hint, I wipe beneath mine and... oh is right, that's never happened before. My nose is bleeding. I recall Gaea's parting words about the sixth element taking a toll. I didn't get the opportunity to ask how much of a toll, But there's no point dwelling on that now. What's done is done.

I wipe the blood from my face and decide to clarify what we're doing. "It's a rescue and a fresh start." I heave a breath. "As far as the rest of the realm is concerned, you died the day the floating islands collapsed at South Tower"

He rubs his chin, gaze flickering over me. "I spent a great deal of my existence hating you and all that you stood for, but in recent years, I've left those thoughts and emotions behind. Thank you for this."

"For the record," I say. "Me and my sisters never hated you. What happened was a horrible misfortune, but we never hated or blamed you. And we never meant for any of it to happen to you."

A mild smile tugs lightly at the edge of his lips. He stands *and offers me a helping hand. I accept, rise, and sway. He grabs my arm, steadying me.*

"Here." *He directs me to the bed, and I take a seat. Unable to not think about the last time I was on this bed, heat flushes my face. Sol looks away, pretending not to notice.* "For the record," *he says, repeating my words back to me.* "I was under the impression that the next Balance Bringer would be born to Prince Marduk, and as far as I know, he has not children."

"Yet," *I blurt.* "In your time, I haven't been born, so... yeah..."

He spins back to face me, one eyebrow lifted. "You can move through time?"

I shrug. "I tried to undo what happened to you, then I tried to undo what happened to Dreya because of that day at the lake." *The day she was cursed.* "But my attempts ended in disaster. For reasons, things needed to happen as they did."

Some reasons are selfish reasons, but reasons, nonetheless. Like Dohlan's mere existence, the creation of Jaden's clan, the health and safety of its members, and Mo. I have yet to figure out what happened to her when events were changed and how those changes affected her to begin with. And those are only some of the reasons born out of my second attempt. The first attempt, stopping the darkness from taking Sol, was an utter disaster.

My heart squeezes tight at the memory of Sol and Jaden's death. But that was then, and this is now. That particular history never happened.

"Do I get to know these reasons?" *he asks.*

My jaw clenches. "Later."

He stares at me, his expression blank.

I need a change of subject. Dipping my head, I watch my hand rub across the bed cover. "This place is a world all to itself. Similar to, yet different from, your floating islands."

"*The islands that your sister Estalla imprisoned me on for centuries,*" he retorts.

When he puts it that way... I sigh. *This place was also a prison for far too long, but it need not be. It can be whatever we mold it into. To do so would simply take a little thought and energy.*

Possibly, a lot of energy.

"*I'm sorry she did that.*" I raise my gaze and find him watching me, his arms crossed. "*I can't even imagine—*"

"*I am not sorry. Not any longer.*" He drops his arms at his side. "*Had it not been for the floating landmasses, the extended lifespan gifted by the ether*"—he tips his head as if conceding to a consideration—"*and my desire to get back at you, I never would have met Dreya. And Dreya, she changed me in endless ways. She became the light that led me out of my darkness.*"

At his words, warmth uncoils in my core, and I can't stop the responding smile. "*Did you tell her that?*"

His head tilts down and away as a grin slides into place on his face; this expression leaning into thoughtfulness. "*I haven't told her nearly enough.*" His attention swings back to me. "*Is she well?*"

My frown is immediate. "*She hasn't been, but she will be if we work together.*"

His shoulders straighten. "*What do we need to do?*"

We're already doing it.

TWENTY-EIGHT

S ol strolls past me, heading directly for Dreya. He whispers her name and holds his arms low and wide in a silent request for acceptance. "Look at you," he says. "Still breathtaking, and still my undoing."

Dreya sucks back a sharp breath and then squawks. All her walls and false faces shatter. Her entire body slackens, and breath quickens. In that moment, she looks nothing like the villain who has been hunting me, nor does she look like the queen from the alternate timeline. She's something completely different, younger, and... yes... far more beautiful.

She's in love. Pure, unadulterated love. The truth is evident all over her face. An emotion that creates a glow, in and around her. The sight of her almost makes me forget the pain that is tugging on every part of my body.

Sol and I planned the reunion this way. The surprise and her hopeful glee.

Nothing was to be said to Dreya until she was here and was able to see him with her own eyes. But before I retrieved her, in order to bring this moment to fruition, Sol and I worked arduously to transform Izza's hidden space from the naturistic cathedral into a replica of his home for endless lifetimes—the magical landmasses that once sailed over the realm.

That's where we now stand, on one of the reimagined floating islands. It's a masterpiece of lush gardens and even hosts an ornate tea pavilion.

Before we began, Sol said to me, *"She..."* meaning Dreya *"... told me that she wanted to run away from her royal prison and escape with me. Float away on the islands. And not simply because she felt like a prisoner in her life, but because she wanted the magic of us."*

Those words had dictated our direction when redesigning the dimensional space. All it took was clear intent, a distinct mental picture, and a splash of energy. Or, truth be told, most of my energy reserves.

I really need to rest and recharge. Soon, I guess.

Anyway, ages later, when I had become past the point of exhaustion, a new world was created. I felt a thousand and ten years older and miles away from rested when I returned to the South Tower rooftop and collected my aunt in the midst of our scuffle. And, despite Dohlan tossing her... and me by extension... over the side, I got us here in one piece.

All those moments led to this: the reuniting of Sol and Dreya.

Goddess Gaea, I pray I got this right.

If my theory proves correct, bringing these two back together will spark hope in Dreya's soul once more and result in her turning from her dark ways. Choose a life with Sol over her need for vengeance and destruction. Because, if her memories speak the truth, before Sol's death, she was never that kind of individual. Despite all the injustice she suffered, she was never unkind.

"Is this a trick?" Dreya asks, her voice small and soft. Her gaze swivels from Sol to me then back to Sol.

"No trick," Sol and I say in unison.

If the roles were reversed, I too would be questioning everything. How do I make her believe?

"I saw your memories," I add. Her head swings toward me, and her body goes rigid. "They were a gift from a time chronicler. And I'm not sure I fully understood at the time, but I do now."

Her chin jerks up. "That is a violation of my privacy."

I don't bother to point out she's done far worse. Doing so would only serve to move this situation in the wrong direction. Instead, I say, "Please, don't be mad. Those memories helped me better understand things: your motives and drives." My demeanor softens. "You were dealt more unfair blows than anyone I know, and... well..." I shrug. "I felt you were due a change."

Her muscles tense and her gaze narrows. "Is that right? In light of all that I have done to you, caused for you and yours, and the realm, you thought I deserved some kind of reward?" Her gaze flickers to Sol, then back to me.

I wouldn't go as far as to say that.

The way she holds herself makes it clear that she wants to believe Sol is real, that what I'm offering is real, but she is leery, and that is one hundred percent understandable.

"Listen, *Aunt*." I shake my head. "I wanted, really, really wanted to hate you. But at the end of the day, I couldn't. So... with Gaea's hand on my shoulder, and guiding my actions, I lifted Sol from the realm in the minutes after his death and breathed new life into him." Because you weren't the only one deserving of a second chance. "I am, after all, partially responsible for what happened to him."

She huffs. A reaction that tells me she agrees with my admission.

"We already talked about this," Sol interjects. "Everything happened as the sands of time required and whatever missteps you have taken are forgiven."

Dreya's hard expression wavers. "You expect me to believe you brought him back from the dead?" Her voice seeps with sarcasm, but then she turns to him, and every deep-rooted hope is written on her face.

A flirtatious smile is his response. And the gesture colors Dreya's skin red. She clears her throat and straightens her shoulders.

"And this place?" she says, crossing her arms and starting to turn toward me. Before I even see her face, I can tell she's raising her defenses. And sure enough, when her gaze connects with mine, all the emotion has been tucked out of sight.

"I'll let Sol tell that story. He was, after all, the master architect." I toss him a smile.

Dreya frowns and addresses Sol. "And how do I know you are who you say you are? Restoring life is rather godlike and this female"—she motions to me—"is no goddess."

"Ask me anything." He takes a step closer. "I am eager to pass your tests and get this settled so that I might hold you in my arms once more. These hours without you have been the longest day known to any being."

She huffs and turns her profile to him. "The real Sol died ages ago. I've had close to a hundred years without him." I choke on a breath. "I know not who you are."

"You know me," he replies, taking yet another forward step. "The first time we met, you had fallen out of a tree. We would meet in the garden during your outdoor visits. And it took me several missives before you would engage in correspondence. I lost you for a time, when they took you to South Tower, but when I found you, we spent time as I pretended to be on staff."

Dreya's lips pucker and Sol takes another step forward.

"I have called you wee princess, young princess, princess of water and ice. I would like to call you my princess." Dreya's chest rises and Sol closes the distance, pressing intimately close and lowering his voice to a whisper. "You know I have that—"

I gasp and turn away, pressing my hands over my ears. Nope-nope-nope. I don't want to know those kinds of details about Sol.

I count slowly to ten and turn back around. Sol and Dreya are lip locked. Bodies pressed and hands exploring. Ugh.

I don't want to interrupt and undo the progress we've made. But I also don't want to play the part of a spectator. Seeing them together only intensifies the hurt of missing Jaden. Will I ever get back to him?

Stifling a yawn, I meander over to the pavilion and settle into one of the inviting overstuffed lounge chairs. In my exhaustion, the cushion is better than any bed. The hard part is done, so I close my eyes and wait. Try to stay awake. But, despite my efforts, I nod off.

I awake to a gentle shake of my shoulder.

Sol and Dreya stand before me, their arms wrapped around one another, holding their bodies close.

I stretch and yawn, greet them with a groggy voice. "Did I fall asleep?"

"You did," Sol says, his expression soft.

"Was I out long?"

"A while." Dreya rolls her eyes and wiggles a finger toward me. "You were drooling *and* bleeding."

Oh crap! I jerk upright and wipe at my mouth and nose, clearing away the offending liquids.

Sol extends his hand, offering a handkerchief. "Are you going to be all right?" he asks.

Graciously accepting his offer, I tilt my head back and press the cloth to my nose. "Should be," I reply, my voice garbled. "I've just exerted more energy than usual so I may need a longer than usual recovery coma."

Dreya hums and Sol tugs her closer, which I didn't think was possible, and whispers in her ear. Her responding smile is immediate. I lower my head and fake a cough. Wait a breath for their attention to return to me.

But then I pull my hand away from my mouth and... oh crap... there's a splattering of blood.

My heart skitters in my chest as I jolt to my feet.

Exhaustion, aches, bloody noses, and now coughing up blood? This is so not good.

"Is everything copacetic here?" I drag my hand along the side of my pants, wiping away the blood. "You guys made a decision? Because I think I need to get back." To Jaden, and Zarah, and Bree. Maybe even the master healer. They may be able to help me.

Dreya's gaze rakes over me. "You look exceptionally unwell, Bringer."

I feel exceptionally unwell. Words I keep to myself.

"Do not expect me to show concern for your wellbeing," she continues, to which Sol whispers an admonishment in her ear. She sighs, then adds, "But you should have a healer tend to you."

Clearly, almost a hundred years playing with the dark cannot be erased in a single day. Even if Sol, the love of her life, is the ultra-brilliant light casting away her shadows.

I mock a smile. "With everything that exists between us, *Aunt*, I would never expect you to express concern for me. And do not, under any circumstances, mistake what I did here today as a sign of me forgiving you. You did, after all, kill my family."

"Noted." She smirks. "But they deserved the death I served."

"Did Kaia, my sister? When did she ever wrong you?" Other than falling in love with your son? She shrugs, and for a flash of a second, I suspect I spy remorse in her eyes. "They were guilty of horrible transgressions against you, I'll grant you that, but they did not deserve death.

"In fact,"—I raise a pointed finger—"some might say death was too easy of an out for them." Because torture would last far longer. Not that I should be encouraging her. Isn't this when she's supposedly trying to turn over a new leaf... or turn back to the old, original one?

My knee buckles, and I slam my hand to the side of the pavilion for added support. "Body's trying to get old on me," I joke. Neither of them appear amused by my joke, lame as it may be. "Anyway..." I wave a hand between us. "You two discussed everything and made your decision? You've decided to stay?"

"We have," Sol says, then plants a kiss on Dreya's cheek. "And we will stay, assuming you'll adhere to my condition."

I nod. "Of course."

When Sol and I were transforming the dimension to mimic the floating islands, he had suggested that endless isolation would be bad for both of them, but especially Dreya. I couldn't disagree. Interactions with others is good for the soul. So, when I've recovered and had time to figure out the specifics—where to place the door between dimensions and how to synchronize the time flow between those two locations—I would provide them with the ability to visit outside of their world of floating islands.

If Deona was able to create a door to the Nethers, then I should be able to do this. *Eventually.*

"Oh look." Dreya slaps her palm to Sol's chest. "Sunset is almost upon us, and you know what that means."

Sol grimaces. "After all the years you have been without me, I do not want Flip to be the first to welcome you home."

"Stop," she says playfully. "Jealousy is not a pretty look on you. And besides, he has never—"

Oh my Gaea. I slap my hands over my ears. "*Blalalalalalalalalala.* Don't need to hear your too-personal stuff. *Lalalalalala.* I just need Dreya to hold up her end. Transfer the ether to me so that I can get going."

Sol touches my hand, prompting me to lower it from my ear. Dreya is laughing, most likely at me, but her expression quickly thaws.

"About the ether," Sol says. "There seems to be a bit of a problem."

My brow pinches. "What kind of problem?"

Dreya's shoulders straighten. "I no longer have it."

TWENTY-NINE

M y ears are filled with the sound of blood pumping through my veins. And my heart is dancing in my chest like it's a jumping bean. An all-consuming *shrump, shrump, shrump* is currently my personal soundtrack.

"You're not lying to me?" I pin Dreya with a pointed stare. "You really don't have the ether, the darkness, whatever you want to call it, anymore?"

She shakes her head and sighs. "Something strange happened when I attacked you on the South Tower's rooftop. The ether acted far differently than it had previous times. And when I shot forth a portion, the rest of it followed. As if it were caught on a hook and being yanked."

My shoulders cave inward. Could I have been the reason for the ether's mass exodus? I had essentially opened myself up to the element and summoned it to me. If it had leaped free of Dreya, it should have come to me. Should be with me now. Only, it's not.

My head starts to pound.

"I need to get back to that rooftop." I straighten my backbone and prepare to call on the fifth element *again*.

Sol grabs my arm. "You should rest first."

What he doesn't say, but his eyes communicate, is that my reactions are clearly leaden and my movements are betraying my aches and pains. All true factors I refuse to let slow at present. Not with the ether now out in the wild.

"I'll rest when I'm dead." I don't know why I say that. I always hated that quip and never supported that way of thinking. Only, right now... yeah... I feel like I need to keep going and that push just *might* be the death of me. But this is my destiny.

I don't give Sol and Dreya any further opportunity to sway my actions. I dig deep into my core and amass every ember of energy I'm able to seize. Expanding the burn of that energy, and wrapping it around me, I ignore every crying muscle and bone, and jump into the vortex of time and space.

My mind is focused on the ether. The way the ether played in Dreya's features and the moment the ether hurdled from her palms. The manner in which it came for me.

This time, when I reach my destination, I don't slip adeptly from time and space, but rather fall. Fumble my landing. My feet hit the stone rooftop, my knees instantly giving out. I topple and roll to the side. Pull myself up onto my hands and knees.

The world is quiet and the sky is inching toward darkness, casting the surrounding edges of the roofline into shadow. At this time of day, the stone of the tower appears more black than gray.

Four feet away, I spy Dohlan's ring, lying on the ground, sitting in the open. With all the time I spent working with Sol to alter the other dimension and then get Dreya there, I'd totally forgotten about the ring.

Even with Dreya now removed from the picture, I should

collect it, just in case.

I take a crawling step in the ring's direction.

"Now, that was a curious thing to witness." My head snaps up at the sound of Dohlan's voice. He's leaning against the battlement siding at my left. By all appearances, he's one long shadow of black. "How did you do it?" he asks. "I tossed you over the side of the tower and now you are here. Safe and alive."

He... he threw me over the side... on purpose? My heart seizes. Inside of me, Kaia becomes a whirl of chaos, draining the last bits of my energy. I flip onto my butt so that I may better keep an eye on him, and then inch myself backward, closer to the ring.

My ribs feel as brittle as cracked ice, my limbs as strong as limb spaghetti, and my upper lip is wet. My nose the likely the suspect.

"Wha... wha... what's wrong with you? Wh... why would you thro... throw me over?"

"Wha... wha... what's wrong with me?" he mocks. "I think the real question here, Ana, is what's wrong with you?"

He stalks forward into the moonlight, the delicate glow illuminating his many features. The too-large scar on his chest, the web of black spider veins cobwebbing his skin, and his eyes of black obsidian.

My world stops. And I can't drag my eyes away from the sight in front of me. Kaia isn't talking. Isn't giving any direction. She's just as frozen as I am.

Dohlan doesn't seem to notice. He comes to a stop a foot away from us. "I'm waiting for you to answer the question, Ana. This little trick you did. Over there"—he jabs a point indicating the edge of the rooftop, then swings his pointer finger to me—"then over here, is this a Balance Bringer ability I have yet to become familiar with?"

"Answer my question first." I lift my chin, hoping I look far more steady than I feel.

He brushes the collar of his shredded shirt. "You already know the answer to your question."

I pull the wickedest smile to my lips that I can muster. "Taking after your daddy, I see."

His features tighten and face darkens. An instant too late, I realize I've made a grave mistake. Before I can blink, Dohlan has closed the distance between us. His foot slams into my chest, knocking me flat on my back. Something cracks. Is it a rib? Something more significant?

The voices of countless versions of myself explode in my head as they begin to phase into one.

Dammit. Not a rib, but Bree's pendant. What crap timing.

"*As the one became three,*" Deona whispers. "*So then, the three returned to one. Or the many to the one.*"

"*Love you sister.*" Crystia's words caress my heart and soul while in the background Kaia is screaming. "*I don't want to go. I can't leave him. Not like this. Not like this!*"

I can't listen to them. I need to focus on Dohlan. "I can help you." My voice doesn't sound like my own. It's weak and scratchy.

"Don't want your help. Now shut up and die already." He kicks me in the side of the head. Blood sprays from my mouth, and he exclaims with excitement. Like he's cheering a score at a football game.

I have no response. Words won't come and pain keeps me from moving. My lungs hurt so much, I'm not sure I'll be able to continue breathing for much longer. Truth be, I think death would be preferable to suffering this agony.

Giving in to the weight of my eyelids, I half close my eyes and welcome whatever will be to come.

Dohlan steps over me and starts to reach down. The call of

my name carries over the rooftop, and he pauses, pulls back. My name washes over us again. My eyes pop wide. I recognize the voices. Jaden and Shadow, to name a couple. How did they find me?

Dohlan curses under his breath and then crouches beside me. "He may be coming for you," he says of Jaden. "But he won't be collecting you in one piece."

He rises to a full stand and then, holding back nothing, kicks me in the gut. My body slides against the stone, a hundred thousand needles dragged across my skin. My slide comes to an abrupt stop with a slam at my back.

My vision dims and every piece of me is on fire. Burning inside and out. Despite my impaired sight, Dohlan's thick, black boots still dominate my view as he approaches. Clearly, he's in no hurry.

"Please, Dohlan." I'm not against begging. Begging not for me, but for him. "Some day you'll regret these actions." I turn my head to better see his face, every twisting inch agonizing. His beauty, even infected by the darkness, is heart crushing.

"Maybe so," he replies. "But you won't be here to witness that day."

Those words are daggers to my soul. I don't want to leave him this way. Not for Kaia, or me, and especially not for him. But I have no fight left to give. And what does that fact say about the future of the realms? Of any possible success with regards to my destiny?

"Goodbye, lover." He bends his leg, and the sole of his foot is the last thing I see.

My world goes dark. Jaden's lingering call the last sound whispering through my brain.

Ana Janssen Raine's adventures will continue! Watch for the story's conclusion in EMERGING: THE BALANCE BRINGER, *coming your way in* 2024

If you haven't already devoured THE BALANCE BRINGER ORIGINS books, it's recommended you do so now: The Balance Bringer Origins

To claim your free Balance Bringer Chronicles story THE MYSTIC MAKER and ensure notification when new stories are released, sign up for Debra Kristi's newsletter.
https://www.debrakristi.com/claim-your-free-gift/

DEAR READER,

Thank you for taking the ride that is the latest installment in Ana's journey. If you enjoyed this read, please consider leaving a review on your favorite platform. Your review needn't be more than a line or two, and the simple act not only helps me develop further stories, but helps other readers find what they are looking for... which is hopefully this series.

Readers and reviewers like yourself make up the foundation of our author world, and we love you madly for all you do!

Thanks so much! Until next time, keep the magic real.

∼ Debra Kristi

ABOUT THE AUTHOR

Debra Kristi was born and raised a Southern California girl. She still resides in the sunny state with her husband, two kids, and several schizophrenic cats. Unlike many of the characters in the stories she writes, Debra is not immortal and her only superpower is letting the dishes and laundry pile up. When not busy drumming away at the keyboard spinning new tales, Debra is hanging out creating priceless memories with her family, geeking out to science fiction and fantasy television, and tossing around movie quotes.

Find me online and connect!

Discover more about me and my books on my website: http://www.debrakristi.com/

And join me on my Facebook author page for updates, news, discussions, and more: https://www.facebook.com/DebraKristi.writer/

Follow *The Balance Bringer Chronicles* on Facebook for 'Bringer'-inspired motivational posts and fun series extras and shares: https://www.facebook.com/TheBalanceBringer/

THE BALANCE BRINGER
CHRONICLES

USA TODAY BESTSELLING AUTHOR
DEBRA KRISTI

THE BALANCE BRINGER CHRONICLES
ORIGINS

"In my humble opinion, this is one of the best, if not the best, fantasy adventure series I have read. Each book is a masterpiece in itself and captivating and addictive."

- LooseBoots, Amazon Reviewer ★★★★★

Gifted Girls

**Magic. Adventure. Family Secrets.
And Dangerous Supernaturals.**

Plus, unexpected twists that will keep you guessing
and turning the pages late into the night.

Series complete!

"Each book in this series just gets better."
-D Nerriman, Amazon Reviewer ★★★★★

MOORIGAD

He walked into Hell's fire for me. I would burn the world for him. I'd even give up my dragon.

In this action-packed, paranormal fantasy romance about two coming-of-age would-be lovers, Kyra and Sebastian's union and strength of character will be put to the ultimate test. The stakes? Everything and everyone that ever mattered to them.

Series complete!

"Adventure, romance, suspense, colorful and engaging characters. A very captivating [trilogy]."
- *Donna Lane, Amazon Reviewer* ★★★★★

GLOSSARY OF TERMS

- **Aubadetruss:** Wristband that harnesses the sun
- **Aura:** The invisible energy radiating from an individual
- **Balance Bringer:** Chosen individual born to the warrior and Fae races, bringing balance to the realms at the hand of a higher power
- **Bidse:** (slang) A malicious, unpleasant, selfish person, especially a woman
- **Chronicler:** Created at the beginning of time by the Elven Queen, chroniclers record the passage of time and events and deposit all historical information in the Urn of All
- **Dream Incubus:** A demon who takes on the appearance of a man in order to syphon the energy of women
- **Dream Walk:** Living an experience, past, present, or future, in a dream state
- **Empath:** An individual who feels the emotions of another soul
- **Elenari:** The first of all elven kind. The first original families of nine, later to become seven
- **Era:** A measure of time marked by a calendar of events
- **Equinox:** Time of year when day and night are of the same duration
- **Faun:** A half man, half goat lustful creature

- **Feline Preservation Center:** Home for large, endangered felines
- **Fires of Guardoone:** Eternal flame capable of killing immortals
- **Gaea:** Mother Earth, the universal mother and goddess
- **Gradnar's Honor:** Hiddenkelian warrior cry honoring the great fallen leader, Gradnar
- **Hiddenkel:** Homeland from where Anala Jannsen Raine originates
- **Lightning wand:** Weapon harnessing light used against the Tenebrousian
- **Lles dei Luz:** Hiddenkelian for 'I grant thee light'
- **Mãnah:** Hiddenkelian for 'mother'
- **Ondine**: Water spirits
- **Puteri:** Princess
- **Purusians:** A group of believers that revere the sanctity of virginity and protect their purity through separation from the majority
- **Shadowkin:** Indirect relation, associated through species
- **Tearman:** Madame Marrouske's sanctuary established around the Tree of Life
- **Tenebrousian:** Hiddenkelian name for the dark ones or shadows
- **Treeite:** A resident of Ivey City, the community built high in the trees
- **Toran:** Gateway between worlds
- **Toranik:** Stone marking a Toran defense area
- **Usoda:** One of twenty-four warrior tribes spread across the vast lands of Hiddenkel

ACKNOWLEDGEMENTS

Huge thanks to the wonderful family of people that kept me sane through the writing process and the talented group that helped bring this latest book to fruition.

Thanks to my husband and #1 fan. I would be huddled in a corner if not for your endless patience and support. Love you, Bud.

Thanks to my mom. You and the hubs fight for the #1 fan spot. *wink* Your endless support, in all areas, has been invaluable to me.

Thanks to my kids (R & A) for your understanding, suggestions, and mental-break interruptions. You two are my world and I love you with all that I am.

Thanks to Rebecca Hamilton for your time, endless patience, and tools for success. It is an absolute joy to work with you.

Thanks to Rebecca Frank for yet another gorgeous cover. I think this one (and the next to come) rank at the top of my favorites. *Big grin*

Thanks to Eden Plantz for always pushing my stories to capture greater depth.

Thanks to the Council of Three (cats Gandalf, Gaius, and Athena) for the endless judging, scrutinizing, keyboard blocking, and chair stealing.

Thanks to the maker of my electric kettle for endless mugs of tea that continued to fuel me through the enter creation process.

And finally, but never ever least important, thanks to you,

the many readers—my ARC team, Immortal Warriors street team, and every reader enjoying the series on their own—you all mean the world to me and I can't thank you enough.

Special thanks to my muses and the universe for making my story creation a possibility.